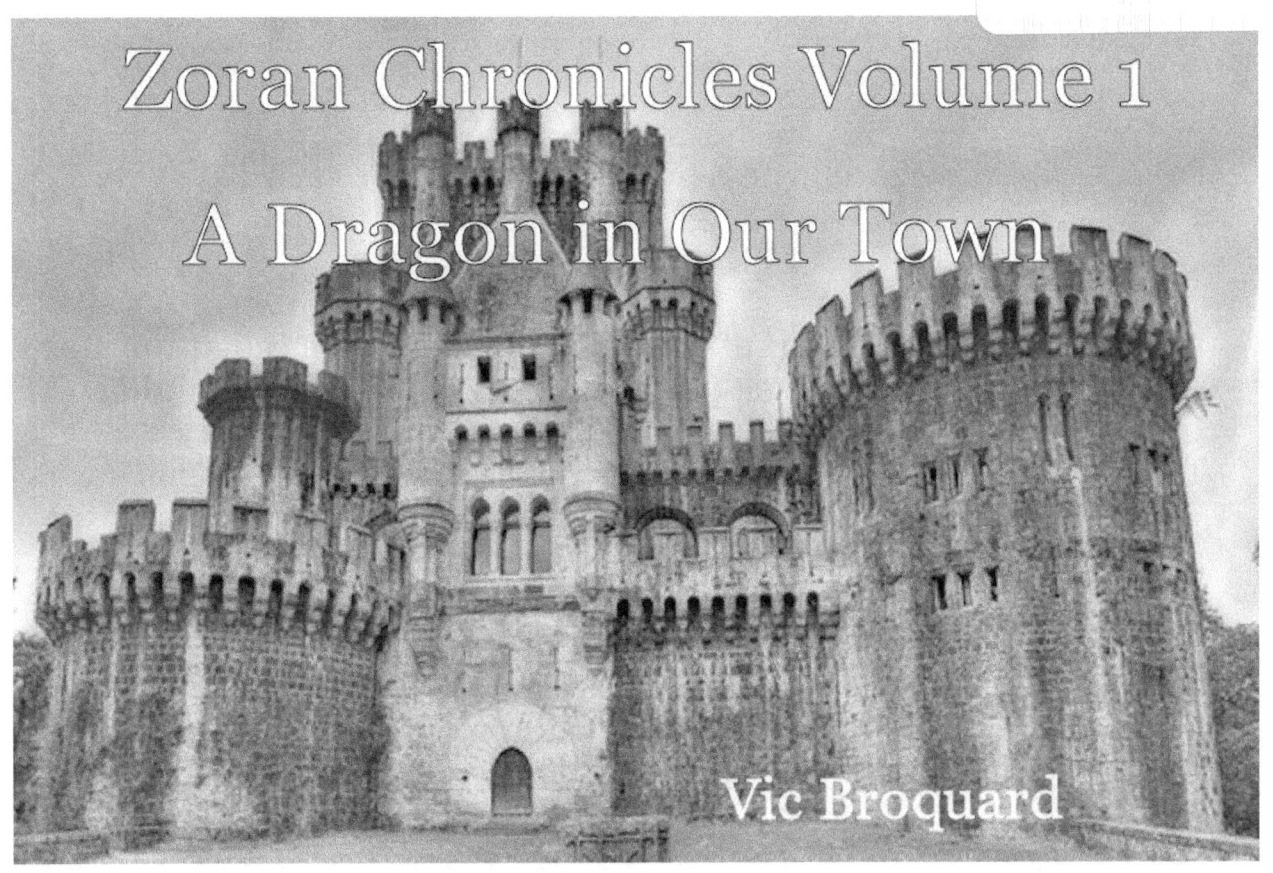

Zoran Chronicles Volume 1
A Dragon in Our Town

Vic Broquard

http://www.Broquard-ebooks.com
Broquard eBooks
103 Timberlane
East Peoria, IL 61611
author@Broquard-eBooks.com

Artwork by Crooked Willow Studios.

For Morgan and L. Ron Hubbard

Table of Contents

Chapter 1 Decision Reached

Cold and black was the night. An icy rain fell; rivulets ran down Zoran's grey outer cloak depositing even more water on his already soaked boots. The eighteen year olds pace was rapid; all thoughts were on the Coddle Inn — its warm fire, its warm ale, and his two friends. Well, okay, his thoughts also drifted more than once onto the barmaid Beta and her golden hair and intense blue eyes. The cobblestone street sloped to either side draining water into the sewers beneath the city. He passed Flagstone Hall; only two more blocks and he'd be out of this miserable early spring rain.

Out of nowhere his inner sense blasted his full attention on this instant of time forcing his head to look upwards. His eyes focused on a large stone block that was falling directly towards his head! Instant reactions from his youthful training kicked in; he dove to his left and rolled as his shoulder hit the cold, wet, unforgiving cobblestones. High atop Flagstone Hall through the opening made by the falling stone, he saw a cloaked, hooded figure suddenly vanish. Crash! The three foot by one foot chunk of polished granite smashed into the street crushing cobblestone, shattering the block itself, and missing his leg by mere inches.

One quick fighter movement and Zoran was on his feet, his sword drawn. His eyes darted in all directions, but the street was deserted. No one was venturing out on a night like tonight unless they had urgent business. "Damn!" he cursed. He shook more water off of himself; his pants were now soaked as well. A minute later he entered the Coddle Inn, shaking off his cloak and clothes at the door. Stale pipe smoke and spirits assailed his nostrils along with that of burning pine logs.

"Hey, over here, Vladislov," the cheery, but slightly drunk voice of his friend Miklos called out to him using his surname. "Come over and warm up by the fire. Ale's waiting!" Miklos and Kornel had the table closest to the inn's large fireplace, perfect for nights like tonight, Zoran thought, and joined them.

"Hey, what happened to you? Fall into a puddle did we?" Kornel joked, noticing that his friend was rather drenched.

"Gimme an ale! Someone just tried to kill me again," Zoran replied angrily, downing one mug in a single guzzle.

"What? Did you see who it was this time?" Kornel suddenly came to attention, struggling to fight off the effects of the three ales that he had already consumed.

"Are you all right?" Miklos added, also becoming alert, his eyes scanning everyone in the inn as if they might be an assassin as well.

"Gonna have a sore shoulder in the morning. No harm done — missed me." Zoran related his narrow escape with death minutes before.

"Damn, you sure are the luckiest guy I know," Kornel stated. "Incredible of you to just happen to look up when you did! Grey cloak and hood — not much to go on this time either." He refilled Zoran's mug.

Zoran was the youngest child of Baron Kazimir and Baroness Katerina Vladislov, the rulers of the main continent of the planet Adapazan. His twenty-one year older brother, Radek, was already named by Baron Kazimir to be his heir to the throne. Like peas, Zoran always said, ruthless tyrants, controlling the planet with an iron glove. In stark contrast to their harshness, his twin nineteen year old sisters, Rayna and Lida, were like gentle flowers in the spring. Yet they were not without power; they chose to use it wisely, from Zoran's point of view. Baron Kazimir ruled from this huge city of Dorum and his giant stone castle Dorumova in which Zoran had his own room.

While the fire began to warm him on the outside and the ale on the inside, he and his two friends chatted about this new attempt on his life. Zoran's mind could not help but drift back to the previous two attempts. Three weeks ago, at dinner, he took a chunk of bread that was on the table before him. However, his inner senses had warned him something was not right. So startled by the suddenness of his surprise warning, he had dropped the bread on the floor. His old pet dog had eaten it and immediately began vomiting and died within two minutes. Someone had tried to poison him at his own dinner table!

Baron Kazimir laughed off the whole incident, but did at least investigate. He found nothing of significance, even though the Baroness insisted that he leave no stone unturned to find the assassin. Assassinations were commonplace within the Federation of Planets.

Then, last week, as he was practicing his combat skills, going hand to hand with the Baron's sword master, Josef, once again, his inner sense kicked in; he reacted by making a rolling dive into the dirt. Just in time, an arrow thudded into the ground where he had been standing. Josef called out the guards, but the archer simply vanished. Other than the arrow, no trace of the assassin could be found. Well, that was to be expected of an assassin, if they knew their craft. Now tonight the unknown assassin had tried it again and almost succeeded. Zoran was more than a little annoyed and upset; he bordered on hostility. Who could possibly want him dead?

"Probably Radek's behind it," Kornel was speculating, as Zoran's mind finally rejoined his friends. "Everyone knows that Zoran is just the opposite of him and the Baron."

"Why? I am not in line to be heir to the throne," Zoran pointed out for the tenth time to his friends. "Look, the Baron," he had long since stopped referring to Kazimir as his father, "has already named Radek as his heir. Even if something happens to him, more than likely it would fall to Rayna or Lida. I'm fourth in line at best, if the Baroness doesn't claim it before it comes to me. I can't see any reason for Radek to want me dead. Sorry fellows, I don't buy it."

"Well, someone sure does, Zoran. This is the third attempt! Sooner or later, they are going to succeed. What the devil are you going to do about it?" Miklos asked, concerned for his childhood friend.

Perhaps it was the ale talking. Zoran found himself saying, "Perhaps I ought to just disappear for a while until I can figure out who is after my head."

"Say, that's not a bad idea," Kornel replied, then hiccupping loudly from the ale. "Go undercover and all that. I like it."

"Yes, but he is Duska. He can just go anywhere in the Federation just by magic. We sure can't go with him and protect him, now can we, Kornel," Miklos replied, rather annoyed that Zoran was suggesting what sounded like a grand adventure and that the two of them, being only Adepts, that is beginning wizards, could not follow. Not unless Zoran chose to magically bring them along. He was hoping his slight hint would register with Zoran who would then offer to take them with him.

"Sorry fellows. If I go, I have to go by myself. If out there something happens to me, you both would be stranded! I could never live with that, sorry. I must do this alone," Zoran replied to his friend's subtle hint. They knew that he was right. Zoran was Duska; they were not. Four years ago, he'd come of age and had been given the Ceremony of Ascension, during which his special gland at the base of his body's brain activated. Through the guidance of the Priestess, he'd been initiated into the Shadow Walk, which allowed him to walk through space to any of the sixteen planets within the Federation. His first trip was nauseating, but by the last walk, he had mastered his fears and was now a true Duska, a Shadow Walker, which was his birthright. All those who ruled throughout the Federation were Duska.

Duska were special, multi-talented, different human beings, gifted by birth with an oversized gland, which, upon puberty, set them apart with special powers and abilities. Perhaps the greatest of these was their ability to Shadow Walk, in which they could transport themselves and others, if they chose, from one planet to another within the sixteen in the Federation of Planets. Their reaction times were phenomenal, and males usually made use of this by becoming master swordsmen. All male Duskas were given standard fighter training from about the age of six onwards.

Magic was also prevalent throughout the Federation, though it took many shapes and forms. Although no one ever made an accurate assessment, popular opinion held that one in ten of every inhabitant had some latent magical skill, though often this amounted to little more than having a spoon stir a cooking pot, starting a fire in the fireplace — little useful sort of things. From among those with magical skills, a relatively few had gotten some magical training and were able to cast limited formal spells; these were called the Adepts. Often they made their living by trading their spells for room and board or gold coins. Here on Adapazan, a heavily forested and mountainous planet, forest fires were a common hazard, and Adepts could make a good living by using their spells to help douse fires.

Even fewer still had the funds or backers to make a full time study of magic. These were called Mages. Armed with an array of spells, often power spells such as Ball of Fire, Lightning Bolt, and Killing Vapors, these men and women frequently found lucrative employment within the ruling baron's army of enforcers or even their armies proper. Those who did not were often employed by the many warlords who controlled lands currently beyond the dominion of the barons and baronesses.

Rare were those in the third category, the Archmage. These individuals had gone far beyond the mundane use of magical powers and spells, extending their knowledge of arcana to unknown limits. Wherever possible, every baron had one Archmage in their employ. Baron Kazimir's Archmage was Milos, now in his seventies, a tight lipped man with a nasty temper and zero tolerance for mistakes. Milos also detested all those without any latent magical skills and thus fit in well with the Baron's subjugation plans for Adapazan.

The court's Archmage, Milos in this case, had several official duties, one of which was to train the royal children of the ruling family. Indeed, Archmage Milos had trained Radek, Rayna, Lida, and had just begun training Zoran. Radek rapidly picked up the power spells which would aid him in battles with warlords and their rabbles. His sisters, while they could cast such spells should they one day find themselves rulers, excelled in other forms of spells, beneficial ones which would help others. Zoran also tended to favor the same spells that his sisters had, much to the annoyance of Archmage Milos. Yet to say that Zoran's training was complete would be an utter falsehood. No, he'd only learned a few spells to date. "Another five years, Zoran, and you will be skilled as a Mage," Milos had drilled this into his head only three days ago.

Around one in the morning, Zoran left the inn and headed home. The rain had stopped, but the cold night ushered in a thin layer of ice over the cobblestones, making walking treacherous. He slipped his way along to the entrance gates of Dorumova Castle, flashed his duke ring to the guard, entered, and walked the halls and stairs that led to his private room on the third floor west wing. Magically enchanted torches illuminated his way. As he pushed his door open, he felt the presence of another behind him. His nose caught the scent of lilacs; Rayna quietly tiptoed up to him.

Dressed in her white cotton nightgown, Rayna had long brown hair and blue eyes. She put her finger to her lips and caught his attention. Zoran motioned her inside and she silently slipped past him. Once they were inside and the door shut, she whispered, "You've been to the inn; it's on your breath, Zoran."

"You would too if someone just tried to kill you tonight," he grumbled.

"Oh no! Not again! Are you hurt? Ought we tell dad?" her voice changing from one of antagonism to that of deep sisterly concern. Both she and Lida loved their little brother, but mostly despised the rest of their family. Zoran repeated the short story of this latest assassination attempt.

"Oh Zoran! What are we going to do?" Rayna whispered, her voice showing a deep worry for her brother's safety.

"You aren't going to do anything, sis. I've made up my mind. I'm going away for a while. Just disappear completely," he said determinedly. It was not the ale talking, she observed.

"But your magic training isn't done? Where will you go? What will you do? Oh Zoran! I don't think this is such a good idea," she pleaded. Noticing it didn't get the response she'd desired, tried another approach. "You know as well as I that you absolutely must finish your magic training. Lida and I still have a couple years to go before we are finished. We must have all the power we can possibly acquire, you even more so."

"What good will magic do me if I'm dead?" he countered. She resorted to tears since this didn't work. Zoran finally melted, taking his sister in his arms. "Please don't cry. I didn't mean to upset you. I know I have to learn all the magic I can. At least you and Lida have a good chance of marrying off planet and getting out from under Kazimir's thumb. Look, no matter where I go, you can contact me. Use your Mind Join spell, sis. Keep me informed of the happenings here around the court. Just tell them I ran away because I was afraid the assassin would kill me. After tonight's narrow escape, they ought to believe me." Zoran cleverly gave her a job to do and she stopped crying.

"When are you leaving?" she finally asked, as he wiped away her tears with his handkerchief.

"Got to pack first, then I'll go — an hour or so," he replied.

"You've got to have food. I'll sneak down to the panty and pack you something," she volunteered. She cast a spell to make sure that the hallway outside this room was empty, then left. Hastily, Zoran began packing, knowing that if he sat around thinking about it, he might lose his nerve. He had no idea where he was going or really what he would need. He changed into his traveling leather pants and shirt, stuffing a dagger down each boot leg. He strapped a pair of throwing daggers onto his back and laid out his pair of short swords. Zoran had defied his father's wishes and had taken up using two short swords instead of the traditional bastard sword, for which his father was famous. Radek had followed in his father's footsteps. Just to defy them both, he'd taken up the two short swords — a thief's or brigand's choice.

He packed a change of clothes, burying several gems in his spare socks. He put a sack of gold coins in the pack as well and tied a simple money pouch around his waist. Zoran made a bedroll from several warm blankets, stowing his few other possessions in his backpack. He didn't need a lantern or any fire starters; the few spells that he knew would handle any such physical needs. He took off his duke ring, fastened it around a thong, and put it around his neck, beneath his shirt. No sense being recognized everywhere he went. Indeed, one glance at his finger would tell all that he was a duke and a Duska.

Presently Rayna returned with a pile of bread and dried meats bundled in a dish towel. "I got this for you. Not much, but it should last you a couple of days. Do be careful, Zoran. I love you and . . ."

Zoran cut her off, "I know sis. We three are alone against our parent's tyranny, but I'll be careful. At least out there, no one will be trying to kill me. Has to be safer than staying around here. You keep me posted on events, okay. Be brave. Tell Lida I love her too." He gave Rayna a long hug. "You better get back to bed before you get discovered." Fighting back her tears, she gave him another hug and then quietly left.

"I'll miss you and Lida," he whispered after she was gone and he stood alone in his darkened room. Indeed he knew that he would. Those two had helped him keep his sanity all these years. Now he had to make the decision on just where to go. Back at the inn he'd suggested to his friends that he might go visit his Uncle Milan on the forest planet of Gladno. He'd always gotten along well with Uncle Milan, who he respected. However, as he stood there in his room, he realized that as soon as Kazimir discovered he'd taken off, he'd certainly contact all of his relatives, searching for his son. No, he'd have to go somewhere where he would not be known or recognized.

Ah, that was the key word: recognized. He couldn't go to any of the court cities; by now, everyone knew the youngest son of Baron Kazimir Vladislov. His freedom would be brief indeed. No, he would have to go to the Wild Lands somewhere. Wild Lands was their term for lands not yet under the control and rule of a baron or baroness. Yet, somehow he had to learn more magic — that was his uppermost worry. He just could not forsake further training.

Suddenly an idea formed. As if by some magic, Zoran remembered that there was an independent Archmage Oldrich who controlled a section of the Wild Lands here on Adapazan! Brn, yes, that was the town, located in the mountains far, far from Dorum — at least a thousand miles. That ought to be enough distance to keep my father from finding me, he thought. However, Zoran knew that he would have to be cagier than to merely Shadow Walk to Brn!

No, any Duska worth their salt could easily track his Shadow Walk, and they'd be on him in a day! There was only one way he could Shadow Walk without anyone being able to follow his magical energy trail, but that was terribly dangerous to his own life. He would have to trace the Circle of Ascension, much as he had done during the ceremonial rites that had activated his gland and make him a Duska. When walking the Circle of Ascension, shadow energy lines intertwined and mingled, leaving no trace of ones exit point. However, walking the Circle of Ascension without a priest present to guide him could well leave him insane or dead or lost in the Shadows of the ether. Yet, it was a risk he would have to take. He took a deep breath and opened his mind, picturing the colorful Circle of Ascension located in the basement of Castle Dorumova. He stepped onto the Circle. His body flew through space and arrived there in the basement, dimly illuminated by a Continuous Light spell. Memories of his own Ascension six years ago swam through his mind. He forced them out, concentrated, and began his Shadow Walk.

Space seemed to blur into a dizzying whirl of places, castles, mountains, lakes, hills, plains, swamps, towns, and villages — all mingled into one giant mass on top of each other as he gradually traversed the Circle of Ascension. To the uninitiated, nausea would certainly follow intense dizziness, and then madness. After making several rounds, he concentrated on Brn and stepped out to that place. Snowcapped mountains rose around him on all sides. Before him were the orange granite outer walls of the city of Brn. Being the middle of the night, Zoran knew that he could not gain entrance.

Some distance from the gates, a dense patch of forest grew. It beckoned to him, and he quietly walked among the tall pine trees. He found the forest floor thick with an accumulation of years of pine needles. Here he made camp. Actually, he wrapped himself in his blankets and dozed, leaning against a tree. His magical instincts would wake him if trouble found him. In the morning he would enter the city and seek his fortune; that was his plan.

Chapter 2 Starvation

Aldrick gracefully swooped and landed before the cavern's entrance, dropping the carcass of the antelope on the ground. His giant claws could have held much, much more. Slim pickings indeed, but it would have to do for now. Sunlight reflected off of his golden scales. Sofie poked her head out, stared at the carcass. "Is that all there is?" she asked of her mate, though she already knew the answer. She, too, had been out hunting, returning with empty claws.

"Divide it between the kids, Sofie," Aldrick suggested, knowing that their kids were going to howl and whine like mad. His stomach couldn't remember when it had last been really full. It was a miracle that the two had been able to sustain their twins, Emil and Renata.

Indeed, the two young golden dragons complained bitterly and loudly, but not until they had devoured the small antelope, ravenously. "Dad, we haven't had a real meal in, well since we can remember!" Emil howled angrily.

"Yeh, dad, we haven't!" Renata added just as vehemently.

"Okay, okay. Family meeting is now in session," Aldrick said in his commanding tone of voice, bordering on a magical spell, though just shy of it. Still fuming, the kids laid down on their cavern floor. Four huge heads were but feet apart.

"You know that for the last three years, I have been continually bringing up the overpopulation issue with Rainer and the Bostoff. (They were a part of the council of the elders which was made up of members of each race. Rainer was the leader of the Golds, the race to which these four belonged.) What I have been preaching to the elders has finally come true. We've overpopulated our world, Voss, and we are all doomed to starvation. We've eaten all the hoofers, and now they cannot even breed. There are too few of them left and too widely scattered. I searched one hundred square miles to find that miserable antelope."

"So what do we do now? Just lie down and starve to death?" Emil said angrily.

"Not at all son, not at all. I know a place that is rich in hoofers — so many that you could feast for years and not diminish them," Aldrick stated, knowing that he now had their fullest attention.

"We must move from here, taking everything with us. However, there is another thing to consider. What do we Golds treasure nearly as much as gems, my twins?"

He saw the light in their eyes once more. "Magic, dad! Magic!" Renata hollered before Emil could do the same.

"You both are now eighteen, and it is high time that you learned all the magic spells you can fit into your heads! I know that I've managed to teach you five spells, but I am not a very good teacher; neither is your mother. What you kids really need right now is to study under an Archmage! Yes, a real master of spells, whose knowledge vastly exceeds that of any of our species."

"You mean those frail humans, dad?" asked Renata, somewhat disgustedly.

"Yes, for all their frailties, Renata, some of them command vastly more magical powers than any of us, their Archmages. Plus, some of them are superb teachers, kids. In fact, I know that my old teacher is still living, though she is getting very old in human years. I propose that we pack up everything and move to her world, where the food is also plentiful. It is nearly springtime there, which is when she accepts new students. I believe that she will accept both of you. I have a little inducement for her, which, if I know Archmage Oldrich, she'll jump to get it."

"Cool, dad!" Renata came out of her hostilities, beginning to imagine first a full belly and then learning arcane magical spells.

"Yeh dad, brilliant. How come we didn't move sooner?" Emil added, still a bit hostile.

"Because you two were not quite old enough. Now you are ready, so what say you? Shall we abandon Voss for another world?"

"Dear, one small matter," Sofie interrupted. "In a few years, Renata will get her first heat. Where will she find other Golds with which to mate?"

"Why worry about that now, love? Let's worry about that when she is." Renata snorted; she wasn't the least bit interested in boys, not yet anyway. They were just too rowdy for her likes.

"Okay, that's settled. Now this is very important, kids. Humans are terrified of our kind, well most of them are. If they see our true shapes, they will likely drop everything and attempt to hunt us down and try to kill us. Humans kill what they fear, instead of trying to understand it. There are exceptions as always. So while we are on their world, we must be very, very careful not to let humans see our true forms. We can live in that same cavern where I stayed when I was getting my magic training from Archmage Oldrich. I think it is still here. Your mother and I will stay there while you are in school. Of course, if she accepts you, she will want you to live in her tower. However, she will allow you time to feed once a week. Just make sure that no one sees you change or sees you flying about; we don't want packs of humans trying to hunt us down. I know that they are puny and easily defeated, but that will surely force Archmage Oldrich to cancel your magic training. Now then, let's practice your morphing skills, kids."

The two grumbled, having done this minor spell many times before. It was one that their father taught them first. Now they understood why; it would allow them to mingle with the denizens of other worlds than their own. "When do we move, dad?" Renata wanted to know.

"Just as soon as I am convinced both of you know what to do and how to get along on her world. Sofie, will you start packing our pile of gems, please?" Aldrick asked.

The next day, satisfied that his kids knew what they had to do, Aldrick cast shrink spells onto their many sacks. Sofie then tied them securely to her legs. "How do we get there, dad?" asked Renata.

"We use our skills to move between worlds, though you must know your destination. I don't want you kids to go trying this on your own now. You might get lost and never find your way back! Once we are airborne, take my claw in yours and Sofie will take yours. When you are all attached to me, I will move us between Voss and her world."

"What's it called, dad?" Emil asked.

"Adapazan, son."

"Weird name," he replied.

"Whatever you do, don't let go until we arrive. Okay, up and away from Voss we go!" Aldrick took a running leap into the air, extending his magnificent wings to the fullest extent, some hundred plus feet across. He soared high into the air then hovered, waiting for Sofie and the kids to join him. One by one, they locked claws, and at last he began to move between worlds, as any good dragon could.

A black swirling mist hid everything from view. Both teens felt terribly uneasy, though they didn't panic. However, both realized that it would be very easy to panic and become trapped here in the nowhere, lost, disorientated, and confused. Everything looked the same — unrecognizable swirling masses of blackness. Suddenly, ahead of them, a blue light appeared, first as a small round object. Steadily it grew in size, larger and larger, until Aldrick pulled them into its sky, soaring high above the towering mountains, forests, and streams. Spring melt had come at last. Even from this height, Renata spied numerous hoofers grazing on the first shoots of spring. Food! Her dad was not kidding them. Her stomach growled once more.

Four golden dragon circled high above the deserted mountain tops, descending at last to a large cavern near one nearly inaccessible peak. "Ah, just as I left it some forty years ago," Aldrick announced and entered to check it out. Presently, he sounded the all clear bellow and the other three joined him. "I know it is rather small for the four of us, but soon the kids will be staying in the tower. Think we can manage Sofie?" he asked playfully. She gave him a swipe of her long tail.

Ah hour later, stomachs finally full for the first time in several years, the four dragons dozed for several days. When they awoke, Aldrick once more grilled the twins on how they were to conduct themselves. Satisfied that they knew how to avoid drawing attention to themselves, all four morphed into human forms. He handed Emil the giant emerald and Renata the small money pouch containing a number of gold coins, which he had left here in the cavern some forty years ago. Aldrick had no interest at all in gold, but he explained that humans highly valued it and that the twins should first purchase some more fitting clothing in the town.

Cocky, Emil bragged, "Dad, stop worrying. We can handle this. No problem at all. We'll see you in a few days when we need to feed again. You are right; this place is food heaven." Sofie smiled and hugged her twins. Then, the two morphed back into their golden forms and flew down until they were within walking distance. They landed and morphed back into their human forms and began the long walk into the town of Brn.

This remote town of some ten thousand people lay cradled between three tall peaks. One heavily traveled road led down into the dense forests and to other towns and villages of the Wild Lands of Adapazan. The twins stared at the tall granite outer walls; they'd seen nothing like this in their lives. Once they passed through the gates, the city streets were swarming with humans of all sizes and sexes. Soon they realized some were men, some women, and some children. Shops upon shops lined either side of the street.

Emil asked for directions to the Stodgy Inn, where the candidates would cluster in the spring in hopes of being chosen by Archmage Oldrich for their magic apprenticeship. Around noon the two entered the inn and acquired a room. So far so good, Emil thought.

Chapter 3 Many Meetings

Shouts and steel clanking upon steel roused Zoran from his sleep. He guessed the road and headed towards the noise, swords drawn. As the trees thinned and the rutted roadway appeared, he spied four wagons loaded with goods being attacked by twelve men. Each wagon had a driver and a guardsman, both of which had gotten off to repel the attacking bandits. However, three of them had quarrels sticking out of their sides or chests and were now mostly trying to protect the wagons as a last line of defense.

Three of the rough looking men were down, arrows protruding from their foreheads. Twang! Make that four bandits down; his eyes caught the flash of some bowman far to his right. Without thinking about it, Zoran launched himself into the fray, his pair of short shorts flashing rapidly. Taking the nearest by surprise, his blades sliced deep into the man's gut and his neck, dropping this bandit instantly. Twang! A fifth went down, as Zoran engaged the next bandit.

The double teaming bandits, realizing that their simple heist was going all wrong, turned tail to run back into the woods. However, the one he was facing had no choice but to attempt a fighting retreat. His broadsword swung defensively against the incredibly fast slicing motions of the twin blades. Fear crept into the man's face; he stopped making any attempt to swing his blade, merely trying to use it to block those razor sharp blades, moving so fast that if he focused on the path of one, the other became a blur. Pain. Pain again. Darkness. The bandit dropped as the sound of snarling, barking dogs came from the direction of the fleeing bandits.

Zoran looked over at the teamsters. Two waved a greeting, but began attending to their companions' many wounds. The archer stepped out of the woods. Zoran blinked twice. A woman wearing a leather top and pants similar to his, tall and with long blonde hair tied back, and sky blue eyes came walking towards him. She had a long bow and an arrow notched, though it was pointing downward at the moment. She took graceful, well placed steps as she approached, her eyes darting from fallen bandit to bandit. The dog growling and barking grew louder.

Suddenly the remaining five bandits came running as fast as they could from the trees, followed by a pack of large brown and black dogs. A man with a drawn sword was right behind them. "That'll be Bernard, most likely," the woman's alto voice called out to Zoran. "Don't attack the dogs."

The bandits, seeing Zoran and the archer before them and the wild man and dogs behind them, dropped their crossbows and swords. "We give up! Call them off!" one yelled frantically as a dog, teeth snarling, saliva dripping, slowly approached his leg.

"Heel, Amos. Heel," the man in the cloak called out. "Heel. Here to me. Here to me. Good dogs. Guard. Guard." Zoran was impressed with the behavior of the six dogs. The one that was threatening to take a bite out of the man's leg backed off. All six scampered like playful pups to the man's sides and sat down. When they heard the word "guard," they sat at attention, like scouts, watching the five men closely.

"I wouldn't try nothing," Bernard called out to the bandits. "Amos will take your leg off." Zoran rather doubted this, but the bandit obviously didn't. He shook with fear and stared at the dogs constantly. "Hail and well met again, Zdenka. Our paths cross once more."

"Aye, and to you too," the alto voice called over the battlefield to Bernard. To the five bandits, she called out, "Tend to your wounded men!" To Zoran, she said cautiously, "Hail stranger. Best be tending to the guards and drivers." Zoran nodded, already moving toward the victims of the attack, who were assisting their wounded men.

All four guards had sword wounds in their arms, legs, or chests. Three drivers had quarrels still protruding, as if they were a woman's pin cushion. The uninjured driver was hastily trying to stem the bleeding from his guardsman. "Here, let me at him," Zoran insisted, taking over. Quickly, he worked on getting the crude bandage tied tight enough to stop the bleeding. From the corner of his eye, he spied Zdenka attending to a quarrel victim.

"Hold him tightly. This will hurt a bit. On three. One. Two. Three." The man groaned; Zoran knew the quarrel had been extracted. "Ah, no blood being coughed up, good sign. Here, tie a wad of cloth to his wound." She moved on to the next one.

Bernard attended to another wounded guard, fastening make shift bandages to his arm and leg. Meanwhile the six dogs kept a vigilant eye on the bandits, occasionally growling, if they thought one was getting too far from the wagons. A half hour passed and Zoran heard the sound of several horses coming their way from Brn. "Ah, bout time," Bernard called out. Eyeing Zoran's curious look, he added, "Brn patrol. They'll take these vermin from us. Good thing too; we won't have to march them in to the Sheriff." Zdenka flashed a smile, though he didn't see it.

Four mounted riders wearing chain mail rode up. One called out, "Strom, what happened here?" The unwounded drover explained that they were attacked by the dozen bandits, and the four guards took charge of them at once. Five with arrows in their heads were quite dead. These, the guards quickly searched, confiscating weapons, coin pouches, and anything else of value. That same guard, evidently the one in charge Zoran assumed, ordered the remaining bandits to start digging five graves.

He then came up to Zdenka, "Your work, I presume, Zdenka?"

"Aye. Twelve against four is hardly a fair fight," she replied conservatively.

He chuckled, "Aye. Glad you were around. This is the third attack in a month. Sheriff sent us out to patrol the road, hoping to find them. You've taken all our fun away, ma'am." He teased her. She smiled. "Here, present this stuff to the sheriff, and you and your friends will get the reward. Get the wagons moving soon; those guards need physician attention pronto."

"Aye. Soon as we have them temporarily bandaged. It won't do to have them bleed to death before we get to Brn," she replied. She helped several get up onto the wagons, as did Bernard and Zoran. The three stood and watched the four wagons begin moving on down the road into Brn.

At last, Bernard said, "I'm heading into Brn, Zdenka. By the way, thanks stranger."

"Zoran, sir. Mighty well trained dogs you have there. I'm heading into Brn myself. Just got here late last night. Slept in yonder woods, when I was rudely awakened but the swords. How far is it into Brn?" Of course he knew precisely where the walls were located; he'd seen them when he had arrived last night, but he wanted to play the role of traveler. Far less questions, besides, if he said he'd Shadow Walked here, everyone would know he was a Duska and royalty. That was the last thing he wanted revealed about himself.

"Hail Zoran," the mellow alto voice said, as she walked up beside the two men. Bernard's dogs now trotted out in front of the three, slowly walking down the road some distance from the wagons ahead. "Nice swordsmanship. Don't see many with a flashy style as yours in these parts, let alone two short swords. Some say those are not a 'man's' weapons." Zoran recognized her teasing probe. Indeed, he had defied all traditions by not choosing a broadsword, bastard sword, or possibly a giant two handed sword.

He grinned, "I'm not from around these parts. By the way, that was some incredible archery you did back there. Impressive, to say the very least."

It was Zdenka's turn to smile, "Aye, but I was off my mark twice. The shots were supposed to be right here," she put her finger right between Zoran's eyes on his forehead just above his nose. "I missed by an inch both times."

Bernard chuckled, "Ah, Zdenka, you are slipping!" She grinned. "I'm called Bernard Dragan, Dog Master. She's Zdenka Lavos, Archer. I'm heading into Brn for the Picking."

"You too?" Zdenka commented curiously.

"Aye, but I don't suppose that Archmage Oldrich will choose me," he said rather bored. "This will be my third try. I'm not sure why I keep coming to the Picking, but I seem to find myself walking this way. She'll probably not pick me this year either, but I reckon it don't hurt to try."

"Well, if you want to learn magic, Bernard, you just have to keep on trying. I'm going to the Picking this year too. I'm fed up with my life. Magic may be what I am seeking. Guess I will see. What's your business in these parts, Zoran?" she asked politely. Bernard was also eyeing the stranger.

"I've come to see Archmage Oldrich myself. I want to see if she will accept me as a student. What's this Picking thing all about?" he asked, hoping to get some information.

It was Bernard who replied. "Each spring, about now in fact, Archmage comes to the Stodgy Inn to interview all those who wish to become magic apprentices. Been doing it as long as I can recall," he explained in a monotone voice. "Some she chooses, some she don't. She didn't pick me twice before, and I don't know why she might pick me this year, though, but it gives the dogs a nice outing if nothing else."

"How does she choose the new apprentices?" Zoran asked, though he saw that Zdenka also was very curious as well.

"Oh, she asks you funny questions," he replied, bored.

"Like what," Zdenka asked, curiously.

"Dunno. Cain't remember them. Funny thing, been asked them twice now, and I can't remember what her questions were! Isn't that just the strangest thing?" Bernard replied, himself suddenly becoming curious for a moment, before slipping back into his usual boredom.

"Probably cast a Forget spell on you," Zoran suggested. "That would account for your not being able to recall her questions. Maybe you'll get them right this time."

"Maybe so, maybe not," he replied. "Least the dogs like the long walk, especially Amos, there. He's the oldest. Right smart dog." Zoran noticed that, when talking about his dogs, Bernard was anything but bored.

As they approached the gates, Zdenka said, "Say, you two follow me to the sheriff's office. Part of the reward money belongs to both of you as well. Please, I insist."

"Thanks, Zdenka, but you did most of the kill'n. I only rounded up the strays," Bernard replied.

"Yes, but that means those five won't be robbing and hurting others for a long time, Bernard. Zoran, you got some yourself. Please, I insist. Then, Bernard, you can lead us to the Stodgy Inn. I don't know exactly where that's at — Brn is rather large."

"Okay, if you insist. Maybe it will pay for my room and board," Bernard replied.

"Thank you, Zdenka. I've my own funds, but if you insist. Thanks," Zoran replied. "I have no idea where this inn is located. Never been to Brn. I can see it's quite large, isn't it?"

"Aye, that she is," Bernard replied. "Stranger, best watch your money pouch. There's pickpockets hangin' round these streets. Unsavory types too, but I reckon that you can deal with them with your fancy swords. Me, I depend upon my dogs. They can smell a foul beast a mile away. Now this one time. . ." Bernard began relating a story of how his dogs helped capture two thieves here in Brn. Not long, Zdenka halted before a brick building. A large sign spelled Sheriff in large letters. She asked them to wait, while she went inside. Zoran resigned himself to listen to the rest of Bernard's tale.

Not long after that and just before Bernard was about to launch into yet another dog story, she reappeared. "Not bad for a morning's work, fellows. I'll split it with you." She handed each of them twenty gold coins. "They fetched a nice price indeed. Okay, Bernard, lead on — to the Stodgy Inn and a bath for me. Say, is this an expensive inn?"

"Well that all depends on the accommodations you want. Me, I always take the cheapest lodgings. Why waste money on fancy rooms? Especially when you don't have it," he replied. "Course, it all depends on how soon the Picking will be, too," he answered in a non-committal tone. Zdenka pressed him, and he added, "Well, where I usually stay costs a gold piece a week, but the fancy rooms, now they run more like five."

"Say, since I am new to town, how about I treat both of you to some good rooms? I've plenty of funds — been traveling a lot," Zoran lied. "I would like some friendly company while we all wait on this Archmage. What do you say? Friends?" He held out his hand and Zdenka shook it, though she was still a bit reserved. Bernard gave a hearty shake, thankful for a nice room for a change.

"Thanks, Zoran. After I get a bath, we can meet in the main bar room. I'll spring for lunch," Zdenka.

"Oh no, that means I spring for dinner and that costs more," Bernard lamented jokingly. "Say, now you can see the Archmage's tower pretty good from here. Look. Impressive, isn't it? I wonder what all goes on in there? Maybe this time I will find out," he added.

The three involuntarily stopped to gaze at the orange granite circular tower which rose five stories above the street. Zoran estimated it was at least a hundred feet in diameter, and it occupied the northernmost part of the city. The outer walls butted up against the sides of the tower. He realized now that this city belonged to Archmage Oldrich, who had probably founded it half a century ago and was likely it's protector out here in the Wild Lands. With any luck, he would be living inside that tower soon. If not, well, there were other Archmages he could try.

The Stodgy Inn was the last inn before the tower, but also a fairly good one. Just inside the main doors was the commons, where meals were served, games played, and, of course, ales had. The barkeeper jovially called out, "Oh no. It's Bernard and his dogs again! Must be close to the Picking time again. Gonna try it again this year, Bernard? Who's your pretty friend there?" He nodded to Zdenka, and then politely nodded to Zoran.

"Yes, trying it again. This is Zdenka Lavos, an Archer from the Dark Forest, here for the Picking too. She just managed to capture the bandits this morning on our way here, with our help mind you. Oh yes, this is Zoran, a fighter, who helped. Say when is the Picking going to take place?"

"This Saturday. Good luck. You be wanting your usual room?"

Zoran spoke up, "No, I want three of your finest rooms for these new friends of mine — three in a row, if you have them. We'll be staying through Saturday. Come for the Picking."

His eyebrows rose. "Fifteen gold, on account of him have'n those dogs 'o his in his room. Makes a mess; maids have a hard time getting dog smell out of the rooms." Zoran smiled, figuring something like this might happen. Most inns wouldn't let dogs inside. He counted out the coins and the man bit one; satisfied, he chatted away.

"Rooms ten through twelve, top story, them stairs over there. Yea gets a hot bath with it and free meals — for *people*, though," he stared at Bernard, who forked over a gold coin for scraps for his six dogs.

"Didn't get your surname, Zoran. Where yea be from?" the barkeeper chatted away, though Zoran knew that the man was intensely curious of strangers. All barkeepers were, at least all those that he had seen.

"Just Zoran, sir. Only Zoran. I come from a town far to the east, been traveling a long time. Heard this Archmage Oldrich is tops. Figured why not learn from the best? Don't you think?" He cleverly avoided the question and sent the conversation in another direction, which the barkeeper was only too pleased to explain just how great Brn's benefactor was.

A bit later, the three headed up the steps to find their rooms. Inside, he deposited his pack and studied the room. First rule of survival drilled into his head was to know your surroundings well. The only entrance was the door. The long hall could be a death trap as there was no other way to the stairs. Looking out his window, he spied what he was looking for — an alternative exit. He could use the drain pipe to shimmy down to the alley behind the inn, if necessary. Satisfied, he rang for a maid and a hot bath in the barrel. His room, while far from the comforts of Castle Dorumova, were acceptable, though not what any Duska would choose.

Lunchtime. The three refreshed new friends headed down to sample the food. Several dozen others had stopped by to dine as well. Some, Zoran noted, looked to be wealthier types. He minded his courtly manners and helped Zdenka to sit, which surprised her. She eyed him more closely after that gesture. Sitting opposite of each other, they could now study each other.

Zdenka must be about nineteen perhaps, he surmised. She was well built, with strong arms and legs, probably by virtue of having become an archer. About his height, she had undone her long hair, and Zoran found himself even more attracted to this woman. She now wore a thin cotton blouse instead of her travel leather top.

Bernard, he judged to be twenty-one, with bowl-cut, short black hair and eyes to match. His face appeared bored more often than not, though he was observant. His eyes animated the instant one mentioned dogs.

Zdenka observed this stranger. He was young, perhaps eighteen, certainly not in his twenties. He still had that teenage youthful look about him. About her height, he had long brown hair that just touched his shoulders. Remarkable blue eyes seemed to penetrate her, she noted. She'd never seen such eyes before. His face was handsome, that she knew. Tall and well-muscled as any fighter ought to be, she concluded. Yet, there was something different about this youth, something that intrigued her. She continued to stare at him, when he wasn't looking at her. Presence, that was it, she realized in a flash of intuition. He had more presence than anyone she'd ever met! Who was this Zoran? Where did he come from? Why was he really here? She had more questions than answers at the moment.

"So tell me, Zdenka, how did a pretty woman like you become an archer? I've rarely seen such a terrific shot as you are," Zoran broke in on her reverie. Either she answered or Bernard would — she knew that for a fact. What the heck, she thought to herself, someone's got to go first.

"Dad and I live in a cottage deep in the Dark Forest, some fifty miles from here. He wanted a son and got me instead," she jested, but Zoran detected there was a deep truth in those words. Mom died when I was young; dad blamed himself. A bear got her while he was out hunting. He insisted that I learn to take care of myself. I can handle a short sword a little, but I didn't like it. Archery, now that turned out to be great fun. I've won the Brn Archery Championship five years running. I decided not to enter anymore, no competition. Besides, I take away all of the fun from all the other archers."

"I'll say she did," Bernard jumped in. He'd seen her last match. "Boris thought he had won the match last fall. Shot one in the bull's-eye at three hundred paces back. Zdenka stepped up and put all three shots dead center in the bull's-eye. You should have seen the look on Boris' face."

"Yes, that's why I am not entering anymore. He was devastated. I don't see any reason to do that to anyone, you know. No point in it," she replied.

"I like your attitude, Zdenka. Why show off? I avoid match challenges like the plague," Zoran replied. Her surname, Lavos. Somehow it sounded familiar, though he just could not place it. Perhaps someone or one of his friends had mentioned it. Yet, this Wild Lands was a thousand miles from the court and civilization. "Say, what is your dad's name, Zdenka?" he asked, wondering if that might help.

"Janos, Janos Lavos. Have you ever heard of him? I doubt it; we've always lived deep in the Dark Forest. Hardly anyone knows of us," she replied. His mind raced. That name sounded familiar, like he ought to know it. Janos must be fighter trained if he was able to teach her to fight and become an expert archer. Yet, why hide out in some forest here in the Wild Lands? Highly skilled fighters ought to be in demand nearly anywhere. Zoran finally left this as a mystery to be solved one day.

"Me, I live in a cottage about five miles out of town, small village of a hundred of us. Got a nice place there. Raise dogs, if you haven't guessed. Guard dogs and hunting dogs are my specialty. Folks come for miles to get one of my pups, though I am pretty picky about who I sell one of mine to — gotta treat them right and give them a good home and lots of attention." He would have gone on at length, but Zdenka cleverly cut him off.

"So what about you, Zoran? What's your story?" she smiled at him, her alto voice enchanting.

Zoran was on the spot. He hated to lie; it was not in his nature. Yet, he couldn't just tell them the total truth. "Like I said, I've come a very long way. I was getting fighter training and had some magic training as well. I know a few spells, but I didn't like the wizard or his attitude, so I came searching for greener pastures, as they say. Well, that's not the whole truth, exactly. Can you two keep a secret?" he asked, knowing that in all likelihood they couldn't, but it would serve his purposes. Both nodded and leaned closer.

"I've run away from home! Yes, I just up and left everything behind me. I just can't stomach the lies, the deceit, the constant warring, and the evil ways of so many rulers. I can't even stand the way that the Baron runs Dorum, let alone all these warlords out here in the Wild Lands. So I up and ran away from it all. I heard this section of our Wild Lands was better off and that Archmage Oldrich was a good monarch, so I came here. It can't be any worse that what I left behind. Just don't tell anyone that I've run away, please."

"Oh, I promise I won't tell anyone, Zoran. I swear that your secret is safe with me, right Bernard?" She sounded so sincere. Zdenka thought to herself, "I knew it! He has to be some nobleman's son! His manners are too refined for around here. Now I wonder which nobleman? I'm going to keep my ears open."

"Dad and I also don't like all the heavy handed tactics used around here by the various warlords either," she confided, part of her wanting to let him know that she felt much as he did. She wondered why she had such a strong impulse to do so. "Honestly, it seems that all of the men in power on this whole planet are cruel, sadistic beasts! We are very fortunate to be in the lands controlled by Archmage Oldrich. She is a benevolent monarch for sure."

"Aye, that she is," Bernard confirmed her declaration. "The Brn Land is about the safest place to live out here in the Wild Lands, though we often get raiders coming in from the surrounding areas."

"What do they do when they raid? Steal everything of value?" Zoran asked.

"Some, but often they steal young men, kidnap them, probably to become slaves in their ever growing armies. I know recruiters often come around telling us to send our young men off to get trained because soon the evil Baron's forces will come invading into the Wild Lands. He will, you know, come a conquering sooner or later. Just study your history. He's already captured the lands once owned by ten warlords, albeit those that were around Dorum mind you," Bernard explained. Zoran cringed slightly. He knew well what his father was doing with Adapazan.

Just then a husband and wife passed by their table on their way out. The man was distracted by something she said and he bumped into the trio's table. As he suddenly turned around to see what was happening, his arm accidentally knocked over Zdenka's ale mug. Zoran's eyes followed the tipping mug. It ought to have fallen over and emptied its contents in her lap. Instead, the mug froze mid-fall and then righted itself, as if an unseen hand had caught it just in time. "Pardon me," the man said and left with his wife.

Zdenka saw Zoran staring at her mug, and she blushed. "Well, I can do a little magic myself," she admitted, though she had been keeping it a secret.

"I say well done," Zoran complimented her. "Fast action. I like that. Besides, you just had a bath." She grinned. She liked this nobleman, if that was really what he was. Bernard excused himself; he needed to tend to his dogs.

"Well, we have lots of time to kill," Zoran began, a little unsure how to proceed with her. He just wanted to somehow get to know this woman better.

"Well, I promised myself that no matter what else happens on my first trip into Brn that I would go to their dance hall. I've heard stories about how fabulous the place is. and I've just got to check it out. However, it is a pretty fancy place from what I gather, so I am going to have to go in search of a dress this afternoon. I presume the barkeeper can tell me where the dance hall is located and how to get there. Care to tag along?" she asked, hoping that he might. If so, it would only add to her theory about him being a nobleman somewhere.

"Sure. I'll go ask for directions. We can go together, if you don't mind my tagging along, Zdenka," he replied.

Later that afternoon, after the two had visited both a dressmaker's shop and a tailor's shop, each purchasing suitable attire for the dance, they were returning to the inn. The streets were rather crowded with townsfolk, many heading home for the evening. Overhead, Zoran spied a large hawk circling. Strange place for a hawk, he thought to himself.

A little further on, the two saw a thief snatch a money pouch from a well-dressed man. A knife flashed and cut its thong from the man's belt. The thief deftly caught it as it began to fall, and then made a mad dash through the crowd, making his escape. Just at that point, the hawk began to dive. Both Zdenka and Zoran watched mystified by the suddenness of the bird's dive. The hawk dove straight for the pick pocket, who was running away as fast as he could go, often pushing or shoving aside others who were in his way. In one perfectly timed swoop, the hawk snatched the pouch from the thief's hand and soared into the sky.

"Now there's something you don't see every day!" Zoran exclaimed. "Did you see that hawk just take that money pouch from the thief? Or am I seeing things?"

"No, I saw it too, pretty incredible. Look, the hawk is coming down again," she pointed out. The two watched as the bird came down and landed on a tall, thin man's arm, releasing the pouch.

"Sir, your pouch," the man caught the attention of the victim, handing him back his pouch. From this distance, the two could not hear what was said, though they did see the grateful man giving something to the tall, thin falconer.

"Come on. I want to meet that man," Zoran exclaimed, having never seen such a feat before. "Excuse me, sir. I saw what your hawk just did. Fabulous training. Are you a falconer?"

"Damnable thieves," he said angrily. Tall and thin, he had black hair and eyes, with a peculiar goatee. He was probably in his early twenties, Zoran guessed. "Yes, *master* falconer," he corrected Zoran. "My card. Name's Karel Ambrose. I patrol these streets about this time of day. Streets are not safe anymore, damn thieves anyway. Think they can just steal anything they want. Well, I am showing that they can't get away with it!" The man was mad, no doubt of that. "Excuse me, but I need to patrol some more. This time of day is prime time for the pick pockets!" He launched his bird into the sky once more and moved on down the street. The two looked at each other and headed on back to the inn for supper. The dance was tomorrow evening.

At suppertime, the inn rapidly filled up with guests and locals. Once the dinner hour passed, a number came in to drink ale and chat with friends. Zoran spied a card game getting started. As he looked at the dealer, his inner sense kicked in — something was not right here. He decided to play a round. "Zoran. Mind if I join you?"

"More the better, Zoran. Hope you don't mind if I take your money, stranger. New around here, haven't seen you in town before," the dealer said. "Name's Bedrich." Three other players introduced themselves, but Zoran's attention was drawn to a black haired woman, who was watching them from a distance. She looked like she was trying to make up her mind about joining them. Her short hair was nicely brushed, and she was slightly thin. Then, she walked over to the table.

"Room for one more?" she asked calmly; her eyes darted from man to man, lingering on Zoran for an instant before concentrating on the dealer. She was twenty-two, four inches shorter than Zoran, and fairly attractive.

"Sure why not. Ladies always welcome. Hope you don't mind my taking your money, little lady," he said in a cocky manner.

"As long as you don't cheat and play fair, I don't mind," she replied a little icily. He gave her a sideways glance, but continued shuffling the cards, then dealt them. Zoran got lucky on the first hand and pulled the few coins to his side.

Three hands later and the stakes were raised considerably. Sweat poured off of two of the other players. The dealer coyly asked, "Cards?"

"Yeh, three," both men said. They had a substantial wager already on the table. Zoran discarded one and accepted a new one. He noticed that the woman had said very little all this time. However, she watched every motion that the men made.

"Dealer takes two," Bedrich said matter of factly, rapidly placing two cards before him.

In a flash, the woman had a dagger in her hand and plunged it down into the dealer's hand, sticking its blade on down into the table. Bedrich howled in pain. Zoran yelled, "What's going on?" ready to knock the woman across the floor.

She snickered, "You almost lost your shirt to this card cheat. Look at the card he just dealt himself." Zoran slid the card out from under the man's bleeding hand. He was holding it tightly, trying not to move his hand. The pain was intense. Zoran flipped over the very Ace that he had just discarded.

"Hey, that's the card I just tossed back in. You, Bedrich, are cheating!" The other players became quite angry, and the barkeeper came rushing over to the table.

"Caught him cheating did we?" the apron-clad man exclaimed.

The other three players angrily told the whole story. The barkeeper pulled the woman's dagger out of Bedrich's hand, but not gently, causing him to howl even louder. "You are lucky that I am not going to turn you over to these players. Get out of here. If I ever see you in this inn again, I will have you killed. Do you understand me?"

"Whataboutmymoney?" he screamed, running his words together.

"It belongs to those you tried to cheat. Get him out of here now!" Several strong arm dragged Bedrich out and tossed him into the street.

Wiping off the woman's dagger, he handed it back to her, "Thanks, Jarka, well done." He tossed her a small money pouch, which she deftly caught, a sly grin on her face.

"Anytime, Fredrich, anytime." Zoran picked his coins that he began with off the table, while the other three men followed suit.

"Why don't we split Bedrich's coins five ways?" Zoran suggested, hoping to defuse the situation further. After doing so, the three grumbled and headed to get a round of ales.

"Jarka, Jarka Mitova," the woman said, putting her dagger away.

"Zoran. Excellent work, Jarka. I sensed something was amiss, but couldn't put my finger on it. So the barkeeper hired you to catch this card cheater?"

"Yes, he claimed he's had a lot of customers complaining about Bedrich always seeming to win the bigger pots. So a couple days ago he hired me to investigate. Been watching him from the sidelines last couple of nights, saw him cheating. I figured I'd catch him in the act. After tonight, he'll not ever again be so agile with that cheating hand. Stabbed him right where his nerves are at. Yes, it'll heal, but he'll find he has more or less a bum hand." She snickered, "Serves him right, the cheat."

"Well, you certainly have a very keen eye and a lightning draw, Jarka. Thanks."

"So, Zoran, you new town? I've not seen you before," she asked rather covertly.

"Yes, I just arrived late last night. This morning I helped Zdenka and Bernard capture some bandits trying to heist some wagons heading into town. Are things always this wild around here?"

She gave him a strange look. "This *is* the Wild Lands. Where are you from anyway? No, things are pretty tame around here, Archmage Oldrich sees to it."

"Long way to the east. I'm here for the Picking, hoping to apprentice under the Archmage."

She chuckled, "Well, good luck with that. I'm throwing in my hat this time as well. One never can tell who she will pick. Well, it's still early; best be going. Lots of pockets to pick out there tonight," she teased or did she? Zoran couldn't tell.

As he picked up his coins, Bernard came over to the table with two mugs of ale. "Ah, I see you met Jarka. She's a thief, you know. Good one too, by all accounts. Some say that she is in the Archmage's pay, thieving back from the thieves, but who knows for sure. Kind of dull in here isn't it?" he explained in his boring tone.

As Zoran sipped his ale with Bernard, he began to miss his two friends that he had left back in Dorum. It just wasn't the same drinking with Bernard. He retired early.

By the evening of the dance, Zoran was incredibly bored himself. Back at the castle, there had always been many things to do, sword practice or even taking off for a horseback ride. Here, he just sat around staring at the walls. He donned his new suit and satisfied himself that he looked presentable. He then knocked on Zdenka's door. "Just a minute," she called out and then opened her door.

"Well, you look — well just great," Zoran replied, rather shocked at the transformation. Gone were the leather pants. In their place, she wore a light blue cotton dress. She'd let her hair down and had brushed it. Golden locks fell over her shoulders.

"Thanks, shall we?" she replied.

"Of course," he offered her his arm and walked her out of the inn. Again, she noted the highly refined moves that came natural to Zoran, further convincing her that he just had to be a nobleman. Both enjoyed the dance, and she found that Zoran was an excellent dancer, ten times better than her father who had taught her. By the time that they returned to the inn, Zdenka was convinced beyond all doubt that Zoran was a nobleman in disguise.

All three sat around a table enjoying a long lunch the next day. What else was there to do except wait? Just after the noontime crowd left, two others walked into the inn. Both caught the trio's eyes immediately. Both were teens, probably not much older than himself, Zoran thought, but his inner senses began working overtime, so to speak. They seemed to have a lot of facial features in common; he hazarded a guess that they may be twins. However, it was their skin color that most attracted his attention, a pale yellow, bordering on bronze or gold. He'd never seen anyone with such skin color, though he had heard of other races around.

One was a young man, who had jet black hair and the blackest of eyes that he'd ever seen. The other was a young woman, who also had the same black hair and eyes, though hers was quite long, reaching the small of her back. Their hair was rather thick and coarse. Neither looked like they quite knew what they were doing. He walked up to their table, since hardly anyone else was now here.

"Excuse me, can you tell me how my sister and I may obtain a room?"

"Sure, just go ask the barkeeper over there. He's in charge," Zoran replied, adding as an afterthought, "Say, once you two are settled, why not come down and keep us company? We're all waiting for the Picking this Saturday. Come join us. Not much else to do but wait on the Archmage."

The lad thanked him, and he and the young woman walked over to the bar. Zoran tried to listen in on their conversation but could only hear the lad say, "Which coin is it? We are new to Brn." The barkeeper pointed the way to the stairs, and the two left to check out their rooms.

Once they were out of earshot, Zdenka whispered, "Those are the strangest people I've ever seen! Did you see the color of their skin? They must have come from very far away indeed!" Both Zoran and Bernard admitted they had never seen anyone like these two before. "Glad that you invited them to join us. Maybe they will tell us where they are from." All three were very curious — none more so than Zoran, who was mystified by the pair.

Sure enough a short while later, the two newcomers came back down and over to their table. Zoran hastily got another chair and helped the woman get seated. Strangers or not, he minded his manners when it came to a woman. Zoran quickly introduced the three of them.

"I am called Emil Vogler. This is my twin sister, Renata. We have come a very long way to meet with the Archmage Oldrich," Emil said in a rather aloof manner.

"Ah, so you are here for the Picking too. Say, where are you from?" Zdenka asked. Zoran watched the eyes of the two teens closely.

"We are from Voss, a very long way from here. I'm sure that you have never heard of it," he replied.

"Say our clothes look so different from yours. How do we get clothes like yours?" Renata asked. The conversation got going well at last. Zoran was certain that he did not lie, but their eyes. There was something strange, foreign even, about them. He and Zdenka volunteered to take them to the tailors and the dressmakers. It would give them time to find out more about these two.

When Zdenka and Zoran had supper together, they had their first opportunity to reflect in private on these two newcomers. "They are the strangest pair I have ever met," Zdenka began. "She had no idea how we put on dresses! Honestly this place they are from, Voss she said, must be the strangest place. I caught her in a slight slip — well I think it was a slip. I asked her what style of clothes she was used to wearing in Voss. You'll never guess what her answer was, Zoran. She said, 'We don't wear clothes.' But she caught herself at once and said, 'I mean dresses like these. Ours are more different.' I asked her about them, but she pretended to be more interested in how she looked. We also got her a leather outfit as well."

"Good. She will probably need both. That sure is strange. Emil seemed to be easily confused about normal simple things too. He had a devil of a time trying to tie his shoe laces. But then I guess if we came from a foreign land, our customs would seem odd here too," Zoran acknowledged. "Still, it's their eyes that trouble me, Zdenka. I cannot put my finger on it, but their eyes intrigue me."

"Sure are black, but I know what you mean. Still, both are friendly enough, actually bordering on naive might be a better statement. Oh well, I guess foreigners are just foreigners. Archmage Oldrich is famous, after all, and probably attracts all manner of want-to-be apprentices from all over the world," Zdenka concluded conservatively.

"Well, tomorrow's the big Picking day. We'd best turn in early. I wonder what her questions will be?" Zoran mused aloud. The two headed up to their rooms. Try as he might, he could not get Emil's eyes out of his mind. Something about them fascinated him, but what?

Chapter 4 The Picking

Around ten the next morning, the inn was filled with all those who wanted to apprentice with the Archmage. To get the opportunity to learn magical spells moved one up in the entire society, either to Adept or even Mage status. Both earned one a vastly better living. Hence each year many came here hoping to be chosen this year.

Precisely at ten, Archmage Nadia Oldrich made her appearance, suddenly appearing in their midst. Zoran suspected that she had most likely used a teleport spell. She was old, seventy-five, with long white hair tied into a bun on her head. She leaned on a staff, probably magical, Zoran concluded. While her body was old, her mind was sharp as was her eyes. The barkeeper led her to a side table in one corner, where she would conduct her interviews. Unfortunately, she was now on the opposite side of the room from where Zoran and his new friends were sitting.

"Darn, we'll be last," Karel spat on the floor, a bit angry that he had not chosen a better location, closer to the Archmage. Zoran was beginning to think that Karel was often angry or at least was easily annoyed.

"Patience, Karel," he whispered, straining to hear what the Archmage was asking a small boy.

"She probably has a quota," Bernard commented in his usual monotone. "Hope it isn't filled before she gets to us."

"Look, she is definitely casting a spell on them after she's finished with them," Zoran pointed out. "You can see the tiny flash of magic." All watched the next young man as he was interviewed.

"Right, I missed that," Zdenka commented.

"Well, I see it too," Karel added. "I'll make it a point to tell her not to cast spells on me when I get my interview!"

"We saw it too," Emil added softly.

Zoran was calm; either she would accept him or not. If she didn't, why, he would just move on elsewhere. Yet with his new friends, he saw just how much they really wanted and needed to be chosen. Even the two strange twins were extremely eager to be chosen. Time passed as one by one the many others in front of them met with the old woman and then peacefully left the inn. None that left seemed the slightest bit upset about not having been chosen, Zoran observed. He concluded that must be part of her enchantment spell, a wise move to defuse disappointment, anger, and resentment. More left. He began to wonder just how selective she actually was going to be!

By the time only their small group remained, only one woman in her mid-twenties had been chosen. With long brown hair and blue eyes, she was sitting over by the bar, patiently waiting. The look of utter elation told all that she had been chosen this year. When it was finally down to their group, Karel got up and rushed over to the Archmage, before anyone else could get up. Zoran smiled and decided that he'd go last. To everyone's utter amazement, Karel punched his fists high into the air, calling out, "Yes!" He quickly joined the young woman by the bar.

Jarka quickly took his place, before the others could react. Zoran suspected that the thief, no matter her skills, was not likely to be chosen to become trained in magic. She would be his last choice. To his surprise, she too, grinned widely, and swinging her hips seductively, walked over to the bar, joining Karel, who punched the air with his victory fist once more for her sake. "Guess I might as well get it over with now," Bernard said, rising and walking toward the Archmage. "Good luck to the rest of you."

A minute later, one very surprised Bernard looked back at the tiny group and smiled, moving to join those at the bar. Now the twins took their turn, both going at once. Zoran suspected that the Archmage would chastise them for coming together. After all this was a one on one interview. Indeed, she appeared to be about to do just that, when Emil pulled something from his pocket and handed it to her. To his surprise, the Archmage motioned for both of them to step closer. They began talking, talking for quite some time.

"They are taking far longer than anyone else, even if you take into account that there are two of them. Well, they are strangers. Perhaps she is having a more difficult time deciding about them," Zdenka concluded.

For ten long minutes the Archmage talked with Emil and Renata before finally motioning them to join the others by the bar. Both twins had a pleased smile upon their yellowish faces. "Go ahead, Zdenka; give it your best shot," Zoran urged her forward. At first, Zdenka was a bit timid, but then strode forcefully over to the Archmage.

Zoran found himself praying that Zdenka would also be chosen. He wondered why? He'd only just met her, but he did like her — quite a lot. She was, well, she was fascinating. Zoran couldn't think of any better term. Then she too joined those at the bar, and it was his turn to face the Archmage Nadia Oldrich. He walked up to her and sat down as she motioned for him to do.

"Name please and origin city," she asked, as if she had asked that question a million times before, which she probably had. "No lies please. Merely the truth. What you say will be held in the strictest of confidences."

"I am Zoran. Er, I'm not sure if I ought to answer the rest, Archmage Oldrich. You see, such knowledge may well put you in some danger."

"I see. Son, I am now seventy-five years old. Been an Archmage for over half a century. Let me be the judge of all that, if you please. However, I sense that I need to say more. You have my solemn word that what you say to me will not be repeated by my lips under any circumstances."

"How about mentally to others?" Zoran found himself blurting out. As a Duska, he could well read other's minds, if he just had to do it. Certainly, he and his sister could communicate mentally across space. As soon as he said this, however, he realized that he had made a grave mistake. Her eyebrows rose sharply, and she stared even harder at him for a moment.

"Yes, mentally as well. Now, I repeat, your full name and origin city."

"Zoran Vladislov of Dorum."

"I thought as much, Duska, youngest son of the tyrant Baron Kazimir, are you not?"

"Yes, Archmage. I have been trained for a year or so under his Archmage Milos, but I cannot stomach his attitude and his blind following of Kazimir and now

Radek. I want no part of their ruthless ways. Besides, someone has been trying to kill me. Tried three times now. Obviously failed. I've run away. I have been very careful to cover my tracks; no one will be able to follow my Shadow Walk. Here, I am called just Zoran, no surname. I want my identity to be a secret, if possible."

"I do know some twenty spells, but I must know more. I would be very honored indeed if you could take me on as one of your students. I know that you are against the Baron and all that he stands for; we are allies, more or less. Please accept me. I will work hard and do as you ask."

"Thank you for being honest with me. I suspected as much. Simply Zoran it is. Now then answer me this. You enter a room only to find a table with a bag containing one thousand gold coins in it. Sitting at the table is a young man who is bleeding badly from a sword wound. You see no sword in the room. Cowering against the back of the room is young mother, shielding a small child. What do you do?"

"I go to the man and apply pressure to stop the bleeding and bandage him. As soon as possible, I ask the woman what has happened here and if she needs assistance," Zoran replied without hesitation.

"What about the bag of gold?"

"Who gives a darn about a bag of gold anyway? We're talking about people's lives here, not money. You can always work and make more money, but it is very hard to create life once it is gone."

"Fine. I accept you as an Apprentice Mage, Zoran. Please bring the others to my tower's door in an hour. I will meet you all there. It's been a pleasure speaking with a true Duska for a change. The world is full of rotten Duska's these days. Until then." She vanished as suddenly as she arrived.

"Did she take you?" Zdenka asked.

"Yes, I am to bring us all to the tower's door in an hour. I guess we have an hour to get our things together." Zdenka smiled, very pleased that her nobleman was also selected.

"Well, I must admit we are the strangest bunch of new apprentices that she's accepted," Bernard commented, slightly interested.

"Yes, I have to admit that," Jarka agreed. "A thief, an archer, a dog trainer, a falconer, a fighter, and two total strangers to these parts. Weird indeed, but then who can say?"

"I am Zuzanna. I am to be your maid and am going to become an Adept!" the young woman added, not wanting to be left out.

"Forgive me, Zuzanna. I am called Zoran," he said apologetically and introduced the others to the older woman. She then left in a hurry to go pack her things, while they did the same, though most had little to pack.

Right on time the group stood before the towering stone circular building. Zoran knocked on the door, and a man in a robe opened. "Hi all, I am Marek, door warden. If you will follow me, please, I'll take you to the meeting room." He led them down a short hall which opened into a large, square room, fully carpeted and with numerous chairs.

Archmage Nadia was there waiting for them. "Welcome new apprentices. First, Marek will show you to your private rooms here on the first floor. Bernard's yours will be the closest to this room and the front door. I trust you will keep your dogs in there until you get the chance to take them back to your kennels. After you drop off your things, meet back here, and we will discuss many things. Marek," she motioned with her hand and he led them through the first side door on their left.

Indeed, a long circular hallway lay before them. Each was given a small dorm style room, perhaps ten by fifteen feet, with bed, desk, and chair, frugal by any standard, but comfortable. Zoran suspected he would be spending very little time in here, sleeping mostly. Five minutes later, they sat down in the large meeting room.

Chapter 5 Beginning Lessons

Archmage Nadia began her explanation, "I suspect that you are wondering just why I chose all of you this year. I admit, with a couple exceptions, you are indeed an unusual set of choices. However, I will do my best to teach all of you as much magic as you can comprehend. You see, the limiting factor is really your intelligence, not how diligent you are at studying, or how well-bred or wisely read that you are. You may expect that the spells each of you learn will not be the same as everyone else in your group. Personal identity plays a role in this as well. Do not concern yourselves if one of you cannot learn a specific spell. It is not a reflection on them, rather on their areas of interest and needs."

"Three of you already have had some training. I'll be up front with you. Emil and Renata know around a half dozen spells of varying power and casting difficulty levels. Zoran has already done serious study with another Archmage and has two dozen spells at his command. You seven are a team. You will work, study, eat, and play together for the duration of your stay here. I will expect that you will assist one another with any and all things. If one or more members of your team fails to act as a responsible team member, I reserve the right to discharge him or her from my tower. Every team must have a leader; yours will be Zoran. Do not ask why I have chosen him. In time, you may understand my choice. Questions?" No one said anything, though Zoran wondered why he had been chosen. Could it be because he was Duska?

"Now then, times are changing. Events are unfolding at a more rapid pace than ever in the past. I find that I must change my methods as well. This part you may like, but we shall see. In the past, I would take my time training those that I deemed worthy of learning magic. However, now I find that speed of training has become most vital. Hence, you may expect that I will be pushing you hard to grasp and use magic. Much may depend upon your group mastering magic very quickly. If you find the pace too difficult, please let me know. In a way, you are all my guinea pigs in this. I am not too old to change my ways; that is a joke by the way. I am seventy-five years old, if you didn't know."

"In addition to your studies, from time to time, I will have missions for you to execute. Some of these may well prove exceedingly dangerous to your lives. I wish that I did not have to do this, but as you can see, I am far too old to travel very much. Because of the critical nature of events unfolding across Adapazan, I must ask you to undertake these in my place. I will do everything that I can to ensure that you have the skills to be successful in the mission. Yet, I cannot emphasize enough that danger does lie out there."

"I have carefully picked every member of this team. Each one of you brings some special skills with you that the others lack. In the end, this may well be of tremendous value to you and your well-being. Enough of the doom and gloom. Here in my tower, I wish that you will remain on this first floor until meal times. Our dining room is directly above us on the second floor, where the kitchen and grounds staff dwell. The third floor is where the more advanced teams live and study. I live on the top floor, the fourth and fifth floors are off limits for all students unless I accompany you there. Now then, let's begin at the beginning. That door there leads to the study room, where each of you may begin your study of magic. Shall we proceed?"

She led them into a large library room. Hundreds of books and scrolls lined one wall. Magical illumination made the room very bright, easier on the eyes for so much reading, Zoran thought. "Now then, even though three already know some spells, I was not their teacher. Hence, I wish that you three would also study the beginning materials as well, just to be sure that there are not any holes in your education. When we get to the actual casting of spells, if you already can cast a given spell, I trust that you will assist me in helping the others attempt to master it. Now here is a checklist of what you are to study. After you feel that you know and can use one of these on the checklist, you are to place your initials beside it."

"I wish that I had enough copies of everything you need to read and study, but I do not. So you may skip around on the checklist until you have covered everything on it. Finally, if you already have studied thoroughly an item, you may sign it off. Incidentally, you are welcome to read and study everything in this room. I will leave you to it for now; I need to assist the others in some casting. If you need anything, pull that string and Marek will come. I'll check back with you later." She left the seven to their study, and Zuzanna entered with a much smaller checklist.

"Hi, I am going to be your maid and look after your things, but first I have to study all these things too. Isn't this just the greatest thing in the entire world?" she bubbled total enthusiasm, like a child with a long desired new toy.

Everyone settled down to begin their study of magic. Zoran already was totally familiar with over half of the items, which he checked off and began with a *History of Magic on Adapazan*. While mostly light reading, Zoran found it interesting, as the author presented the advancement of magic in chronological order. Zdenka was also reading the same book. Towards the end of the long afternoon session, Zoran noticed that her face turned beet red. She hid her face; something had really embarrassed her, but now was not the time to ask her about it.

Instead, he continued reading, wondering what in the book had caused her wild reaction. Not very many pages later, he read, During the famine of 2140, General Janos Lavos was given the order by Archmage Milos to carry out his Baron Vladislov's orders to take the food supplies requested by Archmage Milos, supplies desperately needed to feed all of his many apprentices. General Janos Lavos refused to do the Archmage's order, claiming that would cause the villagers to starve to death during the winter. He was then tried for high treason and sent into exile in the Wild Lands. Thus, when given a direct order from an Archmage, do not presume to know better. These are the wisest, most powerful wizards on Adapazan. They see the whole picture, not one small snapshot.

Zoran's face flushed. Now he remembered where he had heard that name, Janos Lavos. Archmage Milos sometimes brought up that incident as a warning to his new apprentices! Damn! This was her father and more importantly, he was still alive. I've got to meet him, he swore to himself, and then plotted out a time when he could talk privately to her about it.

Shortly after this, Renata commented to her brother, "Gosh, Emil. There are fifteen other worlds with hoofers besides this one!" Emil leaned over to look at the passage she pointed out.

"What's a hoofer?" asked Bernard. Of course everyone else wanted to know too.

Slightly embarrassed, she replied, "Our land's word for antelope. Sorry, I sometimes use our words, not yours." Now Zoran began to wonder why they were both so excited about deer. That made little sense to him, only adding to the mystery surrounding the twins.

At supper, they joined nearly two dozen others in the second floor's spacious dining room. Nothing about these first two floors was either elegant or exceptional; everything was purely functional, quite the opposite of what Zoran was used to back at Dorumova Castle where elegance was everywhere. There, even the hall candle mounts were made of gold. Still, here he felt human warmth, a glow that was nearly totally absent back at the castle. Only when he was around his sisters did he feel as he did continually here.

All of the other students introduced themselves and chatted away as if everyone was a lifelong friend. More importantly, the conversation was stimulating, as many discussed things that they learned today. The very atmosphere here was so completely different than in Archmage Milos' tower that Zoran thought he was in a different world.

"Just so our new arrivals know, you all have Sunday's off from your studies. You may use the day anyway that you desire. Oh, and one more small thing. Emil and Renata have permission to depart in the very early morning hours on Sunday. Do not be alarmed if you rise and they are gone. They will be back sometime after supper. Now if you will excuse me, my old body is quite tired enough for one day." She left and one by one the others followed suit.

Zoran took this opportunity to chat with Zdenka about her father. He gently held her back, as she got up to follow the others out. She turned and smiled, picking up his subtle hint that she should dally. When they were alone, he said. "I read that bit about your father in the history book today. I just wanted you to know that it is totally bull, just the kind of thing I detest utterly. They had no right to force those villagers to starve to death. I think your father did the right thing by refusing to carry out those evil orders."

Tears swelled, though she fought hard to keep them at bay. "I know; dad's told me about it. That's why he came here where no one knew of his past. Maybe the rest will miss that connection when they read it."

"Yes, but they might not make the connection with you. Zdenka, one day I must meet your father! So few ever take a stand against the Baron or his Archmage, I really need to talk with him one day, okay?"

"Sure, but I don't know when we will get the chance. I can see that we are going to be incredibly busy here. I've never read so much in one day in my life. My head is swimming in facts."

"Don't worry, it will get easier. This is all background information that puts spell casting into proper perspective. The really hard stuff will come when we have to learn the spells," he warned her.

The next morning, Zoran rose and dressed. He found that during the night, his clothes had been somehow cleaned and were fresh for him. At the castle, he would just leave his room as it was — bed a mess, dirty clothes piled everywhere. Someone would later come in and clean it for him and make his bed. Now he was in a place that he truly respected. He looked at his messy bed and made it, then tidied up his few possessions. As he was heading off to breakfast, Zuzanna knocked.

"Oh, you've made your bed. I was supposed to do that for you, sir."

"You don't have to, Zuzanna. I am perfectly able to make it. Tell you what. When I need clean sheets, I'll leave it unmade. How's that?"

"Oh thank you, sir," she grinned. Zoran skipped up to the dining room for breakfast.

Days passed. On their first Sunday, their day off from studies, Zoran noticed that both Emil and Renata had long ago left. The doorman confirmed that they had awakened him to let them out at three in the morning! One more mystery piled itself on top of the others. Zoran decided that he would spend the day studying. Zdenka stayed behind as well, "I've got nothing to do in Brn. I know that Karel wants to check on his many hawks, likewise with Bernard and his dogs. Jarka told me that she wants to nose around and pick up any news of what's been happening in Brn during the week. Honestly, I think she's a big gossip."

"Glad you are with me," Zoran found himself saying, though he didn't know why. "Say, how far is it to your place in the Dark Woods?"

"Three days travel, less if you have a horse, which I don't." That put any chance of a visit with her father out for the time being. True, he could just take her hand and Shadow Walk there in a second, or better once he learned to teleport, they could go that way. To Shadow Walk now would completely blow his cover. Only a Duska could Shadow Walk, that was common knowledge, even if the average person had no clue what it meant.

Days passed into weeks, as they immersed themselves deep into the world of knowledge, magic, and spells. On the day that everyone had at last signed off on *Creatures of Adapazan*, Archmage Nadia held a conference to discuss what they had learned and to put it into perspective.

She said softly, "Why are the Wild Lands of Adapazan called the Wild Lands?"

Zoran spoke up at once, images of his father strong in his mind. "Centuries ago, we landed on Adapazan and, under the reigns of a number of evil barons, began subjugating all of the other people here by force of arms, deceit, and treachery. Baron Kazimir is continuing to extend his dominion over the planet. He calls those lands not under his iron fist of control the Wild Lands, because here warlords run even worse viciousness on the people living out here."

"Flunk, Zoran. You have given me an answer that I would expect to hear from one who has been brought up in the so called *civilized* lands of Adapazan," she stated flatly and without emotion. Her comment raised the eyebrows of both Jarka and Zdenka, but for different reasons. Zdenka thought that this only confirmed her deep suspicions that Zoran was indeed a nobleman, probably from the civilized lands. Jarka, on the other hand, snickered; he was not such of a hot shot after all, and he certainly was not from around these parts.

"Would anyone else like to answer my question?" she asked softly, her keen eyes pausing for a moment on the others.

Zdenka decided to try. "Originally, Adapazan was populated by the Yellers, who built what one might call population centers. Highly intelligent, these were the first true civilizers of the planet. Then we, the humans, came here and began killing them, driving them off of the most fertile lands, forcing them out of the zones that we controlled. As the barons continued to enlarge the areas they controlled, the Yellers were forced further out into the less desirable portions of Adapazan. The Yellers now hate humans with a passion and fight us whenever they get the chance. They get their name from all the wild yelling they do when they attack us. Also driven from their old haunts are other nasty creatures, the banshees, the megalowolves, the slithers, and the paleowasps. All of these combine to make living in the non-civilized areas of Adapazan quite dangerous — hence the name Wild Lands."

"Very good, Zdenka. Precisely so. The Yellers are more than justified in attacking humans. After all, we are slowly committing genocide of their kind. Now then, has anyone ever seen a Yeller? Can anyone describe what they look like, what they are afraid of, or how we mages may defeat them if we are attacked?" she asked.

Again, Zdenka replied first, "I had to kill one once. It came after me and my dad when we were out in the Dark Woods hunting for deer for our winter's meat supply. It was at least eight feet tall, really hairy, like a giant ape. I hit it with five arrows to its head before it dropped."

Bernard added, "According to our studies, Yellers are mean and vicious towards humans. They are afraid of fires; they scare easily, and are quite easily fooled by illusions. So fire based spells, fear causing spells, and illusions of same are our best defense against them. They are stronger than two of our fighters and can easily rip a man's arm off. They have a very nasty bite as well. We should avoid all close combats with them, keeping our distance. Oh yes, they are known to use clubs as well."

"Very good. Both of you. Now then, who can tell me about banshees?" she asked.

Zoran wanted to redeem himself, he answered this one. "Evil spirit like creatures, feminine in nature, it is said. Solitary creatures, they only come out at night, seeking male prey. Their screeching cry can paralyze their victims, which they then eat their flesh raw. I once saw the remains of a man who fell victim to a banshee, a really bloody, almost unrecognizable body. They are afraid of bright lights and can be more easily killed by electrical attacks and even water. It is said that they dare not cross water. The book suggests that is because they are terrified that they might see their reflections in the water."

"Very good, Zoran. That is correct. Now how about the megalowolves?" she asked, continuing down the list of creatures.

Bernard answered this one. "I've run into these rather often when I am out with my dogs. They are an oversized wolf, really, with giant fangs that can rip flesh from bones. They often hunt in packs, which is when they are most dangerous indeed. They fear light and fire, so any spell that creates bright lights or fires will drive them off."

"Very good, Bernard. Now then, how about the slithers?"

Emil chose to answer this one, reciting mostly what the book had said about them. From his description, he'd never actually seen one. "These are snake creatures, whose fangs deliver venom that paralyzes a person. Unlike normal snakes, these grow to be three feet in diameter and can reach thirty feet in length. Because of their girth, they can easily eat a human, which makes them dangerous. They are most easily slain by swords and by spells that do cutting type damage."

"Good, Emil. Finally, how about paleowasps?"

"I'll answer this one, because my hawks and I frequently run into these nasty flying creatures," Karel growled. "They are a giant sized wasp, really, the adults reaching three feet in length. Their stinger delivers a nerve agent that first paralyzes the victim and slowly shuts down all bodily functions. If possible, the females then lay their eggs in the carcass so that their hatchlings will have a good supply of food upon hatching. Earth based spells and anything that cancels their flying makes a good defense against them. Also, my hawks are excellent at catching them while they are in flight."

"Excellent. Now that you have an appreciation for the lands in which we live, it is time that we begin learning the spells necessary to protect ourselves and others," she replied, knowing from all the smiles that her students were very ready to begin learning spells.

In early June, Zoran's sister made telepathic contact with him for the first time. *Zoran, can you talk?* It was Rayna! At once from that gentle mental touch, Zoran realized just how much that he had missed his sisters all these months!

I'm here. Yes, please! I miss you and Lida loads. How is everything? Are you two okay?

Yes, we are fine, really we are. How about you? Lida and I really miss you too!

I'm doing great. I'm studying under a terrific Archmage, but I best not tell you who right now. I've made some new friends and am learning spells like never before.

I am so glad that you found a way to continue! Magic is so important. Well, dad was furious when he finally figured out that you ran away. He sent out messages to all the other barons inquiring if they had seen you. Of course, none had. He called on Milos to attempt to track you, but you did a good job of covering your trail. He even went so far as to ask the priests to track your Shadow Walk. He was fuming when they couldn't pick up your trail! I've never seen him so mad. Radek isn't of the same mind though. He keeps saying good riddance and all that. I think he really does dislike you, Zoran. Perhaps he was behind the three assassination attempts. Lida and I are keeping an eye on him.

Any news from the Court?

Well, dad held a secret conference with some other barons. He is now planning a big summer offensive against the Sholov Province and warlord Mikolas. He thinks that he can take that whole province this summer. I hope he loses big time. Oh! Mom's coming. I best stop for now. More later when I know something. Love you, Zoran.

Love you too, Rayna. Tell Lida I love her too. The connection was suddenly broken. Zoran sighed, "I sure do miss my sisters." He pulled his covers up and drifted into sleep.

Having finished their study of basic background information, the group began to work on learning actual spells. Archmage Nadia followed the same pattern as had Zoran's previous teacher, that is, she began their education with the simple, useful spells that one might use around the home or workplace. Spells such as Mend, Warm, Chill, and Clean were easily learned by everyone in the group, though Zuzanna found them challenging. Zoran realized that Zuzanna was only going to be able to master the very beginning spells and would have to be content to be an Adept, which status she greatly desired.

Once they began to tackle the real spells as Bernard called them, things began to take a fascinating turn, at least as far as Zoran was concerned. When he was getting his training from Archmage Milos, he was the only student. Now he had the opportunity to work with his new friends and see how well others mastered the spells. The results he found surprising and unexpected.

Each person seemed to be able to learn only a subset of all possible spells, excepting himself, strangely enough. Then, perhaps not, he thought; I am a Duska, so perhaps that has something to do with spell casting. In fact, the ease and speed with which any given individual mastered a given spell varied in a way he began to find interesting. So much so, that Zoran began charting each spell that his friends mastered.

He was not too surprised to find that Jarka tended to rapidly pick up any spell that had anything remotely to do with thieving. For example, the Intruder Warning, Alter Appearance, Charm Another, Understand Foreign Languages, Detection of Magic, Grow and Shrink, Erase, Gentle Fall, Hold Door, Identify Magical Item, Jump, Wizard Message, Create Magical Shield, Climb, and Scare spells she excelled at and learned very rapidly. Whereas with the key beginning attacking spells of Magical Arrow, Flaming Fingers, and Sleep, Jarka struggled mightily to learn them, nearly giving up on them.

Zdenka excelled with any spell that allowed her to exercise a good measure of control over an object. She readily picked up the Magical Arrow and Sleep spells, along with such spells as Alter Fires, Grow and Shrink, Gentle Fall, Hold Door, Jump, Fog Cloud, and Move Object. In fact, she realized that all along she had been using magical energies to move her arrows to hit the bull's eye. "Every time I shoot an arrow, if I see it going off a little, I sort of pushed it back on track. No wonder I always won the archery contests!" she exclaimed in a rush of realization. On the other hand, she could not seem to master the creation of illusions at all.

Bernard picked up any spell that dealt with animals or of the earth very rapidly, whereas Karel rapidly caught on to any spell dealing with the air, such as Fly. He also picked up spells that dealt with animals quickly. Both men found spells that altered men's minds nearly impossible to learn, such as Charm Another.

Emil and Renata also had a predictable side as well as an unpredictable aspect, Zoran soon discovered. Unlike the others, the spells that they managed to learn were far fewer and seemed randomized. For example, while they were able to learn Alter Appearance, they failed to learn Grow and Shrink, two closely related spells. With these two, Zoran soon learned that if the spell had anything to do with fire or electrical charges, these two were certainly among the first to learn it. Strange indeed, he thought to himself. Well, they are different and come from some distant land, he rationalized for a time.

On into June, this same pattern continued, as they all progressed through the fundamental spells through what Archmage Nadia called Grade 3. Zoran was very surprised to find that Emil and Renata were able to cast a Ball of Fire almost as soon as they read the casting details! Similarly, when these two got to the Lightning Bolt spell, both picked it up immediately, shocking all of the others, who really had to work with these two spells, their most powerful spells to date.

Of course by the end of June when they all finished up their attempts to learn the spells of Grade 3, everyone else had strange ideas about Zoran. He saw himself merely filling in spells that he had either not seen under Milos or had not yet had the time to learn. His friends didn't see it that way, however. One afternoon after a particularly frustrating session, Karel griped, "Zoran, what's with you anyway? You are mastering every darn spell we come across! No one else here is able to do that! Not Zdenka, not Jarka, not Emil, not Renata, not Bernard, not myself. Only you. What gives with you anyway? How come you are able to do all these spells, over a hundred of them now and we can't? What do you have to say about that?" He was angry as usual.

"Yes, how is it that you are the superman?" Jarka sneered rather covertly.

Zdenka was going to suggest that this was because he was a nobleman, but thought better of it. After all, most noblemen couldn't cast any spells. She was as baffled by it as the others.

"Probably because we are not as smart as he is," Bernard added rather bored with the whole discussion. "Besides, he already had a good deal of training before he came here. He's just ahead of us, that's all." Emil and Renata eyed Zoran, eager to hear his answer, perhaps wondering if he might share his secret for spell mastering with them.

Zoran couldn't risk speculating; it would come too close to what he was. Instead, he picked up on Bernard's statement. "Bernard's right. I have studied under another Archmage a while back, so I already knew half of the spells. This time, I picked up some of those I missed and a few that he didn't teach me back then. He and I didn't get along, rather nasty fellow for my liking." This seemed to appease them, but Karel still grumbled about it all and shot him a dirty look.

On the next Sunday, their day off, Jarka came back with some startling news. "Hey, you all need to hear what I just found out!" She was more animated than normal. "Dragons are back!"

"What?" exclaimed Zoran. Many other expressions followed in rapid fire.

"There's no such thing as a dragon. It's just stories made up to scare kids," Zdenka added.

"No, really," Jarka insisted. "Evzen, the Hunter — he was out hunting near Devil's Peaks, and he saw one flying over the peak carrying something. Everyone's talking about it. Dragons are back. Honestly, go to any inn and ask. Everyone's heard about it now. Happened a week ago Friday night."

"Jarka, there *aren't* dragons around here. They are just a myth. No one has ever seen a dragon," Bernard said, having already become bored with this talk of mythical beasts.

"I don't even know what a dragon actually is," Zoran added. "What do they look like anyway? Are they dangerous? Have any of you seen a dragon?"

Everyone shrugged their shoulders; no one had seen one. "I agree with Bernard," Zdenka spoke up. "Honestly, Jarka, if dragons actually existed and if a dragon was around here, why hasn't anyone else ever seen it? Answer that. Really, I think Evzen probably saw something unusual and is calling it a dragon. Maybe it was a paleowasp that he saw. Maybe he was really drunk and hallucinating. There could be lots of reasons."

"I'm dead serious! I asked some of the older folks about dragons. Katerina, who works as a maid at an inn — she is in her sixties. She remembers seeing a dragon around here more than a quarter of a century ago. Go ask some of the older townsfolk. They'll tell you so."

"But what do they look like? Apparently they fly," Zoran asked again. "Are they dangerous? How big are they?" He got no answers, except that they must fly, since that was how the hunter saw it. He decided to send a Message to the Archmage asking her about this news. Shortly after he sent it, she materialized into their study.

"What's all this about someone seeing a dragon?" she asked. Jarka repeated what she had learned.

"Well, well, so we have a dragon in these parts again. Fascinating," she said in her usual quiet manner. Zoran glanced at his friend's faces. Strange, but Emil and Renata had not said even one word this whole time, and their faces were slightly flushed, he thought. She went on, "Yes, dragons are very real and very, very powerful creatures, highly intelligent, and many are deeply involved in magic, able to cast many of the spells that we cast."

"However, Jarka and the rest of you, I caution you about drawing many conclusions from one lone sighting. That may well have been any number of things. I suppose that you all should get educated about dragons. I'll never hear the end of this if I don't. Come on; up to the third floor library."

Oh's and ah's echoed. Never before had any of them been to the third floor, where her more advanced students lived and trained. Eagerly they followed her up the steps, though she took them excruciatingly slowly from their point of view. They entered another library similar to the one that they had been using. Book shelves lined the walls, along with a large scroll holder. She retrieved one small volume and laid it on a desk so that everyone could crowd around and see. Zoran read its title, *A Treatise on Dragons*, by Archmage Nadia Oldrich.

"Incredible! You wrote this book?" Zoran asked, very much impressed with her, far more so than ever before.

"Yes, I wrote this over a quarter of a century ago in my youth. You see, I once taught magic to a dragon. Yes, right here in this very tower. I traded the teaching of magic for inside knowledge on dragon kind. Now then, some simple facts. Dragons are usually between fifty and seventy feet long, with four legs, a long neck and tail, and a wing span of over a hundred feet. Huge indeed. Their bite can crush a human; their razor sharp claws can easily puncture all forms of armor known to man. Still, they possess something remarkable in the animal kingdom to which even we belong: what I call a breath weapon. Some dragons breathe out fire — a fire so hot it can melt iron. Others breathe out electrical charges akin to the power of our own Lightning Bolt spells. Other shoot out air so cold that our bodies would freeze into a solid statue in seconds. Still others pour out a stream of very caustic acid, one drop of which can burn through flesh down to the bone. A few shoot out a slime that causes living flesh to just rot away. One should highly respect dragons and *never* provoke one."

"Now then, there are a number of different species of dragons, just as there are a number of types of humans, though I don't know the entire story here. It has never been studied by a human. From our point of view not theirs, each species has a different temperament and disposition towards we humans. The only types which truly enjoy our company are the golden dragons. The one that I taught here was a golden dragon. You see, their species are differentiated by the color of their hides. They simply do not interbreed. Now the ones with the nastiest temperament towards we humans are supposedly the red dragons and the blacks. Reds shoot out hot flames, while the blacks spew out the caustic acid. Both the white dragons and the brown dragons are ambivalent towards us, usually ignoring humans. Only the green dragons totally ignore us entirely."

"Finally, all dragons tend to love magic and spells and strive to learn all that they can. This basic drive is second only to their love of gems and sometimes valuable metals, such as gold and silver. The golden dragons collect only the finest of gems and could care less about metals. Many of the other species also covet gold and silver as well. Generally, each dragon has their own treasure hoard along with magical items they have found. Now then, Jarka, did your sources tell you what color this dragon was?"

"No, he claimed it was too far away to see it clearly," she replied, wishing now that she could have asked more about its color.

Zoran asked what he had been mulling over while she told them about dragons. "What is a dragon's life span? Do they have any natural enemies? Can they be killed by humans?"

She gave him a curious look, and then replied, "Again, life spans vary with species. Golden dragons may live for five hundred years; some others may live somewhat less. You might say, Zoran, that a dragon is at the top of the food chain. Their only enemies are other dragons who desire their treasure, not unlike the criminals and barons of our world." She couldn't resist a dig at the ruling establishment here on Adapazan and Zoran's father. "Can they be slain by us? Probably, but certainly not easily. I suspect that a creature of these proportions can sustain wounds which would kill a human twenty times over. Don't get any wild ideas, Zdenka; arrows merely bounce off their thick hides. Sword strikes might pierce their skin, though I know of no one who has been stupid enough to test that theory."

Zoran still had more questions forming in his mind. All this was totally new to him and potentially very critical information. "If there has not been a dragon around here for a quarter of a century, why has one come here now?"

"I suspect, Zoran, that if you could find the answer to that question, we would all be far wiser. Who knows what goes on in the mind of a dragon? Certainly not I, even though I trained one in my youth. Now unfortunately, this is the only copy of my book. Please read it together; look over each other's shoulders if you must. It should only take you an hour or so to learn all that I know of dragons. It is very little, actually." She left the group crowding close together to read this incredible book.

Zoran said what they were all thinking, "We are learning something that no one else on Adapazan knows!" No one noticed that Emil and Renata stood well back of the other five and only pretended to read.

That night, Jarka pulled Zoran aside. "We need to talk, talk privately. Come on." She pulled him into her room, closing the door, but only after making sure no one was in the hallway.

"Look, don't you think that Emil and Renata are doing something really weird? I just found out from the doorman, Marek. Those two really *do* leave around three in the morning on Sundays. They don't get back until at least midnight on Sunday. They've been doing that *ever* since we began our training. Now don't you think that is just a *little* weird? *I* certainly do. Whatever could anyone be doing leaving in the *middle* of the night, eh? Nothing is even open, I mean stores and shops and stuff. Where *can* they be going? I've never seen them with horses, so they must go on foot. I just *know* that they are up to something. You are *supposed* to be our leader, so investigate or something. I'm sure the others are just as concerned about those twins as I am, although they haven't said anything about it to me yet, but I'm sure they don't trust them either. I certainly don't trust them."

She would have continued, but Zoran cut her off by putting his finger on her lips. "I'll see what I can find out. Until then, we have no reason to distrust them, but I admit they are a little strange. Still, Archmage Nadia seems to trust them leaving and returning at those hours, so I think we should extend them the same courtesy — at least until we know what they are up to going out at that time. Okay?"

She flashed him a smile, "Okay, but *do* check on them. Where *can* they possibly going and doing?"

Back in his own room, Zoran realized she did have a valid point. He was their supposed leader, and two of their team were certainly acting strangely on this one day of the week. Perhaps they knew how to teleport; if so, they could go anywhere on Adapazan, but why?

When the next personal day came around, Zoran decided to try and follow the twins. However, he was sound asleep at three in the morning. After grabbing breakfast, he too left the tower. Outside, he cast Invisibility on himself and then cast Fly and flew up high over the city. His plan was simple: see if he could spy the twins down there among all of the ten thousand who lived in Brn. Exhausted, he returned at suppertime.

"Well?" Jarka asked. She had once more cleverly gotten him into her room.

"I searched the whole city all day long. I saw no sign of them, but they could well have been indoors during the day. I overslept, but then I don't know if Marek will let me out that early."

"Well, *I* did a bit of my own searching. No one in town has *ever* seen the twins since the day we all entered the tower! Now isn't that even stranger? They go out and no one sees them? Really!"

"Okay, okay, I'll keep trying, Jarka. Honestly, I think in the end they will have a valid excuse, though we just cannot foresee what that might be. I'm pooped. See you in the morning."

Chapter 6 A Service

Two days later, Archmage Nadia called the group into the study. "I have a small mission for you. I know that you have been cooped up for months. This will get you out into the fresh air. I need you to provide protection for a wagon. Laval Mining produces many fine raw gems and gold. Each year about this time, they make a delivery run to Brn, carrying an entire year's worth of product with them. The value of their cargo is larger than normal this year, something bordering on perhaps three hundred thousand gold pieces. The owner has requested that I provide security for their trip to Brn. I agreed, as I always do."

"The mine is located about seventy-five miles from here by road, shorter if one could go in a straight line. It is down range from here and around on the other side of the mountain. You will have to travel a good distance along the twisting mountain road and then pass through nearly forty miles of the Dark Forest, before the road winds along up our long valley road, passing numerous patches of pine forests. The laden wagon will make only about fifteen miles a day, so you ought to be back here late Saturday, if all goes well."

"Of course bandits are well aware of the mine's yearly shipment. Perhaps more than one group will attempt to waylay it, who can say. I doubt that you will encounter Yellers; our patrols have pretty much driven them out of Brn territory. However, banshees are known to inhabit some of the mountainous areas through which you must pass. As Zdenka knows well, the woods is home to packs of megalowolves. Both will be nighttime threats, while I would anticipate that the bandits would prefer daylight attacks."

"I would be surprised if you didn't get a chance to exercise your magical spells this trip," she coyly hinted. Zoran knew every aspect of this trip smelled of danger, real danger.

"After you all get your things together, I will open a Mystical Door from here to the mine. You simply step through the door and you will be there. The owner will provide you with horses for the return trip to Brn. If anything bad happens that you cannot handle, send word to me. Also, I will send along three healing potions with Jarka, just in case of an emergency. Now go pack what you think you will need."

Fifteen minutes later, the very excited group gathered around Archmage Nadia in their dining room. All wore their leather outfits, packing all of their weapons along with a change of clothes. Eagerly, they watched her every motion as she cast a very complex spell. Zoran had not heard of Mystical Door before and naturally had a professional curiosity about it. Unfortunately, he got no clues from its casting. One by one, each stepped through the door only to find themselves stepping out before a wooden mine shack and at a much higher elevation.

Several guards, both heavily armored and holding many weapons, stood guard around an open wagon. A burly man stood nearby, waving each arrival towards him as he or she suddenly stepped out into an unfamiliar place. That they were high in the mountains was obvious immediately. Zoran noticed that the air was both thinner and less humid. A brief round of introductions followed.

The owner, the burly man, explained, "I've a good horse for each of you. Milan is the driver and Tomas goes along as his guard. They are carrying a week's worth of food for all of you and some water, but there are many streams along the way. Thanks for protecting this shipment. I must say that this has been our best year ever. Go with God."

Milan and Tomas came out of the nearby stables leading a pair of horses each. Two other men led three more. The wagon had two large draft horses pulling it. The two handed the reins to Zoran, Zdenka, Jarka, and Karel; then headed for their wagon. The other hands brought the remaining three up to Bernard and the twins.

As they drew close to the three, suddenly the horses began neighing wildly and rearing up, refusing to move any closer. No matter how the men pulled, the horses only grew more upset. Bernard called out, "Hey. Hold on; don't force them. Back off." He walked up to the frightened animals and began petting them and talking soothingly to them, one at a time. Quickly, the three calmed down under his expert handling.

"Let me," he said and took the reins of one horse. Still talking soothingly to it, he slowly led it up to Emil and gave him the reins. The horse was very nervous but didn't act up. Bernard repeated the action with the next horse, finally giving the reins to Renata. Then, he fetched the last one for himself. "Okay, Emil, Renata, mount up. They should be okay now. I don't know what got into them. Something sure spooked them."

"Er, Bernard," Emil whispered, "we don't know how to ride. How do we do it? We've never been on a horse or seen anyone riding."

"Zoran, little help here?" Bernard called out. Zoran rode up to them, fighting to keep his horse from acting up as well, as it drew closer to the three. Quickly and softly, Bernard explained the problem to Zoran.

"Everyone, get going; we will catch up to you in a couple minutes. We are going to walk them a bit to get the horses over their skittishness," Zoran called out. At once Milan obeyed. After giving the four a strange look, the rest of his team moved out, Karel taking up the point position with Zdenka and Jarka on either side of the wagon. He heard the three chatting about what was going on.

"Okay, let's follow on foot. Lead them like we are," he explained to the two very nervous twins. Once out of sight of the mining camp, he explained, "It's okay that you don't know how to ride. I am having us walk for two reasons. One, it will give Bernard and I some time to teach you to ride — well the basics anyway. Two, I didn't want to embarrass you further back there, what with all the men watching you."

"Thanks, Zoran. I really appreciate it. We've never ridden a horse before," Renata explained.

"Think nothing of it," Bernard added. "Probably half of the folks living in Brn have never been on a horse either." Zoran noticed that this really seemed to bring a measure of relief to both of them. Now he began a crash course on riding horses. Ten minutes later, the four caught up to the others, though both Emil and Renata looked petrified sitting in their saddles.

"Hi all, they've never ridden before," Zoran explained to the others. The others took it in stride, though once more Jarka gave them a queer look.

The day passed mostly uneventful, save one minor situation. In the early afternoon, a swarm of paleowasps crossed their path. Before anyone could react, Emil handled them by shooting off a Ball of Fire, incinerating the lot. He was teased for reacting with total overkill, however, but Emil took it in stride, a smile on his face.

Around five, they began looking for a place to camp. Tomas, who had traveled this route many times, knew just the spot, only a short way off the road. They pulled in to a small half-moon shaped glen where three pine trees struggled for life amid the high altitude granite mountain side. Nearby a small stream bubbled its way on down the mountain.

As they pulled into the glen, Zoran's inner sense kicked in, signaling danger to him. "Someone's watching us," he called out. "Stay alert."

"How do you know?" Zdenka asked him.

"Just do," he didn't directly answer her. He wanted to say because I am Duska, but dare not. The group made camp; the twins were more than glad to scour for firewood, leaving Bernard and Karel to deal with the horses, eventually tethering them between the trees.

Milan asked, "Say, one of you ladies wanna do the cookin? Otherwise, yea'll have to eat my miserable attempt."

"Oh brother, okay, okay, move over. I'll do it, only you get to wash the dishes," Zdenka resigned herself to the task. No way was she going to eat lousily cooked meals for five days!

Since no further danger seemed apparent, Zoran chatted with her while she began cooking their supper. "I do it every day for dad and myself," she explained.

"Smells good. I'm famished," he chatted away. Still, his inner sense continued to gnaw in the back of his awareness. Something was out there and watching them, but what?

A while later, the group dined on the best trail cooking that Milan and Tomas had ever had. Milan didn't grumble at all, when afterwards, he had to wash the many pots, pans, and dishes. As darkness fell, the two put their bedrolls beneath the wagon and hit the sack, leaving the rest to guard them.

Zoran gathered the six to him. "Okay, I am sure that it's still out there, probably watching us. I get the sense that it's alone, so probably not a megalowolf pack or bandits. Archmage Nadia said not to worry about Yellers, so my money is on a banshee. Let's have two of us on watch each shift. Zdenka and I will take the first shift of three hours. Then Bernard, you and Jarka relieve us. Then Karel, you and I will take the dawn shift." While Zdenka protested that he would get short changed on sleep, he shrugged it off. If a banshee was out there, he wanted a double watch.

While the others slept, he and Zdenka sat around the small cooing fire, periodically stoking it. They killed the time by chatting a bit about their lives, though he found it difficult to relate many things that he wished he could share with her, concentrating on some of the funnier episodes that he and his two buddies had gotten into before he had fled. At last, they roused Jarka and Bernard and turned in themselves. Zoran fell asleep at once.

Around one in the morning, his inner sense sounded an alarm in his head, almost as if someone were screaming him awake. He sat up; it was screaming! Jarka had thrown more logs on the fire and cast a Light spell, illuminating the whole small glen. Bernard dashed around the campsite looking for the banshee, while holding his ears.

The others got up rapidly as well. Then, Zoran saw her; the banshee was sliding down the slope to their camp. Ghost-like, wearing a gauze of a nightgown, hands more like claws, and fangs, long pearly white fangs, she seemed to float towards them, shrieking her piercing, paralyzing call. With great effort, Zoran forced his nearly immobile muscles to draw his swords. Zdenka's arrow flew true to its mark, piercing the banshee right between her eyes. To everyone's utter amazement, the arrow went on through the banshee as if she were indeed a ghost!

Jarka, seeing that everyone was moving in slow motion as a result of the banshee's call, acted. She cast a Scream spell on herself, then a Magnify spell. Now she began singing and yelling, "La di da di do di da!" Her greatly amplified voice drowned out that of the banshee. Zoran felt his strength returning and rushed the banshee, slicing her twice with his short sword pair. Both blades cut through thin air. She in turn tried to grab him with her talon claws. His intuitive combat training kicked in, and he dove to the ground on her right, hit, and rolled out of her reach.

At that moment, Bernard and Karel both shot Lightning Bolts at the creature; it staggered and shrieked in great pain. Recognizing this was working, Renata, Emil, and Zdenka shot their Lightning Bolts nearly simultaneously. The banshee's ethereal form shook violently in many directions and slumped to the ground, lifeless. A moment later, a giant puff of smoke rose from where its body had lain. Ashes were all that remained of the banshee.

Jarka cancelled her spells. "Well done all of you! Wow. So that was a banshee. Great going gang."

"Fabulous idea, Jarka, you more or less canceled her paralyzation cry," Zoran praised them. His inner sense was now totally quiet. "I think she was what I was sensing when we stopped here, so we are probably safe, but let's continue the guard duty." However, none could relax, for they were way too keyed up over the battle.

As they chatted, Zoran realized his mistake. "Sorry gang, I reacted with my swords, which I always used to do, instead of using magic. You all were great, saving my butt."

"Well I did too," Zdenka added. "Until now I never met something my arrows couldn't handle. I ought to have remembered and shot my spells."

"Hey, don't knock yourselves," Bernard interrupted, though becoming a bit bored once more as the excitement died down. "You reacted the way that you were trained. It takes time to undo training patterns in dogs. I suppose it is the same with us."

An hour after first light and breakfast handled, the group began rolling on down the mountain road once more. In the distance, the dark green color of the Dark Forest loomed. They would reach it by noon. Here, Zoran expected to confront the bandits, who would use the cover of the dense woods to their advantage.

As they entered the Dark Forest, Zoran and Zdenka took the point position, some hundred feet in front of the lumbering wagon. He had Jarka hang back a hundred feet to their rear just in case bandits made a rear assault.

Around three in the afternoon, Zoran's inner sense tingled once again. "Stay alert, something is up!" he called out. The seven's eyes constantly studied the dense trees near the road, but a bandit could well be within ten feet of them and they wouldn't be able to see him. Many trees were two feet across and quite densely packed, giving the woods its name. Slowly the wagon rolled along the rutted road.

Not long after this, around a bend, Zoran and Zdenka reined in; ahead a large tree had fallen, blocking the road. "Trap. Stay alert," he called out. His inner sense told him that many individuals were lying in wait. As they drew closer, it was clear that the tree had recently been felled and was going to be difficult to move out of the way. Two feet in diameter, the tree totally blocked the road and would need the draft horses to move!

"They are in the trees; I caught a glimpse of one," Zdenka whispered urgently. "What do we do now?" She struggled to get her bow out, but Zoran could see that it would be nearly impossible to use while mounted. He had to make a decision immediately, before these raiders did it for him. If the enemy were on foot and if his forces were trained to fight from horseback, the ideal scene would be to remain mounted. If the enemy were on horseback and cavalry, they stood a better chance if they too remained on horseback. Then again, Emil and Renata could barely stay on their horses. No telling what would happen to them if their horses spooked or they were attacked.

"Ride up and dismount quickly!" Zoran ordered. "Pull the wagon in closer and form a circle around the wagon." Quickly, everyone did as ordered, drawing weapons and circling the wagon as it pulled up. "Tomas, Milan, take cover in or under the wagon. This is our fight." The drover and his guard did as ordered; obviously a big fight was about to occur any second. The seven waited, but no attack came. Still, Zoran's inner sense told him it was eminent.

"What are they waiting for?" Karel whispered angrily.

"Probably want us to think that it is not an ambush — that the tree just fell there. When we finally think it is not an ambush and go to move the tree, then they will strike," Jarka espoused her theory, based on what she would do, given similar circumstances.

Zoran smiled, "She's probably right. Okay, Zdenka and I will go see about moving the tree. The rest of you, prepare to attack them as soon as they attack us. Come on; keep your bow at the ready. I'll pretend I am dealing with the tree."

"Be careful. I've got you covered," she whispered. Cautiously they approached the huge tree lying across the road. Nothing happened. "No birds. Men must be nearby," she whispered. "It has to be a trap."

"Of course it is. I sense a large number of men close at hand. They are waiting for the right time. Okay, I am going to pretend to lift the tree." Zoran tried to budge the tree, but all he could do was make a few branches wiggle. It was a heavy tree, carefully chosen to form an ideal barricade. His inner sense screamed and forced him to turn his head sideways, just in time to see two arrows heading for Zdenka and himself. Once more his lightning fast training kicked in. He dove towards Zdenka so that the arrow coming at him would miss, and as he was falling towards the ground, his right hand snatched the arrow that was heading for her chest. He hit the ground and rolled several feet before springing to his feet, while drawing his pair of swords.

He was in time to see a pair of arrows strike Emil and Renata squarely in their chests. His only thought was, "They will be out of the action." Both arrows merely bounced off their chests, after punching a hole in their leather tops!

At the moment that Zoran attempted to move the tree, two dozen men moved out from behind the trees. Ten fired off a volley of arrows, while the others raced to close the distance to the seven who were protecting the wagon. Jarka, Karel, and Bernard both barely escaped arrows meant for them, mostly because of the haste with which they were fired. Dropping the bows, the ten headed into the combat as well.

Jarka, totally unwilling to go hand to hand with these bandits, cast her Fly spell and rose above the battle. Karel and Bernard had no choice but to draw their swords and engage in a sword battle. Their opponents gave them no time to cast a spell. Zoran seeing Jarka's brilliant move, ordered, "Zdenka, I'll hold them off; get up there with Jarka!" He became a whirlwind of blades, fending of two men coming after him plus two who were headed for her. He bought her enough time to get airborne. He had no time to look back and figure out a way for the twins to save themselves. He realized that neither even had a dagger on them. Surely unless they could Fly out of the melee, they would be killed outright. He'd have that on his conscience for the rest of his life; he failed to protect two of his team!

Now fighting four men, Zoran focused all his attention on his foes, his twin swords in rapid continuous motion. Seeing an opening, he lunged, struck, and retreated, allowing the man to drop to his knees in pain, blood flowing rapidly from a gut slice. Zoran intended to give no quarter to these men. Another moved in to take the fallen one's place.

Hovering stably, Jarka fired off a Sleep spell; ten of the men around the central area dropped to the ground and began dozing. Their respite didn't last long; another bandit rushed over and began kicking them awake. Zdenka began shooting her Magical Arrows at the men who were giving Bernard and Karel a very hard time. Both men already had blood tricking down their arms and wouldn't be able to hold on much longer. Jarka now took her lead from Zdenka, firing off her Magical Arrows at the same group of men, hoping to give Bernard and Karel more breathing room.

While all this was going on, three men each rushed towards the twins, who stood there unsure of just what to do. At first, they looked at the holes in their tops, annoyed that their nice leather tops now needed mending. Two men drew up to Emil, while another two reached Renata. All four men took a mighty swing, intending to cut these two down right where they stood. Loud cracks of breaking steel resulted. Four blades broke, although both now had large slices in their tops, not just a puncture hole. Swung with such force, all four blades simply shattered upon contact with their bodies.

"Damn you. You ruined my leather top!" Emil cursed and swung his fist at the man closest to him. His fist totally smashed in the man's head and sent him flying backwards ten feet. On his left, Renata did basically the same thing. She swung her fist at first one and then the other of her attackers, achieving the same result as her brother. Now, both were broiling mad and began going directly after other nearby bandits, who saw two unarmed teens charging them with clenched fists, not even holding a weapon. None had time to reflect upon what happened to their men behind the charging duo. One blow and their heads were smashed and their bodies went flying backwards.

Three minutes later, Zoran had slain three of his opponents and was dueling the last one, when Emil walked up to the man and punched him in his head. Zoran got to see the result; the man's head took on an entirely different shape, as his body flew back some ten feet. Emil grinned. "Ruined our new leather shirts, they did. Made me mad."

Sweat pouring off of him, Zoran gasped, "Amazing. Thanks." He looked around for more opponents, but saw none; all were lying around the immediate area, all quite dead. He saw the two flying women landing.

"Who's hurt?" Zoran called out.

Jarka yelled, "To Bernard and Karel! They took a beating." All rushed to the two men at the side of the wagon. Bleeding from several nasty wounds in their arms and legs, they had slumped to the ground, leaning against the wagon wheel.

At once, Zdenka and Zoran began ripping up makeshift bandages out of their bedroll sheets. Emil and Renata watched, for neither had any notion of what needed to be done. There was no time to waste explaining. The two needed immediate attention. "I'm going to use two of our healing potions on them," Jarka called out. "Their wounds are deep and nasty. Hang in there a minute, fellows." She retrieved her pack from the wagon, pulled out two flasks, and raced to the men. "Drink!" she commanded. Both men did as she asked.

"Wow. This stuff really does work, Zoran!" Zdenka exclaimed as the blood flow began to subside. She could see the wounds starting to close right before her eyes.

"Well, of course it works, Zdenka," Jarka sneered. "It *is* a healing potion, after all. What did you think it would do?"

"Still, they ought to be bandaged up, just in case they don't fully close because more than one potion might be needed," Zoran added. Five minutes later, their bleeding ceased, though both men were still weak.

"Now let's see your wounds, Emil, Renata. You took several nasty chest cuts," Zoran said.

"No wounds. Look, see?" Emil took off his rather cut up leather top. "Now I guess I will need to use my Mend spell."

"Oh here, brother, let me do it. You'll mend it goofy-like," Renata interrupted him. She had already mended her top, and only barely visible lines showed where the sword cuts had struck her.

Zoran rubbed his hands through his hair. "How on earth did you two manage not to get mortally wounded? I mean by all rights, you both ought to be lying on the ground bleeding to death."

"Hey, ask them how come the bandit's swords *broke* when they hit them?" Jarka called out. "All *four* of their swords no less. While you are at it, ask them how come their fists totally bashed in the bandits' heads and sent their bodies flying? I've never seen anything like that before. Man, Emil literally crushed their heads in. How *is* this possible? Ask them *that* why don't you?"

Bernard, now feeling a bit better, spoke up, "Well maybe the bandits had really cheaply made swords. It has been known to happen, Jarka."

"Yes, but all four? Bernard, that potion is making you hallucinate," Jarka retorted.

"We are stronger than we look," Emil fumbled around for a plausible explanation. No way was he going to tell them the truth. His dad's words echoed in his mind.

Jarka, spreading her legs apart in a defiant stance, retorted, "No one is that strong, Emil. You and Renata smashed in their heads, and you don't even have a red mark on your fists!"

"Oh, are we supposed to have red marks? What ought they look like?" Renata said naively, looking her hands over and seeing nothing unusual about them at all.

"We are just strong, Jarka," Emil continued his lame explanation. "Look." He picked her up with one arm, holding her high over his head.

"Put me down! Put me down this very second!" Jarka exclaimed very much annoyed with Emil. How could he possibly be doing this raced through her mind. He doesn't even have muscles to speak of!

"I don't get it either," Zoran broke up the confrontation. "Let's worry about all this later on. Jarka, you search the bandits for anything useful. Zdenka, use your Dig spell to start making some graves. I'll help them unhitch the draft horses and use them to try to get that huge tree out of our way." Jarka agreed, mumbling to herself as she began searching the two dozen bodies.

Emil asked Zoran, "We need the tree out of the way so the wagon can get through, right?" He nodded. "Well, let Renata and me see if we can move it first. If we can, it will save us lots of time." Zoran agreed, and ran his fingers through his hair once more. Everyone watched the twins walk to the huge tree. After a bit of discussion, they each grabbed a hold of a thick branch and lifted together. Right before everyone's eyes, the tree rose three feet from the ground. With some effort, the twins pushed and shoved the tree off to one side, paralleling the road.

"How's this?" Emil called out to Zoran. As the twins looked back at their friends and the two from the mining camp, they saw seven gaping mouths. All seven were completely speechless, none more so than Zoran, who had tried to budge the tree right before the bandits attacked.

"That's not possible," Zdenka whispered.

Zoran called out, "Perfect, thanks. Saved us at least an hour or more. Good going." He had to make them feel that they had done a good job, which of course they had. He kept his total amazement to himself. How can this be? Where were these two from? Was everyone in their country this amazingly strong? He had so many unanswered questions that he just focused on the here and now, intent on getting the wagon moving as soon as possible. The rest of his team would undoubtedly ask the very questions he had.

In silence, the stunned team mechanically resumed their chores. The drover and guard rounded up their seven horses. Zdenka dug a mass grave with her spell, though she had to recast it several times to make a sufficiently large hole. Jarka continued her scavenging operation, but she asked, "Zoran. What do you want us to take? I mean we can confiscate weapons and sell them in Brn, probably some of their clothes too. Might make a few gold pieces on it."

"No, let's not bother with that; just get their valuables and such. Are you checking to see if anything is magical?"

"Of course, I am always *very* thorough," she replied in a snide tone of voice. "Are you going to go looking in the woods for anything else they might have had, like *horses*?" she asked, knowing that he probably had not thought of this. From the surprised look on his face, she knew she'd guessed right.

She went on, "If they didn't ride flea bitten nags, we ought to get ten gold for them. Probably yield us all a hundred gold pieces. I, for one, could *use* the extra money."

Zoran reflected on her suggestion and then spoke, "Ordinarily, Jarka, I'd say go ahead. However, we have two of our team laid up, and we are under orders to get this wagon to Brn in three more days. I think the wisest course is to leave them for now."

Bernard spoke up, "Boss, if they have horses tied up out there, those creatures will be in grave danger. Wild animals can get them or they might die of thirst or starvation. We cannot simply leave them be."

"Okay, okay," he grinned, "I know when I am outvoted. I don't want to harm animals any more than you do. We'll spend a bit of time checking on them, okay?" Bernard smiled as did Jarka.

"Hey, this is my woods. Let me go. I can backtrack the men and find their horses rapidly," Zdenka called out. "I'm done digging anyway. Someone else can bury them."

Zoran hesitated to send Zdenka out there alone, but he couldn't see Jarka burying the dead bandits either. "Jarka, you go with her. If you come across any more bandits, send us a message immediately, got it?" They nodded and the two women vanished into the dense trees. "Emil, lend me a hand with these bodies, will you?"

A half hour later, Zoran cast his Dig spell and finished covering them up, forming a nice looking mound. Just then, they heard horses coming and a pair of smiling women rode up, leading two long strings of horses. "Found a pile of gems in one of the saddle bags," Jarka called out. "Good horses and saddles. Probably we can each make ten gold pieces for our efforts." She was now in good spirits. After tying the string of horses to the wagons, along with those of Bernard and Karel, the group once more headed on down the road through the Dark Forest.

That night, they made camp near a small stream, which they forded first. Around the campfire, they chatted about their big battle. Zoran kept it light, however, "Well, we sure are an unusual team, that's for sure. Jarka's idea to fly above the battle casting spells worked perfectly. Good going, you two." Zdenka smiled too. "As for our twins here, you were amazing. I honestly thought that I would be burying you two back there, if not from the arrows, then from the sword strikes. You two are a powerhouse in a small package! No question of that. I will have to remember that. Are all of the people in your country as tough and strong as you two are?"

"Oh, more so, we are like you, only in our teens. We will get stronger as we grow up," Emil explained. He was telling the truth.

"One day, I would like to visit your country of Voss," Zoran decided. Neither twin replied to that comment, however.

They chatted until long after dark. Zoran insisted that both Bernard and Karel sleep through the night. Emil and Renata took the first watch, and then later Zoran and Jarka watched their camp. In the dawn hours, Zoran promised to wake Zdenka and let Jarka get some sleep. Instead, Tomas insisted that he be allowed to stand watch with Zdenka so Zoran could get some sleep.

Zoran was sound asleep when his inner sense forced his eyes instantly open, senses alert. He lay still listening. It was Emil and Renata's guard duty. Had something happened to them? No they were sitting back to back near the rear of the wagon, occasionally poking at the small fire. Then he heard a light sound, padded feet upon the forest floor. Many of them. He was about to call out "Megalowolves!" but decided to see how the twins handled it.

Drawn by the scent of so many horses, a pack of twenty came to investigate and see how easily they might scavenge a meal. However, as one crept slowly up to the campsite, it stopped suddenly and sniffed. Then, it beat a hasty retreat! All of the pack followed, leaving the campsite in utter silence once more. Strange, he thought and then went back to sleep, confident in the twins.

Around one in the morning when he and Jarka had been on duty for several hours, Jarka finally began to say what was on her mind. Talking in a very low voice, she said, "Okay, they have to be asleep by now, Zoran. Now do you see what I mean about *them* being really, really strange? Have you ever known *anyone* whose chest can stop an arrow? Or how about anyone whose chest *breaks* swords without getting a scratch on themselves? Eh? Know of anyone who can do that? *I* certainly don't."

"Archmage Nadia did say that the twins knew some spells. Perhaps one of their spells somehow protects them against missiles and swords? I believe that there actually is such a spell, only we haven't yet gotten to it," he confided in her. She bit her lip; she had not thought of this.

"Aye, you have a point. Okay, then how do you explain that those two could lift that tree? Both draft horses would be needed if we had to do it. *Explain* that one, if you can," she replied and asked.

"Again, could be some kind of Strength spell that they had on themselves. That's possible, you know," Zoran replied.

"Damn, you are right again. Yes, I've heard of Strength spells too. That may be the answer. But why wouldn't they just come out and say, 'Look gang. We have cast a couple of spells that you all don't yet know on ourselves, which make us into supermen.' Or something like that. I mean, if *I* could do that, *I* would certainly tell you all about it. Well, okay, but that still doesn't explain why they just disappear every Sunday and what they are up to, now does it? I still think that they are hiding something, and I aim to find out what," she said defiantly.

"Let me know when you find out," Zoran replied sincerely. She smiled.

Around noon the next day, Zdenka said, "Zoran, see that faint trail there to your left? That tract leads to our home. It's about half a day's travel to get there from here." He smiled and thanked her for showing him. He really did want to visit the ex-General, though he was not sure just why at this point. A gut feeling told him that he ought to talk with the man.

Shortly after that, a band of five riders passed them. Later in the afternoon, they stopped to help another wagoner repair a broken axle. Nothing else of significance happened that day or night. Both Bernard and Karel insisted on standing watch, claiming that they felt nearly as good as new, though Zoran doubted that very much. Both were still healing, but he allowed them to stand watch.

Mid-morning, they finally left the Dark Woods proper behind them. While there were still plenty of patches of forest, the dim daylight was now replaced by sunshine, and the peaks in the distance quite visible and spectacular. Zoran found himself frequently gazing at them. This Brn country was very picturesque.

During their last day of travel, several lighter wagons passed by them on their way into Brn, while several heavily laden wagons lumbered on past them coming from Brn. Three sets of riders also past by them as well. At no time did Zoran get any sense that trouble was near at hand. At last, they rode into Brn late Saturday afternoon. Inside the gates, a dozen city guards took over for them.

"I'll get rid of the horses and stuff for us; meet you at the tower," Jarka suggested. Bernard volunteered to lend her a hand.

"We want gems please, pretty green ones," Renata called out to Jarka.

"Make mine clear gems," Emil added. Jarka smiled; they would be small ones, unless these horses were worth more than her initial guestimate. At suppertime, Jarka joined them in the tower.

"Okay, we got around eight hundred gold pieces worth from all their stuff. That amounts to one hundred fourteen for each of us. We were able to pick up seven gems worth about a hundred each. So here, have your pick. Each pouch has fourteen gold coins in it." She dumped seven glittering gems onto the table.

"Ah, so small," Renata sighed, as she picked up an emerald.

"How big did you want it?" Jarka teased her.

"Oh, this big," Renata put her hands together, indicating a softball size. Everyone roared with laughter.

"You'll need five thousand times more gold pieces than we got today to get one that size," Jarka estimated for her.

"Oh! Ah well, this is very pretty, and it is my first, very own gem. I love it. Thank you Jarka," Renata bubbled, very pleased with her small emerald.

Now the team went back to their studies once more.

Chapter 7 Sholov Province

Archmage Milos walked into the Baron's War Room, a windowless, heavily guarded square room, located deep within Castle Dorumova's walls. Metal shielding lined the walls to prevent mental spying by other Duskas. Metal tended to block their telepathy, or so the Baron had long ago decided. At least it did for him. Actually, Milos was responding to the Baron's summons.

Milos closed the door behind him and sealed it. Baron Kazimir was talking with his top general, Bor Wenceslas. On a large table was a mockup of the Sholov Province and the fortress-castle Mik, where Warlord Mikolas ruled the province. Well, not for much longer, Baron Kazimir was making his last minute preparations for his assault on Sholov. Milos studied the three dimensional map, noting where the warlord's fortifications were located and where the Baron's powerful army was currently stationed. The fortifications he himself had worked out, having made numerous flights over Sholov Province while Invisible. Milos observed that none of the small army men and pieces of equipment had been moved from their previous positions. He took this as a good sign. The Baron was not changing plans at this late date.

"Ah, Milos. Thank you for coming on such short notice. We are ready to begin the assault on Sholov Province. General Bor wants to move the launch date up one week. He believes that spies have already gotten our planned staring date back to Mikolas, so this move may take him by surprise."

"I told you that we should have used magic to locate those spies before they could elude our borders," Milos replied, feeling that his previous position in this spy matter was now vindicated. The general overruled him, believing that his scouts could intercept the spies while they were en route back to Sholov Province.

"Hell, it doesn't matter one iota whether we attack today, next week, or next month!" Baron Kazimir bellowed boastfully. "Mikolas will be crushed utterly. Now then I have two questions for you, well three really. Are your Mages ready to hit the field?"

"Aye, the seven are packed and awaiting your orders. I believe that they are anxious to show you and the world the kind of destruction that they can wreak on stonework," Milos answered.

"Good, good. Now then, is Radek really ready? He's insisting on personally commanding a regiment himself, but how goes his magic training? I don't want to risk him if he is not up to Mage standards."

"I believe that I have taught him everything that he can learn. He is not the most intelligent Duska I ever taught, which is limiting his ability to grasp the top power spells. So yes, I cannot teach him anything further. Your daughters, they still have a year to go." He knew that the Baron cared little for them; his only plans for them were to marry them off in some manner that benefitted him with stronger alliances. The Baron grimaced at the notion that his favored son and appointed heir, Radek, was not so bright. Yet, he knew this to be true; his facial muscles tightened and then relaxed. There was nothing he could do about that, unless he wanted to take another wife and try again, but then there was the age problem. He was now approaching sixty. Even if he did manage to remarry and father another boy child, he would be long dead before the boy reached adulthood and would very likely be assassinated long before then. No, it was Radek or nothing and certainly not the bastard son, Zoran, who had run away like the true coward that he was. Pity the assassins had failed, he thought.

"Your third question, Baron?" Milos nudged him, after two minutes of silence filled the room.

"Oh, any news on where that cowardly bitch of a son of mine has disappeared to?"

"No, no trace of him as yet. Spies are alert for his appearance in all of the Courts. Nothing as yet. I will let you know the moment he is spotted."

"Good. Good. One day I will beat some sense into that fool of a kid! Now where were we? Oh, yes, launch date will be on Sunday. Have the Mages report to General Bor's field position by seven a.m. That will be all."

"Aye, Baron." Milos unsealed the door and left, casting a Mystical Door back to his tower adjacent to Castle Dorumova.

On the 1st of July, Baron Kazimir donned his finest military uniform, assisted by his wife, Katerina. He had gained some weight since he last wore it two years ago, and she had to make some last minute adjustments, which only aggravated him further. Radek knocked and was allowed into their quarters. "Hi dad. How do I look?" He wore a very fancy uniform, green with red stripes, befitting a field commander.

"Just great son. Do me proud, son, but don't take chances. You are the heir to the throne. I ought to have my head examined for allowing you onto the battlefield," the Baron argued.

"Yes, dad, yes. If you don't, how will I ever gain the firsthand experience and knowledge that one day I will need when you are gone and I have to tackle the unconquered provinces that remain, eh?" His mother gave him a stern look, indicating that his father was not in the best of moods at the moment. He changed his tact. "Sure dad. I will be extra careful, and you, you be careful too. I don't want anything to happen to you just yet. While I know all the magic I need, I am still learning how to manage a whole army from you. So please stick around a while longer, dad." He grinned and knew that he'd just pleased his father. Radek knew just how to handle the old man. He'd had years of practice doing it.

"There, now you are all tucked in," Katerina declared. "Off you boys go to have your little battle. Please be careful and not get hurt." She kissed both men. The Baron resisted making a snide comment; the Baroness was often "not all there," when it came to matters beyond the simple managing of the castle life. Perhaps that was a result of the bad spill she had taken many years ago, when her horse had stumbled and broken its leg. She'd hit her head on some rocks and had never been quite the same since. He'd never say it out loud, but she was now very dim-witted, bordering on ignorant. Ah well, she was still good in bed and dressed up nicely for the formal affairs. Indeed, she still got numerous comments about her beauty when she appeared at these affairs.

The two men did a very short Shadow Walk and stepped into General Bor's tent. Shortly after that, Commander Radek stepped into his own field tent, where his aides were awaiting his arrival. Radek had one thousand men under his direct command. Good seasoned soldiers, well-armed, and well-armored. One handed him his field glasses and Radek surveyed the enemy's position across the valley from his position. Between them, a V-shaped valley with steep sides lay; a small river flowed at the very bottom.

Radek was on the far left flank of the main assault, which would be focused on the barrier wall erected to prevent the Baron from entering Sholov Province by the main mountain road. Radek's task was simple. Once that wall had been breached, Mikolas would certainly begin pulling his troops garrisoned here across from Radek on down to help fight the Baron's main army. Radek would then assault their position, overrun it, and begin a sweep of his own, marching towards the rear of the enemy troops on the march to stop the Baron's advancing army.

Baron Kazimir never told Radek that this particular assignment was not very dangerous and that in all likelihood the troops he would be facing would head south to help stop the Baron's forces. If he did manage to get his regiment down to join up with the Baron's main army, there would be plenty of glory for the commander. If he did not succeed, nothing much would be said, except that they met heavier than anticipated resistance.

The real battle would take place first at the fortified barrier wall, where the team of seven Mages would attempt to breach the stone wall and gates. Of course, if Mikolas had any Mages on his side, they would counterattack the Baron's Mages. By all reports, Warlord Mikolas had only one Mage with him. Thus the odds were heavily in the Baron's favor.

The Baron, resplendent in his uniform, saluted his men and bowed to his team of Mages. He decided against giving any last minute speech; he had already let it be known that he was offering a reward of ten thousand gold pieces for the man who brought him the head of Mikolas. That should ensure an otherwise certain victory. He raised his right hand high and then brought it down sharply, the signal to commence the battle for Sholov Province. It was ten in the morning.

His Mages teleported to their positions, and from General Bor's tent he could see the thousands upon thousands of his men marching down the mountain side or riding down the road, all bent upon smashing through the barrier wall on the opposite side of the steep sided gorge. Soon, mighty explosions were heard as his Mages began detonating their spells against the granite stone of the walls and the heavy, iron re-enforced pine gates. Arrows filled the air like a summer's rain, falling down at last onto the Baron's men. While it was impressive, the arrows had little effect on the heavily armored shock troops that the Baron placed here at his spearhead assault.

General Bor had two thousand cavalrymen at the ready. The moment the shock troops smashed their way through the barrier, the cavalrymen would charge and create a massive breakthrough. The main foot soldier army, another five thousand strong, would follow along behind, dragging the large siege engines needed to assail the mountain fortress-castle wherein Warlord Mikolas was sure to hold up.

Among the many officers, a betting pool had sprung up on just how soon the battle would be over. One month was the going favorite; however both one week and three months had the highest payout odds. Baron Kazimir had placed a bet on one month.

All the rest of the morning, explosive detonations echoed though the valley, as the Baron's Mages did their work thoroughly. Early reports came back. The opposition Mage was killed after he had killed one of the seven. Now the six had an unimpeded opportunity to smash the barrier to rubble, which they enjoyed doing.

At noon the shock troops stormed through the many breeches, and the battle for Sholov Province began in earnest. It was not until three in the afternoon that Radek spied large troop movements on the opposite side of the gully. As predicted, they were making haste to help stop the Baron's shock troops. Radek gave his first official battle command, and his regiment headed on down the gully.

By suppertime, the battle broke off for the day. The Baron's forces had suffered their first setback. "Spike jacks, sir," the field messenger reported. Evidently, the entire land just beyond the barrier wall had been filled with steel spikes, like a child's jacks. When his shock troops attempted to crossover them, the sharp spikes often punctured their boots, laming them completely. Fully five hundred shock troops were being treated. Worse, many of these spikes appeared to have been poisoned! Thus, many of these top fighters were not expected to live!

"Well, that was a surprise move," General Bor explained over dinner with the Baron. "Got to give Mikolas some credit; he is a brilliant warlord. Tomorrow we will deal with these spike jacks. Have no fear, Barron."

"Well, take your time, General Bor. If you had conquered the whole province in a week, I would have lost a fortune on the betting. I'm holding out for one month." Bor laughed heartily; he, too, had placed a wager on one month's duration for the war.

Chapter 8 Revelations and Actions

On the first of July, Rayna contacted Zoran. *Happy birthday, baby brother! How are you?*

Thanks. Doing fine. Miss you and Lida. How's everything? Keeping up with your magic studies?

All fine here. Baron has launched his war against Sholov Province this morning. Radek is now a field commander. Maybe we will get lucky and both will get killed.

Ah, not likely, they are Duska too. Wishful thinking. I'm into the midrange spells now, making really good, fast progress, according to the Archmage at least.

From her tone, he knew that she was impressed. *Wow, you have caught up to us, Zoran! That makes you at least a whole year ahead of the usual training level around here. Excellent progress. Wish we could come and get trained with you. Lida has been having strange dreams.* He sensed that there was something far more ominous that mere dreams behind her simple message.

Can you tell me about them? Have you had them too? Please, be honest with me. I can't look out for you from so far away, but I will try, sis.

She — she is seeing mom falling and falling. Lida thinks that mom is going to die somehow.

Baroness Katerina was not quite all there after her head wound; Zoran knew that his mother had not recovered at all well. That was plainly obvious to everyone. Her passing would be a blessing for her in many ways. She no longer could Shadow Walk or even cast any spells, not even Clean. About all she did was look petty for the Baron, not a life for a true Duska. Zoran sensed there had to be more to this. *Is this all that Lida has been dreaming about, sis?*

Well, no, not really. She was hesitant, so Zoran sent her a feeling of calmness and tranquility, an image of the white swans floating on the reservoir beside their castle. He sensed Rayna sighing. *She is seeing something happening to the Circle of Ascension, all the Circles of Ascension, Zoran, all of them. Something strange, something powerful, but she cannot tell what. You know the priests, they never tell us anything, though Lida has asked them about it. I'm sure is it really nothing. Should I try joining with her when she is having another one of her dreams, Zoran?*

Sure, why not. Let me know all the details. It may, as you say, be nothing at all. Then again, it might be important. Who can say? Probably it is just her imagination running a bit wild —you know, with the Baron on his insane conquer the world trip and all that. Thousands more are going to die this month. God, the blood that is on his hands and soul!

We know, Zoran. How can we keep all that blood off of us? I feel so horrible about it. So many innocent families are going to suffer. I hate the summers now; that's when he fights his battles.

I know, but then half of the other barons are doing much the same on their worlds too, Rayna. Have faith; someday something will change. The Baron cannot live forever.

Yes, but Radek is following in his footsteps. One tyrant replaces another. That always seems to be the way of things. Yes that cycle did seem to perpetuate itself among the ruling houses, Zoran noted. What could he say to make her feel better? Alas, he could think of nothing. A long pause followed. *I'll let you get back to your studies. I just wanted to say happy birthday, little brother. Love you.*

Thanks, love you too, Rayna.

"Hey, you looked like you were off in dream land or something," Zdenka whispered to him. They were studying away, now up on the third floor with the many other advanced apprentices. Ever since they had returned from their guard duty errand, they had been allowed up here. The more advanced spell materials and texts were housed here on the third floor. Still, the Archmage kept their group isolated from her other students, though Zoran had no idea why. Marek did give them a clue, however. One evening he mentioned slyly that their team was progressing almost three times as fast as all the previous groups the Archmage had trained or was training. Zoran then wondered why the rush.

"It's my birthday," he admitted. "My sister sent me a message just then, wishing me a happy birthday. Nothing important, really," Zoran replied.

"Gang, it's Zoran's birthday today!" Zdenka playfully called out.

Jarka couldn't resist and started to sing "Happy Birthday to you." Soon they all got in on it, hamming it up, much to Zoran's embarrassment.

"Okay, now you've gone and done it. Just you wait until I find out when all of your birthdays are, then you'll get it!" he threatened jokingly. Everyone laughed and returned to their studies. Today, they were learning how to create a Killing Cloud, which was a fog-like cloud whose vapors poisoned all living creatures that breathed it into their lungs. It was a nasty spell indeed.

All were more excited about the next spell on the list, however. It was the Teleport spell, one which would elevate them all to Mage status, as well as giving them the freedom to travel anywhere on Adapazan in an instant. Everyone hoped and prayed that they would be able to learn that spell — that key spell of all other spells — all except Zoran, who really did not need it. He could Shadow Walk anywhere on the planet as well as to all of the other planets in the Federation of Planets.

Much of the early weeks of July were spent working on this single spell. Archmage Nadia insisted that every member of the team learn to Teleport. While Zoran picked it up first with great ease, some of the others had a more difficult time with the spell, particularly Bernard, Karel, and Jarka. Interestingly enough, both Emil and Renata picked it up almost as rapidly as did Zoran.

The last Saturday in July was success day. Bernard finally mastered the spell. All seven were now awarded their Mage status, a high honor indeed. Since Sunday was their day off, Zoran exclaimed, "All right, Mages, one and all! Tomorrow, I want to throw you all a really big celebration party at the Stodgy Inn. I've reserved the inn for our use from ten to one. All you can eat and drink is on me! I've hired some musicians to play for us as well. Congratulations to us all! My fellow Mages! This is a once in a lifetime celebration, for Mages are we! Emil, Renata, maybe you can delay whatever it is that you have to do on Sunday for a while and join us. After all, you are part of the celebration too, you Mages." Zoran felt alive, happy, and even a touch elated that every member of his team had made it. The twins looked at each other and then at their five friends.

"Sure we can delay it for a while," Emil grinned. "All we can eat? Are you sure you can afford our tab?" Everyone roared with laughter. They had seen that these two could put away enormous meals without batting an eye.

"Great Emil, Renata. Yes, all you can eat and drink. Time for a real celebration. You are the greatest bunch of friends that I've ever had."

On Sunday, they all headed to the inn — that is, they all Teleported there at the stroke of ten. The musicians were already on hand and played a triumphant march as the seven arrived. Drinks and food flowed from the barkeeper, who was making a very tidy profit this day indeed. Zoran moved tables out of the way making a dancing area. He took Zdenka onto his new dance floor, and they began to dance to the tunes. Not to be outdone, Bernard swept Jarka, protesting all the way, onto the dance floor as well. But her protests were all show; she began to enjoy herself as well.

Karel asked if Renata wanted to dance. "But I don't know how to dance," she replied.

"Darn if I know either, but let's just follow them. At least you can twirl around some," he confided in her. She let go of her hesitation and they joined in, leaving Emil standing and watching. Shortly, one of the barmaids, who was serving the drinks, took Emil by the hand and pulled him onto the dance floor as well. She got caught up in their frolicking fun as well.

A while later, Emil and Renata stopped to eat. Only after letting out a tremendous burp after his seventh serving did Emil finally push his plate away. "Guess that will hold me a while." Everyone roared and handed him another ale. Renata had six servings, Zoran noted. How they could put away all that food was beyond him, but just now, he cared not at all. He was happy, having fun, and was with his friends. The world was beautiful and cheerful. He had no idea this would be so short lived.

The next morning, everyone was nursing a slight hangover, excepting Emil and Renata, of course. After breakfast, all felt somewhat better and were about to resume their studies, when they received a Message from the Archmage. "Meet me in the first floor study immediately." The tone of her voice sounded serious; they looked at each other hoping that one of them had some clue about what was happening. None did. They rushed down to their old study room. All of the many books and scrolls were neatly in their proper places. Archmage Nadia looked very serious and very old this morning. Something was very wrong. Zoran didn't need his special sense to know that something was happening.

"Have a seat, please. I have some really bad news to share with you, and I am afraid that I will have to beg you to undertake a vitally critical mission fraught with danger, especially to Zoran. As everyone now knows, Baron Kazimir," Zoran noted that she purposely did not use his last name, probably for his sake, "has invaded the Sholov Province. Warlord Mikolas has put up a valiant defense, costing the Baron dearly for every mile that he has conquered. However, that is not why I have called you here. No, it is far, far, far more important than the fall of yet another warlord of the Wild Lands."

"There is a side effect, one of immense magnitude, but one which only Zoran here can fully appreciate. Because of the nature of this situation, Zoran, I ask your permission to tell the others your identity and secret, if I may. I swear to you that I am not taking this lightly and that it is vital to everyone's understanding of the situation we are facing at this very moment that they know your story. Will you free me from my pledge to you, Zoran?"

"But that will expose them to — well, you know what I mean," Zoran cringed. More than anything, he did not want to burden his friends with his own troubles or open them wide to assassinations as well.

"I am well aware of that aspect, Zoran, but the sheer magnitude of what is happening and what will happen if we do not intervene within hours far outweigh the danger to your team members."

"I trust your judgment, Archmage Oldrich. I so release you from your word," Zoran spoke clearly and decisively. He rather wished that she had taken him aside and told him what was going on and allowed him to reach the same conclusion as she. However, she hadn't and now he began to wonder why.

"Would you or would you prefer me to tell them, Zoran?" she asked in her soft, calm voice.

"I ought to since they are my friends." He sighed; in a minute they would become part of his secret life, fraught with all of the dangers and even assassination attempts as well.

"I have never told you my sir name. I had my reasons which I will tell you about now. I am really Duke Zoran Vladislov, son of Baron Kazimir Vladislov. Here is my ring to prove it." He pulled his duke ring from its thong around his neck and showed it to the others. Many gasped.

Zdenka exclaimed, "I knew it! I knew you were a nobleman!" She flushed and was silent.

"More than a nobleman, I'm afraid. I am a Duska and fourth heir to the throne of Adapazan. I am sorry for having withheld this from you, but I had no choice. You see, I hate my father and older brother. I am nothing like them; neither are my twin sisters, Rayna and Lida. I was being trained by Archmage Milos, but he is an idiot and despot compared to Archmage Oldrich here. Before I came here in secret, an assassin tried to kill me three times. Obviously, he failed on each attempt, but the attempts on my life were increasing in frequency. I had no choice but to run away. I took great, great pains to hide my tracks so that no one could ever follow me here. Indeed, I didn't even tell my sisters, who I dearly love, where I went. They still do not know where I am. I know that Baron Kazimir has got many spies fanned out throughout the entire Federation of Planets searching for me. If and when they find me, there will be hell to pay, that I know. Just by my having revealed this to you has now placed all of your lives at risk. You too may well be targets of assassins, if the Baron or whoever is behind these assassinations ever finds out that I am here and that you are my friends. I never, ever wanted to place you in this kind of danger. I am Duska. I have an inner sense when danger is at hand and have lightning fast reactions, which has saved my life three times now. I am truly sorry that I have now placed all of you in such danger. You do not deserve it."

"Who is trying to kill you? Tell us about the assassination attempts," Zdenka urged him on. She was staggered by the magnitude of just who he was! A Duska, that explained so much about him — why Archmage Nadia chose him to be their leader and why he could sense when danger was near. Yet he was nothing like his father, the Barron. Zoran was the kindest, most gentle man that she had ever met.

"I have no idea at all who the assassin might be or who has hired him to kill me or even why someone wants me dead. The Baron," he could still not think of him as his father any longer, "could care less about me. He just ignores me like some fly buzzing around the dinner table. Rayna, my sister, thinks our older brother, Radek, might be behind it, but I can't see why he would want me dead. I pose him no threat. He is the heir to the throne of Adapazan, not me. Heck, my two sisters are in line for the throne before I am."

"The first attempt was poisoned bread at our dinner table. I accidently dropped it on the floor, and my old dog ate it and died within minutes. Then, the assassin tried to shoot me with a poisoned arrow while I was in the middle of an intense fighter training round with real swords fighting against our sword master. I barely avoided that one. The last time, he tried to drop a three foot stone parapet block on my head while I was walking down the street going to an inn. I dove out of the way and it missed my leg by mere inches. That's when I decided that I had had enough and ran away."

"I Shadow Walked to get here. In the basement of Castle Dorumova and in the most secure location in the entire castle, lies the Circle of Ascension, which is the key to our ability to Shadow Walk. I purposely retraced my initiation steps, passing through all of the intertwined lines that connect the many planets of the Federation, before I stepped out and here to Brn. That way, not even a priest can determine just where I went. Ordinarily, if one Shadow Walks, a priest can see the energy lines and ascertain the destination. Honestly, there is no way anyone can trace me here directly. I think we are still safe for a time." He wanted to alleviate their fears of imminent assassinations.

"Holy crap! We've had a real Duska with us all this time!" Karel finally burst out his surprise and awe. He had been in complete shock until now.

"Wow! Incredible!" added Jarka. "Say, does that now mean that we have to call you Duke Zoran and treat you as a super-nobleman?" she couldn't resist a stab; after all he had been hiding this from her all this time.

Zoran grinned, "Jarka, if you call me duke, I will have to cut out your tongue." She flushed and then giggled, getting his joke. "Honestly, that would give everything away. The assassins would be here in no time, and you'd probably find your throats cut, once he forced my whereabouts out of you. Never call me duke or Duska, please. I'm just plain old Zoran."

"Hardly plain," Bernard teased him, with a big grin on his face.

"So you can walk between planets?" Emil asked curiously.

"Yes, just as easily as you all can now Teleport anywhere on Adapazan, Emil. We are born with a special gland at the base of our brains. When we reach puberty, the Ceremony of Ascension is conducted by our priests. Essentially, they lead us around the Circle of Ascension, which activates our glands. I was awfully sick at first, but it soon passed. Without the guidance of the priest, I would never have been able to master it by myself."

Emil reached a decision. His father could do this thing too, this Shadow Walk or at least something similar. Emil knew that, while his father would teach him this, there would be limitations. Aldrick told him that he could only travel to planets that he knew about, and here was a man who could move between at least sixteen of them, far more than his dad ever mentioned. Emil wanted to be able to go to all sixteen and thus he reached his decision. "Archmage Oldrich, perhaps this is a time for additional revelations."

She smiled, "Perhaps, Emil, it is so. Would you like to share with your team?"

"Yes. Gang, Renata and I are not what we seem to be, humans. Actually, well, ah, we are really gold dragons, young ones, in our teens, just like some of you. We are here to learn magic spells, as did our dad many years ago. He brought us here to learn from his old teacher, Archmage Oldrich."

"What? Dragons?" exclaimed Karel.

"Well, that explains a whole lot!" blurted out Bernard. "No wonder the horses were so skiddy around you two!"

"Ah ha!" Jarka whispered rather loudly.

Zdenka merely said, "Oh my!" She was genuinely surprised.

"No wonder you had such hard times with all our customs and actions," Zoran replied. "Your secret is safe with me, you two. Thank you for telling us. So that's why you two were not injured by the arrows and swords. No wonder you could lift that tree. Incredible. You two must be very strong indeed."

"Say, can we see what you really look like sometime?" Jarka asked, dying to know just what they did look like. "And what's with all this sneaking around on Sundays? Where have you two been going? I've looked around town, but I have never seen you here in Brn."

"Er, feeding," Renata answered, slightly embarrassed.

"We get really hungry by then. Normally, we need to eat once a week. I'm afraid that we would have to eat all of your food if we didn't take off on Sundays to hunt and feast," Emil explained.

"What do you eat?" Jarka inquired, curious. She hoped it was not on people that they dined.

"Hoofers," Renata replied, "antelope."

"Okay, we got lots of them around here, just glad you didn't say people," Jarka teased them, but with a serious overtone. "So it was one of you that the hunter saw flying in the mountains a while back?"

"Er, no, not us. We have been very careful. No one has seen us. It was dad; he slipped up and allowed the hunter man to see him flying back with an antelope for mom," Emil explained, and then realized that he had said a bit too much. Oh well, they might as well know the rest. He went on, "Mom and dad are here too, living in the cavern where dad often stayed when he was here years ago studying magic."

"You see, our planet Voss is, as dad puts it, over-populated by we dragons. We've eaten all of the hoofers of any kind there. Before we came here this spring, we were starving to death, really we were. The Council wouldn't listen to dad who tried to warn them about our over-population problem years ago. Now all dragons on Voss are slowly starving to death. That's why dad brought us all here. He can travel kind of like your Shadow Walking, I think. Zoran, one day, I would give anything if you would help me develop that skill. Dad is going to teach me what he knows about it, but you know far, far more than dad does. Please, help me when the time is right, please."

"Me too," Renata added.

"I'll see what I can do, when the time is right," Zoran promised, though he did not know whether this was a good call or not. Certainly the time would not be right in the foreseeable future. "Anyway, team, let's all swear to keep their secret safe with us. After all, think of the problems that would arise if the whole town knew that we have four dragons living among us."

Jarka nodded, that was an understatement if she'd ever heard one. The five all agreed. Renata then suggested, "Next Sunday if you want, you can come with us and meet our parents, that is, if you don't mind watching us eat. We do have to eat, you know." Everyone was only too pleased to be asked.

The Archmage allowed them to chat about these amazing revelations for a brief time. Then, she resumed control of her meeting. "Okay. Now why have I decided all this must become known just now? The answer lies in the Circle of Ascension that all of the Ruling Houses of the Federation have. Without these Circles of Ascension, it is doubtful if any of their special glands could be activated. They are the root of a baron's powers. Without a Circle of Ascension, a baron's line would end, as none of his children could have their special gland activated. There would be no more Duska children, no more heirs, no more powerful leaders, no more Shadow Walking between planets. This is why the barons so heavily guard and protect their Circles of Ascension, they are extremely vital."

"With this in mind, I now have someone from the Sholov Province that I want you to meet." She cast a brief spell and Marek opened the door, showing the guest into the room. Dressed in brown monk's robes, the hooded man entered and bowed to Archmage Nadia Oldrich.

"Mages, I would like you to meet Brother Jiri Zar of Sholov Fortress." He removed his hood and bowed to the assembled Mages. His hair was cut very short, his eyes, brown, probably in his mid-twenties, Zoran guessed. His robes hid his physique, which was that of a fighting monk. His last name, Zar — it was familiar somehow — something to do with history, as he tried to recalled.

The monk's eyes met each of the Mages in turn as he bowed to them. When his eyes reached Zoran's, he reacted with surprise. "Zoran? Duke Zoran?"

"Yes, but I am keeping my identity around here a secret, known only to those here in this room, please say nothing of this to others," Zoran quickly replied.

"My lips are sealed. Archmage Oldrich, this is even better that I had expected, a duke is with us; perhaps there is yet hope." She smiled and bade him continue his tale for the Mages.

He stood tall and began his well-rehearsed speech. "My name is indeed Brother Jiri Zar, a holy monk of the Ascension. I am the great-great-great-grandson of Bandar Zar, who built the very first Circle of Ascension on the forest planet of Gladno so long ago. Unfortunately, the knowledge of how to build these Circles of Ascension was lost when he died, though he built sixteen of them, one on each of the sixteen planets of the Federation. Since that time, no more have ever been built; the knowledge was lost."

"My wife, Priestess Anezka, has already performed one Ceremony of

Ascension and is skilled in their use to mature the young Duska. Three years ago, Priestess Anezka and I were called in secret to this planet and to Warlord Mikolas at his mountain fortress. His fortress is an ancient one, dating back to the founding of the barons and the Circles of Ascension. While renovating the old fortress, buttressing it against this day which has now come — that is, an all-out assault by the Baron's army — Mikolas uncovered a secret chamber beneath the fortress. There he found numerous ancient scrolls and books covered in dust. The author of several of these was Bandar Zar."

The monk paused allowing the importance of this to register with the Mages and with Zoran in particular. "Realizing the potential importance and value of his find, he sent for my wife and me. Yes, these are the long lost writings of Bandar Zar. More importantly, in them, he describes how to build a Circle of Ascension!"

Zoran gasped. The sheer magnitude of this find was incredible! Brother Jiri continued, "We three, my wife, Mikolas, and I, held long discussions and Mikolas first suggested the idea. Why not build a new Circle of Ascension right there in his fortress, creating a new power position and a new House of Duska, one to compete with Baron Kazimir, one to finally rid Adapazan of this tyrant? Once the Circle of Ascension was completed, the Council of Houses would have no choice but to recognize Mikolas and Sholov Province as a new member of the Council, effectively stopping Baron Kazimir from his planet-wide conquest of power."

"To that end and as dictated in the writings of Bandar Zar, I began construction of the first new Circle of Ascension in centuries. It is not yet done. Oh, had I been faster in learning how to build it. Oh, if only it was in operation now, then Sholov might have been saved, but such was not to be. The Baron's army is on the doorstep of Mikolas as I speak."

"Mikolas, Priestess Anezka, and I all agree that under no circumstances whatsoever should these priceless documents and the partially built Circle of Ascension fall into the hands of Baron Kazimir! His only Mage was killed in the opening salvo. Now we have no way to Teleport these things from his fortress. I was forced to make the journey here overland, costing us precious time — time that we do not have. Priestess Anezka communicates with me daily, and I am afraid that time has run out for us. As we speak, the Baron's army is besieging the fortress. We have at most hours, maybe only minutes, to rescue these things."

"Mikolas will dedicate his life to buying us time to safely remove these items from the Baron's grasp. He now realizes that he will not live to found the newest House, but is donating his fortune to us to help build that new House elsewhere. I have come to ask you to immediately come to the fortress of Mikolas and help us remove these things to safety. Please will you help?"

"Absolutely. Let's get going. I can Shadow Walk us all there, but maybe it would be better if we Teleported, less chance of being followed," Zoran replied.

Archmage Oldrich said softly, "Thank you. I have offered them all safe haven here at my tower. Please bring them and their precious materials here, which is still beyond the Baron's long reach. After that, we can decide what to do with them. Quickly, get your things together and yes, use Teleports. We do not want your Shadow Walk to be traced back here."

Three minutes later, the team raced back into the meeting room, armed to the teeth, so to speak. Brother Jiri said, "The only problem now is just where to arrive. Already parts of the castle are being overrun. We don't want to materialize in that portion now controlled by the Baron. Let me contact Anezka." A minute later, he said, I have the arrival location in my head. How am I to relate this to you so that you can know your destination point?" he looked befuddled. Yet another obstacle barred his mission, which had been fraught with barriers to overcome.

"Allow me," Zoran replied. He focused his mind and touched that of Jiri. "Yes, Jiri, hold that image in your mind. I'm going to put his image into your minds, gang. It won't hurt." One by one, Zoran found the minds of his friends and tied them into the image being held on to by Jiri, who focused all his attention onto keeping that image in his mind. "Now, cast our Teleports. I will bring Jiri with me." He cast his spell and within seconds of each other, the eight vanished from Archmage Oldrich's tower. They did not see her praying and crossing her fingers.

They arrived in a stone room. Smoke and foul fumes drifted in through the open windows. A distressed young woman stood beside a man wearing chain mail armor, well-armed. Noise of battle echoed through the room. "Oh Jiri! It is almost too late!" Anezka exclaimed, rushing to her husband's side. She had shoulder length blonde hair and pale blue eyes. She looked a priestess.

"Zoran? Zoran Vladislov?" Mikolas exclaimed, utterly shocked to see the duke. "You're not dead?"

"Very much alive. I've come to rescue the Zors and your precious find. I can take you with us as well, if you like. These must not under any circumstances fall into my father's hands!" He knew that he had to rapidly convince Mikolas that he was not in his father's employ. "I've been with Archmage Oldrich. She is training me. We are all Mages here. Let us lend you a hand."

"Come, it is in the basement. We can still get there, but much of the fortress is already overrun. There is so little time and I am needed here to coordinate our last lines of defense and our retribution. Jiri, take them there. Let me know when you are leaving, that I may find peace at last, knowing that our discovery is safe! May God be with you all, thank you."

"This way," Brother Jiri called out. They rushed down a very long stairs. The command post, where Mikolas was standing viewing and coordinating the last defense, was seven stories above the basement, where the remodeling had uncovered the precious cache. Down they descended, sounds of steel upon steel echoed loudly as they passed exits to the various floors. Soldiers were fighting inside the fortress rooms. So little time.

At last they entered the hidden room. Zoran and his friends surveyed what had to be done. "We need at least a half hour to safely pack everything," he voiced his best guess.

Jarka concurred, "At least a half hour. Can Mikolas hold out that long?"

Zoran made telepathic contact with Mikolas and asked him. "No way gang; the first floor has been lost; they are now climbing the stairs upwards. Any moment they might head down here. We have minutes at most. Ideas? Suggestions?"

Emil volunteered, "What if dragons appeared and began attacking? Would that slow them down?"

"Wow! You bet it would! Can you do this, Emil?" Zoran asked.

"Yes, as long as they don't need this stairs any longer. We can fit through it, but will likely bring part of the ceiling down as we wiggle through."

"Okay, when we are ready to teleport out of here, we will let you know. You can then teleport back in here and join us. Okay?"

"Fine. Renata, it's time to show these humans what a dragon can do!"

"Well, teen dragons, Emil. Remember, we are not fully grown yet," she teased her brother. "You all stand way back. It will be a tight fit until we wiggle up the stairs."

Jarka squeezed herself into the farthest corner of the room! The others flattened themselves against the back wall. All watched in utter fascination as the golden hued Emil morphed back into his normal body, a forty foot long, golden dragon. Emil stood twenty feet tall; his claws would indeed skewer a man easily. With great effort and crumbling stonework, Emil squeezed himself back up the stairs to the first floor, now controlled by the Baron's Shock Troops. As Emil came out into a large room with soldiers running in many directions, he let out his loudest howl and belched forth a cone of broiling flames, frying a dozen men dead in their tracks. He destroyed two more groups before moving on out of the door way and took flight. Renata was right behind him.

The shock, total surprise, and utter awe completely stopped the entire siege of the fortress. Flying side by side, the twins swooped over concentrations of troops, blasting them with their giant cones of superheated flames. For variety, they occasionally let lose a powerful bolt of electrical energy at some of the fleeing soldiers. Mass pandemonium broke out, as the Baron's soldiers ran from the fortress, fearing for their lives. Many never made it to safety. Again and again the twins circled the mountain fortress, burning or electrocuting the baron's men. They didn't have to worry about accidentally getting Mikolas' men. Those that still lived were on the upper floors of the fortress.

On the top floor, Mikolas gathered the last of his men with him, only fifty remained. "My god! Dragons! Oh, if they could have only come sooner!" exclaimed Mikolas.

"It's a miracle! Real dragons! They are real! Look at the revenge we are having. How sweet this is!" one wounded fighter yelled. "Go get them! Kill them all!" he yelled to the dragons, who couldn't actually hear him. They were too far away.

"Men, loyal, free men, while we have only a few minutes of life within us, God has shown us a miracle. The dragons have returned, and they are on our side! Behold miracle of all miracles!" Mikolas called out to his men. Somehow, though he had no idea how, he had been able to give his men a dying miracle. Perhaps some of his fleeing people, now high in the mountains, would also see these magnificent golden beasts coming to fight for the people of Sholov Province. He hoped that some did and would spread the word far and wide. A new day was beginning, though he knew he would not live to see it. Merely seeing the dragons and their wrath was comfort to Mikolas. His long struggle was not in vain.

His last remaining aide called out, "Boss, the last of our people has reached Bazir Pass. It is time." A half hour had now passed, and the dragons vanished as suddenly as they had appeared, leaving behind masses of smoldering men. Over a thousand soldiers were dead or badly injured. Flames continued to burn around the outer areas of the fortress.

Mikolas touched a burning torch to one pile of black powder and then to its companion. "Here you go, Baron Kazimir. I hope you like it," Mikolas spat on the floor. The flashing, sputtering of the gunpowder disappeared from the room, following the long ago carved channels cut into the stone for this very purpose. One ran up the mountain towards Bazir Pass, while the other ran on downhill to the tall pine forests that surrounded this end of the valley and fortress.

With the dragons now gone, the Baron's forces regrouped and once more charged the fortress. As they reached the top floor where Mikolas and the last of his fighters prepared to battle to the end, an explosion shook the fortress. High up by Bazir Pass, an explosion brought tons of granite cascading down, totally blocking the pass. No one, no army could follow the retreating folks, who once called Sholov Province their home. The adjoining Orlovia Province was safe from the Baron's army for now. He'd have to find another way to attack that warlord.

To the south, the pine forest with its centuries of dried pine needles erupted into flames. Indeed, the entire southern edge of the forest was soon ablaze. Mikolas was burning down the whole forest. There was no way out of this valley. Baron Kazimir would have to wait for days for the fires to burn out, leaving him nothing but an abandoned wasteland. Some prize to hold up, Mikolas sneered, and swung his sword at the oncoming soldier.

Meanwhile, in the basement, Zoran and the others began packing the priceless artifacts for transport. Complicating matters were two things. Beyond the documents, the partially constructed Circle of Ascension had to be dismantled and packed. Also, and much to Jarka's delight, Mikolas was donating his entire treasury to them to help build this new Circle of Ascension. Five hundred thousand in gems and jewelry had to be packed as well. They were forced to leave behind the gold, however. It was too heavy to get on such short notice. However, there was not much of it; most had been converted into gems. Perhaps Mikolas had foreseen this day and had prepared.

A half hour later, they were finally ready to go. Zoran telepathically let Emil and Renata know that they were ready for them to join them in the basement. A minute later, the two reappeared, quite out of breath from their exertions. "I'm so hungry I could eat two hoofers!" Emil exclaimed rather excited about his adventures.

"Please, don't eat us," Jarka begged, worried that starving dragons might just let their stomachs dictate their actions.

"Relax, Jarka, we don't eat humans. You taste really bad," Emil replied honestly.

"Really you do. Dad says humans taste more like dragon dung. Who would want to eat that?" Renata added to her brother's explanation. Jarka visibly relaxed, very glad to hear that!

"Come on; we got to get out of here now. Grab as many bags as you can safely carry. Teleport to our meeting room in the tower. I will bring these two with me," Zoran ordered. He waited until the others had all gone and made sure that no bags were left. Then, Zoran took Jiri and Anezka's hands and cast his teleport spell. Nothing but a few hundred gold coins remained in the room, and nothing that would indicate the precious documents of Bandar Zar had ever been here.

"You all smell like a battle," Archmage Nadia said softly, after they all arrived in her meeting room on the first floor. "I take it that you were successful?"

"Close, but with the timely help of two gold dragons, who bought us the time we needed, yes, Archmage, we have returned with the whole lot. We left nothing behind, not a trace of this discovery will be found. It remains a secret to the Baron and the Houses," Zoran reported.

"Good, good. No one is hurt?" she inquired.

"We are starving," Emil blurted out. "All that flying and belching flames has worked us up quite an appetite."

Everyone chuckled. "Okay, why don't you two take off and find some hoofers. Get back as soon as it is feasible," she suggested.

"Okay, but we want to know what goes on next," Renata said, torn by her curiosity and her hunger. Hunger won out. The two teleported away.

"Let's put the sacks into the study in the next room. Then, how about baths for all of you? I don't want the stench of battle smelling up my tower. Marek will show you two to your room and the bath." Quickly the five headed to wash up and change. Zoran noted that this would also give the twins time to get back. They wouldn't miss anything, he hoped.

An hour later, everyone gathered back in the main entrance room. Quickly, Zoran recounted what they had done, though he deferred to Emil to relate what the dragons had done. Next, Jiri explained what had led up to this and what had very likely occurred after they left. "You see, Mikolas didn't want all of his people in Sholov Province to become slaves of the Baron. Over these past many months, he had all those that wished to move quietly head up the Bazir Pass and down into Orlovia Province. He had assurances from the warlord there that his people would be welcomed and allowed to migrate elsewhere or settle in his province. What warlord would not desire a doubling of their population?"

"The last of them were near the pass when you all arrived. Once the last one had cleared the pass, Mikolas intended to blow up the pass, bringing tons of the surrounding granite mountainside down on the pass, effectively blocking passage into Orlovia Province from Sholov Province. That was the bargain he struck with the warlord there. Now the Baron will have to find an alternative route to assault Orlovia."

"Simultaneously, Mikolas was to set fire to the entire southern line of the pine forest just south of the fortress. The Baron will find that he is now the proud owner of a wasteland, devoid of nearly all its inhabitants, crops, and commerce. He wins a partially destroyed stone fortress and a hundred gold pieces that we left behind. I hope the Baron chokes on this." Many chuckled as they heard just what the Baron got for his slaughter of so many men.

"What Mikolas and we were trying to do is to create another Circle of Ascension and thus a new rival House, complete with its own baron to rival Baron Kazimir. Once we had the Circle, we are certain of gaining the respect of all the other Houses, which Mikolas hoped would put an end to the Baron's constant conquering of lands surrounding his own. That was the plan. In the end, when we realized this was not to be, Mikolas converted all of his treasury into gems and jewels for easy transport and has donated it to Anezka and me to fund the construction of the Circle

Zoran Chronicles Volume 1 A Dragon in Our Town

of Ascension elsewhere on Adapazan."

"If your people would like us to remunerate them for their timely rescue of us and the partially constructed Circle, we would be more than willing to pay. Just tell us," Jiri continued.

"No payment needed. Just glad we could help," Zoran spoke up before anyone else could. No way was he going to accept any monetary gain. Having the chance to stop or delay or create serious problems for the Baron was vastly more important, as was saving these precious documents. He knew that Jarka would ask for something and this took the opportunity away from her.

"What plans do you have now for the relocation of this new Circle of Ascension, Brother Jiri?" the Archmage asked softly.

"We want to finish what Mikolas and we started out to do. We see this as the only real way to stop or end the Baron's reign on our world. We must have our own Duska and baron, our own recognized House among the High Council," Jiri answered her.

Priestess Anezka added, "Now we are at a loss on where we should go to build it. The more people that know of our incredible and precious find, the sooner others are going to come after us to steal it for themselves. These documents are utterly priceless. Honestly, we are a bit at a loss on just how to proceed now that Mikolas is gone and cannot protect us any longer. I would hate to just turn all this over to the Ruling Houses and let them have these documents."

Archmage Nadia sighed and then began, "Truly we find that we are at a crossroads — all of us gathered together in this room. What we decide or fail to decide here will have an enormous, if not utterly profound impact, not only on us but on the entire Federation of Planets. You are quite right. As soon as news of this find leaks out, every House in the Federation will be after those documents, one way or another. If they cannot outright buy it from you, most certainly they will send in their assassins to secure it."

"You cannot go from warlord to warlord offering to build it at their fortress. None of them alone could possibly stand against the Baron's army, a multitude of assassins, or even other Houses who might Shadow Walk their armies here to take it by force of arms."

"Yet, if somewhere the Circle of Ascension could be built and then presented to the Federation's High Council, you stand a good chance of being recognized and added to the High Council, but you would need at least one Duska to become the baron there. I assure you that if you did not have a bonafide Duska, the High Council would appoint one of their own as your Duska, which is not desirable either."

"We are besieged with seemingly insurmountable barriers and an equally lofty goal worthy of our best efforts. Times like these, I wish the world had a fortune teller!" This brought a grin or chuckle to everyone.

Zoran knew what he had to do, though he didn't want to do it. At last, he spoke quietly. "I'll be your Duska. Build the Circle of Ascension, and I'll be your Duska and go before the High Council, forcing them to recognize the new Circle and House. Heck, the assassins are already after me so what are adding a few more going to do?"

"You — you would do this?" Priestess Anezka exclaimed both shocked and surprised. "You would be giving up forever your own birthright to Baron Kazimir's throne and setting yourself against your father and his army!"

"Hey, not much chance of becoming a baron by birthright. I'm fourth in line. Radek's already been chosen as his heir apparent. My sisters are next in line. If anyone ever harms my sisters, I will wage total war against the perpetrators, no holds or laws barred! However, I really do not want to be a baron, but as the Archmage said, we must make the attempt to reach that lofty goal. It could well put an end to Baron Kazimir's subjugation of the whole planet. I have no choice but to make the attempt. I could not live with myself if I didn't stand up for you. I am a Duska after all. That means that I am supposed to be held to a higher responsibility level than everyone else. I'll be your Duska. You build the Circle of Ascension."

Brother Jiri said very officially, "Duke Zoran Vladislov, we hereby accept your gracious offer to become our Duska should we successfully build another Circle of Ascension." Both he and his wife bowed low to Zoran, who felt slightly ill at ease and embarrassed by their bows.

"Well, one insurmountable barrier has been lifted," Archmage Oldrich said softly. "Now where should it be built?" The room was dead silent. While there were many warlords here in the Wild Lands, dealing with them was fraught with problems, to say nothing of their having a suitable castle, such as Castle Dorumova, where the Circle could easily be protected.

Inspiration struck! Zoran said, "Here, we should build it here in Archmage Oldrich's tower!"

She looked shocked, "Why on earth here? This is not a castle or a fortress. Brn Province has neither anywhere in it."

"I know. For one thing, it minimizes those who already know about this discovery of Zor's documents. Two, Brn is over a thousand miles from Dorum, making it difficult, though not impossible for the Baron and his army to reach us in the near future. Three, what better protection than to have the Circle defended by an entire Archmage and all her many Mages living here. Even I would think twice about attacking an entire Archmage tower! Once we succeed and are officially recognized, perhaps then we can set about building something more suitable. What do you think, Archmage Oldrich?"

"Wait before you say anything further," Emil interrupted them. Everyone turned to face the gold dragon teen. "You forgot number four. Fourth, you can have a number of gold dragons protecting the tower. I am sure that our parents would be willing to provide protection as well, making four of us. If you need more, dad might be able to bring some of his friends from Voss here. There are plenty of hoofers for many dragons here in your forests, really there are."

"Wow! Thanks, Emil," Zoran replied, becoming excited about this aspect. "Once everyone in Brn knows that the dragons are here to protect them from the evil Baron Kazimir, they will readily accept them! After what I suspect these two dragons did to his army today, I am certain that any baron would think more than twice about making any kind of takeover of Brn by force of arms. Magic and dragons shall be your protection. What say you to our offer, Archmage Oldrich?"

She smiled, "What can I say but that I accept this offer. This is the highest honor I have ever received in my life, and it carries with it the highest responsibility I have ever borne. I will bear it with pride."

Zoran rose to the occasion; his formal court lessons had not been totally wasted. "Thank you Archmage Nadia Oldrich for your generous offer. As the new Duska, I accept your offer." He gave his best courtly bow to her, which brought a smile to the old woman's face. Long had it been since she received a Duska's bow. Zoran continued, "We should keep the project totally secret until the Circle is activated, at which point I am sure all of the other Houses will instantly know of its activation. At that time, we should be prepared. We should meet with the twin's parents soon to get their agreement. We should have a general in charge of creating a small garrison of men to help with any physical guarding that may be needed. I believe I know just the man for this position."

"Certainly not my son," the Archmage gently interrupted. "My son is the mayor of Brn, a fine diplomat and solver of city problems, but he never took to magic, I am sad to say, and he is not much of a fighter. He does run Brn extremely efficiently and is very well liked by the city folk. Please don't ask him to do this."

"I promise I will not. I have another in mind, but I would like to meet with him first. I hate to ask this of you, but could my team have a few days off right now? We should meet with the twin's parents as soon as possible, for they play an integral role in this. Plus, I would like to meet the other that I have in mind for the general's position. Once these two things are handled, I promise you that we will continue our studies uninterrupted. Please allow us a few days off."

For the first time, the Archmage actually laughed. "My dear boy, I have been pushing all seven of you harder than I have ever pushed any students in these past forty years! Yes, yes, lessons will resume on Monday. Will that be sufficient time?"

"Probably more than enough, thank you. Gang, we ought to go visit their parents now and make sure this is acceptable with them. Meantime, why don't you and Brother Jiri see if there is a suitable location for the construction of the Circle of Ascension? We will report back as soon as we know anything."

This was quite agreeable. Emil cast his spell and sent a message to his father, explaining that he wanted to bring his team to meet his parents and that this was to be an extremely vital meeting. "Dad says it is fine with him. We should teleport there, but first, he wants me to have you all swear that you will never reveal the location of his cavern to any others."

"I so swear," Zoran said without hesitation. The others followed his lead. Satisfied, Emil and Renata took their team member's hands and cast their two teleport spells, arriving at the entrance of the cavern, high in the mountains south of Brn, and overlooking the whole of the Dark Forest.

"Please stand back. Dad wants us to assume our normal dragon forms, and I don't want to accidentally bump you down the mountainside," Emil asked. A minute later, the five were dwarfed by the two teen golden dragons.

"Follow us inside," Renata said, a proud and excited tone in her voice. The five did so. To say that Zoran and the others were impressed with Aldrick and Sofie would be a total understatement. Aldrick's body was over fifty-five feet long, ignoring his very long neck and even longer tail. He towered over his twins. Sofie was only slightly smaller. For the conference, the dragons laid down in a semi-circle, positioning their heads close to one another. The five sat down before them. Aldrick's head alone was bigger than Zoran's body. Yes, the older dragon could have swallowed him whole! This fact was duly noted by all five. Their size and power was almost beyond belief.

Zoran and Emil outlined what had happened earlier this day. He also explained fully about himself and that he was a Duska. Aldrick, from his earlier training under Archmage Oldrich, knew about the Duska and their ability to Shadow Walk, as well as the fact that they were the rulers of many planets in the Federation. Finally, Zoran explained what they were about to do, build a new Circle of Ascension right here in Brn.

Emil then explained what he had offered to do, provide overt protection. Yes, the entire town would constantly see golden dragons flying about their city and tower. Zoran then said, "We would like to ask you to join in the protection of this province. Also, if you have some trustworthy dragon friends who might like to join, they would be welcome here too. There is plenty of antelope to go around. I understand that on your planet obtaining sufficient food has become a very serious problem. This might be an opportunity for more of your honorable friends to join us here."

"Well, it is rare that dragon-kind mingles with humans, mostly for magic and gems. However, the food crisis is most serious indeed. Sofie and I do have some trustworthy friends back home who may jump at this opportunity. We will check on it. How many others would you accept? We do not want to overpopulate your land either," Aldrick explained.

"You've seen the surrounding lands. How many of your kind can it support easily without any problems?" Zoran had no choice but to trust the dragon's judgment in this matter of sufficient antelope.

"Perhaps no more than a dozen more. Now if they could settle in nearby mountains, many more, but I believe that land belongs to other provinces."

"Okay, then let's start with up to twelve more. You make the decision on who to ask. For now, it is best for you to continue maintaining your low profile until the construction work is finished."

"Might I ask for something in return?" Aldrick ventured, knowing that Zoran had little choice but to honor his wishes.

"Absolutely. If it is within my power to grant, it is yours."

"When the time is right, I wish that you would assist my twins in their version of what you call Shadow Walking. Show them all of the planets in the Federation. Your language has no word for what we dragon's do. Planet hopping is the closest I have ever found. Can you do this for my children?"

"As long as we can figure out how to do it, I promise you that I will do so." Zoran knew well what this meant. Once he had shown them the sixteen planets, from then on, they would be able to travel there on their own and show other dragons the way. Was he opening the door to a massive dragon resettlement? Was he creating an insurmountable problem far into the future? He had no real choice but to agree to this request. After all, once the Circle was completed, realistically, it would be the threat of the dragons that would guarantee the safety of the Circle and the new House. It would take years and years to build a proper castle and an army to protect it. He knew that without the aid of the dragons, the new House would be short-lived.

"Excellent. A bargain is sealed," Aldrick pronounced. With the formalities finished, they then chatted a while before returning to give those in the tower the good news. Golden dragons would protect Brn, something no other House on any planet would have, an ultimate weapon that could guarantee them some measure of security, if only for a time.

Chapter 9 Janos Lavos

The next morning, the team met for breakfast. "Where are we off to today?" Jarka asked curious about this mysterious person, who Zoran wanted to become their general.

"Unfortunately, he is a very private man at the moment. I must ask you to wait here while Zdenka and I meet with him. If all goes well and if I find him suitable, then I will message you for you to come to us and meet him yourselves and give me your assessment of my choice. I hate to restrict you this way, but for the man's sake, I am asking you to allow us this first meeting."

"Do you know who he is talking about, Zdenka?" Jarka asked a bit peeved that she was not asked.

"No, Jarka, I really have no idea at all or why he wants me, but I am glad that he is taking one of we Mages with him. He should never be allowed to go traveling about without at least one of us there to help protect him. After all, he is now going to be our Duska." Jarka could not argue with that and resigned herself to wait.

"Go for it," Bernard said in his usual bored manner.

"If trouble finds you, send for us immediately, do you hear me?" Karel said with a slight snarl. He meant it. Zoran and Zdenka agreed and left, walking out of the main door into the sunlit morning.

"Where too?" she asked.

"Let's walk to the gates and step outside the city first, please. It's a beautiful day to be walking with a fine young woman," he complimented her. She blushed and took his offered arm.

A half hour later, they left the city behind them and were walking down the main road that led out of Brn. "Okay, no one can overhear us now. Take me to your father, Janos. I must talk with him."

"What? You want my dad — the general? Really? Are you sure?" Poor Zdenka was taken completely by surprise and was terribly confused.

"I told you long ago that I wanted to meet him. Now is as good a time as any."

"Well, okay then. I will teleport us to our homestead. Mind you, our place is absolutely nothing like — well anything that you are probably used to. I mean — well you will see. Please don't hold our homestead against me or dad."

"Of course not, Zdenka. Lead on." She concentrated and cast her spell. A moment later, they arrived deep within the Dark Forest. Gone was the bright sunlit day, replaced by deep shadows of the wood. The air was slightly musty and noticeably cooler. They stood in a clearing among the dense woods.

Before them was a crudely build log cabin, a split rail fence enclosing the clearing, and a barn, constructed similarly of logs. Two horses were grazing on the grass. A number of chickens pecked at grain on the ground within their fenced cage. A big black dog came bounding across the grass towards them. Zdenka knelt down to greet him. "My dog, Pik. Hi, I am glad to see you too, big boy." He came up to her and began licking her hand and face, welcoming her home at long last. A pounding noise came from the barn.

"Dad's probably in there inventing something. Come on. I'll introduce him." They walked across the clearing to the barn, whose doors were opened. Inside, a small foundry was burning. A man was bent over an anvil, pounding away. Sweat poured down his shirtless back. Even from a few feet back the heat was intense. "Hi dad. I'm back for a bit. Brought someone who wants to meet you." He looked up and doused the metal in a bucket of water.

"Zdenka! What a surprise. Everything going okay at the tower?" he asked, concerned that his daughter had returned so soon. Worry lines creased the brow of this tall, well-muscled man in his early fifties. His hair was similar in color to hers, but he hadn't shaved for a few days. His body hid what he was working on and Zoran sensed that this was on purpose.

"Sure dad. Had some real excitement yesterday. We'll tell you about it, if you can take a break. I have someone I want you to meet," she changed tactics as her father visibly relaxed, knowing that she was not in some kind of trouble on this surprise visit. "This is Zoran, Zoran this is Janos Lavos."

Wiping his hand on a rag, he offered it to Zoran, who shook it firmly. He'd asked her not to divulge his last name just yet. After all, Janos probably held a good deal of hatred against the Baron. No sense starting out on the wrong foot. "Well met, Zoran. Excuse my appearance. I wasn't expecting my daughter or a visitor. Come on up to the house. I'll wash up and Zdenka can brew us some tea. Sorry, don't have anything stronger to offer you. The mead is gone until the fall batch is done."

Long used to stone castle walls and stone buildings of Dorum, Zoran found the inside their cabin to be the crudest building in which he had ever entered. Mud filled the cracks between the logs. Yet, there was something else in this main front room, something intangible but very real, a feeling of real warmth and love, as well as security and a distinct peacefulness, which was totally lacking in Castle Dorumova, except around his sisters. "Mom did most of the decorating in here; we've left it pretty much as she had it," Zdenka explained, as she began fixing their tea and noticed Zoran looking around the room. "Got two small bedrooms; mine is up above your head, the loft. Dad's is in the back room. It's probably nothing like you've ever encountered. Sorry."

"Hey, there is nothing to be sorry about, Zdenka. This place has both charm and unique warmth about it. I can really feel it. Cold granite cannot compare one iota to your house." She blushed and hurriedly busied herself with the simple task of getting tea ready.

By the time she was carrying the pot and mugs into the pine roughhewn table off to one side of the large main room, her father came out of his small bedroom; he'd rinsed and put on a shirt. She served the tea and the three sat down. "So what do you do, Zoran?" he asked.

"Long story, but at the moment, I am the team leader of we seven Mages. By the way, Zdenka is now officially a Mage," he replied.

"Well, isn't that something! My little archer has become a full-fledged Mage as well. Congratulations, Zdenka. You did it. I always said there isn't anything my Zdenka cannot do once she sets her mind to it." He was quite proud of her that was readily apparent.

"We've got quite a story to tell you. I'll let Zdenka tell you about the other day's adventure. I think you will enjoy it." Zoran cleverly allowed his daughter to relate the lengthy story. Zoran wanted time to study the man. He had not grown soft living all these year out in the wild away from all civilization. He was still fit.

When she got to the part where the golden dragons made their appearance, Janos did not look at all surprised. After she finished relating that they had gotten back safely to the Archmage's tower, she said rather annoyed, "Dad, you aren't totally shocked and surprised about the dragons appearing!"

"I know honey, but I've been seeing them on occasion out over the forest about a dozen times since you went off to study magic. I've been going to tell you about those magnificent creatures the next time you came home for a while. Haven't had the chance yet today. I will say this: Warlord Mikolas had more humanity than all the Baron and his cronies have combined! Brilliant move of his to evacuate his whole province. I hope most chose to leave; subjugation under the Baron's rule is neigh on to slavery. Yet, maybe there has been a subtle shift in the balance of power with the appearance of these dragons. Undoubtedly, the Baron's losses were horrific, compared to what his original estimates must have been. I am sure this will slow him down in his plans to subjugate the rest of the Wild Lands."

"Undoubtedly so," Zoran replied, now taking up the narrative. He'd reached his judgment of Janos and was very pleased to see that anger and hatred had not festered in the ex-General who had been exiled for treason. He then began a careful and lengthy explanation of what the Brother Jiri and Priestess Anezka Zar were going to do, build the first new Circle of Ascension in several centuries. "As soon as it is built, all of the other sixteen Houses will instantly know of its existence. A new power will suddenly appear, shaking up their rigidly fixed world outlook. Of course, the new House will have to have a Duska. I have volunteered to be their Duska." He paused, letting the magnitude of his simple statement register.

"Who are you anyway?" Janos asked, his eyes piercing into Zoran, as if he had not yet seen him.

"Zoran Vladislov, unfortunately Baron Kazimir is my father. I aim to put a stop to his tyranny here on Adapazan, if I possibly can."

Janos opened his mouth to respond, but sat speechless. Wild emotions ravaged through his mind. Here was the son of his enemy sitting at his table, the son of the vilest, wickedest, most sadistic man he had ever had the misfortune of serving. Yet, the son was not his father, slowly that idea rooted and took over control of his mind. As it did, he stood up and gave Zoran a long unused, courtly bow, as he once had done so very long ago, when he was a young man in his early twenties. "My duke," he bowed a second time, embarrassing Zoran even further.

"Please, just Zoran, and please, you don't have to bow to me. Rather it is I that ought to bow to you — you who alone had the will and courage to defy the Baron's orders to further ravage poor villagers. I am honored to meet you, General Janos Lavos." Zoran rose and bowed to him. Zdenka looked totally shocked at both men, not knowing how to react. That her father had bowed to Zoran filled her with surprise and a little awe. She had never known her fiercely independent father to bow to any man, yet he did to this young lad. She felt ill at ease, courtly manners and rules she had never known and suddenly felt that she was somehow dishonoring Zoran by not — well she didn't know what she ought to have been doing, she concluded.

"Now then, Janos. Once the Circle of Ascension is made and activated, a new House will come into existence. As you know, the Baron's Circle is deep within the heavily fortified Castle Dorumova. Ours will be in a simple Archmage tower; there is not anything remotely like a fortress in this whole province. Yet, it will be guarded by the Archmage and all us Mages. Plus, I have made a deal with the golden dragons of Voss. They will then become visible to everyone and fly protection for the tower. Let's see an army even try to attack Brn then! However, I will also need some handpicked, well-trained guards to help with physical security. I need a General of Security. Janos, I would be highly honored if you would consent to become my new General of Security. Please give this serious consideration. I know of no one better qualified than you in this entire province."

He grinned, "How can I possibly refuse your offer? My daughter is now a Mage and will be protecting the tower. I absolutely insist that I lend a hand. Not only for her sake — she is all that I have left that matters most to me — but also if this will in some way help put an end to the Baron's continual subjugation of the free peoples of this world, I must lend my assistance to this strange adventure. You, sir, know how to strike a hard bargain," he teased Zoran, while a broad smile brought out his age lines on his forehead.

"Thank you General Janos. I don't have any idea how long it will take Brother Jiri to actually get this Circle constructed. I suspect some time. Money ought not be an object."

"We have time then. What sir are your orders?" he asked formally.

"Come and look the situation over at the tower, if you are not familiar with it. Make your own judgments on what number of security forces we ought to have. Pick your own men, equip them as you see fit, train them as you desire. We have money enough, within reason at this point. As soon as we have an estimate on the finishing date, I'll let you know. Probably we have at least six months before we need security in full."

"Completely my decisions? I am going to enjoy this service! Incredible difference between you and your father, who left me with little or no choices at all in such matters. I promise to do my very best. I want to finish up my little project here for my daughter. I'll head into Brn in a few days, if that is acceptable."

"Absolutely."

"What project, dad? You never told me about any project for me?" Zdenka was suddenly quite curious.

"A little surprise for my lovely daughter, now a Mage. I will wait for the right time to give you my little present, Mage Zdenka Lavos. Your mother would be so incredibly proud of you dear. I know that I am the proudest father on Adapazan."

She blushed again, but her curiosity went unquenched, which slightly annoyed her. "What present? Daddy, come on, what present?" she pleaded and begged. Zoran was glad it was not him who was offering her a present! At last the besieged man gave in. How could any man resist her, Zoran wondered.

"Come on. I'll show you. I've got a dozen done already. It was going to be a surprise for when you graduated, but since you are now officially a Mage, I guess this is as good a time as any. To the barn. I was working on them when you came." While the three strolled to the barn, Zdenka had her arm around her father, continually trying to get him to walk faster, which he playfully refused to do.

Inside the barn, he handed her a beautifully handcrafted quiver of arrows. A dozen arrows were already inside it. "I know that Mages can enchant magical weapons, but I also know that those items must be of the finest quality. Each of these arrows meet the highest standards. I ought to know. I am making you two dozen, enough to fill this quiver. If you can then enchant them, you will have two dozen magical arrows on which to fall back, should magic spells be insufficient."

Both Zdenka and Zoran examined the shafts and tips. Indeed, he had done excellent work. The tips were actually hunting style, that is, with two interlocking planes, yielding a four razor sharp edges to pierce even the toughest armor when she used her powerful longbow to propel them. Even if they were not enchanted, these were a superb set of arrows. She hugged her dad and thanked him repeatedly.

"Now you two ought to get on with your magical training. You've wasted enough time with an old man. Get going. I'll head into Brn in a few days and leave word where I will be staying," he insisted.

"Okay, I want you to meet the other members of our team, including the dragon twins. Is it all right if I have them come now to visit for a short while?" Zoran asked.

"Sure, I would love to meet the others who are part of Mage Zdenka's team. It is rare that anyone has a Mage team. Besides, I'd love to meet these golden dragons in person. Few can ever say that they have talked with a dragon. It would be something to tell my grandsons about, if I ever get any," he teased Zdenka, who again blushed.

Two minutes later, five more teleported to her homestead. "Bernard, great to see you again!" Janos shook his hand vigorously. Zdenka explained to the others that they gotten their dog from Bernard. One by one, Zdenka introduced Karel, Jarka, Emil, and Renata. The dragon twins were obvious, for the golden hue of their skin gave them away, now that everyone knew that they were really dragons.

They even morphed back into their real forms for him, enjoying his lavish attention. Zoran then explained to these five who Janos was; they had not made the connection from their history lessons. Now that it was pointed out to them, all five realized that Zoran had indeed picked an excellent man to become their General of Security.

After chatting about their recent adventures, the five teleported back to the tower, leaving Zdenka to say goodbye to her father. That done, Zoran, still holding her arm, led her out onto the clearing before casting his spell. He whispered, "It is so peaceful here, Zdenka. I can see why you love it here in this forest."

"Yes, a kind of peace that is hard to find in bustling Brn. I really do miss it, but our magic studies mostly fill my mind. The spells are getting so hard to learn aren't they?" she mused.

"Yes, they will only get harder. I supposed that we ought to get back." Rather reluctantly, Zoran teleported them back to the tower.

Chapter 10 News from Home

That night, Rayna made mental contact with Zoran. *Zoran! Dad's back. All sorts of vital news! Radek's been badly burned! Golden dragons appeared — breathing fiery brimstone — killing soldiers — burned Radek horribly!*

Calm down, Rayna. That's it, slow, deep breaths. Okay. Start at the beginning.

Dad came back a while ago. He had to Shadow Walk back, carrying Radek in his arms. He said they were just about to take the last level of the Warlord Mikolas' fortress, when out of nowhere these two golden colored dragons came flying up and out of the basement level. They shot fire and flames from their mouths. Some said it was more like lightning bolts, though I don't know how anyone can mix up those two effects. Thousands of troops were killed or badly injured, burns mostly. Radek was one of them. He was badly burned. Gosh his face looks horrible. He's at the healers now.

Then, somehow the whole southern forest around that fortress turned into flames, blocking everyone's retreat. However, the explosion which dad says was supposed to bring the mountains down on him and all his men failed. It only blocked a high mountain pass. We guess he got lucky on that one. His men are still trapped there until the fires die down. It's too big to be easily put out.

Dad says that he now controls Sholov Province. I asked him what is there. I got a strange answer. He said empty villages and towns. When I asked him where did all the people go, he shrugged and suggested they were all forced into the warlord's army. Zoran, are they really making children fight their wars now?

No, I highly doubt that, sis. Maybe the villagers fled. I know I would if I knew the Baron's army was coming to conquer the province. I'd rather move elsewhere than live under the thumb of that despot. Probably all moved away, that's all. He didn't want to disclose the fact that he had been there or why. It was too risky, for Rayna might let something accidentally slip.

I'm going to check on how Radek is doing. I'll get back to you in a bit.

Although Radek was his brother, he felt little sympathy for him. Undoubtedly, Radek had killed or ordered killed many brave men who were fighting for their freedom. Zoran laid in his small bed and stared at the dark ceiling. *Am I really going to take on dad and Radek? Someone has got to or this senseless killing will just continue until there's no people left that he doesn't control their very lives.* Imagined images of fighting his father and older brother floated through his consciousness. Such unnerved him, could he actually fight either one?

Sometime later that night, Rayna made contact with him once more. *Radek is recovering. He's lost his right eye and his face will be badly scarred, the physicians say. They are more worried about his fighting arm and legs. They say from now on, all three may be terribly sensitive to both heat and cold. He'll never be the fighter that he used to be; they all agree on that.*

Dad was furious and, Zoran, he beat the physician who told him that something awful — broke his jaw and arm! I overheard him telling Archmage

Milos to quadruple his efforts to find you. I think dad wants to somehow have you replace Radek. I believe that dad thinks he can somehow force you to be like Radek. Leda and I are becoming afraid for your safety. We both know that you are never going to go along with him and be like Radek, propagating his savagery on others. What are you going to do?

Nothing. No one knows where I am at and I intend for it to stay that way. This was all getting too close to home. Zoran desperately wanted to change the subject. *How's mom? How's she taking it?*

Not too good. She's been sitting beside him all this time. Leda finally got her to go to bed; it's late. Maybe mom will feel better in the morning. We can hope so. I'm going to chat with Leda now. I heard her coming back. More later. Love you. Bye.

Love you too.

For some time, Zoran lay in his bed thinking. Could he be found? Could someone find him here? Until now, he figured they wouldn't be all that interested in finding him and thus he was safe here. Now — now things had changed, if, and this was a big if, his dad actually thought that he could somehow manipulate Zoran into stepping into Radek's shoes, becoming everything Zoran detested. If so, then his many Mages could systematically visit every province looking for him. Yes, they could go invisible and hang out around a town, looking and listening for any word of Zoran. He realized now that he had been foolish to have kept his first name. He ought to have abandoned it too. Hindsight can be a wonderful education, he mused, angry at his own foolishness.

For a few minutes, he considered going around to all those in Brn to whom he had told his first name and casting a forget spell on them. He began tallying them up and soon faced the utter futility of that. Far too many people had now crossed paths with him.

He had visions of one of the Baron's Mages coming to Brn, casting a disguise spell on himself and making inquiries about Zoran. Have you seen a young lad now nineteen with shoulder length brown hair and blue eyes that seemed to penetrate you? Oh, how foolish not to have cut his hair, grown a long beard, anything so as not to resemble himself.

"Hey, Zoran, time to rise!" Zdenka called to him through his door. Morning already!

Chapter 11 More Studies

"Gosh, you look awful," she commented when he joined her and his friends for breakfast.

"Didn't get much sleep," he grumbled. "Radek was burned in the attack. My sister talked with me last night. She believes that the Baron is going to redouble his efforts to find me. I had nightmares about that, I guess." He admitted the truth, well mostly.

"Despots will do that to you!" Karel growled angrily and stabbed another piece of bacon.

Zoran was only too glad to enter the third floor study room, if only to gain solace in studying. A slight musty odor permeated the room. Valuable scrolls holding advanced spells beckoned to them all, and his team dove into their studies once more.

This time, the check lists they were given seemed vastly longer, much more to study and digest. Zoran found solace in this, in that he didn't have to think about the future and what it might hold for him. Could he actually duel his father?

The spells were becoming far more complex to cast. Now they began to realize all of this extra reading material was providing a solid framework, a reference base, which would make the casting of the actual spell easier to handle. Bernard was exuberant when he discovered that he could now Conjure Animals, that is, bring animals into existence, even if their lifetimes were short lived. He was most impressed with their dedication to fighting to protect him from danger.

Oh the other hand, Jarka was wild about the ability to Make a Suggestion to a Crowd. With a casting of her new spell, she could place a suggestion into a crowd of people, who would then act upon it. Of course, the closer the suggestion was to their reality, the better they followed it. Zoran had visions of Jarka suggesting that everyone in the inn donate a gold piece to her funds and her sitting back collecting them. He grinned as the images played through his mind.

Two weeks later, Zoran successfully cast a spell that he deemed highly useful for himself. At last he was as exuberant as Bernard had been with his conjured animals. He could now project his image some four hundred feet away from where he was standing. Others found it difficult indeed to tell the difference between the image and him! He realized that if he ever did have to fight his father, he could gain an advantage for a short while by having this image of himself doing the fighting while he took a different tack. Then, he realized that this spell could be used to good avail by an actual assassin! Imagine the image of the assassin attacking his prey, while the true assassin stabbed the totally distracted prey in the back! Somehow Zoran knew this was going to be a powerful spell. He then set to work on finding ways and means to detect the image from the real person and how to thwart it.

A week later, the team began tackling another highly powerful and useful spell, the ability to Erect a Contingency Spell. That is, if a specific thing happened, immediately the chained spell would activate. Their scrolls suggested numerous uses. For example, in case I get badly wounded, teleport me to my bedroom. In case I get blinded, teleport me to a place of safety. If I am about to be stabbed in the back, move my body ten feet away. If I am falling over ten feet, cast levitation on myself. If I am drowning, cast Swim.

Jarka made up a new one, "Gang, how about this one. In case I get caught picking someone's pocket, teleport me to my home." Everyone moaned in mock protest. She called out, "Hey, even better, in case I get caught, cast Forget on everyone present." They all roared with laughter.

"Hey, then you will forget too!" Karel pointed out to her and everyone roared once more. She glared at him and then realized her mistake and laughed along with everyone else.

Slowly the days passed. As August came to a close, Zoran began noticing that Jarka and Bernard's check lists had more and more unchecked off spells on them. As their team leader, he took the opportunity to examine this phenomenon more closely. Indeed, each had only been able to learn one spell out of the last fifteen! The blanks were only increasing in frequency. Karel's list also contained a lot of blanks, but not quite the same frequency. The twins were following their usual pattern of seemingly random spells being learned, perhaps one in five.

At last, although he really didn't want to, he examined Zdenka's list. He found himself wanting her to be somehow different, but didn't know why. He forced his eyes to confront her list. While she too had gaps, they were nowhere as large as the others! He breathed a huge sigh of relief and then wondered why he did that? Why am I so relieved, he thought to himself. Finally, he looked at his own list and blinked twice. He had a gap here and there, particularly on spells that he considered too evil to cast, such as turning dead bodies into walking, attacking mindless zombies.

At last, as their leader, he requested a conference with the Archmage. "You have something on your mind, Zoran. Out with it, please," she said softly. Now that he thought about it, she never ever had raised her voice! Somehow she could accept anything that happened in her own quiet manner. Amazing.

"Oh, it's these gaps in their check lists," he said and began a lengthy explanation of what he had observed. "What does it mean? Ought we all go back and help them master the ones that they cannot seem to get the first time through?"

She smiled her all knowing smile. Gosh, I wish she wouldn't do that! He thought to himself. It rather unnerved him. He'd just made a startling discovery that she apparently already knew all about!

"Remember what I said about intelligence and the ability to learn to cast magical spells? In case you have forgotten it," she explained.

He interrupted her; she was not going to get away with this one. "Yes, the more intelligent a Mage is, the better able he or she is to learn advanced spells."

"Precisely. You see, Jarka and Bernard have almost reached the end of the advanced spells that they have the potential to learn. Karel is also getting near that point, but he still has a little ways to go. I admit that I am a little surprised that Zdenka is still doing so well." Zoran felt a sudden wave of pride in her, but again he didn't know why that should be.

"Now the twins, well they are dragons and have vastly different minds than ours. Yet, they both are highly intelligent and are picking up the advanced spells in the same way that they picked up the easier beginning ones. No surprise there.

Aldrick was the same way. I made note of that in my treatise, if you will recall. I see that you are making good progress still."

"Well, yes, I seem to be getting most all of them. Why? Is that unusual?" he asked, wondering if he was somehow different.

"I don't know, Zoran, truly I do not. Perhaps it is because you are a Duska. I have never taught a Duska before. However, if that were all that was occurring, then why haven't all the many other Duskas in the Federation done the same thing during their magic training. No, I do not have an answer for that one, Zoran. Perhaps one day you may find it for yourself. If you do, please let me know. Now you ought to get back to your studies."

The rest of the week did not go well for either Jarka or Bernard. Not one spell did they even get close to working right. At this point, the Archmage stepped in to talk with the frustrated team. "As you have seen, both Jarka and Bernard have reached the highest spells that they can master. This is no reflection on them as people or as Mages. All Mages have their limits. The wise know when they have reached it. However, this does not necessarily mark the end of their training. There are other things that you can attempt to learn that are vastly easier than these top level spells. I believe that you, Jarka, would be interested in learning how to make magical potions, many of which mimic similar spells."

"Yes, I've always wondered how magical potions are made. Is it possible to learn how to do it? I'm game if there is. I am really burned out on these terrifically complex spells!" she replied.

Archmage Nadia smiled, "Yes, dear, you should find the making of potions fairly easy. We shall start you in on that line of research today, if you are ready."

"Absolutely!" her enthusiasm had returned. "I want to learn how to make healing potions! Now that would be a super skill to have!"

"Bernard, you have always been keenly interested in history, am I right?"

"Ancient history is more like it. I am fascinated about how our planet was settled and all that."

"Excellent, I suggest that we start you in on an in depth study on the complete history of Adapazan." He was more than willing to do so at once.

Karel glared, "I aim to keep on trying to master some more of these. I am not giving up yet, Archmage!"

"No, please do not. Keep at it and see what more you can learn to cast. However, if later on you discover that you have reached your limit, please come see me. Now then, let's get back to work. You two, come with me." Eagerly, Jarka followed her, while Bernard shuffled behind her.

Chapter 12 Kidnaped

"Help! Everyone, Brother Jiri has gone missing!" a very distressed Priestess Anezka wailed, interrupting the five who were struggling with another spell. Startled, everyone instantly stopped and turned to look at her. Extreme distress caused tension lines all over her face, and she continually wrung her hands over each other, as if she could somehow make her husband reappear.

"Relax, Anezka," Zoran said attempting to mimic the soft tones which the Archmage always used. Whether or not he seemed like her, it did have some effect on her. She stopped fiddling with her hands and sat down.

"Jiri ought to have been back an hour ago. I asked Marek to go and check on him. He's vanished! No trace."

"Where was he supposed to be going? What was he doing?" he asked.

"He said he needed some lead and charcoal. He promised he'd be back in just a few minutes. Marek said that he never arrived at the metal smith's shop or at Zea's Charcoal. Honestly, I think something terrible has happened to him. Please, you must help find him. So much is at stake," she pleaded, though they all knew just how much they were depending upon Brother Jiri.

Just then, Jarka and Bernard burst into the room. "I sent them a message," Zdenka whispered to Zoran.

"What's this about Jiri vanishing?" Jarka asked. Zoran quickly explained.

"First, let's use our spells and see if we can find out what's going on with him," Zoran suggested. "We should use magic instead of running aimlessly around Brn. Let's use See Through Another's Eyes and Hear What Another Is Hearing. Clues, gang, look and listen for clues." At once, the seven began casting their spells. Emil could cast the see version, but not the hear, while Renata was the other way around. The others could cast both. The See spell produced nothing but blackness, so Zoran assumed that Jiri must be blindfolded. He quickly canceled that spell and cast the Hear version, others did likewise.

Zoran began hearing what Jiri was hearing at this moment. The sound of a hand slapping flesh suggested that Jiri was being beaten, especially when a moan followed almost at once. A harsh voice barked, "Tell me what you are doing in that Mage tower? Tell me!" Another loud smash followed along with a moan that was distinctly softer. Jiri was slipping into unconsciousness. "Tell me! I followed you here from Mikolas' fortress. I saw you go in that tower. What are you doing in there? What are you hiding? Did you take something from Mikolas?" Crack. "Damn, he's passed out. Stupid monk." Zoran heard the sound of a chair sliding across a floor, then only silence. He canceled his spell; one by one the others did as well.

"Damn assassin has probably got him. Beaten him unconscious already, if he's not dead," cursed an angry Karel, pounding his fists together. "We've got to rescue him!"

"Yes, but where is he at?" Zoran asked. Everyone shook their heads.

"Leave that to me," Bernard said now slightly interested. "Anezka, go find me a dirty shirt or sock that he's recently worn. I'm going to fetch the Nose. Back in a minute." He cast a teleport spell and vanished.

"What's he doing?" Zoran asked, but Zdenka shrugged her shoulders. No one had any idea. Anezka left to do as Bernard had asked, while the others hastily grabbed their weapons and made ready to go after this assassin.

A minute later, Bernard reappeared holding a small brown dog on a leash. "I'm back with the Nose. Meet Zeb, best tracking dog I've ever raised. I know, he's getting a little old, but his nose is something else." He was about to launch into one of his many tales, when Anezka returned carrying a slightly smelly shirt.

"Ah, perfect." Bernard held the shirt to Zeb's nose. The dog reacted at once with a short series of high pitched barks. "Okay, he's telling me that he's got it. Come on. Let's follow where Jiri went." Bernard led the way out of the tower and into the crowded streets. Again, he held the shirt in front of Zeb's nose and then commanded, "Seek Zeb. Seek." At once, Zeb barked and began trotting down the street, his nose in a continual sniff.

Five minutes later, they approached Zea's Charcoal shop. However, just before the shop, Zeb stopped and turned down the alley, pulling hard on his leash. "This way, this way," Bernard called out, although he did not need to have said a thing. It was obvious that the dog was following Jiri's scent. Zoran speculated that here at the edge of the alley the assassin had taken Brother Jiri prisoner.

As Jarka made the turn into the alley, following along behind as she was wont to do, she paused and picked up a tiny dart. She sniffed it. "Zoran, here. I found this dart. Got some residue on it, probably something that would subdue a person. I will analyze it when we get back to the tower."

On went Zeb, trotting merrily along the alleys of Brn. For a half hour, they went down one alley only to detour into another alleyway. This assassin was making it very difficult for any tracker to find him, Zoran noted, hoping the assassin had not counted on a dog. At last Zeb halted and seemed confused. He headed toward a street, back tracked and headed down the alley again, then backtracked once more.

"What's happening? Has he lost the scent?" Zoran asked.

"No, it's likely that the assassin has crossed paths with himself. Probably came this way earlier. What's out there on the street?"

"An inn, though not a nice one," Jarka called out from the rear. "Probably the assassin was staying there, it's cheap."

"Okay, he can't beat Jiri up in the inn," Bernard concluded. He convinced Zeb to continue following the trail down the alley. The dog was off once more. Five minutes later, Zeb stopped by a back door that led into some kind of warehouse. While Bernard kept his dog quiet, Jarka doubled back to see the building from the main street. She sent them a message saying she didn't see anyone around. No lights were on inside the front and the door was locked.

Cautiously, Zoran tried the back door. It, too, was securely locked. While they were conferring on the best way to break in without losing their element of surprise, Jarka reappeared behind them. "Move over. Let a master at it," she coyly teased them. "Have you figured out what we're doing once the door is opened?"

"We rush in and cut him to pieces!" Karel growled angrily.

"No, wait, if we do that, he might just kill Jiri," Zoran cautioned. "Stealth. First objective: find Jiri. Once we find him, some of us stay with him and protect him while the rest of us go after this assassin. Cast Invisible and let's fan out inside, looking for Jiri. Whoever finds him, message the rest of us." Quickly, the seven cast their spells, and then Jarka masterfully picked the lock. Bernard decided to stay outside with his dog, just in case the assassin tried to make a hasty exit. Invisible and with his sword drawn, Bernard waited patiently in the shadows, though it looked a bit strange to see a dog on a leash being held by an invisible hand. Bernard soon realized this and cast another spell on his dog as well.

"Ta da," Jarka whispered her tease to the others. The door creaked a little as it opened. All seven stole inside, feeling the bodies of others who were in front of them. After all, they were invisible and couldn't see each other either.

In the dim light inside coming from some mica windows up front, Zoran saw boxes piled around the sides of a large space. It was a warehouse, no doubt of that. The question was: where was Jiri being held? As the seven moved about the large space, the floor boards occasionally creaked. Zoran guessed that if this assassin was any good at all, he would hear their noise and know someone was sneaking around inside.

Minutes passed, sweat began dripping from Zoran's forehead; the warehouse was hot and very stuffy. He realized that he was now leaving telltale drops on the floor! Where were they anyway?

I found him. Southeast corner behind crates! I'm teleporting him to the tower! Zdenka cast her message spell to the others and prepared to cast her teleport spell. Out of the shadows a man dressed in black stepped, his right fist delivered a solid blow to her jaw, sending her flying backwards, stunned. He slipped back into the shadows. Hastily everyone rushed to the southeast corner.

"Damn!" Zoran cursed, breaking his silence. Zdenka lay sprawled on the floor near the chair to which Brother Jiri was tied, blindfolded, and now unconscious. Although he was now quite visible and he had not yet seen the assassin, he added angrily, "If you've hurt her, I will personally make you pay dearly, assassin!"

From the top of a crate a hand tossed some powder down onto Zoran. His inner senses forced his body to again dive to the right, rolling as he hit the floor. The powder, which had been intended for his eyes, blinding him, fell harmlessly to the floor where he had stood. With a pair wicked, S-shaped daggers dripping a black liquid, one in each hand, the assassin jumped down to stab him in his back. Out of position, Zoran began rolling as rapidly as he could, hoping to buy enough distance so he could get to his feet.

Suddenly, the assassin cried out in pain; his back went stiff as a board; both daggers fell to the floor. Jarka appeared behind him, her invisibility lost because she had now attacked. Her dagger had cut deep into his back, severing his aorta. In slow motion, the assassin slowly dropped to his knees, his eyes closed. As the last bit of life pulsed from his body, he slumped forward, face down on the dirty warehouse floor. Jarka held on to her dagger, which slid out of his body as he fell forward. Jarka spat on the man, "Foul assassin, death is too good for you."

"Way to go, Jarka! Thanks, I was in a bit of a tight spot there," Zoran exclaimed. "Zdenka's been hurt." He got up and rushed to her side. "I'll take her; you all bring Jiri. To the tower immediately." He cast his teleport spell and he and Zdenka disappeared.

Karel brought Jiri with him seconds later. The twins followed on their own. Jarka, however, remained behind. First she sent a message for Bernard to join her. Then, she began to search the dead assassin. Bernard soon stood over her looking, and she hastily explained what had happened and where the others had gone. "We're going to examine him, first. Then, we need to dispose of his body. Whatever you do, don't touch those weird daggers; they are covered in some kind of poison."

Carefully, she began searching him, confiscating a number of items, including his money pouch. She found an empty vial, which she determined had contained the poison, along with two more bottles as yet unopened. Bernard commented, "You know, we ought to get rid of the poison. I mean what if some worker stumbles and falls into it and gets it on his hands or something? There are cracks in the floor boards. I'm going to conjure some water and wash the poison into the cracks. I don't reckon it will do any harm on the dirt underneath the warehouse."

He cast his spell and water began flowing over the daggers. Sure enough it slowly drained beneath the cracks. Seeing that this was being successful, Jarka grinned and began dumping the other two vials of poison into the waters as well. For good measure, he cast the spell a second time, washing the area once more. "There, that ought to do it. Now what, Jarka?"

"Well, perhaps we ought to bring his body back to the tower. Someone might recognize him, which may prove useful. If not, we have to find a way to get rid of it."

"Okay, I'll do the dirty work and teleport him back. You ought to lock the back door. No sense in letting whoever owns this warehouse think that they have been robbed," Bernard suggested.

She grinned, "I'll make a good thief out of you yet, Bernard." Both chuckled at her jest. Bernard then cast his spell and he, his dog, and the dead assassin vanished. She collected up the items she had confiscated and headed back out the back door, locking it after her. A moment later, she too vanished from the alley, arriving in the main first floor meeting room of the tower.

Zuzanna was holding an ice pack to Zdenka's jaw. Everyone else was tending to Jiri, when Jarka arrived with the assassin's things. "How are they both doing?" she asked.

"Oh, my jaw hurts, but I'm okay," Zdenka said, though it hurt to even talk this much.

"Brother Jiri has taken a bad beating, but no bones are broken. I think he'll be alright too, but probably plenty sore for days," Zoran answered her. Leaving him to his wife, Zoran now turned to the dead assassin. He stared long at the man's face. "I've seen him before. I think that he is or was one of Baron's Kazimir's spies. Well, he won't be telling him about us that's for sure. How are we going to get rid of the body?"

"I'll take care of it," the soft voice of Archmage Nadia startled them. She had silently entered the room. "You have not yet gotten to the perfect spell to vanish a body: move it to a position on the surface of the sun, where it will vaporize instantly. Fitting end for a foul assassin, don't you think?" She grinned. Zoran realized that the Archmage was still more powerful than any of her apprentices. Quiet yes, powerful, even more so. A minute later the body vanished from her tower. No one saw his body materialize just above the sun's surface and disintegrate within a split second.

"It looks like the Baron has sent spies into Sholov Province ahead of his attack. One must have seen Brother Jiri leaving and followed him overland. When he entered the tower here, for a time, he was out of his reach. Patient assassin, I'll give him that," Zoran concluded.

"What if during his stay here, he sent back messages to the Baron, telling that Brother Jiri came here and was staying in the Archmage's tower," Jarka asked, hinting at something far sinister. "Suppose that now there are other assassins and spies of the Baron's around Brn? Suppose that more are on their way here, perhaps sent by the Baron to check on what Brother Jiri is doing here?"

"Damn!" Karel cried out, "Sure is likely that he has!"

"We should never go about the city alone anymore," Zoran concluded. "It might not be safe. Zdenka, let your father know what has happened today. Tell him we could use his services sooner than expected. Brother Jiri is going to need to get what he needs for his work, but I want him to have bodyguards with him anytime he goes out of the tower. In the meantime, some of us can escort him until Janos is ready."

"Thank you all. I thought I was a goner there," Brother Jiri said, though it was also painful for him to talk. His face was a mass of bruises as was his chest. "I still need some lead and charcoal." Zoran chuckled. Beaten to a pulp, Brother Jiri was still engrossed in his work on the Circle of Ascension.

"Okay, tell us what you need exactly and we'll fetch it for you," he replied.

The next week, Zoran used some of the gems donated by Warlord Mikolas to purchase the houses on either side of the tower, paying the two families far more than their buildings were worth. Here, he had Janos stationed with his men. At first, the new general only had chosen two strong fighters who could handle swords well. As the weeks went by, Janos slowly added more men to his security garrison force.

Chapter 13 Fall's Ups and Downs

Days of study flew by the group. September brought the harvest season to Brn. Wagons of grain and other crops arrived daily from the nearby farmer's fields. All fields were small and rocky, of course. Winter would soon be upon them, here high in the mountains.

"Look for first snow around the start of October," Zdenka explained to Zoran one Sunday afternoon in late September. They were enjoying their day off, having teleported to her homestead, deep in the Dark Forest. Already, the air was quiet chilly, and they held each other close for warmth as they lay on the grass staring up at the multicolored canopy above them. Reds, yellows, and browns in many hues transformed their homestead into a marvelous sight. "I just love the trees in the fall, so many rich colors."

"Yes, spectacular indeed, Zdenka, but they all pale compared to you." He looked into her eyes and finally got up the nerve to lean over and gently kiss her waiting lips. She responded, squeezing him tighter.

"I thought that you would never get up the courage to kiss me," she whispered a bit later. "I've longed for this for so long, Zoran."

"I've been — well, I didn't know if you — well, liked me like I like you," he fumbled his way through totally unfamiliar territory. He'd never kissed a woman before, much less dated one. If he had been back at Castle Dorumova, he would have asked his sisters about how best to proceed.

"I love you, Zoran," she whispered.

"I'm so madly in love with you that I can barely concentrate on learning new spells when you are so close to me," he admitted.

"I know. I've seen you watching me when you didn't think I was paying any attention to you," she giggled. "We girls notice these things, you know." He grinned.

"Seriously, Zoran, I haven't said anything before now, because — I mean between you and I — is it allowed?" she asked

"You — you would? Well, first I have to ask you, I think that's how its done. Zdenka, will you marry me?" he asked.

"That's what I mean. Can we marry? Is it allowed? I mean, I'm not Duska. Don't you have to marry another Duska?" The worry in her tone pierced his heart.

"Absolutely not! Actually, marrying a Duska is not such a good thing; too much inner marrying between cousins has already has produced many miscarriages and worse. I am free to marry anyone I choose. I choose to marry for love, not for power or station, as so many do. I want to marry you because I love you. It's that simple, but you haven't given me your answer. You don't have to, if you don't want to. We can wait longer and see. . ."

She put her fingers over his lips. "Of course I will marry you!" She kissed him passionately.

"When should we do it?" she eventually asked. "What kind of wedding did you have in mind?"

He sighed, the practicality of their situation interfered. "We best wait until we get done with our magical training."

"I agree, it could easily get in our way. It's hard enough to concentrate when you are close to me now. Think how it will be if we are actually married!"

He grinned and gave her a gentle squeeze. "A simple one," he added. "How about you?"

"What's it like getting married in your castle? I mean, if you were marrying there and all that?"

"Oh it's more like a week-long celebration. Partying, expensive gifts, elegant clothes and dresses, fancy ceremonies. I once went to a cousin's wedding. I thought that it would never end, but then I was only six at the time." She giggled, imagining a small boy amid a giant wedding.

"Won't you miss it? I mean a fancy wedding as befitting a Duska?"

"Not in the slightest. I just wish my sisters could come. Someday, I hope you can meet them. I know you will like them and they will certainly like you too."

Since it was starting to get dark, they reluctantly rose and teleported back to the tower and dinner. That night, Zoran made mental contact with Rayna. *How's Radek doing?* He asked first, unsure just how to tell her that he was getting married.

He has recovered as much as possible or so the physicians say. His face is gruesome to look at, and he wears a patch over his right eye now. His sword arm can barely hold a golden goblet, and he walks with a severe limp. Dad hardly gives him the time of day anymore; honestly, he is really depressed. How's everything with you?

He still had not figured out how to tell her, so he just blurted it out mentally. *I am going to get married, Rayna.*

What? Incredible! Way to go! Who is she? Do we know her? Who is this woman who has stolen my little brother from me? She was teasing, of course.

Er, I best not tell you her name right now. I can send you her image, if you want to see what she looks like? Rayna begged him to show her what she looked like. He formed up an image of Zdenka's face as they had lain beneath the colorful trees.

Oh she's beautiful! Wait until I tell Lida. She will be ecstatic too. When are you getting married? Oh, and just where? Lida and I most definitely want to come. You cannot deprive us from attending your happiest day. Please, Zoran you can't deny us that day.

We are waiting a while, until — until a certain thing is finished. When we know the date and time, I will see if it can be arranged. Honestly, I don't want anything to happen to you just because you discover where I am staying. I couldn't live with myself if something did. Trust me a little longer, please, Rayna.

Okay, gotta go. Mom's calling. Lida and I will chat with you later tonight when we are free and not being watched.

On the 2nd of October, Brn received its first snowfall of the long winter season. Zoran and Zdenka paused a minute to watch the large flakes fall. Then, it was back to study once more. Both were now having considerable difficulty with the spells. Karel continued to forcefully stick with it, hoping he might master the next spell. However, over a dozen had passed by him without one sticking. In contrast the twins continued on their seemingly random pattern of a spell here and a spell there.

The second week in October, Rayna made contact with him around noon. *Zoran, sorry to bother you while you are likely studying, but I have to. Radek has just died. He jumped off the top observation deck of the castle. Committed suicide. Mom's taking it hard. Dad just said good riddance. Zoran, he is pulling out all the stops trying to find you. Do be careful!* He conversed with her a little longer before breaking contact.

"What's the matter?" Zdenka asked, sensing something was wrong. He explained about his older brother.

"So the Baron is now looking high and low for you? Does that mean he wants to make you his heir?" she asked.

"Who knows. But I will not let him bypass Rayna and Lida. It is their birthright. They are second and third in line by all Duska conventions. If he tried to make me his heir, he'd be robbing my sisters. No way will I let him do that! Not ever. Let's finish eating and get back to that darn spell. Honestly, these are so darn hard; it's a wonder that anyone can cast them."

"It's a good thing that they are. Honestly, you don't want lots of Mages going around wiping out people's memories! Nasty spell indeed," she replied.

As the days grew shorter, November came. Outside, the ground was buried under six inches of snow, which Zdenka claimed would not melt until spring came at last. He noted that there seemed to be more snow here at this time of year than back at the lower elevation of Dorum.

Karel continued to effort his way through these very advanced spells, as if somehow his fighting will would compensate for his lack of intellect. It didn't, but he doggedly continued hoping the next one would work for him. Zoran was now pleased that he too could cause an object to vanish by having it appear just above the surface of the sun. In this, he felt somehow equal to Archmage Oldrich, a tiny victory.

However, the spells which they now began researching and eventually attempting to cast were the most powerful of all magical spells. All five of them eagerly dove into the scrolls and tomes, trying to grasp the concepts and what was required of them to be able to cast such spells. Intense concentration, ultimate conviction, these were among the criteria they would have to muster.

One day, Zdenka had a sudden insight and then attempted to cast the spell she had been working on for days now. Of course Archmage Nadia was with them constantly as they attempted these most powerful of all spells. Zoran had not really paid much attention to that, she'd just began appearing with them of late. Magical energies flashed, a giant gloved hand appeared and began to crush into dust the sample rock that the Archmage had given her for this spell. "I did it! There is a Crushing Glove! Wow! Super!" she exclaimed, wild with excitement. Everyone patted her on the back and congratulated her over and over, including Nadia herself. The old Archmage was overjoyed with Zdenka and showed more emotion than Zoran had ever seen her display.

The next day both twins succeeded with their spell, but to cast it, they had to stand on the tower's roof. They had each conjured a swarm of meteors, fireballs blasting onto the slope of the steep mountainside behind the tower. Once more their success was celebrated by one and all.

The very next day, Zoran's spell activated. Compared to the fireworks and visual sights of the other three's spells, Zoran's seemed to do nothing at all, until they all realized that all magical spells and items within the tower no longer functioned! He had Interrupted Magical Effects! Of course, the magical items returned to being once again magical after he canceled the spell. The Archmage had to recast her many protection spells which she had always kept on her tower. Such was a minuscule price to pay for her student having mastered this powerful spell!

Though there were still another half dozen spells to attempt to learn, the Archmage called a temporary halt, here on the 10th of November.

"May I have your attention," she said formally. "Zdenka, Emil, Renata, Zoran: it gives me the greatest of pleasures and honors to notify each of you that you have officially reached the status of Archmage. Being able to cast one of these power spells has put you into a unique category of magical skill use. You four are joining a very elite club. There are but twenty-four of us, make that now twenty-eight of us, among all of the Planets of the Federation! It is rare indeed for any Archmage to have trained another to such a level. Yet, somehow, I have gotten all four of you there. Perhaps yet Karel will join you, as there are still a few more spells to attempt."

"However, at this time, I would like to gather everyone in my tower together and announce your tremendous achievement to everyone. This is the greatest day ever for Oldrich Tower!" While Zoran simply sat there stunned, along with Zdenka, who nearly fainted from the news that she had become an actual Archmage, all of the other apprentices, Adepts, and Janos and his guards, along with the Jiri and Anezka crowded into the dining room. All were buzzing with chat about what this special announcement might be.

Archmage Nadia Oldrich pulled the four up to the front of the room at her side. In a loud voice, one that Zoran had never heard her use before, she said, "I have the most important announcement to make that I have ever made in my life. It gives me tremendous pride to announce to all of you what has been achieved by these four. I give you Archmage Zdenka Lavos, Archmage Emil Vogler, Archmage Renata Vogler, and Archmage Zoran Vladislov!"

The room literally exploded with shouting, cheering, clapping, and whistling! Janos had tears flowing down his cheeks. His little Zdenka was now one of the most powerful people in the entire Federation; only a Duska had more. However, the chills going down Janos' spine did not come from his daughter's success, rather from Zoran's. He waited until he could get a chance to share a word with him. At the moment, the four were shaking hands with dozens of others.

Eventually, he got his turn. "Congratulations, son. Yours is an incredible achievement as are the others. However, yours is utterly singular and terribly critical. Zoran, do you realize what you have achieved here?"

"Er not really. Archmage?" he fumbled, trying to grasp where this was leading.

The General of Security said calmly, "No Duska has ever in the entire history of the Federation of Planets achieved the status of Archmage. You have just joined together two totally separate worlds, that of magic and that of the Duska. Potentially, Zoran, you may well be the most powerful Duska to ever walk the sixteen planets!"

Zoran was impressed, "No one else has done this before?"

"None, sir. None. Mage status, yes many. Archmage status, only you. May you use your power wisely."

"I will sir. By the way, I have been meaning to ask you something. I have asked Zdenka to marry me when we have finished our magical studies. I would like to ask your permission to marry your daughter."

For an instant, Zoran thought that he was going to have to keep Janos from keeling over. He staggered a moment, before catching his breath. "Sir, it would be the highest honor I could ever imagine for my daughter. Yes, yes, you have my permission, though ought you choose another Duska instead?" Zoran found that he had to explain the same thing to her father as he had to Zdenka.

Convinced that the marriage was indeed ideal and permissible, he asked, "Who also knows? Since I am only finding out now, I presume you two have been keeping it a secret from everyone, security reasons?"

"Yes sir." He kept it short and to the point.

"Say, what are you two talking about? Dad's face is nearly red!" Zdenka came over to take her dad's arm.

"I've just asked him for his permission to marry you, dear. He has agreed," Zoran explained. She immediately hugged and kissed her father, and he beamed, as any proud father would.

"What's all this fuss?" the Archmage, in particularly good humor said, as she came close to the three.

"Okay, okay, I can take a hint," Zoran said with a mischievous grin. In a loud voice he called out, "Everyone, I, well we, have an important announcement to make." The room became silent. "Zdenka and I are going to be married as soon as we finish our magical studies."

Once more, their friends yelled and whistled. One by one their friends came to shake their hands. Jarka said, "Well, it's about time! We all had wagers on when Zoran would get up the courage to ask you. I won the bet." She grinned coyly.

"Tonight we celebrate; then tomorrow, it's back to work, back to study," Archmage Nadia took advantage of the quiet. Fake moans echoed around the room, followed by laughter.

That evening, while he was taking a much needed bath in the barrel, Lida made mental contact with him. *Zoran. Zoran. You there, can you talk now? It's important.*

Yes, just taking a bath.

Good. Mom has died. Today. She was forlorn over Radek's death. She took it really hard. She jumped into the river, breaking through the ice. Took the guards all day to find her and get her out. Zoran, everyone is dying around us!

Sad. Mom has not been all there for a long time, sis. How are you doing and how's Rayna taking it?

Oh, we are upset. We've been looking after her for the last couple of years as you know. Still, crazy or not, we both loved her. She's never been like dad.

I know. I loved mom too.

Dad's taking it really hard. He's talking of giving her the official Ceremony of Passing at her funeral, you know, the super-formal send off for Duskas. It's his right to do that. He's the Baron. That means many of our uncles, aunts, and cousins will be coming to the funeral. It's going to be held in three days at noon.

I ought to be there too. Zoran knew that he really ought to pay his last respects to his mother, particularly so, because she would be given the highest of honors, the Ceremony of Passing. It would be an affront to everyone, if he were not present.

Oh Zoran, how Rayna and I long to see you, but it is far, far too dangerous. Who knows what dad might try to do to you? You must not come! Oh, gotta go! Dad's on the warpath again! She broke the connection abruptly. He hoped that she was not in any kind of trouble.

Chapter 14 The Funeral of Baroness Katerina Vladislov

"I know just how dangerous this is going to be," Zoran was discussing his decision to go to his mother's funeral in two days with Janos, Nadia, and his team.

"Son, you don't! Every assassin that ever accepted the assignment to kill you will likely be there as well! Everyone would expect that you would show up for her Ceremony of Passing. It's a sure bet. Probably that is why the Baron is holding the ceremony — to flush you out. Lord knows what the Baron will do when he sees you there! You know that they will have every magical protection known to mages in operation. You couldn't even get away with a disguise. The instant you set foot back in Castle Dorumova, everyone will know. Plus, even if somehow you survive, how can you return here without revealing this location?"

"The last is easy. I'll just return the same way that I came to Brn in the first place, a way that cannot be tracked or traced. You are right about all the magical protections, though. They'd cancel any magical disguise I chose to don."

"I'd only feel better about it if we had a swarm of security men totally surrounding you at all times," Janos admitted.

"Look, this is a funeral ceremony," Zoran protested.

Janos thrust his hands through his hair in utter frustration. He knew only too well the deviousness, callousness, the wickedness of his old Baron. Nothing was sacred when it came to the desires of that man. Zoran was still a boy without a clue of court politics and treachery. "Son, think about the situation that the Baron is facing." He knew well not to use the word father to Zoran. "Put yourself in his mind set for a minute. He must have an heir to his throne — that is paramount in his mind. For years he has groomed Radek to step in and continue down the path he is carving. Suddenly, he finds his heir and protégée gone. He looks at what remains, knowing well the traditions of the Royal Houses. He has two choices, your older twin daughters or take the heat and bypass their rights and choosing you."

"He knows that you have fought against him and his methods since you were a lad. You've even run away from home rather than go along with his policies and brutal suppression of his people. Yet, in the back of his mind, a male heir is vastly superior to a female heir. Why? The woman will marry and that husband will inevitably take over the actual running of the planet. Which to choose? My money is that the Baron will make one last attempt to convert you to his way of thinking and operating. Failing that, only one choice is left to him. Do you realize what this must be, Zoran? Think lad, think!"

Zdenka listened in awe to her father's speech. She had never heard him speak so knowledgeable about the Court, the Houses, and their Politics before now. He was talking about an entirely different world from what she knew. She didn't like what she was hearing very much at all. It sounded so utterly ruthless, devoid any freedom of choice which she valued above all, the right to control your own destiny.

Zoran sighed, Janos was right. He was thinking only of himself and his desire to say farewell to his mother, crazy as she had been. "Even if he tries to talk to me, you know I am not going to submit to him, not ever." He thought of his two sisters and paled. "You think that he is going to try to force them to marry someone he's picked to succeed him?"

"I'll wager everything that I own on that one, Zoran. Once he has committed himself to that path, he will let nothing get in his way, not even his own daughters. I'm sure that he would even kidnap one of them and ship her off to the man he's picked to succeed him, forcing her to marry him. He'd drug her to gain her acceptance. He'd do anything to her so that his picked heir can then sit on his throne when he passes on. This Ceremony of Passing is where something will happen so that he can secure his heir, announcing it to all of the gathered Royalty. My money is on it. This so called funeral is nothing but one giant intrigue, his chance to setup his new heir, not in honoring his deceased wife, who he cared for about as much as he does a farmer's pig!"

"He'll meet with you, see that you cannot be swayed, order your execution, force one of your sisters to marry his chosen man, and announce it to the gathered Houses, making it a formal recognition. Neither you nor your sisters will be safe at this ceremony. You simply must not go there."

The mere mention of his sisters convinced Zoran that he had to go now, more than ever. "I cannot abandon my sisters to this despot! I am going and that's final. If need be, I will rescue my sisters. What kind of a man would I be if I abandoned my own sisters to him? No, I go and that's final."

"I'm going with you!" Zdenka said firmly and with conviction. "You need protection."

"Me too," Bernard added. A chorus of "Me too's" came from his other team members.

Karel growled, "Where you go, Zoran, we go!"

"I cannot ask you to go. It's far too dangerous; there'll be assassins everywhere. Besides, none of you know the castle layout. It will be totally unfamiliar territory. All of you will be at a horrible disadvantage there. Janos knows the politics and intrigue and deception that go on there. I really appreciate you all wanting to come with me, but it is simply far too dangerous for you."

"Look, Zoran, if one of us was in danger, wouldn't you come to help us out?" Zdenka asked him pointedly, her hands on either hip.

"Of course, but that's different. I'm a Duska. I can handle myself in tight situations."

"Oh, so you think that just because you are a Duska and that we are not makes us less of a person because of that, do you?" she fumed, knowing that she was hitting a sore spot and that this was precisely why she was worried about marrying him. She was not a Duska, never would be.

His face felt hot, really hot. "No! I don't think less of you because you are not Duska!"

"So it's all right for a Duska to risk his life for one of us, but it is not all right for one of us to risk their life for a Duska?" she retorted angrily. She was fuming and she realized that they were having their first argument.

Zoran looked at her stunned. What was she saying? How was it okay for him to risk everything for one of them and not allow them to do the same for him? Sheepishly, Zoran said, "I'm being prejudiced aren't I?"

Still with her hands defiantly on her hips, she retorted, "Yes you certainly are, Zoran Vladislov!"

"You know what we say around Brn," Bernard added rather bored with this whole pointless discussion, "what is good for the stallion is good for the mare. I don't see what all this fuss is about. You would willingly help us in a crisis so why cannot we willingly help you in a crisis?"

Zoran relented. "Look, any of you who want to come with me are welcome to do so. However, if you would prefer not to come, I will not think any less of you for so doing. This is likely to be very dangerous, and I cannot ask you to come with me into such danger. Yet, if you want to, I will be grateful for your aid. Honestly, I don't have a clue about how to deal with this Ceremony and what may happen there."

"Thank you, Zoran," Zdenka finally relaxed. "Now then, you have two days at most to get us all familiar with the castle and what's where and the Court and all that. Let's get moving."

Jarka, who had been silent this whole time, grinned. She was going to get her first look inside a real baron's castle, the ruler of a whole planet!

"We should begin by sketching maps of Castle Dorumova, Zoran. It's been a long time since I was there, plus I only saw a small portion of it," Janos suggested. The two set to work, hastily drawing out the layout.

They had just gotten a good start when Lida made frantic mental contact with Zoran. *Zoran! Zoran! I got to talk to you! Help!*

Lida! What's wrong?

Dad! He's forcing me to marry that pig Strom, you know, his ally Baron Bogdan Clav's son. Strom is worse than Radek ever was! You know I want to marry Leo.

What did he say, Lida? Zoran's mind was suddenly filled with hatred of his father, picking on his own daughters like they were some cattle to sell.

He said that at the Ceremony, he will announce that I will be marrying Strom Clav in the spring. If I do not do this, he swore that he would first assassinate Leo and then if I still refused to marry Strom, he would assassinate me! Zoran, what am I to do? I don't want anything to happen to Leo! What am I to do? Please, help me.

Damn! Damn! Damn him to hell!

Should I tell Leo about what's happening? I can Shadow Walk over to Castle Matous. Can Uncle Milan protect us, do you think? But then will he try to make Rayna marry Strom? What can I do, Zoran?

Hang on a second, sis. Let me think. I am coming to the funeral. I'll be there to help you out of this mess. Okay, I got it. Don't do anything until I get there. Play along with the bastard; at least don't give him any reason to send out assassins to kill Leo. I think you ought to tell Leo what is going on, but do not let him take any drastic measures, not until he comes to the funeral with Uncle Milan and Aunt Marjeta. They will certainly bring along a lot of security forces with them. That will help. When I get there, we can meet and figure something out. Be brave Lida. We can figure something out. Okay?

Okay, Zoran. Rayna has already told her fiancé, Stefan Pavel, about what's going on, just in case dad has me killed and goes after her next. He's promised to bring along a whole lot of extra security men.

Have Leo do that too. This whole Ceremony of Passing is nothing but a front for the Baron to establish a new heir to his throne. You be careful, Lida. Don't do anything to provoke him, not until I am there, please. He is not above having you killed, Lida.

I know. I'm terrified of him, Zoran. He knows it too. I don't know if I can bear it. I'll try. I'll tell Leo now. Rayna sends her love. Hell, here he comes again. Gotta go. She abruptly broke the connection. White with anger, Zoran related to the others what his sister had just told him. Only with difficulty was Janos able to get him back on making sketches of the castle.

"You know, Zoran, that we have one edge over the Baron," Karel said.

"What's that?"

"None know that we will have four Archmages and three Mages in our group. We can muster far more firepower than they will be expecting!" Karel was thinking ahead to a battle. Zoran grinned; he was quite right. No matter what else the Baron had planned, he did not know that he would be facing four Archmages and three Mages. Poor Milos would be horribly outgunned, especially if Zoran's uncles brought along their Archmages as well.

"Say, what kind of clothes should we wear?" asked Jarka.

"Damn, I forgot about that," Zoran realized another of his goofs. "Since it is to be one of our major ceremonies, everyone will be wearing their most elegant suits and dresses, black of course, but darn, really elegant clothes. We have nothing like that here in Brn, from the little I've seen."

"Well, we can't go looking like we do now," Jarka said with a coy smile. "Does anyone besides Zoran know what these dresses and suits look like?" No one had a clue.

"I know, I will have my sisters round up something appropriate for us to wear while we are there. It will give them something to occupy their minds, give them some little relief from the Baron's treachery. Er, I am afraid I don't know a darn thing about how to tell them our sizes and all that."

"Men! Honestly, how can you be *so* ignorant?" Jarka teased him. "Leave that to us." She Summoned a tape measure. She and Zdenka began compiling a list of their measurements. Then, she also measured the men's waists, in seams, and so on. "Here, send this to your sisters. This ought to be enough for a dressmaker and tailor." He grinned sheepishly and made contact with Rayna.

Who are these people that you are bringing here? Don't you know that dad will likely put out contracts on their lives as well?

They know the danger and are coming with me anyway. Okay, one is my fiancé. You and Lida will get to meet her.

Oh Zoran! Wonderful news! Who is she? Tell me all about her! She must be one fabulous woman to capture your heart! I wish mom were still here. She again broke down at the thought of her mother's death. In spite of her mother's mental illness, she had loved her and did miss her, especially at times like this.

He allowed her some time to regain her composure. *Sorry, for security reasons, I can't tell you more now. I will when we get there in less than two days. Hang in there a bit longer, sis. Love you.*

Love you too. Bye.

"Okay, clothes arranged. Now here is the layout of our bedrooms, the only safe sanctuaries we have in the castle, really. Every place else is under the Baron's control, and he has all sorts of monitoring spells in place. It is not safe to talk anywhere but inside our private chambers." He continued to outline the details that he could remember of the castle and its defenses.

Just then Brother Jiri came to interrupt them. "Good news everyone. I had another breakthrough with the Circle construction. If all goes well, it should be in operation by Yuletide!" That was the last week of December, the traditional week of winter festivities and celebrations. Only a few more weeks and Zoran could at long last put a major damper on the Baron's plans of planet-wide conquest!

Because there would be so many other guests in attendance, Zoran decided that they would go the night before. This meant that he needed access to his own private room, where they could stay, which meant that he had to have his old room available. Again, he contacted Rayna and had her check on his room. Luck was with him; the Baron had left it as he had left it. Presumably, the Baron still held out some faint hope that Zoran would come to his senses and return to Castle Dorumova.

"The instant we teleport there, the Baron will know of my arrival. Because of all of the arriving guests for the Ceremony of Passing, he will have to have lowered the protection spells that prevents one from teleporting directly into his castle. However, he certainly will have Alarm spells activated and in full force. He will undoubtedly be notified the instant I arrive there. Be on your guard the entire time that we are there, particularly so after the Baron finally has a meeting with me. After he makes his pitch and I refuse him, the assassins will be turned lose on us all. It is not too late for any of you to decline to come. I do understand; this is extremely dangerous."

"I've packed my blades," Jarka grinned.

"My sword is ready as are my spells. I aim to kick some butt!" Karel declared hostilely.

"Okay, is everyone ready to go?" he asked. All six nodded. Zoran, holding hands with Zdenka and the others in one long line, cast his teleport spell. Magic flashed, but something unexpected happened.

As he visualized his destination point, his bedroom, he ran into an anti-magic barrier, preventing him from arriving. He and his six team members found themselves still standing right where they had been standing in their tower! "What went wrong?" asked Zdenka, suddenly becoming worried.

"He does not want me to directly arrive in my own room, but in the common teleport arrival location, where he undoubtedly has many security men waiting to take me into custody. I must be cleverer than that. Give me a couple minutes, gang. There is another way."

He knew that he could Shadow Walk them all into his room, totally bypassing the magical barrier. However, this the Baron also knew. Ah, the Baron was being clever. If Zoran used his Duska Shadow Walk, then the priests could easily track from where he had come. The Baron would now know where Zoran was staying. Clever Baron, Zoran thought, but not clever enough. He concentrated on Uncle Milan and made contact.

Hi, Uncle. Zoran here. Can I ask a big favor of you? No questions asked?

Well, Zoran! This is a big surprise. How have you been? The Baron has been relentless in his search for you. Clever of you to have remained hidden from his best spies all this time.

Doing very well, Uncle Milan. I need a favor. I am going to mom's Ceremony of Passing, but I need to use your Circle of Ascension to get there. Can you lower your protections there so I can teleport to your Circle and use it, please Uncle? That way, the Baron will not be able to track me. I promise you that it will not lead him back to your Circle. That's how I escaped in the first place, via the Circle.

Sure nephew. Give me a minute to get the orders relayed. We will be there in an hour ourselves. Leo has told me what the Baron is planning to do. We are bringing along an additional fifty men. If need be, Leo will bring Lida back with us. Are you with us in this?

Absolutely. Lida is in love with Leo. We cannot let the Baron force her to marry that pig's son. We can talk more in my room at the castle. Thank you, Uncle Milan. See you in a while.

"It's all set. Got to wait a couple of minutes for the protections to be lowered. I will be Shadow Walking us there. Hold on tightly. Whatever you do, do not let go of the person next to you. Jarka, take my other hand, Bernard, take hers. There we are evenly balanced now. This will seem strange and highly disorienting to you. If you feel nauseous, it will pass. Just trust in me. First, we will teleport to another Circle, my uncle's. I trust him. He will have lowered his many protections for us. Everyone ready?" Zdenka took a deep breath. The teleport activated and they arrived in a dimly lit room, deep within Castle Matous. On the floor were glowing, intertwining thread-like lines of various colors that seemed to alter nearly continuously.

"Behold a Circle of Ascension," Zoran announced.

"It radiates intense magic," Jarka commented, mostly to herself. She realized that almost no other people in the entire Federation of Planets, other than Duskas, ever saw a real Circle of Ascension! She burned its image into her mind. The others had similar thoughts. It was incredibly beautiful to view; one could stare for hours at the shimmering, changing threads of light.

Zoran began to pace around the Circle, stepping on all of the threads. The room disappeared, replaced with a strange black nothingness, a void. In the distance, periodically a planet came into view and then disappeared, as Zoran followed and mingled with the threads themselves, each of which led to a specific world within the Federation. Only when he felt that he had sufficiently intertwined his path with the sixteen threads did he finally focus on his destination, Adapazan and Castle Dorumova, more specifically his own private room.

His friends fought hard against a total disorientation of all their senses. Awe and hope surged each time a world, tiny in size, appeared in the black void, hope that this was done. Only when the bluish orb began growing did they realize that at last they were finally beginning to arrive. Like a scene observed through a zoom lense, the world grew in size. Then the towering spires of Castle Dorumova appeared, steadily growing in size until it filled all their world. Still it zoomed until a dimly illuminated room appeared and grew to full size.

"Here we are," Zoran announced. "My room. Crap! Pardon the mess; it is just like I left it last year." Indeed, stuff was scattered everywhere. Memories of his hasty packing returned. "I had to leave in a big hurry. No one's been in here to clean up. Okay, first action, search for any hidden spy devices and spells."

At once, spells detonated right and left. They found none. "Well, that's a relief. Okay, I will let Lida and Rayna know that we are here. Undoubtedly, the Baron will soon discover this as well." He concentrated and told his sisters he had arrived.

Rayna explained. *We have to greet Uncle Milan and Aunt Marjeta. Dad is having us perform mom's old duties, greeting our guests. Stay put until we can come to you. It is not safe. Dad has spies everywhere!*

"Now we wait," he announced. Meanwhile, the women set about cleaning up the place. Slightly embarrassed, Zoran lent them a hand. Karel conjured two large sofas so that they would all have a place to sit down and chat with his sisters.

A while later, a knock on his door announced their arrival. Zoran let his two sisters into the room. All three continually glanced around the halls making sure they were not detected entering. Once inside, a three-way hug ensued.

"We've missed you so much, little brother," Rayna whispered.

His team finally got a look at the twin sisters. Now twenty, they had blossomed into lovely young women, who looked nearly identical, save for the way they wore their hair. Rayna had shoulder length light brown hair and sparkling blue eyes. Lida had identical colored hair, but wore hers much shorter, the only way one could tell them apart. Both wore black silk gowns that billowed out below their waists. A hint of lavender betrayed their presence.

Rayna, seeing the six waiting patiently by the sofas, giggled. She saw three women, one with unusual golden hued skin and said, "Okay little brother. Introduce your friends and tell us which one is your fiancé! We are both dying to know and meet her!"

"Okay, okay. I can take a hint. Gang, this is Rayna, longer hair, and Lida, shorter hair, my twin sisters. This is my fiancé, Archmage Zdenka. I will tell you her last name in about a month." Both twins moved to her and gave her a warm hug and embrace.

"Congratulations, Zdenka! Archmage? Incredible! Honestly, we never thought anyone would ever capture little brother's heart. You are really very pretty too. He didn't mention that to us," Rayna teased him. Zdenka blushed slightly, knowing that she was with two Duskas, two very powerful women in their own right.

"And this is Mage Jarka, Mage Bernard, Mage Karel, and the twins Archmage Emil and Archmage Renata. The twins are from a distant land, studying with us," Zoran explained, still fearful of revealing too much about them — no last names for sure, not just yet.

"Wow, three Archmages and three Mages! You sure have come prepared!" exclaimed Lida, as she greeted each of them warmly.

"Four Archmages," Zoran decided to add a bit more hope to his sisters.

"Where? Is someone invisible" Rayna asked, looking around for another companion.

"Me. Apparently I have set some kind of new record. A Duska has become an Archmage."

Both sisters opened their mouths in utter shock and surprise. "Really? Is that even possible?" Lida exclaimed at last.

Rayna finally found her voice, "Zoran! That's never, ever happened. We are still not yet Mages even! How did you do it? You can cast those top power spells? Incredible! Wow! Congratulations indeed!"

"Yes, congratulations, little brother. Does anyone know of this?" Lida asked.

"No, we are keeping it a secret for a month or so before it is revealed to the world. Please keep it a secret a little longer. I just wanted you to have a little more hope. We are sure in a fine mess, aren't we?"

"Oh Zoran, what are we going to do?" Lida sank into the sofa beside her brother. "Leo's here; he told me that he plans on taking me back with him. I'm going to pack tonight and be ready for whatever happens tomorrow. I'd rather be dead than marry that ugly Strom Clav. He's worse than dad and has terribly bad manners and stinks. Yet, if I run off, what will become of Rayna? Dad will only force her to marry the pig!"

"Stefan's not here yet. I think he's coming in the early morning," Rayna explained. "Honestly, if we run off with these families, there will be hell to pay. It could start another dispute and war between these houses!"

"To say nothing of all the assassins running around after our lives and Leo's and Stefan's," Lida added what she feared most.

"We need to stall for time; in another month I will be shaking up the Baron and all of the other Houses," Zoran said defiantly. "Sorry I cannot be more specific just now. I just need to stall a month. If the Baron tries to force either of you to marry, somehow, someway, we have to get you two out of here."

"They would probably be safest with us, Zoran," Zdenka suggested.

"You are right, love, but their boyfriends and our Uncles may see it differently. We cannot tell them just yet why they would be safer with us. I'll talk to them when I get the chance. Just make sure you both keep every protection spell you know on your rooms tonight."

"We will. Are all of your friends going to sleep in here with you? The girls can share our rooms. Besides we have proper clothes for all of you," Rayna asked.

"I'm all for that, Zoran. This way, we can help protect your sisters tonight," Jarka volunteered, eager to chat with either of the two Duskas.

Just then, Zoran's inner sense alerted him. "Dad's coming. Zdenka, go with Rayna. Jarka, Renata, you are with Lida. Shadow Walk them immediately into your rooms. Mages, put every possible protection spell on their doors and rooms. Action now!" he was insistent.

At once, his sisters took hold of the women's hands and vanished. Karel, Emil, and Bernard took up a defensive semi-circle around Zoran, who headed for his door. "It will be the Baron," he said with a sigh, knowing a nasty confrontation was about to occur.

"Ah here you are at last, my one remaining son," the Baron exclaimed as Zoran opened the door and allowed him to enter. Zoran noticed a dozen security men had accompanied him, but they stayed out of his room. They had not been invited inside and wouldn't be unless so ordered by the Baron.

"Baron," Zoran replied, refusing to call him father or to acknowledge the greeting.

"Where have you been son? We have all been so worried that some ill had befallen you?" he continued ignoring Zoran's cold greeting.

"I'm just fine, never better Baron. Thank you for honoring our mother with the Ceremony of Passing. She deserves it." He stayed totally non-committal.

"Well, yes. Good to see you looking fit, perhaps fitter than when I last saw you. I do believe that you have filled out some. Been eating well, I see. I was worried that perhaps you were starving to death in some hole somewhere. You have heard about your brother?"

Ah, now he was getting to the point, he thought. "Yes, Radek followed your ruthless despotism and see where it led him? Burned and crippled for life, unable to fight, barely able to walk. Bet you ignored him and he couldn't take it any longer. He ought to have known better, but then he always did idolized you as long as I can remember."

"Yes, he proved valiant on the battlefield, as any son of mine should. Excellent warrior. It was those hideous, vile creatures that caused his burns. Son, dragons have come to Adapazan! Now is the time for us all to drop our hostilities towards each other. We must join together, if we have any chance of defending our lands and our peoples from these mean, vicious dragon lizards! If we cannot put aside our differences, all of Adapazan will fall into utter chaos and total ruin, destroyed by these vile, evil creatures." Zoran wondered how Emil was taking all this, but didn't dare throw him a glance. Later Bernard told him that Emil fought hard to keep from laughing hysterically.

"Ah, so then these dragons have been attacking other towns and cities here on Adapazan, Baron?" Zoran cleverly inquired.

"Not as yet, just burned Sholov Province to the ground, murdering thousands of my troops. It is only a matter of time before they do advance beyond Sholov Province, which is now completely deserted, by the way. Not a single living person dwells there, a ghost province."

"Your invasion, then, had nothing to do with forcing the people in Sholov Province to flee for their lives to avoid becoming your slave workforce?" he couldn't resist taunting the Baron. However, as soon as he made his outburst, he regretted it. It only antagonized the Baron further.

"Of course not, son. I am slowly bringing law and order to the Wild Lands, which are controlled by wicked, lawless warlords. You know that. These men rape and pillage and steal to make a living. Son, times are bad. Radek is gone. Your mother is gone. I am coming tonight to see if we cannot heal the wounds between us. Come back to me. Join me. Follow my lead, and I will name you my heir at tomorrow's celebration. Don't you wish to one day be known as Baron Zoran?"

"Baron, the true reality is that you are a ruthless, evil, sadistic dictator, a slave master who suppresses all living people to your own ends. I will never follow in your footsteps. You can name me your heir apparent, but as I stand here living and breathing, I swear to you that the moment that I become Baron taking your place, I will undo absolutely everything that you have ever done — abolish every last law you've set down — fire every last person who has ever committed any vile actions against the people of Adapazan and try them for high treason against the people of Adapazan. Go ahead and name me your heir, if you can live with that."

Vic Broquard

The Baron's face cringed with suppressed anger. His face turned bright red from the effort to keep from exploding and attacking his son this very instant. "Very well. You are no longer a son of mine! So be it!" He turned and left, angrier than Zoran had ever seen him before!

"So that's our Baron," Bernard said bored again.

"He didn't take that none too kindly," Karel put in.

"What did he mean by his last statement? Was that a threat?" Emil asked, totally unfamiliar with human relations.

"He meant that he has disowned me and that he will likely be sending out assassins to kill me. At least this time, I will know who is behind the assassination attempts. I never did figure out who was trying to kill me when I was last here."

"Damn," Karel exclaimed angrily.

"Figures," Bernard added in a monotonous tone.

"We best put up every protection spell we can and immediately," Zoran suggested. For over ten minutes the Mages cast spell after spell. Zoran also relayed to the five women what had happened and checked on their protection spells.

"One of us should remain awake and on guard through the night," Karel ordered. "I'll take first watch. Bernard can have the second one." After conjuring some more beds, which pretty well filled Zoran's room, they retired for the night.

Next morning, as the men began dressing in the black silk suits that Rayna and Lida had provided for them, they chatted about the night. "Well, someone tried to break in on my watch," Karel pointed out. "Didn't get past the Alarm spell, though."

"Same on my watch," Bernard added. "Failed miserably to gain entrance."

"Someone tried to Charm me into opening the door," Emil said in a matter-of-fact tone. "The idiot."

The men found it a struggle to get into their suits. There were so many buttons and attachments that they spent an hour getting into them. "Pack up everything else, Shrink them, and stow them in our pockets. We may have to make an emergency escape," Zoran advised and also relayed that in a message to the women, including his sisters.

Now they had to wait on the women, who took even longer to get ready. At last, Rayna sent word to Zoran. "Okay, we move out. Have you all gotten your defensive spells cast on yourselves?" They had. "We will pick up the others and head to the Formal Breakfast in the Great Hall. Keep your eyes open; we could be attacked nearly anywhere." Cautiously, he opened his door. Seeing an empty hall, the four men slipped out and went down the hall to Rayna's room and knocked.

"Wow! Zdenka! You look fabulous!" Zoran was shocked to see how Zdenka now looked wearing her large silk dress. Rayna had done up her hair and given her a green emerald necklace to wear.

"See what I can do, little brother," Rayna proudly teased him. Zdenka blushed and took his hand.

Lida had also helped Jarka and Renata look equally at their best. Bernard swooped immediately to Jarka's side, swearing that he would be her escort. Jarka loved every minute of this. Such a dress she had never worn nor dreamed existed. Renata was mostly bored with all this human fuss. However, she loved the emerald

100

that she had been given to wear around her neck.

They formed into a group, with Emil and Karel walking in front of Zoran and Zdenka. Lida and Rayna followed; Renata followed them, with Bernard and Jarka bringing up the rear, a position Jarka normally desired. It was a long walk to the Great Hall, down one flight of stairs, only to enter another long hall. On the party walked.

Suddenly, Zoran's inner sense kicked in. "Danger!" he whispered. Lida and Rayna also sensed it as well. A man wearing all black became visible as he rushed towards Zoran. He had been invisible, waiting for him to pass by. Unfortunately for the assassin, Emil was in his way. Without breaking his stride, Emil gave the rushing assassin a left punch in his head. The assassin's head was crushed almost beyond recognition and his body smashed hard into the granite stone wall of the hall. The party marched on without saying a word.

Shortly, Rayna whispered, "How did he do that? The assassin's head was crushed! Emil must be super-strong!"

"Archmage," Zoran whispered, finding a clever way to hide Emil's dragon strength.

"Wow!" his sister exclaimed.

At long last they arrived at the main doors to the Great Hall. There was a line waiting to be announced and enter. Zoran could already see the Baron sitting with Archmage Milos at the front table. A number of other barons from other planets who were allies of his had already been announced and had entered, sitting at the tables closest to the Baron's table. As the next party prepared to enter, the Door Speaker announced in a loud voice, "Baron Milan Matous of Gladno, Baroness Marjeta, and Duke Leo." He also announced several more of their children He tried to see them, but there were too many in line ahead of them.

A bit later, the Door Speaker announced, "Baron Viktor Pavel of Valtr, Baroness Ivana, and Duke Stefan." Two other siblings were also announced.

Several other Barons were introduced, and at last Zoran and his friends reached the entrance and waited on the Door Speaker. After a moment, Zoran realized the Door Speaker was under orders not to announce him. He cast a simple magnify spell and announced himself, "Duke Zoran Vladislov, Duchess Rayna, Duchess Lida, and party." Every eye in the room suddenly stared at the small group as they entered. He saw at once that those who were opposed to the Baron were being forced to sit at tables on either side of the room, far from the Baron. Uncle Milan flashed him a hand signal, and Zoran led them over to their table.

While the Door Speaker continued to announce other arriving barons, Zoran formally introduced his uncle and family to his friends. Leo insisted on sitting beside Lida, however. Uncle Milan explained, "We will be safe here at the tables. Every baron of the Federation of Planets will be here shortly. He would not dare try anything at this Last Breakfast for Baroness Katerina. We are safe for a little while. We can talk later."

As soon as the last baron and his family entered, the Baron rose and spoke loudly. "Welcome my fellow Barons, Baronesses, Dukes, and Duchesses to my time of grief and morning during the Last Breakfast for my lovely Baroness Katerina, who we all loved and admired. Enjoy the finest food available on Adapazan. At one p.m., we will meet here in my Great Hall for Katerina's Ceremony of Passing. Thank you all for honoring the memory of a wonderful Duska, baroness, and wife."

His words were all lies. Zoran fumed; not one ounce of truth did he utter. He loathed his wife, especially after her fall had scrambled her mental facilities. He made no mention that she had decided to end her own life.

The table talk was light and friendly. Uncle Milan was fifty-one, a little overweight, with well-trimmed brown hair, more like a business man than a fighter. His uncle was impressed with his friends. "Three Archmages, my Zoran, the company you now keep. Impressive. Have your Archmages accepted employment with any Royal House yet?"

Zoran answered for them, "We are all still in training a bit longer, but yes they have chosen a Royal House, though just yet, which House must remain a secret." He winked playfully at his uncle.

"Well, I must admit, Zdenka, I have never met a prettier Archmage!" Uncle Milan complimented her.

Aunt Marjeta commented, "Well, Zoran, you had us all so worried about you. I had visions of you starving to death out there somewhere in the wilds. It really is so good to see that you are even fitter than the last time I saw you, which was, now let me see, well, it's been at least two years now." She chatted on.

Bernard whispered to Jarka, sitting beside him, "What are you doing?"

"Committing the faces of all the barons to memory. This is a chance in a lifetime, you know. We get to see all of them in one place. Can you imagine a room full of Duskas? The most powerful beings in all the Federation!" She continued to look around at the many faces, some old, and others young. Some of their children were still teens or younger. Jarka had never mentioned that she had a photographic memory. She would be able to recall every face here anytime that she desired.

As the barons finished up, many rose to leave; some would stroll the castle, others would gather in side rooms to chat. As he was about to get up, Uncle Milan requested, "Zoran, remain seated a while longer." When the table next to theirs freed up, Baron Viktor Pavel and his family slowly moved over to join them. Zoran guessed that the two barons had arranged to meet and was right.

Baron Viktor whispered, "Zoran, Lida, Rayna, please join us." They moved down the table a little ways. Barons Viktor and Milan sat with their sons; Stefan and Leo at their sides, across from Zoran, Lida, and Rayna. Baron Viktor was in his early fifties, a muscled man with a black goatee and moustache. His eyes were piercing and black. He asked, "How did it go with your father?"

"He's disowned me. Already one assassin has tried to kill me on my way to breakfast," Zoran answered truthfully.

"Ah, then he will undoubtedly be announcing at the Ceremony his contrived marriage of Lida to that slob of a Duke, Strom Clav. The question before us is what do we do about it?"

"I will stand up and totally refuse to do his bidding!" Lida lividly answered him. Leo tried to calm her, holding her hand across the table.

"Won't he first have to announce that Lida will be his heir?" Zoran asked.

"Ah, yes, you are right. I was putting the cart before the horse. Yes, he will declare formally that she is his heir and then the contrived marriage," Baron Viktor restated it. "If she then rebuffs the marriage, he will have no alternative but to arrange for Lida's untimely death. Once an heir is announced, it cannot be altered without just cause presented to the entire High Council."

"Right, Leo wants to marry her soon and at the very least take her back to Gladno with us today," Baron Milan stated.

"That will bring his assassins to Gladno," Baron Viktor pointed out.

"I'm aware of that. If he does, I may well go to the High Council seeking retribution," Baron Milan replied.

"The question becomes: should we take Rayna with us? She and Stefan have decided to marry as well," Baron Viktor asked.

"I can't speak for you, Baron Viktor. Surely in time assassins will descend upon your House as well as mine. I should think that if you desire to have Rayna as your daughter-in-law, you should act before the Baron does."

"We are packed and ready to go whenever you say," Lida whispered, hoping to encourage them further.

"Please dad, let us take Rayna with us. Lord knows what the Baron will do to her when Lida goes against him too," Duke Stefan pleaded with his father.

"Okay, son. Rayna, we will take you back to Valtr with us when we go," Baron Viktor replied.

"Zoran, you've been strangely silent," Uncle Milan pointed out.

"Barons, uncles, words cannot express how grateful I am for your kindness in looking after the safety and survival of my dear sisters. I know only too well what retribution may come your way. Before I left last year, assassins tried to kill me three times. That's why I fled when I did. It is a tremendous risk that you are assuming."

"Well, it also has to do with politics, son. Our Houses have been warring against Baron Kazimir and his predecessors for at least a century now. Here we are handed a total shift in power. In a few years, Adapazan may be on our side, a gigantic and unexpected shift in power among the Federation of Planets. We have more at stake than the two pairs of love-birds. Just so you understand our motives, duke," Baron Viktor explained.

Zoran grinned. Politics had everything to do with their decision; he knew that well. "I promise you both, that if you can somehow keep my sisters safe and sound for another month or so, I will be shaking up the entire Federation and its balance of power. More, I cannot say now. You will know beyond the *slightest* doubt when that time has come. Trust me; this will be the *biggest* event in centuries. Just keep my sisters safe until it happens, and I will back you all the way."

Both barons grinned. They liked this renegade son of their enemy, their nephew. "We will do our best. First, we have to safely get them off this planet," Uncle Viktor replied.

"If trouble comes, I will create a diversion to allow you to Shadow Walk safely out of here," Zoran promised, though at the moment he had no idea just what that diversion would be.

"We'd better mingle with the other Houses," Baron Viktor suggested and the informal meeting broke up. Lida held onto Leo, while Rayna took Stefan's arm. From now on, they would not be parted from their boyfriends.

Zoran decided the smartest thing for his group to do would be to stay here in the Great Hall. Wandering about the halls would give an assassin another chance to strike. Jarka didn't object. She and Bernard wandered around the huge room, looking at all of the interesting heralds, tapestries, and trophies mounted on the walls.

Zdenka decided now was as good a time as any to try out one of her Archmage spells. She cast it and sat back to see if any Premonition would come. A bit later, she shrieked and that got everyone's attention. "Oh my god! When Lida stands up to reject her father's contrived marriage, an assassin will stab her in her chest with a poisoned dagger! Zoran, we have to stop him! The room will erupt into chaos!"

"Thank you Archmage Zdenka for your timely warning," he said proudly giving her the formal recognition due her and her power spell. "Okay, Zdenka, get close to Lida and cast Skin of Stone on her. That should prevent the blade from piercing her. I'll get to Rayna and do the same. Let's make sure that we are close at hand to retaliate the instant the assassin appears. No holds barred. Kill the assassin," Zoran ordered. Jarka grinned coyly and nodded.

Having been mingling with the many guests, taking on the role that their mother had performed in the past, Lida and Rayna finally were escorted back into the Great Hall, still clinging to Leo and Stefan. Zdenka and Zoran cleverly cast their spells and touched the intended recipients. "Little more protection," Zdenka whispered to Lida, who smiled.

"It tingles," she whispered back. "Oh it's nearly one and here they all come. We should get near the center where mom's body is resting in state."

Unlike the Last Breakfast, many others joined the barons and their families. Archmages, Chiefs of Security, Mages, and even fighters filed in to attend this holy Ceremony of Passing. The Baron stood on a raised platform along with the entombed body of his late wife, though her body was not visible. A solitary chime sounded. Then a choir of two dozen voices singing a religious chant was heard as they solemnly entered from the main doors, headed by the High Priestess, who would conduct the ceremony.

"We are gathered here today to honor Katerina Vladislov, baroness, wife, and mother. Our wishes, dear Katerina, are to see you safely off on your voyage to the hereafter." She spoke about the highlights of the woman's life, the joy that she brought to her children, and so on. Then, she began the official last rites, little of which Zoran could understand. At last, the choir began another song and pushed the floating coffin slowly out of the Great Hall. Magical fires and lights seemed to issue forth from her coffin as it moved, symbolic of Katerina's passing from one realm into another. After several minutes, the sounds finally died down as the choir moved on down the long halls, taking her body to its final resting place outside the castle.

The Baron stood. "At this time, I would like to make a formal declaration. My son, Radek, has died, and it is fitting and just that I formally declare my heir before the assembled Houses. It is my wish that my daughter Lida be my heir to the throne of Adapazan. I do so state with no reservations."

A round of applause gave him their official acknowledgment that his choice had been received by all of the Houses. "Further, I want to announce that I am marrying Lida to Strom Clav within a month's time. Let the happy couple come forward and receive our blessings."

Strom rushed eagerly to the platform; this would be his finest hour. He was about to become heir to the throne of Adapazan!

Lida rose, and all eyes turned to her. "I want to declare before all of the gathered Houses, that I, Lida Vladislov, will never, ever under any circumstances marry that pig of a man, Strom Clav, not if he was the last man in the Federation! Rot in Hell, Baron!" She was acidly vehement in her pronouncement. The stunned crowd gasped nearly in unison as they reacted to this unexpected turn. His own daughter was publically defying him! Worse, the continued alliance of House Vladislov with the Baron's allies was suddenly flipped over to their enemy's alliance! This is what actually caused the stun, not so much her refusing to marry Strom.

Suddenly, as in her premonition, a man covered entirely in black with only his eyes visible appeared in front of Lida, his hand held a dagger that dripped black oil onto the floor. He plunged the dagger into her heart, while the stunned assemblage tried to grasp what was happening here: an assassination right before their very eyes! The dagger did not pierce her skin, however. It broke in half so forcefully was it plunged! Lida fell backwards from the force of the blow, giving the impression to one and all that she had just been stabbed!

A split second later, a throwing dagger flew straight from Jarka's hand, plunging into the assassin's forehead, followed by a barrage of Magical Arrows from the other six. The assassin was dead several times over one second after he had struck!

Six seconds later, mass pandemonium broke out, as the realization of an assassination struck home to all those in the room. Zoran saw nearly every user of magic in the room beginning to cast spells. His inner sense picked up the idea that men and women on both sides were going to use this opportunity to slay others on the opposite sides. Baron versus baron and so on down the line, a giant battle was about to break out in seconds. He had to give Milan and Viktor their much needed diversion, time for them to Shadow Walk themselves, Lida, and Rayna out of here. He concentrated and fired his spell.

Suddenly, every single magical spell, every single magical protection, every single magical item, such as a ring, was neutralized! No magic whatsoever triggered or detonated, further shocking everyone present, excepting a few. "Now!" Zoran's voice rang out and his second spell detonated. The room suddenly went totally black, no light at all.

Zoran listened for his team's brief chanting of their teleport spells. In rapid fire, all six teleported back to their tower, Zoran followed immediately, arriving a few seconds after his friends. "Well that shook them up!" Karel exclaimed enthusiastically.

"Good throw, Jarka. Man, you are a killer with your throwing daggers," Bernard complimented her. She raised her eyebrows a couple times and winked at him.

"I can't believe that they were just about to battle it out with each other!" Zdenka exclaimed, totally shocked by what she had just witnessed.

"Hey, just got word, they are all safe on Gladno and Valtr. Mission accomplished," Zoran replied, greatly relieved.

"That was a great move, canceling all those spells in one shot, Zoran. Incredible, just incredible. Wish I could do that," Karel out flowed a bit of enthusiasm, which he seldom did.

"Say, do we get to keep these incredible dresses and necklaces?" Jarka asked, realizing that they were all still wearing their very fancy clothes, albeit black was not her ideal color choice.

"Yes, enjoy," Zoran said. "Compliments of the Baron's pocketbook. Well, he now has something to think about. All three of his remaining direct heirs have abandoned him. I just hope that he now doesn't try anything stupid."

Archmage Nadia Oldrich walked in and said, "Okay, how did it go? Then, it's to your studies. Time is precious, I do believe." Zoran chuckled, indeed it was.

That evening, both Lida and Rayan joined with him telepathically. Lida sent, *Thank you for saving my life and helping get me out from under dad's thumb. I owe you a big one, little brother. Whatever did you do there? Who hit the assassin with that throwing dagger? Not even Uncle Milan can say for sure. Everything happened so quickly, I didn't have time to dodge, but it was awfully hard to do much while wearing that confining dress.*

Jarka got him first with her dagger. We were a split second slower with our Magical Arrows. When I saw the place was erupting in a war of spells, I used my top spell, Interrupt Magical Effects, which nullified all magic in that room for a minute. I cast Darkness to give you all a chance to duck out of there unseen.

So it was you then! You really are an Archmage! Rayna sent.

Yes, sis.

Tell Jarka thanks for me, please. Lida added.

Okay. She and Zdenka love the dresses, by the way.

Zoran, she's a dream! You chose well, little brother, Rayna added.

Indeed, I really like her and we've only just met. I wish we could spend some time getting to know her better. Just who is she anyway? Lida asked.

Be patient a few more weeks. Lida, whenever you are going anywhere, please get the Skin of Stone spell cast on yourself to help prevent assassination attempts. I know Uncle Milan will do his best to keep the castle safe. Just humor me and take that extra precaution, please.

But I don't yet know that spell, Zoran.

Well get Uncle Milan's Archmage to teach it to you tomorrow. You too, Rayna. As you saw, it is very useful against assassination attempts. Let me know when you have learned it, both of you. If they can't teach it to you, let me know, and I will send someone to you who can. It is imperative that Lida remains alive. You are now officially his heir and the only way that can be undone is if you die. So stay alive, sis! Both promised.

Say, is Leo Uncle Milan's heir?

No, Leo's older brother is, so it works out perfect. He and I can run Adapazan.

But what about Rayna?

Don't worry about me. Stefan is Viktor's heir, so it all works out okay.

That's a relief.

Yes, but you won't be a baron, Lida protested. *We've worried about that many nights, haven't we, Rayna?*

Don't worry about me. You'll see why in less than a month. I got to go. Keep me posted. Love you both. Indeed, Zoran had a lot to ponder as he fell asleep.

Chapter 15 Yuletide

"Well, there are only a few more spells to attempt to learn," Zoran mused. The five were once more in the third floor study room. Their checklists were rapidly coming to an end.

"This one looks really good," Karel muttered. "I wish I could get this one, very useful spell for me."

"Which one, Karel?" Zdenka asked.

"Change Shape. Well, let's get cracking." Karel showed more enthusiasm on this spell than many others, Zoran noted. They spent the day studying the background data and the particulars on its casting. The next morning, they began to attempt its casting.

After a long but precise chant, Karel finished the spell, making the proper hand motions. Magical energies flashed. Zoran and Zdenka blinked. Karel was not there! They were staring at a large falcon! A Mystical Door opened and Archmage Oldrich stepped into the room and stared at Karel as well.

"Where did that bird come from?" Emil looked up and his sister, likewise. Both were studying its casting.

"That's Karel! He's actually done it!" Zdenka exclaimed, hardly believing her eyes. The falcon paced the table top, strutting its importance. Then magical energies flashed again, and there was Karel standing on the table top.

"I did it! I did it! I did it!" Karel whooped it up, impressed with his own spell.

"Can you do it again?" asked Archmage Oldrich, softly as usual.

Karel calmed down and proceeded to go through the intricate chant. Magic flashed and the falcon reappeared! When he resumed his human form, Archmage Oldrich exclaimed with a good deal of enthusiasm, "Well, I would not have believed it had I not seen it with my own eyes. Congratulations, Archmage Karel Ambrose!"

Everyone began talking at once, patting him on the back. As the rest of the tower came into the room, Jarka rushed up, pushing others out of the way, and gave him a big hug and planted a kiss on his cheek. "Way to go, Karel!" He seemed a bit unnerved by all this sudden attention, however.

"Me, an Archmage? Who would have believed it?" Karel yelled in disbelief.

"Students, there is a lesson to be learned here. Karel persevered in spite of all signs that he would not be able to learn any more spells. He just doggedly kept at it until he finally succeeded," the Archmage commented to her gathered students. She also saw that no more studying would likely occur and gave them the rest of the morning off to celebrate. Study resumed after lunch.

That afternoon, both twins also succeeded with this spell. Zoran speculated that their success had a lot to do with the fact that, as dragons, they inherently could change into human form anyway. Now they could change into any form desired, and they were smugly pleased with this, because neither of their parents could cast this spell.

Zoran and Zdenka, alone of the five, continued to have trouble casting this spell. The Archmage encouraged them to continue practicing it during the week. By

Friday, both finally gave up and stopped trying and suddenly the magical energies flashed at nearly the same instant. A pure white horse appeared, shoving the tables aside, while alongside stood a grey wolf! A minute later, the two returned to their normal selves, laughing hysterically. Then they hugged each other, followed in turn by Karel, Emil, and Renata.

Emil suggested, "Now you three can change into a golden dragon like us and we can all go flying together!"

"Yes, but we would be real dragons, wouldn't we," Zdenka was hesitant. "And that would mean we would need to eat like a horse."

"No not a horse, silly, a hoofer, an antelope. Tasty morsel, really, you ought to try it," Renata suggested. Zdenka turned up her nose slightly, deciding she'd rather be a bit hungry instead.

They worked on the remaining few spells with little success. As the third week in December approached, Zdenka alone managed to learn the last spell and she did it in a remarkable fashion. Her spell functioned. She saw the four moving in extremely slow motion compared to her. Hastily, she tied her hair ribbon onto Zoran's hair, making a small ponytail out of it. She took Renata's sweater off of her and put it on Emil, and then quickly tied Karel's shoe laces together. She rose just as her spell terminated.

"What?" exclaimed Zoran, pulling on the back of his hair. His hand returned with her hair ribbon. Zdenka giggled.

"Give me back my sweater, Emil!" Renata said annoyed, but couldn't remember having given it to him or his taking it from her. Karel began laughing and stood up only to trip and fall over. When he saw his laces tied, he roared even harder. The other three now realized what had happened and laughed along with him, before congratulating Zdenka. In the end, she was the only one would could exercise intimate control over time, but then she was into controlling things anyway, Zoran concluded.

At last Yuletide week arrived. The seven had finished their studies, except that Jarka and Bernard wanted to continue their studies of potion making and scroll making after the new year began. All of the magic students went to the Stodgy Inn on the first night of the festival to celebrate. They all had much to actually celebrate, and even Archmage Nadia joined them, one of her rare excursions out of her tower.

Sipping a heavy stout, she explained to the five, "Tomorrow I must send your names into the official registry. After that, the entire Federation will know that you five are indeed officially registered Archmages." All five thanked her for all that she had done for them. A bit later, Aldrick and Sofie joined their children and friends to celebrate as well. Janos arrived later that night and brought Zdenka her surprise present: a beautifully made quiver with two dozen arrows of exceptional quality, ready for her to enchant them, turning them into magical arrows.

On the fourth night of Yuletide, Zoran and Zdenka sat in a corner of the inn chatting. He said, "You know, love, I really want to get you a special present, but I don't have all that much money, and I can't go shopping without taking everyone else with me."

"Same here. I suppose I could slip away for a bit, but I don't have much I can spend either. We have all been really supported by Archmage Oldrich all this time," she replied.

"I know, why don't we go shopping tomorrow and we can each get a little something special for each other?" She liked the idea. After all, Yuletide was the season for giving presents.

Their shopping spree didn't last too long. At the jewelers, they spied a matching pair of rings with a pale blue gemstone in them. Spontaneously, they both decided this was it. Grinning because they each had the very same idea at the same time, they bought them. Gently, Zoran placed one on her finger and she, he. "Now we are a matched set," she proclaimed. "I can't wait for the other ring," she teased him. He passionately kissed her right there in the store. Jarka made some coy cat-calls, however.

The fifth night of Yuletide, Brother Jiri visited Zoran. "Duke, it is done, I'm proud to say. No way to know if it will work though. It has to be activated in a ceremony conducted by my wife and a Duska — that'd be you. I guess I'm saying we're ready whenever you are ready to attempt to activate the first new Circle of Ascension in centuries!" Brother Jiri was quite proud of his achievement and rightly so. If it actually worked, he would become incredibly famous indeed.

The next morning, Janos, the Zors, Archmage Nadia, and the seven gathered in the basement of the Archmage's tower. One section, roughly thirty foot square, contained the new dormant Circle of Ascension. The back side of the room was curved, the outer wall of the circular tower. In the center of the room, a circle precisely twenty feet in diameter lay etched into the stone floor. Brother Jiri had removed part of the floor here, installing his creation. "Duke Zoran has picked the color for his ribbon, sky blue. Each House has their own color." Two weeks earlier, Jiri had asked Zoran what color his wanted to use for this tower and Circle. To avoid confusion, Brother Jiri suggested that he pick something other than the sixteen already in use. Zoran had picked sky blue.

"This House, whatever it is going to be called, is indicated by the sky blue thread. If we are successful, these seventeen threads will intertwine and activate Shadow Walking between the seventeen Circles of Ascension," Brother Jiri continued his explanation. "If it works, this will be the first new Circle of Ascension since the time of my great-great-great grandfather, a monumental event to say the very least."

He advised, "Zoran, the moment we activate this you must be prepared for all of the consequences. I've discussed this with my wife and we owe it to you to prepare you for this activation. All of the other Houses will know that this one now exists the very instant ours is activated. That a new Circle of Ascension has been built will be most profound, and many, many others are going to want to know how it is done, will demand that more be built, attempt to come and steal Bandar Zor's detailed instructions, and so on. My wife and I, plus these documents must be protected. I do not want to find myself being coerced into making another Circle by barons such as your father."

"There are many other factors to consider as well. Obviously, the other Houses, barons, and their families are all going to want to come and see this one for themselves, if only out of intense curiosity since this is historic in nature. It also opens this place up for invasions, that is, assassins can be brought through by barons or the baron's men and wizards can be brought through or even attempts might be made to steal it from you — the list is endless. Great protections must be put in place to either prevent these from happening or to at least sound an alarm if enemy forces or unwanted people arrive here."

"Then, there are all of the political ramifications of a new House being established. I am not remotely qualified to even discuss such things. All this will happen the instant we activate it. Are you prepared to deal with all of these things, Zoran?"

"No, but I have no choice but to ask some barons that I trust for their help and assistance. Janos, how goes our meager Security forces?" Zoran asked.

"I have sixty good men trained and ready for service, Duke Zoran. They will be split into three shifts, so that this tower is guarded day and night, every day. Twenty will be on duty for eight hour shifts. The only problem I foresee is if we are attacked or invaded, these will be wholly insufficient," Janos replied honestly and a bit worried about this possibility.

Aldrick spoke up, "I have a dozen golden dragons ready to move here from Voss as soon as you are ready to have them stationed here. Of course, they will be desirous of receiving gems for payment."

"Terrific, Aldrick. Yes, the Security men and the dragon guards must be paid. We still have some of the funds given to us by Warlord Mikolas. We'll use that as long as it lasts. Obviously, I must quickly find a source of funding. I didn't realize just how many problems creating this new Circle of Ascension was going to create."

Archmage Oldrich commented softly, "You are yet young, Zoran; you have much to learn besides magic. Here in Brn, I provide the protection for the province. Each fall, I receive a small amount of monetary support from each household. While not large, this allows me to survive well and provide what is needed for these people to live in safety. However, I have never promised them that I could stop Baron Kazimir's army, if and when he should decide to invade Brn Province. With this new Circle of Ascension, you, Zoran may be able to provide that guarantee that they can live in peace and prosper without fear of an invasion. It would be reasonable, then, that the households provide a little more each year to help pay for their security."

"But where will we live?" Zdenka asked the question uppermost in her mind. She knew nothing of politics and armies and money, she only wanted to be able to setup a household with Zoran and soon.

"Er, I haven't worked that one out either, dear," Zoran apologized.

"You may stay here in your rooms for as long as you need," Archmage Nadia offered and was thanked. Still, Zdenka knew this would have to be short-lived.

"Say, Brother Jiri, I have a question. Once we activate this Circle of Ascension, suppose that I am able to build a better place to house it nearby. Can it be moved? Can a Circle of Ascension be moved slightly from where it began to someplace nearby?" Zoran asked, wishing that he had thought of this far earlier.

"Yes, if it is only a little ways," Priestess Anezka answered, since this was her province not her husband's. "It is often done to obtain a more secure location within a castle. The Circle of Ascension is tied to this location, this vicinity. You cannot move it to, say, Sholov Province."

"Well, that is a break. I seem to have found myself embroiled in a multitude of problems," Zoran laughed nervously. "Say, once we activate it, can it ever be deactivated, perhaps for a little while?"

"Obviously it can, if you are going to relocate it," she replied. "However, all of the other Circles of Ascension will still have your sky blue ribbon in them. Anyone could come here to investigate. The only way to remove the identifying ribbon is to destroy the Circle."

"Well, that was a good idea at least. Oh well, I guess we have little choice but to step into the big unknown," Zoran concluded. "We'll just have to solve each problem as it comes up. How long will the ceremony take to get our Circle activated?"

"I've never done the Activation Ceremony, Zoran. No one has, not for centuries. Maybe an hour? I don't know," she replied, a little nervous about attempting a ceremony about which she had only read but never actually done.

"Okay, tomorrow at ten o'clock in the morning, we activate the Circle of Brn," Zoran said decisively. "Prepare the city for what's coming; have the gold dragons circling the tower at ten; have all sixty guards on duty. We're going to give the Sixteen Houses of the Federation of Planets a Yuletide present that they will never forget! I'll make some arrangements with my Uncles; I believe that they will lend us some support immediately upon activation. Mages, we will need to formally welcome those that will be coming to investigate, as well as protect our new allies and ourselves from assassins and treachery that may come with some of those that come to investigate the activation."

"But none of us have a clue about how a court should welcome such visitors, Zoran," Zdenka stated the obvious, rather nervously. "We need to give them a good impression of us, don't we? I mean, many will be Duskas deserving of high honors — well, some do anyway."

"Ours will be a different court, dear. No rituals slavishly followed, not for us. We will just all be ourselves. If they don't like it, that's their problem. Besides, the magnitude of what is happening will totally overpower any and all rituals and traditions. Those will be the last things about which these barons will be thinking — I assure you of that!"

"I shall see that the dining room is prepared so that you may offer some guests food and drink," Archmage Nadia said softly, backing him up. "Admittedly, it is going to be a far cry from the type of dining these barons are used to enjoying." She chuckled to herself. Her facilities were totally functional and inexpensive, no frills. After all, the money for her support came from these hard working men and women here in Brn, whom she had protected all these years. She refused to spend their money frivolously.

She continued, "If I may make a suggestion, Archmage Zoran, why don't you let us all lend you a hand? Once the Circle is activated, every one of us here has a stake in it, for good or ill. I think that I speak for us all, we want to help shoulder some of this burden of yours."

"She's right, you know, Duke Zoran," Janos added. "Making use of us all would be wise. There are far too many details for one man to handle in so short a time."

Zoran sighed. "Yes, I know, it's overwhelming, but my worst fear is the danger that I am putting you into the moment the Circle is activated. Okay, friends, division of labors it shall be. Who wants to do what?"

Archmage Nadia spoke first, "My son, Mayor Bogdan Oldrich, should be contacted immediately and fully informed about what we are doing. To avoid panic, someone must address the citizens of Brn, informing them of this Circle, the political ramifications, the dragons, and what this will mean to them and their families. I will arrange this meeting at once. As I said before, I will see to the food and dining arrangements for tomorrow."

"I'll see to the physical security aspects," Janos volunteered.

Aldrick added, "I will make the arrangements with the dragons. Payments and living arrangements must be worked out and I will deal with those."

"We Archmages and mages will set about security arrangements and magical protections for this Circle and tower," Zdenka volunteered.

"Thanks, everyone. I'll see to the political ramifications of a new House appearing and see what allies I can obtain," Zoran concluded.

"Now you are talking!" Jarka said coyly. "Let's get this show on the road." The group divided up and began working on specific details.

Zoran sat down in a quiet corner and began making mental contacts. Not everyone was available for a conference this instant, but he finally got all four of them all joined up a half hour later. Uncle Milan, that is Baron Milan Matous, Uncle Baron Viktor Pavel, Lida, and Rayna.

Thank you all for allowing me to join us together for this conference. I assure you this is of monumental importance. First, I am an official Archmage. Archmage Nadia Oldrich has sent in the official documents of registry for us five who have achieved this status. It is now official. I guess that I am the first Duska to become an Archmage.

Uncle Milan congratulated him, *Incredible! That's fantastic news indeed, Archmage Zoran.*

Very impressive indeed, son, especially since you are on our side and not your father's, Uncle Baron Viktor said what he felt.

So it was you that canceled all of the magical effects at the Ceremony? Uncle Milan asked.

Yes, that is one of my top power spells. I also cast Darkness to give you cover to escape. I did promise you a diversion, Zoran chuckled.

Amazing, simply amazing indeed. Well done, nephew.

Thanks, but that is only the tiniest thing that I wanted to tell you all. Brace yourselves, I have perhaps the most startling news ever.

Okay, we are all ears, Baron Viktor replied, eager to hear the real reason for this unusual conference.

I want you all to be watching your Circle of Ascension tomorrow morning around ten in the morning. We are performing a ceremony at that time, though my priestess is not sure just how long it will take.

Son, you are not planning to harm our Circles are you? Uncle Milan exclaimed angrily, worried that Zoran was up to some mischief.

Not in the slightest, Uncle. If all goes well, you should see the appearance of the seventeenth House, a sky blue circle. If so, please come to us at once. I will be desperate for your aid and advice! Plus, you will see a sight never before seen within the Federation of Planets.

What! Exclaimed Baron Viktor.

What? This is not possible! A new Circle of Ascension? How? How Zoran? Uncle Milan nearly screamed mentally back to Zoran.

Oh my god! Lida excalaimed.

Zoran! Fabulous! put in Rayna

I am in possession of the actual documents of Bandar Zar, which tell how he built the sixteen Circles of Ascension and how to actually construct them. All I dare say at this time is that a friend of mine has built one and a priestess friend will be performing the first Ceremony of Activation in centuries tomorrow around ten in the morning. If it actually works, I want you four at least to know of it the very instant that it becomes operational and to please come to me at once. Obviously, in short order, all of the other barons will know about this historic event. Honestly, Uncles, Baron Viktor, Baron Milan, I need your help and advice, if it actually works.

Oh my god! Zoran! I'm speechless! This — this is of monumental proportions! Uncle Milan replied, totally aghast.

Holy gods, Zoran! Do you know what you are doing? This will shake up the entire Federation of Planets! You can count on me being there with you the instant your Circle is operational! What forces should I bring with me? asked Baron Viktor, sizing up the situation rapidly.

Yes, what do you need? We'll be there the instant it is operational. Do you want us to come to wherever your Circle is at ahead of time? Uncle Milan asked the obvious, wondering how Zoran could possibly protect such a find and a new Circle of Ascension.

No need to come ahead of time. If the Ceremony does not work, if there is something amiss in its construction, we will need time to remedy it. I believe that I have enough to protect it for a short while, but after it is going, well, come and see and I will be grateful for any and all advice that you can possibly give me. I am a bit overwhelmed with the responsibility that is landing in my lap. I'm not sure what all must be done, let alone the political ramifications of a new House suddenly appearing without warning. I suppose that all of the barons will attempt to come and see for themselves where this new Circle is located.

Yes, that cannot be helped. Just make sure that you have enough protections in place, enough security men present so that none will be tempted to execute a coup on you, Baron Viktor advised.

Do be careful, little brother, Rayna added.

We'll see you tomorrow, Lida sent.

Okay, I hope this will do much to get the Baron's assassins off of you two and your fiancés. See you tomorrow, if all goes well. He broke the connection. Zoran smiled; he knew that those two barons would be conversing like never before between themselves! He'd certainly shaken them up!

"Zoran, we need you a minute," Zdenka nudged him out of his thoughts. He looked up at her, smiled, and rose, realizing the stone floor was awfully hard and cold. He rubbed the circulation back into his rear, while following her into the Circle of Ascension room.

"Okay, we've constructed a really safe and secure location in which to store Bandar Zar's documents and journals. You stand here, before your Circle, and say 'In the name of Bandar Zar, appear.' Go ahead, try it, Zoran," Zdenka insisted, her alto voice full of excitement.

"In the name of Bandar Zar, appear," Zoran spoke. To his amazement, an extra-dimensional room appeared right in the center of the dormant Circle! They stepped through the shimmering door into the twenty-foot square room. The walls were white; twenty globes of light provided excellent illumination. One wall contained a locked scroll cabinet and a locked box contained the journals. A third ornate box held the ceremonial books that the High Priestess needed. A mahogany desk and chair sat in the middle of the room.

"Now to open the cabinet and box, you say, 'In the name of Brother Jiri Zar, Open,' and 'In the name of Priestess Anezka Zar, Open' to have them open up. Once you close their lids, they automatically reseal. Pretty cool bit of magic that we've whipped up, don't you think?" Zdenka asked, proud of their work. The other Archmages had quietly come up behind them to see Zoran's reactions.

"Incredible! Fantastic! Terrific job! All of you," he turned to face his friends. "This is perfect and a really good hiding place for these valuable things! Thanks to all of you!" Everyone was pleased; their faces showed it.

Jarka added, "When you step out and close the door, the whole room vanishes, leaving no trace at all that it is here. Pretty neat, don't you think?"

"Absolutely neat, Jarka," Zoran replied, testing it out and watching the room simply vanish after he shut the door. "Oh, Aldrick is looking for you, something about the dragons."

The group headed up the steps and out the main doors. Here, Janos and Aldrick were conferring. "Ah, there you are, Zoran. I'd like you to meet the rest of your dragons," Aldrick explained. "They are waiting for you in the Security barracks next door."

"Thanks, let's go meet them," Zoran replied, eager to see more golden dragons. In many ways, he was depending upon them for their ultimate security from overland assaults. Janos and Aldrick led him into the converted home next door to the tower. Sitting around a table were six adults and three young teens. Their skin tones matched that of Aldrick, he noted.

Aldrick introduced him, "This is the new Baron and Archmage Zoran Vladislov. Archmage, this is the Osterhagen family: Roth and Jutte, and their daughter, Raffaela. This is the Weiss family: Nagel and Madde, and their daughter, Ursel. This is the Muller family: Kuefer and Sascha, and their son, Lang." Zoran shook hands with each, very pleased to see them all. Now he would have thirteen dragons around the province. Enemy barons would think twice about bringing an army to take Brn by force.

Zoran then explained in detail what he was doing and what their tasks would be, though Aldrick had already told them nearly all of it. "We would like a few of you to spend the night in a room next to our Circle room, in case of any nocturnal invasions. You can rotate who is sleeping there every night, if you like. I can't imagine that you would prefer to sleep in human form all that much. Now, I suppose we ought to discuss your payment?"

Roth cleared his throat. "Well, yes, Aldrick said that you would pay us in gems, which is precisely what we desire. However, we understand that you are just getting established here and probably are low on funds. We would like to suggest an alternative to a lot of gems. Our son and daughters are going to be the right age for learning magical spells. Aldrick has explained that you have six Archmages here at this tower. If you would consider training our three youngsters when they are old enough, we would lower our gemstone requirements significantly, to say five hundred per month per dragon."

"Now that would suit us ideally! You have yourselves a deal. How soon will they be ready to learn magical spells?" Zoran replied, unable to conceal his elation over the vastly lower expense of having the dragons in his employ.

"Not for another year or two," Roth answered. "Another detail, we need a large cavern, of course. Three of them. We've been scouting the mountains north of your tower, and there are a number of promising locations where we could make our real homes. Is this acceptable?"

"Of course. And you can have the mining rights to any gems that you may find there. Those peaks are nearly inaccessible to humans, so I think that makes it a perfect location for you."

Roth seemed very pleased. Raffaella asked curiously, "Are Emil and Renata really Archmages too?"

Zoran smiled, "You bet they are. We seven studied really hard, six long days a week, and they made it. Each knows some of the topmost power spells. While I cannot guarantee you that your three will be able to learn such spells, we all will do our very best to help them make their attempts. All I ask is that you don't eat all of the antelope in one location; rather spread your hunting around the whole area, please. We like to dine on them as well, though not nearly as much as you folks do."

"Really, this is hoofer heaven," Lang pointed out. Zoran grinned.

One by one, Zoran shook their hands, sealing their bargain. He and Janos returned to the tower, while the dragons left the house to go exploring the mountains and begin excavations of their new caverns. "I've got the sixty men ready for your review, Zoran. Honestly, fifty gold a month is quite a lot for their services."

"I know, but I want them well paid, Janos. I'll give them more when I can afford it." Janos shook his head. This young duke was paying these men at least five times what they could get as fighters elsewhere.

"You will certainly have their loyalty, Duke Zoran," Janos chuckled. The two men reviewed the well-armed men who stood in several ranks for inspection. All wore chain mail armor and carried a variety of weapons. After reviewing them, Zoran gave them a few words of appreciation. Then he was needed inside for the mayor had arrived.

When Zoran entered the room, Archmage Nadia was sitting in the dining room with her son, Mayor Bogdan Oldrich. Bogdan was in his late forties, well-dressed and well-mannered, as befitting the town's leader. As Zoran entered, he rose and shook his hand, "Congratulations on becoming an Archmage, Zoran. I understand that this is a terribly difficult thing that you have accomplished. Me, I never did like magic, much to mother's eternal dismay," he said jovially.

"Thanks mayor. I'm afraid that I am about to shake things up around here, for the better I hope."

"Yes, mom said that it was urgent that we meet. What's up?"

"First, I should tell you my sir name and then go from there. I am Duke Zoran Vladislov."

"What? The Baron's son?" exclaimed Bogdan very much taken by surprise and startled.

"Yes, his youngest. Please, I am not the Baron Kazimir. I hate his guts as much or more than everyone else does. An assassin tried three times to kill me back in Dorum, so I ran away from home and came here to study magic from your mother. You've heard how Sholov Province fell?" He nodded and Zoran continued. "It seems that warlord Mikolas came upon a monumental find when he was renovating his fortress there. He discovered the long lost writings of the man who created the Circles of Ascension, from which the Duskas gain their power. There has not been a new House in centuries. Mikolas was attempting to build a new Circle and House at his fortress when the Baron invaded."

"Thanks to your mother's timely intervention, we arrived there just in time to rescue the partially built Circle and the priceless documents. Mikolas was trying to build a new House to combat Baron Kazimir and put an end to the Baron's conquest of the Wild Lands. He gave his life that we could have the chance. I promised Mikolas that I would carry on his work. It's done; in the basement of your mother's tower is the first new Circle in hundreds of years. Tomorrow morning we plan to activate it and bring a new House and baron into the Federation. I've volunteered to be the baron, and I am dedicated to bringing down Baron Kazimir's iron fisted domination of Adapazan."

"But all of the Circles lie deep within heavily fortified castles, if I understand this," Mayor Bogdan interrupted. "We've not even a fortification anywhere in the Brn Province, mere stone walls around Brn. Will not the Barron just come and take over your new Circle and bring doom down upon us?"

"No he won't dare. You've heard the rumors circulating about town that there is a dragon around here somewhere?"

"Well, yes, but those are just rumors, you know," Bogdan replied. "There are no dragons."

"Unfortunately, dragons are very real indeed. For the last year or so, there have been four gold dragons in Brn Province. Your mother has trained two who are now Archmages themselves. Those two were the dragons that attacked the Baron's army in Sholov Province. I've hired more to help protect Brn Province. Thirteen in all, Mayor. I'd like to see any army try to advance upon our province now! The twins knocked off over a thousand of the Baron's troops in just a half hour. Think how much damage six times that number could do! I am doing my very best, Mayor, to ensure that Brn Province remains a free land."

"Oh my! Thirteen dragons in our town? Oh my! Will they harm us by accident?" Bogdan looked worried.

"No, they do not eat humans; we taste really bad, so they say. Their preferred food is an antelope a week, and there are plenty of those in our forests. I will have some walking among us, staying at your mother's tower, in case someone tries to take over the tower by force. Mayor Bogdan, you now have an ultimate defense force protecting our province."

"Now this is good news. Say, how much will they cost us? Their services must not come cheap."

"Right now, I am covering it from the gems that warlord Mikolas gave us to help get the Circle setup. They only want gems; nothing else interests them, excepting magic of course."

"Gems?"

"Yes, they value gems highly. The twins only use a bit of gold because that's what the merchants around Brn expect in trade for clothes and inns. Now the main reason I needed to see you today is that tomorrow morning around ten, we are going to try to activate the Circle. If we are successful, many barons will make a trip here to see what is going on. I will have the thirteen dragons flying in circles around your mother's tower. I don't want them to scare the devil out of our townsfolk."

"Right! Oh my yes, it would scare the devil out of everyone. I must prepare the entire town at once!"

"Let them know the truth; it's time to stop hiding. Brn is about to become the center of the free peoples of Adapazan. I hate to bring this up now, but down the line a bit, I wonder if they would be willing to increase their yearly taxes a little to help me offset the cost of the dragons and the security men that I've hired to help protect Brn Province?" Zoran finally got to ask the burning question. Could he expect more funds from the locals or would he have to find alternate means of financing this whole adventure?

"Ah, it comes down to money. Well, let's give them time to digest all this. Allow them to get familiar with dragons overhead and walking the streets. If you can indeed guarantee our safety, I believe that most would offer up a bit more each year, just as long as there is no extravagant spending. Mom has always been quite frugal which helps a lot."

"We will follow in her footsteps. I will do my best to get funding elsewhere for the long term. I am just going to need some financial help in the short term, just the next couple of years."

"Ah, that is even better. Say, can I meet one of these dragons?" Mayor Bogdan asked, becoming curious at last. His fears had subsided.

"Sure, come with me; their leader, Aldrick Vogler, is nearby arranging things for their group." Zoran nodded to Archmage Nadia and led Mayor Bogdan outside and introduced him to Aldrick. The two took a fancy to each other, primarily because Bogdan wore a large green emerald pendent on his suit coat, his emblem of office. The two men began chatting, and Zoran was called away to attend to another situation.

Not long after this, town criers began relaying the mayor's message. "Hear yea! Hear yea! Archmage Oldrich has brought a Duska and gold dragons to Brn to protect us from the evil Baron Kazimir Vladislov! Tomorrow around ten, look to the sky and see our golden protectors circling her tower!" Up and down the many streets of the city the dozen criers went, yelling out the information. Zoran knew that the pubs would be filled with wild gossip and speculations this evening.

Chapter 16 Activation

"What are we supposed to wear?" Zdenka asked Zoran, early the next morning. Lines of worry marked her complexion.

"Yes, what are we to wear?" added Jarka. "This is an important first meeting, and we do not have a clue about dress protocols, manners, court etiquette, none of that. You *ought* to have given us some clues, you know." She chided him.

"I know, I know, Jarka, but I really don't know about women's dresses and things like that. Honestly, wear something comfortable and be prepared for possible attacks or assassins and the like. I'm wearing my leathers in case I need to fight. Time enough later for the court protocols. We have to get this working first," Zoran replied, slightly nervously.

The gaily embroidered, billowing, white, ceremonial dress of the High Priestess swished into the room. Priestess Anezka Zar, holding on to the arm of her husband, Brother Jiri, who wore his suit with twin tails, entered the room. She said, "We are ready to begin, Zoran."

Zoran let out a sigh and replied, "Okay. Then this is it. Down to the Circle, everyone."

In the basement room, General Janos Lavos positioned six guards around the outer perimeter. Others were in the next room. The Archmages and Mages filed in, taking up positions between the guards, spells at the ready. Anezka already had the incense burners going, giving the whole room an unusual smell. Brother Jiri offered the arm of his wife to Zoran, "Good luck, Duke Zoran."

"What do I do?" he whispered to Anezka. Zoran realized that he had not the slightest idea what was needed from him.

"The Ceremony links you to this Circle of Ascension. Just focus on the color of your ribbon on the floor, the sky blue line. I will do the chanting. As it activates, according to the documents of Bandar Zar, this new Circle of Ascension ought to bind itself to you. We are not exactly sure what that really means, however. There hasn't been a new Circle in centuries, so no one really knows anymore just what goes on with the binding process. Ready?"

"I guess so. Let's do it," he whispered. Inwardly, Zoran said a prayer; everything depended upon this Circle coming into being. So much was riding upon it activating. He gently held onto her arm, allowing her to lead him.

Priestess Anezka began chanting in a plainsong sort of way that he had never heard before. He couldn't quite follow her words, however, as she walked very slowly around and around the circles of seventeen colored tiled ribbons on the floor. The intertwining threads formed a circle some twenty feet across. On their third pass, Zoran began feeling a bit nauseous, as he had when he came of age and had his special gland activated. The room seemed to grow darker and darker; the intertwining threads seemed to begin to radiate their own light, captivating his complete attention as the two continued to walk over them.

Alive, somehow these threads seemed to be alive, he thought. That cannot be, his mind struggled with that notion. The seventeen threads began to swirl of their own accord; the treads were moving around the circle, each at a slightly different speed, which only added to the disorientation of Zoran. Dimly he heard the distant voice of Anezka calling to him, "Focus on your sky blue thread. Focus!"

With effort, Zoran attempted to concentrate on following the single sky blue thread as it interwove with the sixteen others. Dizzy. He felt like falling down, only he couldn't say which way was actually down. Other colors fought for his attention, but he concentrated on his sky blue color. Swirling colors intertwined within him, locking onto his sky blue. Now his color dove into the earth, directly below his feet, wherever they seemed to be. Zoran was not quite sure that his feet were even on solid ground; he seemed to be stepping into space within the earth. Now the sky blue color and the earth seemed to fuse into one and into his own body. Just when he thought that he was going to pass out, faint, or vomit, this location, this Circle of Ascension latched on to his body solidly and the swirling ceased. He felt as if he were somehow anchored here, anchored firmly to his very own Circle of Ascension. He was now a part of this location; this spot here on Adapazan was now a part of him, though he did not realize this yet.

The swirling ceased; the room came back into focus. He was still holding the arm of Priestess Anezka; she was still chanting; they were still walking. Zoran looked down at the Circle. The seventeen colored threads were now glowing and undulating; slowly the intertwined threads moved around the circle of their own accord. Anezka finally stopped her song.

"There, it is done. I give you the new Circle of Ascension. Zoran, you must now speak the name by which this Circle and House shall be known." She nudged him slightly, bringing him to his senses.

"This shall be known as the House of the Free People of Brn and Adapazan," Zoran spoke proudly and clearly, giving all the distinction to those who lived here and those who fought for freedom.

Priestess Anezka announced formally, "I give you Baron Archmage Zoran Vladislov of the House of the Free People of Brn and Adapazan!" Everyone began clapping, acknowledging this incredible event that they had just witnessed. Jarka realized that they were fantastically lucky; they had just witnessed something no one had seen for hundreds of years, the creation of a new Circle of Ascension and power. Zoran walked over to Zdenka and took her hand.

"Zoran! Your eyes!" she exclaimed, very startled. Zoran blushed, suddenly all eyes in the room stared at his.

"What's the matter with them?" he asked growing very embarrassed with this surprise attention.

"They've turned sky blue! They match your thread's color!" she exclaimed.

Zoran gave a joking giggle, "Glad I didn't choose purple!" Everyone roared with laughter.

"Zoran, someone's coming through!" the steely voice of Janos called out. Instantly, everyone focused their undivided attention on the center of the Circle, whose threads were now glowing brighter than before, a sure indication that someone was using it to come to this location.

A moment later and four forms took shape. As they fully materialized, the Circle resumed its dull glow. Zoran recognized them at once. His uncle, aunt, cousin, and sister Lida arrived. Zoran spoke ceremoniously, "I give you my uncle, Baron Milan Matous of Gladno, Baroness Marjeta, Duke Leo, and my sister Lida Vladislov. Welcome to the House of the Free People of Brn and Adapazan."

The baron wore his official attire of office, a very fancy suit with many medals pinned to his chest. His smile was infectious, and he could not conceal his excitement. His wife wore an elegant green, silk dress that billowed out nearly seven feet. Duke Leo, his arm around Lida, also wore a very well made silk suit, befitting an heir to a throne. Lida wore a matching light blue dress; her hair done up nicely. She could not contain her excitement.

"Oh Zoran! You did it! You have made history! I am so proud of my little brother!" she exclaimed, rushing to him and giving him a huge hug and kiss. "Your eyes! Oh, I do like their new color!"

"Congratulations nephew!" Baron Milan said, his bass voice echoing in the room. "Well done indeed! This will shake up the establishment!"

"I can't take credit for building this. Priestess Anezka Zar performed the ceremony and Brother Jiri Zar built this new Circle. Come on you two. I want you to shake hands with my uncle." Both timidly stepped forward and shook hands with the Baron.

"Someone's coming through," Jarka announced. Hastily, Zoran moved the four back behind his security guards. All eyes watched for more bodies materializing in the center of this new Circle.

Zoran, his uncle, and others recognized them at once. Zoran announced formally, "I give you my uncle, Baron Viktor Pavel of Valtr, Baroness Ivana, Duke Stefan, and my sister Rayna Vladislov. Welcome to the House of the Free People of Brn and Adapazan."

Baron Viktor wore an elegant brown silk suit, and his grin could not have been broader. His wife wore a matching brown silk dress that also billowed out seven feet. Duke Stefan wore a slightly lighter shade of brown silk suit with twin tails. Rayna, radiant and very excited, also wore a billowing light blue silk dress, matching her sister's dress.

"Oh little brother! It worked! You did it!" Rayna exclaimed, rushing to hug Zoran.

"Well done, Baron Zoran, well done indeed!" Baron Viktor added, shaking his hand firmly. "This will certainly shake up all of the Houses!" At once, he and his party moved to join with Baron Milan, and the two men began chatting, while their wives exchanged words as well.

Lida and Rayna clung to their brother and to their fiancés as well. Zdenka and Jarka felt rather embarrassed. Their simple dresses looked awful compared to these elegant ladies.

"Say, come on. I have a sight that I'd like you eight to see — well all of you ought to see this sight," Zoran interrupted everyone. "This way; let's step outside the Archmage Oldrich's tower." Zdenka took Zoran's arm, as his sisters finally let go of him. A minute later, the large group stood outside the five story, plain looking tower, there at the northern edge of Brn. They were not alone. Everyone who lived in Brn was also outside staring up at the sky around the tower.

Thirteen gold dragons, the sunlight reflecting off of their shiny skin, flew in wide circles around the tower. Such a sight had never before been seen anywhere in the entire Federation of Planets! Some soared up high and then dived, others did barrel rolls. Two of the smaller forms swooped down onto the only empty patch in the crowded streets, there just before Zoran and the tower. After landing, their forms morphed into the two young Archmages.

"Allow me to introduce to all of you to Archmages Emil and Renata Vogler, twin gold dragons," Zoran spoke formally as the twins, grinning, walked up to the group.

"That is the most beautiful sight that I have ever seen, Renata!" Rayna spoke first. "You and the others — why you are just beautiful. I had no idea."

"Indeed, spectacular flying," Uncle Milan added. "Say, can we talk, Archmage Emil? I have a million questions I'd like to ask." Baron Viktor stood beside Baron Milan, eager to hear Emil's answer.

"Of course, though our father is more experienced in dealing with humans. Why don't you chat with him?" Emil cleverly sidestepped the questioning. A spell cast, Aldrich flew down, landing on the street. He morphed into his human form and came up to his son. "Dad, these barons have a lot of questions for us. I figured you would know better how to answer them."

Aldrich grinned; his son was doing just what he had asked of him. "Certainly, barons, come, I understand that Archmage Oldrich has refreshments awaiting us."

General Janos returned to stand guard over the Circle of Ascension. He fully expected that many other barons may come to check out this new Circle, just as soon as they discovered the new sky blue thread addition to their own Circles. The others headed into the first floor meeting room, where the Archmage was awaiting them — she had had her staff prepare various breads, teas, and juices.

"Please, barons, baronesses, dukes, accept my humble hospitality. I have but a simple, frugal tower," Archmage Oldrich said in her usual soft manner. "Now if you will excuse me, my body is a bit tired. I will leave you to your discussions." After the men rose and thanked her, she left.

"Baron Zoran, we have much to discuss, but I would like the opportunity to meet Aldrich first," Uncle Milan explained.

"Go ahead, uncle; it is not every day that you get to talk firsthand with a gold dragon," Zoran teased. Zdenka shot him a grin.

"First, where do you all come from?"

"From a planet called Voss."

"How? I mean do you have means of travel, such as our Shadow Walk?"

"Something that is similar, I believe. I've never been given a Shadow Walk so I cannot say for sure. We can only travel between planets with which we are familiar. Archmage Oldrich was my teacher many years ago. I am familiar with Adapazan."

"Well, it would be my honor to give you a Shadow Walk, say to my planet of Gladno later today," Baron Milan replied.

"And I would be honored to also take you to my world of Valtr," Baron Viktor added quickly, unwilling to be left out. Too much was at stake here.

"Excellent, then I will have a way to compare our travel with yours," Aldrich replied.

"How is it that you need to come to Adapazan? To learn magic?" asked Baron

Viktor.

"Yes and no. We golds prize two things above all others: gems and magic. Our lives are devoted to the acquisition of large gems and learning all the magic we can. Well, we also tend to collect magical items, but those are scarce. So, yes, I brought our twins here to learn magic from Archmage Oldrich. She is a good teacher and it has paid off handsomely. Both our twins have achieved Archmage status, something seldom achieved among golds. That is the yes part."

"There is a vastly more important reason for our coming to Adapazan. Back on Voss, I am afraid to say this, but we have overpopulated our world. There are virtually no hoofed animals left on Voss. Slowly, we are all starving to death. I pointed this out to our High Council over four years ago, but they chose to ignore my dire warning. Sofie and I were barely able to get enough antelope to feed our twins. Zoran has kindly allowed more of us to come and live here where food is plentiful and abundant."

"He is also allowing some of us to establish gem cutting businesses here in Brn. You see, we mine for raw gems and then we cut them into exquisite stones. Golds are particularly skilled at this. He has kindly given us the mining rights to the inaccessible areas of the mountains around Brn Province, where we dig for our both homes and gems. In time, the humans here will come to discover the high quality work that we do. I expect that this will be a very profitable venture for both our races."

A totally unexpected phenomenon occurred within Zoran's mind. He suddenly knew that Baron Aldo Monda of the agrarian planet of Cosma wanted to arrive at his Circle! "Excuse, me, but Baron Aldo wants to come here. I must go meet him."

"Allow him to join us. Also allow Baron Tom Witherspoon and Baron Etienne Gervaise to come; they are our allies," Uncle Milan hastily interjected his wishes.

"I would not allow your enemies to come, if I were you," Uncle Viktor added. "Specifically, Bogdan Clav, Cheng Meerong, Carwyn Alun, Eckhard Hadwig, and your father. The others are neutral."

"Thanks, I have to talk with you about the politics soon, I can see that!" Zoran replied. He and Zdenka left to meet with Baron Aldo. No sooner than Baron Aldo materialized within Zoran's new Circle of Ascension than his senses detected a request from Barons Tom and Etienne. Zoran smiled, he guessed that his uncle had alerted his allies to the possibility of a new Circle appearing. He allowed both men to materialize, but wondered if he would always know who was going to arrive at his Circle.

Shock, surprise, wonderment, excitement, and keen interest shown from the faces of the three men as they shook hands with Zoran and Zdenka. Their faces flickered from one expression to the other, rapid fire. Baron Aldo was in his fifties, a tall, thin man with a black moustache. His planet, Cosma, was primarily an agrarian one. Baron Tom likewise was in his fifties. He was short and stout, but his blue eyes missed nothing. Like Aldo, he ruled over a planet mostly devoted to the growing of crops, Terra. Both Terra and Cosma exported vast amounts of grain to the other planets. Baron Etienne was in his mid-forties. His planet, Gonda, consisted mostly of rolling grasslands filled with horses. Yes, these were primarily horsemen; Etienne was thin with long blonde hair and even smelled of horses.

Zoran gave them his welcome address, introducing the Zars and explaining their roles in construction of the Circle. "We owe everything to Warlord Mikolas of Sholov Province. He discovered Bandar Zar's secret chamber beneath his fortress and commissioned the Zars to build him a Circle. Unfortunately, he was killed this past summer by Baron Kazimir, but we rescued the Zars and the documents, keeping them out of the clutches of my dad. I assure you, Baron Kazimir will never get his hands on them!" All three men replied that this was a very wise decision on Zoran's part.

"Come, you must see the sight of our Circle's protectors. We have over a dozen gold dragons here providing protection for us and the tower." He and Zdenka took the three men outside to view the dragons that were still flying around the general area of the tower. All three men were most impressed with the dragons, especially when Zoran told them that Barons Milan and Viktor were inside talking with them. They insisted on joining the pair, as Zoran knew that they would.

"Ah there you are, Tom, Etienne, Aldo, I would like you to meet Aldrick Vogler, a gold dragon from Voss!" Baron Milan greeted the three as they entered.

Just then, Zoran's Circle commanded his attention. He hastily excused himself, and Zdenka and he raced down the stairs. "Bogdan and Kazimir want permission to come. Damn them anyway."

"Perhaps you should allow them to come and see that we have Archmages and dragons protecting us," Zdenka advised cautiously. "After all, if they see them with their own eyes, they will believe that they are real. Kazimir already knows how devastating two young ones can be."

"You are probably right, dear. Just stay on your guard. I don't trust these men, not even remotely!" Zoran told General Janos who was coming and to be prepared. Janos gave a wry smile, and Zoran realized that the General would be savoring this meeting with his ex-Baron.

The two barons arrived at the center of this new Circle. "You!" exclaimed Kazimir angrily, as he recognized his son and realized that his son now was his rival here on Adapazan!

"Hello Baron Kazimir, Baron Bogdan," Zoran said quietly, still unwilling to acknowledge his familial relationship with this man. "Welcome to the House of the Free People of Brn and Adapazan. You are in Archmage Oldrich's tower, guarded by a half dozen Archmages, to say nothing of all the many Mages here. General Janos Lavos is in charge of our security, along with over a dozen gold dragons. At the moment, the dragons are giving us a flying demonstration. If you two will follow me, I will show you our dragons, which live with us. I believe that Baron Kazimir knows all too well about gold dragons."

"Damn you, Zoran! It was you! You murdered your own brother!" spit flew from the violently shaking, raging man.

"Sorry, Baron, I cannot take credit for that. You murdered your own son by your ill-conceived war against free people. I didn't lay a finger on Radek nor any of your soldiers. I was too busy rescuing the Zars and the ancient documents of Bandar Zar, which told us how to build this new Circle of Ascension. Warlord Mikolas was about to have his own Circle, when you attacked. His dying wish was for me to carry on and build the first new Circle in centuries. With his financial backing, I have done so. Ah, there are the fine gold dragons."

Both men stared up at the five story stone tower, non-descript in all ways, except for the many golden forms flying around it high in the sky. Snow covered mountains lay behind them, outlining their huge forms. "I can have as many gold dragons come to protect us as I desire," Zoran added for emphasis. "Besides breathing fire and shooting electrical bolts, they are also very competent magic users. Two are my dear Archmage friends. I am giving you both and your allies fair warning. Do not attack Brn Province or any of the other Wild Lands of Adapazan. If you do, I will summon hundreds of these fine dragons to incinerate your entire army and then your castles. Do I make myself clear? If you send assassins here, I will feed them to these flying creatures, though one man does not make for more than a cookie snack with these fellows. They have such an appetite. I guess we would too if we were a hundred feet long."

"Son, how could you do this? Why did you not consult with me, your father? I hear that you are in cahoots with those spineless so called do-gooders! They cannot protect you. You and I, we could have been the most powerful men in the entire Federation! Son, it is still not too late to change your ill-thought allegiance," Baron Kazimir attempted to reason with his son one last time. He was terrified of the winged creatures, having seen his army decimated in minutes by just two of them.

"Someone has to stand up for the free people that remain on Adapazan and stop you from turning them into your slaves. Someone has to stop the march of your army across our world. Your days of conquest here on Adapazan have ended. We are entering a new age. I will not hesitate for an instant to sick my dragons on any army that comes marching across the Wild Lands. I give you my word that I will not attack you, your castle, or the lands that you now control, Baron Kazimir — that is, not unless you provoke me by sending assassins here or sending forth another army to conquer the Wild Lands or Brn."

"Baron Bogdan, just so you know, dragons can also Shadow Walk. If you try anything, we will come to Rehor and feast on your men, women, and castle. If you send out assassins to harm my sisters or their fiancés, my retribution will be swift and final. Do I make myself clear?"

"Why should I send out assassins, Baron Vladislov?" the cagy, fat Baron Bogdan whined. "I have no quarrel with you or your sisters. It has been made abundantly clear that Kazimir cannot control his own children. Might I ask, was it you that stopped all of the magic from occurring there at the Ceremony of Passing for your mother, right before everything went dark?"

"Yes, I saw that such was needed. I would not allow my mother's funeral to be so disgraced by men who cannot hold their tempers."

"Ah, excellent, lad, excellent indeed. You prevented a good deal of bloodshed that day. You have earned my respect, young Baron Vladislov. Well done indeed, Archmage," Baron Bogdan feigned admiration with a coy smile. "We should meet one day and discuss the future. Baron Kazimir, we ought not take up more of young Baron Vladislov's time. Thank you for showing us your new Circle of Ascension."

Zoran followed them back into the tower and basement, verifying that they both did leave and not try some trickery, such as going invisible and attempting to kill. When they were gone, Zdenka commented, "Well, I believe that went well, Zoran. Both men realized just how dangerous it will be to them if they try anything, don't you think? Bogdan seemed in far better humor today than he was at the Ceremony of Passing for your mother."

"He's trying hard not to totally alienate me," Zoran replied. "You are right; Kazimir's anger got turned into fear. Maybe he will leave us all alone."

"Son, I would not count on that," General Janos broke in, "always expect the vilest treachery from those men." Zoran smiled; he knew that was true.

When the two and the Zars rejoined the five barons and Aldrick, lunch was being served. Zoran found all six had definitely become friends. Aldrick excused himself; he had a business meeting with the Mayor. Lida changed the topic from business to what interested her and Rayna more, their marriages. "Say, Zoran, Duke Leo and I are going to marry next month, on the twenty-fifth of January. Uncle Milan is hosting our wedding, since mom has passed away."

Not wanting to be left out, Rayna added, "And Duke Stefan and I are going to marry at the same time. Lida and I are combining our weddings. Uncle Milan has offered to host our wedding as well. We're all going to go to his palace on Gladno, a double wedding!"

Baron Milan chuckled, "It is more cost effective for me to host one wedding celebration."

"Yes, and I am quite glad that he's doing it," Baron Viktor teased him. Duke Leo and Duke Stefan looked very pleased.

"So when are you and Zdenka marrying?" Lida asked what she really wanted to know. "I know that this is none of your big sister's business, but Uncle Milan has agreed to host your wedding with ours. We can make it a trio, that is, if it's not too soon for you, little brother."

Zdenka flushed and looked at Zoran. "Dear, what do you think? Shall we take up this offer? We are done with our magic training now. If you think this is too soon or if you'd rather marry here in Brn, just say so."

Before she could reply, Baron Milan spoke softly, "Zoran, Zdenka, your safety is vitally important. I have an ulterior motive in hosting these weddings: your safety. On Gladno, I can guarantee your safety. Here in Brn, I cannot and neither can Baron Viktor or the others. Besides, your mother was my dear sister. I would like to honor her memory by giving you the best possible special wedding day. Please, if only in the memory of my sister."

"That's fine with me," Zdenka timidly replied. "I would love to share our special day with Lida and Rayna. It's just that I don't have any appropriate clothes to wear, you know, fancy court dresses and such, and I don't know a thing about fancy weddings and what I am supposed to do and all that. Honesty, I am totally ignorant of courtly life. I'm sorry to let you all down so badly. I'm just a forest archer, not a courtier."

"Dear, that is not a problem at all," Rayna hastily replied. "We can get you all the things you will need. We can teach you what you need to know. Please, let us do this thing for you and our brother. Trust us Archmage Zdenka; you are hardly a mere forest archer. Besides, I think Uncle Milan and Baron Viktor wants Zoran to come and spend some serious time with them. Please say yes, Zdenka, please," she begged.

Zoran laughed; memories of Rayna's pleadings came back to him. She always got her way when she tilted her head and formed this particular facial expression, like some little angel. Who could resist? Certainly not Zdenka, who grinned. "Okay, you win, Rayna. If Zoran is willing, so am I."

"Good, good, that's settled then," Uncle Milan seemed relieved, Zoran noted. "Now then, Zoran, we have an awful lot to discuss. It is vitally important that you come to Gladno and spend some time with us. Bring the Zars with you, please. Can you possibly come say next Saturday and plan to spend at least a month with us? That will give the women time to help Zdenka learn what is expected of her. After all, Zoran, at the next High Council meeting in March you and she will become Baron and Baroness. She needs to know what is expected of a baroness."

"Yes, Uncle Milan, we will come for a month. Honestly, I do need to talk with you — all of you barons. I built this new Circle in haste, and now I find that I have walked into more problems than I know how to solve! I am in need of some serious advice and soon."

Baron Viktor added, "Yes, some will say that you built the Circle in haste. History tells us that the original barons first constructed a secure castle with many fortifications to protect a Circle of Ascension and only then built their Circles. You've rather done it the other way around. It is a risky gamble, but because of the Archmages and the dragons, son, you may well be successful. Yet, we all do need to discuss many things. Thank you for coming."

After the lunch, the barons took their leave, returning to their worlds and castles. Yet, the visitors and inquires did not stop. Slowly, the other barons became aware of the seventeenth thread now embedded within their own Circles of Ascension. Naturally inquisitive, they also attempted to Shadow Walk to see for themselves. These barons were mostly in the neutral category — those who chose not to take either side of the two warring factions.

Zoran stuck to his earlier decision and allowed only the baron to visit, blocking all attempts by the barons to bring additional security forces along with themselves. Hours dragged on endlessly, as one by one, the other barons visited. Zoran and Zdenka played host to Baron Hinto Yamitiwa of Isi, Baron Adolf Ebbe of Gerde, Baron Alvaro Cencion of Alta, Baron Bran Ahern of Mauve, Baron Aryeh Makeda of Chana, and Baron Hajime Yoko of Asami. The other three barons in league with Baron Kazimir also desired to visit: Baron Cheng Meerog of Jing, Baron Eckhard Hadwig of Dietmar, and Baron Carwyn Alun of Anwyn. To these latter three, Zoran also issued his stern warning about sending assassins to Brn, threatening devastating retaliation if they did.

Night had come when the last of the barons finally left. "Well, time to eat. I'm starved. That was the last of the barons," Zoran announced. "Now they have all discovered that it is possible to have new Circles of Ascension and that I am their newest baron." The group sat around the dining room table, along with all of the Mages and those still in training.

General Janos added his thoughts, "Emil, Renata, I must say that your kind certainly did a fabulous job today. Just seeing all of you flying around has done more to safeguard this place than anything else. I know that word has spread throughout the Federation about what happened to Baron Kazimir's army when he took Sholov

Province. You and your folks may not have to actually fight against humans again; you are perhaps the most powerful deterrent I have ever known. These barons will think twice about attacking Brn. This may well be the dawn of a new found peace on Adapazan. I certainly hope so."

Archmage Nadia spoke quietly as usual, "General Janos, I certainly hope so, but today's deterrent may well become tomorrow's combatants. On another matter, students, I wish to take this opportunity to announce to you all that I am retiring. Yes, I will finish those of you that are still in training, though I am going to pick up the pace. When spring comes, I wish to retire, plant a few flowers, and enjoy the few days that remain unto me."

Zdenka looked stunned, as did Zoran. Neither could believe her. What would this tower be without this powerhouse Archmage? Zdenka looked at her with pleading eyes. She saw them and smiled. "Yes, I know that this comes as a shock to all of you, but seventy-six years is a long time. My health has steadily deteriorated. I am barely able to get around. It is time to pass the mantle of training others in the art of magic on to another."

She continued, "Even though I will be retired, you can still count on me to help defend, if such is needed. Now then, it is customary for a retiring Archmage pass along his or her tower and responsibilities to another. I choose to do so at this time. I have given the matter of my successor a great deal of thought and have reached my decision. Zdenka, I wish you to step into my shoes and become the new Archmage for Brn Province. I give you my tower and all that goes with it, if you will accept the responsibility of teaching others magic. Your first action will be the usual spring picking, choose only four this time, since you are just beginning. What say you?"

Zdenka choked on her ale. "Me? You are giving this place to me? I am to teach others magic? Oh my! Am I really qualified to do all this? Are you sure? Others are so much better than I am at this. I mean, Zoran, he knows nearly all the spells."

"Yes, I am sure, Zdenka. While Zoran does know more spells, he will have his hands full with other matters. I have watched you for almost a year now. You have the dedication, the passion, the patience, and the skills to step into my shoes, dear. You are conservative and not prone to taking risks. Karel has not the patience, though he has the skills. Emil and Renata are dragons and have their own lives and goals that are not human ones. I could not ask this of them. No, Zdenka, you are perfect for the job. If you will not accept this, I will have to look outside of Brn for another Archmage to take over here."

"If you are certain that I can do this, then I gladly will accept, Archmage Nadia, but I really don't know what all I must do," Zdenka replied softly, a bit shocked with the surprise news and more than a little overwhelmed by it.

"Excellent. We can talk later tonight. Your duties will not begin until the first Saturday in April. We have several months to get you prepared. Besides, I will be staying nearby in Brn, so I can help you with anything that you need."

Jarka rose, holding her mug, she called out, "Hail one and all. I give you your new Archmage of Brn Province, Archmage Zdenka Lavos!" Everyone followed her lead, rising and toasting her, much to her embarrassment. Then, the celebration began in earnest.

Later, while Zdenka met privately with Archmage Nadia, Zoran took the opportunity to chat with Brother Jiri and Priestess Anezka. "Say what's up with my eyes changing colors anyway?" He began with the obvious physical change.

"Well," Anezka explained in a non-committal manner, "I think that when a Circle becomes tied to its originator, this is part of the process. It identifies you as its owner."

"Yes, but Baron Kazimir's eyes are not red and his Circle's color is red," Zoran countered.

"I believe that this color change only happens when it is first created and activated. None of the current barons' eye color matches their Circle's color. Just be glad that you didn't choose purple," she teased him.

"Yeh, right. Another thing, every time someone has tried to Shadow Walk to the Circle, I have felt their coming in my mind. It is almost like I have control over whether they can materialize on my Circle or not. Do you know anything about this phenomenon?" Zoran asked what had been puzzling him since his uncle's arrival.

"Hum, well yes, Zoran. We don't know much about just what all the effects are on new owners. You see, there hasn't been a new one for ages and, well, I need to study Bandar's documents further. I suspect that there are going to be a number of very unique things between you and your Circle that are not present with today's barons and their Circles," she backed off from giving him a direct answer. "Do let me know of anything else that seems to be going on between it and you, though," she added hopefully.

Brother Jiri added, "Zoran, we should go over the routine protections that every baron places on and around their Circle." The three spent an hour setting all of them up. Brother Jiri made doubly sure that Zoran knew what to do, giving him a crash course in being a baron with a Circle of Ascension.

The next day, Zoran handled his promise to the twin dragons. "Okay, there are sixteen planets in the Federation, we are on Adapazan now. I will take you to visit the other fifteen now, but we ought to go there invisible. We don't want to attract undo attention. I mostly just know the locations of the various ruling baron's castles so we'll arrive around them. As you know, Adapazan is mostly a hilly and mountainous planet. First, stop is Rehor, which is very like Adapazan in many ways, hilly and mountainous. Hold my hands and I will Shadow Walk us there." Emil and Renata took hold of his hands, and Zoran stepped into the blackness of the spatial void between the worlds. He focused on a grey-white dot, which slowly grew into the world of Rehor. They arrived outside the capital city and Baron Bogdan Clav's castle.

Next, they visited the plains planet of Isi, Baron Hinto Yamitiwa's realm. Here, the twins saw vast grassland plains and many four legged creatures roaming the lands, perfect for dragons. The agrarian planet of Terra was next, home of Baron Tom Witherspoon. As far as their eyes could see, neat crop rows spread out, small stone walls demarcated each field. From there, Zoran took the twins to the swamp planet of Jing, where Baron Cheng Meerong ruled. The castle rose from the many bogs. A low fog hung over the surface of the watery landscape as far as they could see.

Baron Viktor Pavel's world of Valtr was next, a world of vast grass covered rolling hills with horses in abundance. This was a land of superb horsemen. Planet

Gladno, home of Baron Milan Matous, was next on the tour. Gladno was a heavily forested world with both extensive pine and deciduous forests covering the landscape. Forest fires were the biggest worry on this world. From there, Zoran took the twins to the icy and snowy world of Dietmar, home of Baron Eckhard Hadwig. Neither twin wanted to spend any time here, for it was far too cold and barren.

Zoran chuckled as he then took them to the opposite type of world, Anwyn, a desert world. Here, much of the world was vast arid regions; deserts abounded, home of Baron Carwyn Alun. Indeed, the twins laughed, realizing that Zoran purposely went to the desert world after the icy world. Now they arrived on Cosma, another agrarian world. Once more, vast cultivated fields stretched out before them from their vantage point near Baron Aldo Monda's castle. The vast grassy plains of Gonda, home of the horseman Baron Etienne Gervaise was their next stop. Again, horses predominated the scene.

The mountainous world of Gerde, home of Baron Adolf Ebbe, was their next stop. Emil speculated that many fine gems might be found on this world. Baron Alvaro Cencion's world of Alta was next. Here was a hilly world, filled with many hoofers, as Renata put it — a fine place to dine. Zoran grinned. The heavily forested world of Maeve, home of Baron Bran Ahern, was their next stop. The desert world of Chana and Baron Aryeh Makeda came next, but they spent little time here as well. Neither twin liked deserts — no hoofers. Finally, Zoran took them to see the water world of Asami and Baron Hajime Yoko. This strange world consisted of vast waters dotted with millions of islands. There w no substantially large continents anywhere on Asami. The twins were not impressed with this world either. Then, he returned to Adapazan, showing the twins how to find Brn Province.

"Thank you Baron Archmage Zoran," Emil said formally when they had returned to their tower. "We are now unique among our kind. We know of more worlds than anyone else. Thank you very much." Zoran wondered if this was such a good idea, showing them all sixteen worlds, but it could not be helped; he had promised them this tour.

"Yes, thank you, Zoran. You have given us new hope. One day I will mate, and now I feel that I can bring a child into the universe. I had resolved never to do that because we were starving on Voss. Now, there is so much to choose from — so many places where our kind can live in peace and with full bellies," Renata added.

"I'm glad for you. I just wish that we would have known about your plight sooner. Ah well, I think Zdenka is waiting for me," he replied, a twinkle in his eye.

Chapter 17 Court Education

"What are we supposed to wear?" Zdenka asked Zoran, early the next morning. Lines of worry creased her forehead. Today, they were going to travel to Gladno to spend a month with his Uncle Milan and be married. She was very nervous and overly self-conscious, worried that she could not possible fit in with the Baron and Baroness, let alone their court.

"Love, I have no idea either. All this is new to me as well. When I was growing up around the courts, I paid it little attention. We represent the free people of Brn and the Wild Lands. There aren't any fancy courts here, so let's you and I just be ourselves, representatives of those we are protecting. They can have all their stuffy, fancy court etiquette; we'll be ourselves."

"Well, that's easy for you to say, Zoran, but you know that all eyes will be upon us, watching our every move. You don't want them thinking that we are nothing but a bunch of hicks — that cannot be good," she replied.

"I know, dear. We'll just be as honest as we can and be ourselves. The rest will take care of itself. I know my sisters will help you a lot — probably doting over you, if I know Lida and Rayna. Honestly, they really do know more about court and etiquette that I do, so I expect that they will be giving me lessons as well." This seemed to mollify Zdenka somewhat and the two finished their packing.

Shortly, the Zars joined them at the Circle in the basement along with Jarka, who was accompanying them to Gladno. Zdenka had insisted that at least one other ought to come with them, just in case of trouble. Zoran chose Jarka because of her particular skills, leaving General Janos Lavos and Archmage Karel in charge of protecting their Circle during their absence. As Jarka trotted into the room, Priestess Anezka noticed that she was armed to the teeth with daggers. "Expecting trouble, Jarka?" she asked slightly worried.

"Never can tell. I always go to strange places fully prepared for the worst. Safer that way," she said coyly. "After all, politics run the barons, not family ties. Okay, I'm all set."

Zoran took a hold of Zdenka and Jarka's hands, while they in turn held onto Jiri and Anezka. He stepped into his Circle, felt its power flowing through his body and stepped into the blackness. Soon the small greenish orb of Gladno appeared, growing steadily larger. Vast green continents became discernable. Zoran homed in on the largest land mass. Shortly, the heavily forested region of Beroun appeared before them, followed by the large city of Novary. Shortly thereafter, the huge stone Castle Matous rose up like a gray spire amid the dense pine forest and city. White snow covered the ground, contrasting with the green and browns and gray stone. As the castle grew larger, Zoran made for the arrival patio on the outside of the second story of his Uncle's castle. They were standing there awaiting his arrival, he noted.

"Welcome to Castle Matous, Baron Archmage Zoran, Archmage Zdenka, Mage Jarka, Brother Jiri and Priestess Anezka Zar. Welcome indeed," Uncle Milan called out officially. Rayna and Lida rushed to hug their brother, while their boyfriends, Duke Leo and Duke Stefan, grinned and stood officially beside their fathers, Baron

Milan and Baron Viktor Pavel. Zoran sensed that the two barons wanted to hold lengthy discussions with himself and the Zars.

"Zoran, Lida and I have it all worked out," Rayna bubbled with excitement. At long last all three were free from the strangle hold of their despised father. Life soared anew within both young women. "First, we are going to take the girls shopping and get them all a whole wardrobe, suitable for the Courts. We will be getting you outfits as well, little brother. You can't go around looking like this, not if you want to impress the other barons. We are also going to get both of your wedding outfits as well. Lida and I want to thank you for saving our lives, and this is one little thing that we can do for you. The barons want to talk with you and Brother Jiri right away. We will all meet together for supper. Lida and I want you to really get to know our beaus; after all, only twenty-one more days and we will be officially married! So you can't say no, little brother!"

Zoran chuckled, "How can I get a word in edgewise, sis? Okay, okay. Just remember that Zdenka and Jarka will need lots of assistance picking out proper dresses and such. Please, don't get me any purple shirts." The twins giggled, knowing Zoran disliked purple.

A few minutes later, Zoran, Brother Jiri, and Priestess Anezka sat in a formal conference room with the two barons. On the wall was a map of the Federation of Planets. A servant brought in pastries and tea and left them to their meeting. Zoran watched as Uncle Milan cast several protective spells on the room, making sure that nothing that was said could be overheard. "Now, we have complete privacy," Baron Milan began.

"Zoran, we have much to discuss and work out. However, Viktor and I do not wish to waste the Zars' time on your matters, so we are going to discuss some matters that concern them first. After that, they are free to visit my castle or return to Brn or whatever they desire." Zoran nodded, but he suspected what the two men were about to ask.

"Brother Jiri, your discoveries and your successful construction of a new Circle of Ascension is perhaps the greatest achievement in several centuries! You both will be famous, of that there is no doubt. However — and I am now speaking on behalf of probably every baron in the Federation — do you have any plans to construct more Circles? Are you willing to construct more Circles?"

Brother Jiri, having long known this day of reckoning was coming, cleared his throat. "Such knowledge should not be kept from others. The answer to both is yes. Yet, my wife and I wish to retain control over for whom we create new Circles of Ascension. We would rather die than build a new one for Baron Kazimir and several others — those barons whom you oppose."

The sparkle of delight in both barons' eyes told Zoran everything. "Excellent, excellent, Brother Jiri," Baron Milan replied. "Baron Viktor and I both would like a new Circle of Ascension on our worlds. It is my fondest wish that you accept our joint proposal to construct ours as soon as possible. Undoubtedly at the March High Council meeting, you will be besieged with requests from many other barons. We would like to be the next to receive your precious gift of new Circles."

Priestess Anezka chuckled, "We have already guessed that you would be asking this of us. Yes, we will build each of you a new Circle of Ascension as the next two that we create."

"Superb! Thank you!" Baron Viktor exclaimed, unable to restrain his enthusiasm and relief.

Brother Jiri nodded and added, "Of course, there is going to be a charge for our services. The raw materials run about fifty thousand gold coins."

"Yes, of course, we must discuss your remuneration," Baron Milan replied. "Let me add, that while in our services, you will have as much protection as I give to myself and my immediate family. Your safety will be our prime consideration."

"Thank you. I was abducted and nearly beaten to death by one of Baron Kazimir's assassins, while I was building Zoran's. We both appreciate and need top quality protection. War Lord Mikolas donated five hundred thousand gold to get Zoran's Circle built. We feel that it is only fair to his memory that we charge that amount for additional Circles. Will this be acceptable? You see, we owe everything to Baron Zoran and will be giving him half of our proceeds as our humble way of thanking him and his companions."

"What?" Zoran exclaimed, shocked and surprised by this turn. "Brother Jiri, that is an enormous sum! You and your wife are doing all of the work. Surely, a lesser sum is more appropriate."

"Not at all, my dear friend. Without you and your friends' timely assistance on two occasions, I and my wife would not be here. We owe you more than we can ever repay. Besides, we both know that you are desperate for funds to support your new Circle. You have a castle and fortifications to build. This is the very least that we can do for you. Please." Zoran nodded and gave him a hug.

Baron Viktor spoke up, "It is a fair price, Brother Jiri. We were anticipating that you would be asking far, far more than this amount. Frankly, we were ready to pay nearly any price that you would ask! Speaking for Milan and myself, we wholeheartedly support your generous offer to Baron Zoran. Indeed, we have spent many hours working out how he can best defend his new Circle. He's gone about it completely backwards, you see. First, you build the castle and fortifications that will house the precious Circle of Ascension. Then, you build the Circle within this mighty protection. I must say, his Circle is going to be tough to defend. It is merely a simple mage tower. No offense to Archmage Oldrich, but her tower is just that, a simple tower, easily breached and difficult to defend."

"Right. With your donations of this magnitude," Baron Milan added, "we can rest easier knowing that Zoran will be better able to defend his new tower. Well done, Brother Jiri. How soon would you like to start? Viktor and I tossed a coin and I won. Unless you object, you may build a new Circle for me first and when it is done, build Viktor's. I will have your payment for you later this afternoon."

"My, Anezka, they seem awfully anxious to have new Circles, now don't they?" Brother Jiri teased. She smiled, but Zoran expected that they would be asked to build more just as soon as possible. "Yes, honestly, barons, when we came here today, we fully expected that you would be asking us to build you some Circles. We are prepared to begin at once."

"Fabulous, fabulous. Say, how long does it take to build one of these Circles?" Baron Milan asked.

"Well, overall, not counting the time wasted dismantling the half finished one at Mikolas' fortification and moving it, I spent nearly a year making it. However, now that I know what I am doing, I expect that I can have one built in four to six months, maybe less. A lot depends on how fast I can acquire the raw materials needed and so forth."

"Excellent! I will have my engineering staff at your disposal. Let them know what you need, and they will obtain it immediately. If we work together, perhaps the time requirements will be lessened. If I am not too presumptuous, I have an engineer and security detail that are ready to take you to the site. I am having my new Circle built on the opposite side of this continent, where my son and his family reside. There, you will find everything in readiness for your work. I will join you there this evening." After some additional chat, the Zars left to go see the new location and begin their preparations.

"Now then, Zoran, we have much to discuss," Baron Milan began. It was just the three barons sitting at the table. "Viktor and I have given this considerable thought. Your Circle has just upset the balance of power, tipping it over to our side from the evil barons' side. You can expect that your father and his allies will attempt everything in their power to undo what you have done. After all, if your Circle stands and Lida lives, Baron Kazimir's reign of tyranny over Adapazan is ended. Not in well over a century has a baron lost his dominion as Kazimir appears to have done. Believe me; they will stop at nothing to regain it."

"As far as his heir is concerned, he's locked into his proclamation. That cannot be undone, except if Lida dies before he does. We five — you have our word that we will spare nothing to protect Lida and Rayna from assassins. Both of your sisters must remain alive until Kazimir's death."

Zoran visibly relaxed. "Thank you, thank you. That is my greatest fear — that my sisters would suffer because of what I have done. I know that you will do your best. Not because they are becoming your daughters-in-law, but politically."

Both men grinned. Viktor said, "He is getting smarter by the minute!"

"Down to business then, Zoran. You need a fortress and castle built there in Brn immediately," Milan continued. "You need an army to defend it. An army needs military supplies. Brn is really an isolated area, primitive compared to all other capital cities within the Federation. If Kazimir and his allies launch an invasion toward Brn, attacking either the warlord provinces of Lesy or Kin, while your dragons could fly there to oppose them, there is little that you can do to stop them. To get to you overland, they would have to go through Lesy, Radim, and Veklov Provinces or go through Kin, Tehov, and Valy Provinces. The more direct route thorough Orlovia is out because of the blocked passage from Sholov Province. Son, there is no way those warlords could withstand the shock troops of Kazimir and his allies. You are facing monumental problems."

"He is understating it," Viktor added solemnly. "It's grim indeed. We've been working out how we can help since we last saw you. Son, you have allies in this. Would you like the honor, Milan?" he asked, a twinkle in his eye. Zoran wondered what these two men had in mind.

Milan nodded, and spoke, "Zoran, your allies want you to have a chance to hold on to your Circle. It is in our best interests that you do — balance of power shift and all that that entails. We've worked out a scheme which we think will give you the best odds. First must come the construction of a suitable fortification and castle near your tower. Now ordinarily, if we had our engineers design one and then see to its construction, one would expect the most basic shell to be done in perhaps ten years, while its completion would be more like thirty years down the line or more, depending upon the sophistication of its construction and availability of supplies and workers."

"But we don't have either the money or ten years, Uncle," Zoran protested, wondering what Milan was going to propose.

"Indeed, son, we do not. Baron Tom Witherspoon of Terra, Baron Aldo Monda of Cosma, Baron Etienne Gervaise of Gonda, and we have agreed on a plan. All five of us will send our engineers and all of our construction crews to assist you in building your fortification and castle. We will cover all of the expense of our crews and the construction costs. Later on, as your funds come in, you can then set about a repayment plan. Our engineers assure us that in one year's time, you will have a basic defensible shell ready to go and within two — three at the outside — it will be finished. That is, unless you opt for anything really fancy. We're talking a basic fortress that can withstand a siege and a habitable castle safe enough to protect a Circle of Ascension."

The shocked look on Zoran's face told the two men everything. Both knew that they had Zoran right where they wanted him! "I — I don't know what to say! This is, well it is more than I ever dreamed would be possible! Yes, yes, I agree. I will do everything I can to repay you as soon as physically possible! Thank you! Thank you from all of the free people of Adapazan!"

"Good. Good. Now then, before we dive into such details, the matter of an army must be discussed. We five believe that in spite of your dragons, Kazimir and his allies may try to take your Brn by force of arms, probably coming from the south through Lesy, Radim, and Veklov Provinces. The climate is far warmer than the northern route. Again, your allies have asked me to present the following proposition to you. If they attempt to bring an army overland to attack Brn, we five Barons promise to send large armies to come to your defense."

Zoran grinned, "Politically sound. You cannot risk losing this sudden shift in the power balance. If Kazimir comes after me, you have to do everything you can to stop him."

"Told you that he is wising up," Viktor teased Milan. Both men chuckled.

"So what do I have to give up to get this guarantee of support of five armies if we are attacked? There must be a price — besides being politically correct."

"Well, son, of course there is. We five Barons wish two things from you. First, at the High Council meetings, we wish that you would side with us as often as you ethically can. We need your vote. Second, we five Barons wish that you would intercede on our behalf with the dragons. You see, we five would love to have a flock of dragons on our worlds — dragons that would help us defend our lands. We know that the dragons on Voss are starving to death, and we would like to offer some of them sanctuary on our worlds, as long as we have amiable, workable relations, that is."

Zoran laughed, he was taken completely by surprise. "You want your dragons too!" He roared. "Soon, everyone will want my dragons. I cannot imagine why? My two dragon friends only eliminated some two thousand shock troops in a half hour without getting the slightest scratch on themselves. Could that be why?" Milan and Viktor now saw that Zoran was teasing them, both men joined in his laughter.

"Of course, son, why else?" Milan finally replied. "After all, you have just introduced a new unlimited weapon of sorts. I know that this sounds crass and callous of us. Dragons, well the ones that we've met, are highly intelligent creatures. It is just that we would like such allies on our side. Besides, if conditions on Voss are as Aldrick says, they are all starving to death. Think of it as a humanitarian action on your part."

"You have me in a box and you both know it, don't you," Zoran replied a bit testily. "They are not animals or lizards that you can discard when you don't need them. They are more like another highly intelligent race of beings — to be treated as such. Besides, if you eventually wish them to leave, you will have an awfully hard time of it. They are at the top of the food chain, so to speak. If you do not treat them fairly and with great respect, you are likely to be destroyed by them. Are you sure that you want to take this move? I was forced into it by circumstances — the only way I can protect my Circle at the moment."

"Of course, of course. Yes, we discussed this possibility with Aldrick when we met with him. He will be very willing to work with you on this project of resettlement of gold dragons," Milan replied. "I see no reason that our two races cannot get along well with each other."

"Are you sure that you want to do this? Once they come, there may be no way to get rid of them if things do not work out as you have planned, Uncle."

"Yes, we are all very sure of this. After all, Zoran, if Baron Kazimir and his allies know that you have signed a mutual defense pack with us and that we five also possess a flock of dragons, they will think hard about launching an invasion of your Wild Lands. It is the best deterrent that we can devise at this time. Honestly, Zoran, we are doing all that we can to look out for your interests here — as well as our own, as you ought to expect," Baron Viktor added.

"Well, they would be fools to launch an overland assault if they know that you five would send an army each and accompanied by more dragons." Zoran had to admit that their plan was sound. Only fools would dare challenge such an alliance. Perhaps, this would buy him the time he desperately needed. "Okay, I will sign such an agreement."

No longer surprised, Baron Milan handed him several documents that they had prepared in advance for him to sign. Zoran chuckled, "You knew that I would agree to all this beforehand, didn't you?"

"Of course, what other choices do you have? I hate to be so blunt about it, but this change in the balance of power is of monumental importance. We cannot allow it to slip through our hands! Besides, we have tried to make it as painless on you as possible. Honestly, you have so much to handle anyway. How in heaven's name you are going to get all those barbarian warlords under control is beyond us."

Zoran signed the documents and was given a copy of them. "Now, next business is business. Barons Tom and Aldo control agrarian planets and have plenty of grains to trade with you. Barons Etienne and Viktor have hilly planets with thousands of horses to trade with you, while Gladno is heavily forested and I have all kinds of high quality lumber to trade."

"Yes, but what do I have to trade in return?" Zoran asked. This was far beyond his experience; he'd never paid any attention to his father's business dealings.

"Ores, precious gems and metals, son. Adapazan is loaded with valuable minerals, such as iron and copper, to say nothing of gems, gold, and silver," Baron Milan replied, wondering just how ignorant his nephew actually was about his own home world. "Barons Tom and Etienne are particularly keen on trading for these. Such are in short supply in their plains worlds. You will find some of the neutral planets also in dire need of ores. None more so than the water world of Baron Hajime Yoko of Asami."

Seeing how little Zoran actually new about commerce, Baron Viktor added, "If I might be allowed to make another suggestion, Baron Archmage Zoran." He used his full title purposely, "Nowhere in the Federation of Planets are six Archmages under one roof. The sheer magnitude of magical energies that you command is beyond impressive. Yet, you could use that to your advantage. If you could convince your fellow Archmages to devote some time and energy to the creation of magical items, you would find a very, very lucrative market for those within the Federation. Enchanted rings, amulets, swords, and daggers can fetch a heady price. Just something to consider, son."

"Yes, we just want to point out that from a commerce point of view, your situation is far from hopeless," Milan added his justification to the mix.

"Thanks for the ideas. I readily admit that I am most ignorant of this business aspect. As you may well imagine, I stayed totally out of the Baron's affairs. Besides, I spent all my time learning combat skills and magic, as a young Duska is obligated to do. I'm afraid that I am going to need your able assistance with commerce. I don't even know what to charge for our goods, let alone if other barons are taking advantage of my ignorance. Can I count on your advice when trading deals come up?"

Both Baron Milan and Baron Viktor smiled, the latter adding, "Of course, nephew. It would reflect poorly upon us if it became widely known that another baron had taken unfair advantage of my nephew. When you are going to bargain, let us know. One of us will come with you to help out."

"Thanks. Politics again?" Zoran ventured. Both men nodded. "Say, suppose that we do wish to trade ores for grain. How is this accomplished between worlds? I've often wondered just how it's done. I have seen men arriving at Dorum with wagon loads of goods."

"Ah, this is our province, Zoran," Baron Viktor chose to answer him. "Teleportation does not work between planets, as you well know. The only method of inner-planetary travel is using our Duska Shadow Walk. Duskas Shadow Walk a wagon load at a time between worlds. Usually, this is a task that we assign to our sons, once they are trained. Duke Stefan has made many a Walk on Valtr's behalf. Of course, the transaction is fully arranged beforehand, and he takes a number of security men with him."

"Over the centuries, there has been virtually no evil intervention during trading transactions between the planets. The political fallout would be devastating. For instance, if Baron Kazimir should attack one of your shipments from another world, then the entire High Council would completely isolate him. He would be instantly cut off from all further trade with the other fifteen worlds. None of us can afford such draconian measures. We all need things that the other worlds have in abundance. No, waylaying a Duska shipment is tantamount to cutting your own throat. Still, assassins find such times fruitful; hence always take good security measures, Zoran."

"Say, since this is all new to you, what say that we visit my accountants?" Baron Milan suggested. "They can show you some typical transactions that I have recently made. It will give you some idea of how much a wagon of grain is worth and so on. That will take only a few minutes. Then, let's meet with our five top fortress engineers and get to work on designing yours, shall we?"

"Thanks, that would be valuable, Uncle. Say, how can I get a map of the Federation Planets and one like that of Adapazan that you have there on your wall?" Zoran asked. He realized that he knew very little at all about the geography and layout of his own Wild Lands and of Adapazan. This knowledge he knew that he would need almost immediately when they returned to Brn.

The long afternoon was filled with five engineers and their sketches of fortifications and castles. Zoran was amazed at how much information both Barons had accumulated on just their brief visit to Brn and Archmage Oldrich's tower! Each chief engineer came from a different planet and each had different ideas of how best to proceed. However, all five were in complete agreement on the fortification and castle location. It had to be just beyond the current Archmage tower and the city's outer walls there. The rising mountain valley would offer incredible protection on all sides, except from the city itself. To get to the fortress, an army would have to plow through the entire city first. At first, Zoran cringed at this idea; he was supposed to be protecting the city. However, they quickly pointed out to him that the attacking army would be at a severe disadvantage with city street fighting. They could be ambushed from nearly every building and rooftop in the city, taking massive losses long before they finally reached his outer walls. Zoran insisted that there be sufficient room within the fortress walls to house the city folk, if a siege ever came.

Time and time again, Zoran had to insist, "Simple, keep it simple. We do not want anything fancy. No, no gold torch holders, please. Keep it purely functional and lost cost. Brn is not wealthy."

By dinner time, the outer walls had been drawn up. Its circumference was nearly a mile, though its shape was more that of an irregular pentagram, taking advantage of the natural shape of the high mountain valley directly behind the Archmage tower. The main entrance would be to the left of the tower, where Zoran currently housed his small security forces. They assured Zoran that stone cutting would commence upon his return to Brn, even though it was still winter.

Within the walls, a small creek would fill a water pond that would provide for the inhabitants. Many large wooden buildings were designed to line the outer walls, providing housing for horses, security forces, and the emergency housing of the citizens of Brn, should a siege occur. The design of the manor house had to wait for tomorrow. On this, none could agree this first day. Zoran desired another wizard tower, similar in height to the existing one. Yet, the Circle of Ascension had to be deep within the castle or manor house with all manner of protections to keep it secure. A simple tower would never do, they continually pointed out to Zoran.

As everyone headed to their rooms to get cleaned up for dinner, the women finally returned from their shopping excursion, accompanied by quite a commotion. "Zoran, they tried to assassinate Lida," Zdenka explained excitedly, as she rushed up to greet him. Behind the four women, a number of security men bodily carried a subdued assassin standing him before Baron Milan.

"My god! Lida! Are you all right?" Zoran exclaimed. Duke Leo was already at her side.

"Yes, yes, no harm done, just ripped my bodice, but I have purchased several new ones anyway. Skin of Stone saved me again, little brother. My, is Jarka ever fast!"

Jarka, standing beside Rayna, smiled and stayed out of the limelight.

"Come, you must tell me precisely what happened! I cannot believe that they would do this in my own city!" Uncle Milan was furious. His face grew red with anger.

"Well, we were walking out of the last dressmaker's shop when one of the two invisible assassins cast a spell on us," Lida began, eager to relate their adventure. "I believe he was trying to dispel some of my magical protections that I had on myself. It worked, I felt several leaving me, but that attack allowed us to see him. Just then, the second invisible assassin rushed up to me and tried to stab me with his poisoned dagger. Jarka sensed his coming somehow. Man, she is sure fast! Just as the assassin became visible as his dagger hit my bodice, Jarka's dagger went through his right eye. He died instantly. She is incredibly fast, Zoran, believe me. Anyway, Rayna shot several spells at the first assassin, and then I did too. He kept dodging ours, but Jarka finally trapped him in sticky webs. Our security men took charge and captured him. He's not said a word though. Maybe you can get him to speak, Uncle Milan." Lida finally finished her tale, pleased that she had the complete attention of everyone, especially Duke Leo, who still clung to her.

Duke Leo declared, "Dear, from now on, you don't go anyplace without me!" She beamed and squeezed his hand.

"Damn. Assassins in my own city. This will never do. Take him to the dungeon. We'll make him talk. Probably hired by Baron Kazimir," Baron Milan cursed. "Well, this demands action; action they'll get. Take him away and search him thoroughly. We'll make him talk!"

Turning to Jarka, he calmed down and added, "Mage Jarka, you have my profound thanks for saving my future daughter-in-law once again. I will see that you receive a proper acknowledgment. Zoran, you have chosen very able friends indeed. It was wise of you to bring her along with you. Most impressive. Mage Jarka, if ever you seek employment beyond Baron Zoran's realm, please consider working for me. It a standing job offer," he grinned, but knew full well she had no such intentions. This was a political formality, recognizing her services rendered. Jarka continued to smile, proud of her minor achievement.

Baroness Marjeta, a tall woman, elegantly dressed, well-coiffed blonde hair and dark blue eyes, said, "Well, enough excitement for one day. Let we ladies bathe and dress in our new outfits. Dinner will be at seven. Baron Zoran, you have new suits waiting for you in your room. I suggest we all be properly attired for this evening's dinner."

"Yes, dear," Baron Milan replied.

"You too, Viktor," Baroness Ivana, also added with a tease in her voice. She had long black hair and dark eyes. She was a compliment to her baron.

"Yes, dear," Baron Viktor replied in kind, mimicking Milan's voice tone. Aside to Zoran, he whispered, "See what you are getting yourself into by marrying?" All three men chuckled.

"I'll see to our prisoner first, gentlemen," Baron Milan said and left them, following after his security men into the dungeon.

As the young couples exited their rooms to head to the dining hall, Zoran was surprised to see how beautiful his sisters looked in their matching pale blue billowing, ruffle-filled dresses, whose color blended well with their light brown hair. Duke Leo, tall and thin, with long blonde hair and a constant smile, escorted Lida, while Duke Stefan, also tall, but well-built, with dark brown hair, escorted Rayna. He could see why both his sisters were so taken with these young men. They seemed wildly in love with his sisters.

Just then, Archmage Zdenka and Mage Jarka came out of their room, offering an arm for Zoran, who wore a black suit with white linen shirt. His jacket had twin tails. "Oh my! Zdenka, Jarka! Wow! You both look absolutely stunning! Wow!" Indeed, he was shocked at their transformation. Zdenka wore a sky blue billowing dress that precisely matched Zoran's new eye color and the color of his thread in his Circle of Ascension — a fact not missed by Zoran. Jarka looked equally stunning in her brown dress, made of satin which shimmered in the light as she walked. "Wow!" he said for the third time. He missed Rayna's knowing wink at the two young women. Later he learned that Rayna had been instrumental in helping them pick out just the right afternoon dresses. With one on each arm, Zoran proudly escorted them to the dining hall, following the other two young couples.

In the huge room where exquisite tables, chairs, armoires, and other pieces of furniture abounded, one could see the benefits of living on a world where fine quality wood was plentiful. The craftsmen here knew how to make not only a functional object, but one that was highly aesthetic — a work of art. Zoran was impressed. His uncle and aunt arrived last, much to Marjeta's distaste.

"Well out with it, Milan. Then, let's hear no more of it this evening," she cajoled him.

"Yes dear. The assassin is dead by his own poison. However, before he committed suicide rather than face my wrath, I discovered that he is in the employ of Baron Bogdan Clav, not Baron Kazimir, as I first thought. I will deal with Bogdan tomorrow. There, dear, enough said. Time to dine. Oh yes, our court musicians will play for an hour after dinner. I'm told that the young people wish to dance." Zoran grinned at Zdenka, he wondered if she had had any part in arranging this detail.

They got to meet Baron Viktor's other children, more of Zoran's cousins, who had arrived in time for dinner. Andrea was nineteen, while Berta was eighteen; their boyfriends were not present, however. Vana was barely seventeen, while Viktor Junior was twenty. The second Circle would elevate Viktor Junior to a baron as well.

Baron Milan's other children joined them as well. His youngest son, Alfons, nineteen, had arrived from the fortress Raha, along with his young wife, Valérie.

They had been married only a couple of months. Alfons was proud that he married before his older brother, Leo. The new Circle of Ascension was being built there in Raha for him. Also, his young daughters were present: Dusana, seventeen, and Katerina, fifteen. They hovered around Andrea and Berta, and the four constantly chatted and giggled. Although the dinner was quite formal, Zdenka found that it was very friendly and that she fit right in with them, especially with Rayna and Lida. She visibly relaxed and began to enjoy her stay here.

Both Zdenka and Jarka thoroughly enjoyed the long dance after supper, as did the other young couples and his cousins. Duke Leo promised to have the musicians play every night after dinner, and Lida gave him a big thank you kiss for that.

The next day's lengthy design session finally began to make inroads on the actual castle-manor house-tower combination, but it would take the rest of the week to finally get it completely done to everyone's satisfaction. While the girls went out shopping nearly every day, Baron Milan sent along fifty security men with them. However, the women did find time to review the ever growing fortress and castle plans that Zoran and the engineers were drawing up.

One evening as Zdenka and Jarka were going over the nearly final plans, Zoran discovered an interesting fact. Jarka commented, "Shouldn't you have a maze surrounding the Circle of Ascension like at Castle Dorumova?" She sketched the precise layout on a scrap paper.

"Well, yes, that makes its defense easier, but how do you know the castle's precise layout?" Zoran asked.

"Once I see something, I can later recall it perfectly," Jarka replied. "At your mother's ceremony, I studied all of the faces present. I can now identify every one of the barons and baronesses, to say nothing of Castle Dorumova's layout."

"Wow! Incredible, Jarka. You never cease to amaze me. I certainly cannot do that." She grinned and was pleased with his praise.

As the wedding day drew closer, Baron Milan vetoed the boys' request for a last night out on the town — the bachelor's party. It would be the last opportunity for Baron Kazimir to attempt an assassination before his heir married Duke Leo, putting her forever out of his reach. "Too much danger. I cannot allow it. We party inside the castle." Duke Leo grumbled, but could not overrule his father.

As Jarka helped Zdenka get ready for her wedding day, she volunteered, "Do you know that Bernard has asked me to marry him?"

"No, he did? Bout time. He's had eyes on you as long as I have known him. What did you say?" Zdenka replied, curiously.

"Well, I told him I would answer him when I got back. I do like him. I've just never thought that I would, well you know, settle down like that."

"So," Zdenka prodded her.

"Well, I've decided that I'll say yes when I get back. There, I've gone and said it out loud, finally. Why was that so terribly difficult for me to say?" she wondered.

"Congratulations! He is really a wonderful man, you know. I've known him for a number of years. He's kind and considerate."

"Yes, but he is also awfully boring a lot of the time, though since he has become a Mage, he is far less so. But then, I am a sneaky thief," she admonished herself.

"An honorable one that always does good," Zdenka added. "Don't be so hard on yourself. You've changed a good deal too since you became a Mage."

"I guess I will have to get used to having dogs running all over the place," she jested. Both women laughed.

The ceremony was a grand affair, but was soon over, much to everyone's delight, none more so than the three couples. Duke Leo and Lida began packing for their honeymoon. They were headed to Gonda, where Baron Etienne would look after their safety. Other than the couple and the barons, no one knew where they were going. They purposely used the Circle of Ascension to travel there that night, making sure that they could not be followed. A bit later, Duke Stefan and Rayna parted for their honeymoon on the watery planet of Asami, where Baron Hajime would guarantee their safety.

Zdenka, having been privy to the women's discussions of honeymoon places, decided that she wanted to visit Asami as well. It sounded like a heavenly place to vacation, tons of islands and beaches everywhere. However, their honeymoon would have to wait for several months; both had too many pressing obligations back home. Indeed, she was very intimidated by having to begin her first Picking of new magic students in barely two months, let alone all of their training. She was now the owner of the tower, since Archmage Nadia was retiring. The problems facing Zoran were far larger and more pressing.

As the two crawled into their honeymoon bed that night, Zoran promised, "Dear, as soon as we can safely get away, I will take you to Asami. It will be our special place; I think you will like it." She gave him a hug and they began passionately kissing.

Chapter 18 Preparations

The next day, the newlyweds returned home, laden with nearly a wagon full of packages, dresses, suits, drawings, and other gifts. The framed pair of maps Zoran prized, as one gave him his first real knowledge of the overall layout of the Wild Lands and their relation to the provinces occupied by Baron Kazimir. Zdenka and Jarka prized their new wardrobe most highly, as you might expect. After the many congratulations were finished and their numerous boxes stowed, Zoran called for a conference. The engineers and work force would be arriving in the afternoon.

"I've made some deals. The five top fortification engineers of five planets and I have come up with this as the cheapest, most economical design for us. Five crews will begin preparation work this afternoon. How they can in all this snow I do not know. Gather around, let me show you what we are proposing," Zoran explained. He spent an hour outlining all of what he learned, plans made, and bargains struck.

"Archmage Karel, these will be your quarters here on the top floor. There is plenty of space for you to have as many falcons as desired. Bernard, this section is for you and Jarka and your dogs. I assume that you will want to bring as many of them here as possible," he explained. Both men, surprised with this special touch, slapped him heartily on his back in appreciation.

Karel, Bernard, I would like you two to work closely with the engineers if you will. Janos and I are going to tackle the next major hurdle: what to do about the remaining warlords and their provinces. In two weeks, I will have to go to the first High Council meeting, where we will be formally recognized. In the meantime, there is lots to do." He finished his pep talk, and he and Janos retired to stare at the map of Adapazan and the warlord problem.

"Baron, I am very out of touch with the current status of the remaining warlords," General Janos confessed. "Years ago, I had some idea of them. Certainly time has altered situations. When I left Dorum, I came to Brn because it was the best of all the remaining provinces. Some of these rebel leaders are nearly as bad as Baron Kazimir. Ruthless, cunning, vicious, treacherous, these men are attempting to hold on to their Wild Lands somehow. Their forces vary widely. Some are good fighters; others, riffraff. Certainly, each one is terrifically independent and will be very hard to control."

"I figured that they would. Look, this is going to be the House of the Free Peoples of Adapazan. I plan to act that way from the start. I am going to treat them as I would like to be treated. Then, if they go against us, that's their own undoing. I've worked out a plan, but I need to know all of the leaders of Lesy, Radim, Veklov, Ves, Zovou, Valy, Tehov, Tratky, Kin, and Orlovia Provinces. That's at least ten Warlords, maybe more. Your first task is to see if you can find out their names for me. I am going to write up my first message to be sent to them."

While General Janos left to make inquiries around Brn, Zoran began writing out his initial contact letter. Identical copies would be sent to the Warlords. He began by introducing himself and explaining that he was fighting against Baron Kazimir, that he was in Brn, that he had become an Archmage, and that with the help of Mikolas and the Zars, had actually built the first new Circle of Ascension in over two centuries.

He went on to explain what this actually meant, that now Adapazan was no longer under the sole dominion of Kazimir. In fact, this new Circle stood for the Free People of Adapazan. He then wrote, "I have taken it upon myself to stand solidly in the way of any further expansion of Baron Kazimir into the Wild Lands. He shall not attack another independent province ever again. At this time, I have begun to build a fortress and castle here in Brn, but it will be at least a year before it is done. True, I have no armies of my own. However, I am an Archmage and have four other Archmages with me, along with many Mages and a small security force. In order to hold our position against attackers, I have brought over a dozen golden dragons from their home world to Brn. You may have heard just how deadly my two young dragon friends were in Sholov Province. Anyone will think more than twice about attacking us as long as we have dragons to help in our defense. I can invite more gold dragons to Adapazan as needed. I have just signed a mutual defense pact with five other planets. If the Wild Lands are attacked as was Sholov Province, they are pledged to send five armies to help drive the invaders back."

His letter continued, "Enough of me. I am terrifically interested in meeting with you and representatives of your Free Province. Why? I am certain that you might have some really good ideas that can help us all out, and I obviously need some help. I have no idea what is needed in your province, which I am sworn to protect with my life. I have made trading arrangements with other planets in the Federation, but I just don't know what your province needs. Please, contact me as soon as possible. I need your help and ideas. If possible, please come to Brn on the 5th of March so that I can show you the new Circle of Ascension and my dragon friends. Take whatever security precautions you deem appropriate."

Zoran reread his letter and made a few corrections. Then, he cast a magical spell and watched as ten copies of the letter were made by ten ink quills. All that remained was for him to put each Warlord's name on it and find a way to send the letters. Late afternoon, General Janos returned with some names. He was unable to ascertain many last names; most were just called Warlord. His list included: Lesy Province: Warlord Adolf, Radim Province: Warlord Antonín, Veklov Province: Warlord Boris, Orlovia Province: Warlord Gustav, Kin Province: Warlord Eduard, Tehov Province: Warlord Ivan, Valy Province: Warlord Jolana, Tratky Province: Warlord Osvald, Ves Province: Warlord Sabina, and Zovou Province: Warlord Petr.

He was surprised to find two female Warlords, Jolana and Sabina. They ruled two of the three adjoining provinces to Brn. Archmage Karel volunteered to visit each province and post the letters for him. Why? Unknown to his new friends, Karel had traveled widely during his late teens and was familiar with the surrounding provinces. That he could now easily teleport from place to place made the job quite easy for him, and he returned in time for supper.

"Now we wait," Zoran announced to everyone, after thanking Archmage Karel for delivering his messages. Everyone had opinions on what their responses might be, but Zoran mostly ignored them. He'd asked for their ideas and help, something any free person would respond favorably to, he wagered. He certainly would, if he was in their shoes.

Two days later, messages began arriving via warlord Mages. One by one, Zoran received word that the warlord would come on the 5th. Naturally, Archmage Zdenka began making preparations to feed a rather large crowd of people, though it would strain the dining facilities of the tower to its limit. Zoran suggested that any overflow could be sent to the Stodgy Inn right nearby and made arrangements with the innkeeper. It was a wise move on his part, it turned out to be definitely needed!

On the day of reckoning, parties of warlords began arriving, beginning around nine in the morning. All came with their Mage, who teleported their leader and security forces. Most warlords came with five or six security fighters, all armed to the teeth, ready for treachery and combat. Zoran cordially greeted each of the warlords, introduced the other Archmages and Mages to them, and gave them a personal tour of the new Circle of Ascension. Around noon, after the last group arrived and the introductions finished, Zoran had everyone bundle up and step outside into the snow covered street. Before their eyes, Archmages Renata and Emil transformed into their dragon shapes, and Aldrick and his large group appeared, right on cue. The twins took off and joined the others — thirteen golden dragons circling the tower. Just for effect, Aldrick and several others let lose a blast of fire, melting a bit of snow on the granite mountainside behind the tower. Yes, the warlords were visibly impressed. Zoran's first move was to make sure that each warlord really did believe what he had said about the Circle and the dragons.

Because of limited seating in the tower, each warlord was allowed only one companion to dine with them. The others were sent to the Stodgy Inn, where Zoran arranged a feast for them as well. After taking off their heavy parkas and taking seats, not without a lot of grumbling and angry shouts about not sitting by so-and-so, Zoran at last got a good look at his peers. What a dramatic difference from dining with Baron Milan! Uniformly, their clothing was relatively poor quality, but functional. Many of the men were heavily bearded, and some even had a noxious odor about themselves. Zdenka thought that many were long overdue for a bath! She, however, made no mention of this.

After a hearty meal, though by his Uncle's standards, a frugal meal, Zoran at last rose to speak first. "Thank you all for coming today. You've seen that we now have a Circle of Ascension, that I am a Duska, that soon I will be recognized as a Baron of Adapazan, at least the Free People's portion of Adapazan, that I do indeed have golden dragons as my friends, and that they do breathe fire. If you wish to see the mutual defense treaties that I have signed with five allied planets of the Federation, I will make those documents available after our meeting. My aim is to prevent any further loss of your provinces to Baron Kazimir."

"However, I do have problems that I need your help in solving. I most desperately need to know what you need assistance with and what ideas you might have. Truly, a new day has dawned for we free people of Adapazan. First, my problems. It will be over a year before we have a strong fortification built here in Brn to protect the Circle more fully. I have no army as you can see. Brn never has had an army, as most of you know. Yet, I must help you defend your provinces from the ravages of Baron Kazimir and his allies. Most critical are Lesy and Kin Provinces, since any overland assault on Brn must come through those provinces first. I have no contacts in any other province and have no way of knowing if and when any enemy army might assault your provinces. Yet, once I know, I guarantee you that I will bring five armies from our allied planets and the dragons to drive Kazimir's army back, if not destroy them utterly!"

"Further, as your Duska, I can bring trade goods to your province from other planets in the Federation. Yet, I do not know what it might be that you need. So I throw the table open to you ten warlords. Look the situation over and see what ideas you have that can help us all. Let me know what your people need and what can be traded. Ideas, please." Zoran sat down. Jarka, Karel, Bernard, and Zdenka readied their pens, writing down what was suggested.

Warlord Adolf of Lesy Province rose. He was in dire need of a bath and a shave. He growled angrily, "What about taking back the five provinces the bastard father of yours stole from us? What about driving him out of Dorum?"

Zoran replied, "That is going to happen — but not like you think. As you may have heard, his heir, Radek, has died. He then announced my sister Lida as his heir and then tried to force her to marry Baron Bogdan's pig of a son. She refused him and is now married to Duke Leo, Baron Milan Matous of Gladno, one of our allies. Already Baron Kazimir has regretted that move and has tried to assassinate her twice now. When Kazimir finally dies, Lida will inherit Dorum, and she is with us, promising to undo everything Kazimir has done, freeing everyone that is under his dominion today. If we just be patient, warlords, we can win total freedom for all of Adapazan without any loss of life, without even going to war against him. Yes, it may well be the coup of the century."

As far as Zoran could tell, the ten leader's spirits rose considerably. That the death of the hated Kazimir would instantly reverse the years of his ruthless rule came as a complete surprise to these warlords. Warlord Eduard of Kin Province then rose, "Mages are rare in the Wild Lands, but I can have my Mage here send you messages of any possible threats against Kin. We can give you as much advance notice as we get of any impending attack against us." At once, Warlord Adolf also agreed that his Mage could do likewise, and rapidly the others quickly agreed to send messages via their Mages as well.

Good, thought Zoran, this is a start. Warlord Ivan of Tehov Province added, "Since we seem to be in this together, if Kin is attacked, I can send much of my forces to his assistance. It is in my best interests to stop any advancing army in Kin before it gets to Tehov. Many others begrudgingly agreed with his idea. With their combined forces, the dragons, and the proposed other five armies, that any attacking army could be stopped before it got to their province appealed to their self-preservation.

Warlord Jolana of Valy Province, a blonde woman who looked every bit a robust fighter, rose. "What about getting us some of our own dragons? I for one would like to have a dozen protecting Valy. Can you get us some or are the dragons only for you and not for the rest of us?" Her antagonistic tone told volumes of unsaid words and ideas.

"Dragons are highly intelligent and magic users, as witnessed by the two Archmages sitting here with us. They are at the top of the food chain; we are definitely below them. Do not fear; they do not like to eat humans. Antelope are their delicacy. If you agree to treat dragons with great respect and honor, I can certainly get a dozen gold dragons for each of your provinces. However, they demand a price for their services. They are master gem cutters and prize gems above all but magic. As long as you can pay them their required gems, I am sure I can get each of you a dozen of your own. Are you really interested in having dragons about your province?"

This was discussed for a half hour, pros and cons. Every warlord was taken off guard by Zoran's readily agreeing to provide them some dragons. Not one of the warlords expected this. Surely, they thought, Baron Zoran would be keeping the dragons all to himself. They certainly would have if they were in his shoes. Now they faced the reality of the actuality. Archmage Emil presented the terms that the dragons would demand, and they discussed this for some time. In the end, all ten requested a dozen dragons of their own. Zoran promised to deliver them in about two months' time, giving them a chance to either back out or come up with the gems to pay the dragons.

Warlord Ivan bellowed, "Say, what about weapons and armor? We need lots of good quality swords. My warriors have nothing but makeshift leather padding and cannot stand against the steel armor of Kazimir's shock troops. What about that?" Cat calls echoed around the table. Indeed, Zoran expected this request.

Warlord Osvald of Tratky Province, a burly man wearing furry animal skins, perhaps the crudest looking of the group, broke in, "Nay, we need grains. Tratky is the northernmost province, and we're barely surviving. Not enough food, especially grains. My people need food in their bellies if they're gonna fight. And then there's dem damnable Yellers. U'all drove 'em up our way."

"Hey, and our way too," interrupted Warlord Petr of Zovou Province. "Got nothing but problems with Yellers running rampant. Ain't got no time to go a'fighten Kazimir. U'all 'ave given us a huge problem. How's 'bout you taken 'em back into your provinces, eh? See how you like 'em 'ttacking u all duh time."

The room erupted into a yelling match between the warlords. Everyone blamed everyone else for the Yeller mess. Zoran allowed them to vent their hostilities. As soon as there was a lull in the bickering, he spoke up. "Does anyone have any ideas how we might solve the Yeller problem, short of genocide?"

Genocide was their first idea, naturally, but his challenge met mostly silence. "What else can we do about them? They're just a bunch of blood thirsty wild beasts running around on two legs," one warlord broke the silence."

"Well, that's why we are here. To put our heads together and see if we can come up with some bright ideas," Zoran replied. "I must admit that I have not have contact with Yellers. I'm sorry about that. I freely admit that I am mostly ignorant of them. All that I know about them comes from book learning, and we all know how off that can be. Surely those of you who have faced them have some ideas?"

He noticed that both Warlords Sabina and Jolana gave him a most curious look. Here was a Duska, a royalty, a nobleman, who was not dominating or insisting that he knew everything or that he knew best what was needed for them. Both reappraised him.

"Well, we've mostly been driving them out of our provinces," Warlord Adolf replied. "Yeh, I know that we're driving them into your provinces, but where else can we drive them?" More arguing ensued.

"Let me see if I follow what you have been doing," Zoran spoke up during the next lull. "For centuries now, starting at Dorum Province, the Yellers, who were natively here, have been constantly being pushed westward or northward. Today, their largest concentrations are now in Tratky and Zovou Provinces. The warlords in those two provinces now have no place else to drive them. Is this a fair summary?" It was.

"If'n we 'ad a lot of boats, maybe we kin drive 'em over to Dolni Island," suggested Warlord Petr. Give'm their own land away from us." Heads nodded agreement, voices seconded his idea.

Then the alto voice of Warlord Sabina spoke up, "Well, we don't have boats, but we now have the next best thing, we got us a Duska. How about our Duska moving the Yellers out of here, eh? What say you to that, Baron Zoran? You don't have a hankering to genocide, so how about you doing it?"

"Well, this is why we are all here today. If I am to be your Duska, I certainly have to know what your problems are and have lots of ideas of what we can do to work together to solve them. I will certainly see if I cannot find a way to do as you ask, move the Yellers to their own place."

"Ya, but what about getting us more food and better cloth and stuff," asked Warlord Jolana. "You know that we are going to need vastly improved roads between our provinces if all this supposed commerce is going to come from other planets."

"She's right, warlords. If I am to get large trades going with other worlds, we have got to have a vastly improved transportation system between our provinces. How are you going to get your wagon loads of iron ore, coal, and the like here to Brn so I can transport them to the other worlds and bring back your wagons full of grains, cloth, weapons, and armor? I can't have hundreds of your wagons sitting here loaded with your grain waiting for your Mages to come teleport them sack by sack. If you want quantity, you've got to have a good transportation system, to say nothing of a good communication system between you and us here in Brn."

"Yeh, but what are they going to want from us for all this stuff?" asked a warlord.

"As I understand it, the agrarian worlds need ores of all kinds. Iron, copper, lead — just the stuff we have in abundance here. The more wagon loads of ore you can deliver, the more goods I can get in trade. Others will want gold, silver, and gems, especially for horses, swords, and armor. The better the quality of these that you can produce, the more the other worlds will give you in exchange. As time goes on, I will be in a better position to know what else these others may wish in exchange and we can act accordingly," Zoran replied and decided now was the time to get them participating.

"Okay, so there are eleven of us. You've all heard the problems that I am working on and additionally, I will see what can be done about the Yeller problem. If I can find a way to move them to Dolni Island, then I will need each of you to round up the Yellers that remain in your provinces. Well, excepting Zovou and Tratky, where their densest populations are located. I'll work out something special with you two. So what of the other problems that we face are you willing to work on solving?"

"Well, we all need to work on improving our roads," Warlord Jolana volunteered. "We ought to coordinate our plans or else my new road will not connect with Boris' new road." Everyone roared with laughter. She was right in her observation. They all agreed to make a better road system as soon as the spring snow melt began and to coordinate with their neighboring provinces.

"We'd better ramp up our mining production," another suggested. All ten agreed to give this their full attention as well. Several volunteered to get a dozen ore wagons ready within four weeks so Zoran could acquire some much needed grain for Tratky. All agreed to really get going on gem stone production to satisfy their newly acquired dragons. Further, they agreed to have their Mages communicate vital information to Zoran's Mages every week or more frequently as needed. The Warlords of Lesy and Kin Provinces promised to send out spies into the neighboring provinces of Kazimir's to gain advance notice of any army buildup along their borders.

Around four, they finished up and the warlords took their leave, departing as they came. Over dinner, Archmage Karel exclaimed, "Well, Zoran, I just don't believe it. The warlords are an incredibly wild, rebel bunch, and you not only got them in one place but working together along with you as well. I say you just performed a miracle. You realize that no one in centuries has gotten this bunch together as you have done today? Incredible, just incredible. Maybe there is some hope for the Wild Lands after all and not just Brn as I thought."

"Thanks Karel. No way could we get their cooperation by force of arms. People usually respond well if given a chance to help. I gave them that. If they follow through on all that they have promised, just the improved roads will be a strong uniting factor," he replied.

"Yes, but dear, you promised them to deal with the Yellers," Zdenka decided to speak her thoughts. "Just how are you going to handle them? I mean they are more like wild animals."

"I don't know; it will have to wait until the spring thaw. We've got more pressing problems at hand. I am worried that Kazimir is going to try something awful."

"I would expect something at the High Council first, Baron Zoran," General Lavos spoke his mind. "Based on my experiences with that vile man, he is not a total fool. He knows well the devastation caused by dragons. No, I think that you should look for all manner of trouble at the High Council meeting. It is imperative that your Circle be recognized officially and that you are given your proper baron's seat on the High Council. I would look for him to first attempt a political solution from the High Council. If that fails, then you can be sure that, dragons or no dragons, he's going to take more drastic actions. After all, you have him cornered like some wild animal. He's about to lose everything that he and his ancestors fought for and defended: the ruling of Adapazan."

"Damn, I know nothing about the High Council or how it works or its rules," Zoran cursed.

"Don't worry, dear. I am sure that your uncles Baron Milan and Baron Viktor will look out for your interests," Zdenka replied. "They have an awful lot riding on gaining recognition of your Circle, almost as much as you do. It breaks the tie between the two sides. However, I think that you ought to go discuss things with Mayor Oldrich. He's going to have to get better roads built as well, to say nothing of all the workers coming to build the fortress."

Chapter 19 The High Council

On the 15th of March, this year's first session of the High Council of the Federation of Planets was held on the planet of Alta, a hilly planet. Neutral Baron Alvaro and Baroness Anita Cencion were the hosts for the week long meeting at their castle in Puerto. According to the rules, Zoran had to bring Zdenka, his baroness, and was allowed to bring along two advisors who would sit with them at the council tables, along with four security personnel. He chose to bring General Janos and three of his hand-picked men. For his advisors, he chose Jarka and Karel. He asked Jarka not only because of her excellent protection skills that she had demonstrated numerous times already but also because of her photographic memory. Karel came along for two reasons: Alta possessed numerous falcons, and he had a sharp mind when it came to men's motives. Zdenka, with Jarka's aid, dutifully packed their six boxes of dresses and sundries.

"These court dresses sure do take up a whole lot of space and are hard to transport," Jakra complained. "All this just so we can look pretty for the men."

"Ordinarily, I wouldn't give a hoot," Zdenka replied, stuffing another dress into an overfull box and valiantly trying to shut its lid. "Excepting Zoran, of course. But these people are the most powerful people in the sixteen worlds, the topmost rulers. We certainly don't want to have them take a lesser view of Zoran because we look like ordinary peasants from their point of view."

"True enough. Nothing like hobnobbing with the rich and powerful. I just hope they are not all snobs and such. At least his uncles and aunts seem nice enough," Jarka admitted.

With the last of their things packed, the women cast their shrink spells on the six large boxes and put the very small boxes into one of their handbags. "More like it," Zdenka exclaimed; Jarka grinned. Dressed in their very fancy satin ball gowns, which billowed out some six feet around them, they headed off to meet up with the men. Zoran wore his new black suit with twin tails and looked every bit as nice as his uncle, Zdenka thought. The Zars joined them and at last they were ready. All looked at each other, sensing each other's tension and nervousness.

"Well, this is it," Zoran broke the ice.

"I hate to tell you but I am nervous about this," Brother Jiri confessed. "We will be meeting all of those barons, and I'll bet every last one of them will beg me to make them more Circles."

"Well, you are now the most famous man in the Federation of Planets," Zoran admitted, teasingly.

"Nah, Zoran here is," Karel declared, "he's just shaken up two centuries of dullness."

"Now you have me nervous," Zoran joked, and they all laughed. Joining hands, Zoran stepped them all to the planet Alta. Since this was the first time here for everyone, Zoran purposefully allowed his walk to circumnavigate the world, giving them a good overview look at this world, whose land masses were uniformly all very hilly. Periodically, they spied roads streaking across the springtime green hills, like gray lines a child might draw. A few towns came into view before the large capital city of Puerto loomed larger and larger before their eyes. Gray stone buildings predominated as they approached; then the giant gray stone fortress of Baron Alvaro Cencion loomed before them, growing larger and larger. Following his uncle's directions, he focused on the giant gray cobblestone courtyard just inside the fortress gates, and they arrived.

Rimming the courtyard were hundreds of orange pots, whose spring flowers were already growing, adding color to the drab surroundings. On the ramparts behind and above them, a hundred fighters stood, weapons raised, ready for any trouble — Baron Alvaro took the High Council security measures seriously. A tall man in a suit that looked finer than Zoran's stepped forward to meet them.

"I am Esteban, the butler. Whom am I addressing?" he said mostly bored, as if he had been doing this all day.

"Baron to be Zoran Vladislov and party," Zoran replied formally.

"I see. I've been expecting you. If you will follow me, I will show you to your rooms. You are to be at the meeting room at ten o'clock for the opening ceremonies, sir." He led them inside the gaping, handcrafted doors of the main manor house and down long corridors. Periodically, large orange pots hung from the walls with more flowers just blooming. "Baron Milan Matous and party have the room next to yours here, and Baron Viktor Pavel and party are on the other side. Both parties have already arrived, sir. If you will excuse me, others will be arriving." He bowed and left them, walking crisply back down the long hall.

Inside, they found a small home, with a private bath and three bedrooms with a central living room. They quickly stowed their gear, after unshrinking it. The women took one of the bedrooms, while the men divided themselves between the other two. The Mages began first a search for scrying devices and spells. Finding none, they then setup their own personal defenses. Satisfied, Zoran was about to visit Baron Milan when the baron knocked on his door.

"Ah you all look most presentable. That is good. Now then, Zoran, you are about to get a crash course in Federation Politics. Here is how it will begin. At five until ten, a butler will come for you. Baroness Archmage Zdenka, yourself, and the Zars will be expected to follow him. I'm afraid that there will be little for your security men to do this trip. They are allowed to explore the castle and fortifications and even the town, if they so desire. It beats just sitting around in this room. Now then, you four will be taken into the Visitor's Area. Once all of the visitors are in place, a fanfare will announce the arrival of the sixteen barons, who will enter formally and take their assigned seats."

"After Baron Alvaro makes his welcoming speech, the first order of business will be the formal announcement of the new Archmages of the sixteen worlds. When your name is called, you may take one step forward, if you choose. Not all of the new Archmages will be here. It is just a formality that allows every baron to know about all of the Archmages, the most powerful magic users in the Federation."

"Next, the announcement of the new Circle of Ascension and thus the newest House will be made. Expect many challenges to be made by Kazimir and his allies. If and when the High Council votes you in as the newest house and baron, you two will be formally introduced and allowed to take your seat. I have reserved four seats between my group and Viktor's group."

"This will surely be followed by the introduction of the Zars and a lengthy discussion of new Circles. After that, who knows what will be on the agenda. Okay, it is about time. Good luck son." He left just as Esteban appeared.

"If you will follow me, I will lead you to the Visitor's Area." Again, he spoke formally and in a bored manner, as if he had done this a million times. The six followed him down the halls and corridors, of course Jarka memorizing their path. He opened large double doors, required because of the width of the women's dresses. Holding Zdenka's arm, Zoran stepped into the huge meeting room, followed by Karel holding Jarka's arm, and Jiri holding Anezka's arm.

The area was separated from the rest of the room by an ornate wooden baluster wall that stood two feet tall. The barrel vaulted ceiling rose some fifty feet overhead covered with highly realistic artwork depicting various landscapes representing the sixteen worlds of the Federation. "Incredible!" whispered Jarka. None of these six had ever seen anything like this room.

Out beyond them were large, magnificently made tables and plush chairs, arranged in a U-shape with six foot gaps between the two joining corners. Zoran assumed that the neutral Barons would sit along the bottom of the U, while the two other aligned groups of Barons would sit facing each other. All could face the Visitor's Area. Across the way, a line of six uniformed men stood, large brass trumpets at the ready. Precisely at ten, they raised their instruments and began a fanfare. A bass voice bellowed loudly, "Baron Alvaro Cencion and Baroness Anita."

Arm in arm, the two walked slowly and stately into the room, their two male advisors following them. Sure enough, they took seats in the middle of the table that was at the bottom of the U. They stared at Zoran and his friends, however. The trumpets continued their fanfare and the voice announced the other barons and baronesses in turn, as slowly the room filled up. After all of the Neutral barons were seated, Baron Milan and his allies were seated next, followed by Baron Kazimir and his allies. All told, fifteen minutes elapsed before all were seated.

Baron Alvaro rose and spoke. Because of the acoustics in this vast chamber, his words were clearly heard throughout the spacious room. "Barons and baronesses, welcome to the twelve hundred and first High Council of the Federation of Planets. It is my great pleasure to host our meeting. I suspect this meeting will be one of the most profitable and unusual meetings that we have had in centuries! As usual, Baroness Anita will be hosting our evening meals and formal dances. Now let's get down to business, shall we? The first article of business is the formal announcement of the new Archmages of the Sixteen Planets. I am told that we are honored today by the presence of some of these powerful magic users. If you will step forward when your name is called, you can receive your formal recognition so richly deserved."

A fanfare sounded and the bass voice bellowed out. "Archmage Emil Vogler, Adapazan. Archmage Renata Vogler, Adapazan. Archmage Karel Ambrose, Adapazan." Karel took a step forward and received a hearty round of applause from the men and women — so much so that he blushed.

"Archmage Zdenka Lavos Vladislov, Adapazan." She stepped forward and received an even louder round of applause, primarily from the women in attendance. "Archmage Zoran Vladislov, Adapazan." Zoran stepped forward. The room erupted in a thunderous round of applause. Everyone knew that for the first time in history a Duska had achieved Archmage status! He noticed that even Kazimir clapped, though just barely.

Baron Alvaro then resumed control of the meeting. "Next on our agenda is the formal recognition of the newest Circle of Ascension and thus the newest House and baron to be officially proclaimed as such and allowed to join our High Council. As we all know, last Yuletide, a new Circle of Ascension has been created — sky blue its color. The Circle has been inspected personally by us and there can be no argument that it is not a real Circle of Ascension. Likewise, its owner, Zoran Vladislov is certified as a Duska, of that there again is no doubt. Hence, Zoran requests that he be formally proclaimed Baron Zoran Vladislov and be given his rightful seat on our High Council with full voting rights as the rest of us."

Baron Kazimir rose, "We object. This cannot be allowed. It violates our centuries old rule of one House, one Baron, per world. He should not be so recognized. I speak for many of us. Allowing this farce will only weaken and destroy our High Council. It goes against centuries of our illustrious history. I say veto this request." All of the other barons at his table yelled out in agreement, along with two others at the Neutral's table.

Baron Milan rose, "I hate to be the objector to Baron Kazimir's request, but there clearly are no such rules in place. Since the disappearance and death of Bandar Zar over centuries ago, there have been no further opportunities for any of us to build new Circles of Ascension. Thus, you may call it tradition, but the actual fact of the matter is that the technology to build them has been lost to us for over two centuries. There is no such rule in place."

He continued in a formal manner, "On the contrary, Rule 13 states that 'Once a Circle of Ascension has been verified as fully operational, that Circle becomes part of the Federation of Planets and its ruling High Council.' Rule 14 states that 'If the owner of said new Circle of Ascension is certified as a Duska, then said owner becomes its Baron.' Rule 15 states that 'Said Baron then becomes a full voting member of the High Council.' Barons, the rules are quite clear on this matter. Zoran should be fully recognized per our own rules."

Many ranted and raved about these, primarily the barons at Kazimir's table. In the end, they could not dispute the rules. Instead, Baron Bogdan tried a new approach. "Barons, I believe that we all are aware of the official rules. Yet, rules are just that rules. Rules are made to be broken. In this case, many of us feel that they should and must be broken. Look, if we allow this upstart to be on the High Council, look what it does. No longer will one planet be represented by one vote! Adapazan will now have two votes on our most important matters!"

Many catcalls and yells of protest followed, before he could continue. "Look what this does. While we have not yet discussed the construction of more Circles of Ascension, we all know that everyone of us will be begging the Zars to build us more Circles. Within just a few years, why there will be so many new Circles that we will not have room in this hall to seat so many barons! Our tight knit High Council will be watered down by dozens and dozens of new barons. What is to prevent say Gladno from constructing ten new Circles? Do we then give Gladno ten more votes than the rest of us have? I say, no, no, no! It cannot be tolerated!" The room erupted into a raucous cacophony of arguments, pro and con. Order could not be restored for nearly a quarter of an hour!

Using a Magnify spell, Baron Viktor bellowed out over everyone, "I've researched all our rules. There is no rule that says one vote per planet. It specifically says one vote per baron!" Still the arguing raged. Zoran realized fully that these men were in the fight of their very lives, politically that is. Indeed, as more Circles were built, more members would join the High Council, diluting the voting process, lessening the political clout of any one single member. Worse still, no longer could they count on one planet's vote, because in the case of Adapazan, certainly Zoran and Kazimir would vote the opposite of each other! He knew that what was decided here today would have a very far reaching impact on the entire ruling body of the Federation.

Just then, the trumpeters sounded another fanfare, announcing the dinner call. That ended the argument. Zoran and party dined at a separate table from the barons, though the meal was the same, absolutely exquisite, roasted pheasant. When the session resumed an hour later, cooler heads prevailed. Baron Alvaro proclaimed, "Barons, it is clear that we must follow our own rules in this matter. I will add another item to our agenda so that we can work out new rules or perhaps just new policies, but we cannot turn aside from our own rules that we swore to uphold upon taking office." He conducted a vote and only Kazimir and his allies voted against allowing Zoran to take his rightful place on the High Council.

"It is my greatest pleasure in announcing to the world the newest Circle of Ascension of the Free Peoples of Adapazan. I give you Baron Archmage Zoran Vladislov and Baroness Archmage Zdenka Vladislov!" The room erupted into cheers and clapping. Zoran proudly escorted Zdenka from the Visitor's Area to their seats between Milan and Viktor. Karel and Jarka followed behind them, leaving only the Zars remaining in the Visitor's Area.

"The next item of business is to hear from Brother Jiri Zar and Priestess Anezka Zar, the great-great-great grandson of Bandar Zar himself," Baron Alvaro proclaimed. Again, the room erupted into a heady round of applause, causing both to blush. They were given seats before the U-shaped table arrangement. "Please, Brother Jiri, tell us how it was that you have been able to build a new working Circle of Ascension. Spare us no detail!"

For an hour, Brother Jiri outlined what had happened, beginning with Warlord Mikolas and his discovery of the hidden room beneath his fortress. Even the role played by Zoran was related, including the dragons' aid. He outlined how one of Baron Kazimir's assassins very nearly killed him and how Zoran and friends had rescued him. Kazimir fumed, he had not known just how close he had been to obtaining these priceless documents. Twice now, they had slipped from his grasp, though he did not even know of their existence.

He then decided to outline his future plans. That is, he announced that he was going to build other Circles of Ascension, one for Milan and one for Viktor. He explained his requirements for so doing, namely his price, the buyer's obligations, and that he retained control over for whom he would build more Circles. He did not, however, tell them that half of the monetary proceeds of each new Circle would be donated to Zoran. They didn't need to know what he did with his money.

"See, it's just as I said," Baron Kazimir bellowed when Brother Jiri was finished. "Now Gladno and Valtr will also have two votes in our council, not one. This is rapidly getting out of control. Brother Jiri will of course build another Circle for me, will he not?" Kazimir provoked Brother Jiri, knowing full well what he was causing.

"Of course not, Baron Kazimir. I exercise my right not to build one for you. We've enough tyranny on our worlds without my adding to them!" Brother Jiri spoke acidly, playing right into the baron's hands.

"See! It's just as I said. Soon, many of us will become second class barons!" Baron Kazimir fairly screamed at the others. His allies pounded their fists on the table in support of his views.

Baron Alvaro calmly replied, "All in good time, barons. I assure you that this is on the agenda and will be fully covered. Now then, Brother Jiri Zar, Priestess Anezka Zar, the High Council would like to present you both with our highest medal of honor for what you have done, the Golden Eagle Cross! There is no higher honor that we can bestow on anyone, not even we barons. Please come forward and it will be my honor to make the presentations! Such an award has not been handed out in over one hundred seventy-five years!" His was the limelight shared with the Zars. History would remember him as the baron who made this presentation; he savored every moment of it. Each received a jewel encrusted golden amulet in the shape of an eagle on a gold neck chain.

"Please dine with us barons this evening. I am sure that each of us wishes to personally thank you for what you have done," he wrapped up the presentation. Of course, everyone also knew that the other barons would be contacting him this evening about constructing more Circles for themselves! After the Zars left, the topic became what most impacted these men: what to do about the foreseen proliferation of new Circles of Ascension and the balance of power.

Baron Milan offered the first view. "Barons, no matter what we do about this situation, we must follow our three century old tradition. If a new Circle comes into existence and if it has a Duska, he must be proclaimed a baron and given a voting seat on this High Council. To do otherwise is to discard the very foundation on which the Federation of Planets is based! To do otherwise is tantamount to our own destruction!"

"Point well taken," Baron Bran Ahern of the forested world of Maeve and a Neutral agreed. "I agree, the rules on which our Federation was founded must be held sacred and adhered to or we will surely fall into a civil war amongst ourselves.

"But what about the disparity of votes?" put in Baron Aryeh Makeda of the desert world of Chana. "This is a very, very serious problem that we face!"

"And what about the number of Circles that are allowed to be built on each planet?" added Baron Hajime Yoko of the water world of Asami. "Ought we not assign some limits to the number allowed per planet?"

Thus, the political maneuvering began in earnest. Zoran was pleased that they all decided that the ancient rules ought to be followed regarding new Circles and barons. At least that much was still sacred. However, the rest was totally up in the air. By dinnertime, nothing had been decided, though many opinions had been tossed onto the table.

That evening, Zoran and Zdenka dined with the other barons for the first time as their equals. Interestingly enough, the barons chose to sit together, leaving their wives to chat among themselves. With the exception of Kazimir and his allies, the other barons were quite friendly to Zoran, offering him advice, suggestions, and even their help, should he desire it. Many attempted to point out their various unspoken policies of court etiquette.

Zdenka, on the other hand, found herself fitting in well with nearly all of the baronesses. They were most impressed with her achievement of Archmage, a topic that nearly everyone mentioned to her during the evening. Many asked if Zoran really had achieved that status, Archmage. She dutifully pointed out his use of the Archmage-only spell that he had cast at the funeral ceremony for his mother. That satisfied all challenges. She received numerous requests for her and Zoran to come and visit the other planets in the Federation, all except their enemies, that is.

Still the enemy baronesses were not unfriendly towards her, as their husbands were to Zoran. Many offered fashion tips. The young Baroness Liu Meerong of Jing, whose husband was allied with Baron Kazimir, flashed her five inch long fingernails deftly. "My dear, it is the height of fashion to have really long beautiful nails. Look at mine, I've painted them bright red, such an elegant color. You should let yours grow long as well. Mine are the longest of us baronesses."

Baroness Anita Cencion of Alta took a liking to her. She was only a few years older than Zdenka. "My dear, your dress is lovely. I can see the tastes of Marjeta and Ivana in it. Some of us prefer styles like mine. See how much it flairs out, nearly eight feet. And oh, do go for brighter colors, Zdenka. You will look so much more vibrant and radiant in bright colors. Now, your shoes — they are much too conservative! Here, look at my pumps. See the height of my heels? Six inches indeed. They make you taller and far more dainty and graceful. Half of us baronesses are now wearing them. Now we do have to take smaller steps, but we like to think that we are making our spouses slow down and appreciate us all the more." She rattled on and Zdenka found that she could not refuse accepting a pair from her to try out tomorrow. Indeed, before she knew what she was agreeing too, Baroness Anita had her trying on a whole new wardrobe for tomorrow!

At last, a large band of musicians entered and the formal dance began. The others in their party now joined them as the tables were cleared and the dance began. Both Zoran and Zdenka became so in love with the dancing that they vowed to acquire their own band as soon as possible. Even Jarka and Karel got into the dancing, though Karel was definitely not a dancer. He put on a brave face for Jarka's sake. Soon, others began interrupting them, insisting on a dance with either Zoran or Zdenka. By the end of the evening, Zoran had danced with all of the baronesses. He got an earful of suggestions. Why doesn't he allow her to grow her nails really long which is the latest in fashion? Why doesn't he get her the latest in dresses and high heels? Would he bring her and come for a visit? On it went.

On her side, the barons pumped her for information. Where does Zoran stand on this issue and that one? Cleverly she sidestepped these by saying, "He's only just gotten his Circle and is still working to get his own house in order. I'm sure you can explain your position to him far better than I can." On it went, a delightful evening of dance with strong political overtones.

Early the next morning, Baroness Anita confiscated Zdenka, "I'm going to dress your beautiful wife up properly. She ought to be wearing the very latest in fashions!" Poor Zdenka was swept away by Anita, though she looked longingly back at Zoran as she was whisked away, Anita chatting all the way. Zoran chuckled.

Just in time to head down to the morning Council session, Anita returned with Zdenka dolled up in the latest fashions. Her outfit now resembled that of over half of the women in attendance. Her dress did indeed billow out eight feet, reds, yellows, and blues alternated in a colorful pattern that did make her look even more attractive. "It's these shoes," she complained. The heels are so high that I can barely walk in them. Please hold on to me! I don't want to fall down! That would be the height of embarrassment! Go slower. I can only take tiny steps. Supposedly these are the very latest in fashion," she explained.

"We are invited to their ballet tonight. It is some kind of music and dance performance, she said. Anita said that the dancers walk and dance on their toes! I don't see how that is possible, but we are invited. I couldn't say no. Is that okay?"

"Sure thing. You do look gorgeous, my love. Besides the slower we go the more time I can spend with you and not those stuffy men and their politicking." Both laughed along with Jarka and Karel.

The hours passed with more bickering and arguing among the barons. By late afternoon, two motions finally were agreed to be put to a vote. One suggested that they retain one vote per planet and that those with multiple houses had to come to their own voting consensus. If they could not agree or it was a tie in other words, then that planet's vote would not count. The other motion was to allow partial votes. If a planet had two Circles and thus two voting barons, then each one's vote would be a half vote. If one had four, then each vote would be a quarter vote. Either way, Zoran realized, there would only be sixteen actual full votes being counted.

At long last, the two motions came up for voting. The partial vote motion lost, primarily because of the complicated bookkeeping that would be needed to count votes. Thus, from now on, those planets with multiple Circles and thus barons would have only one vote and they would have to agree on it or their planet's vote would not be tallied. This sat well with Zoran's enemies. It was perhaps the best concession that Baron Kazimir could obtain, under the circumstances. Still, with the Adapazan vote now no longer counting, since the two would likely never agree, the balance of power shifted to Baron Milan's side, by one vote, ignoring the Neutrals, of course. They would still have to be carefully courted to obtain enough key votes, but that was one vote easier now.

That evening, Baron Alvaro and Baroness Anita came to fetch Zoran and Zdenka to take them to the ballet, along with Karel and Jarka. Zdenka kept an eye on Anita to see how well she managed walking on these terrifically high heels. She was amazed at how graceful Anita actually was, though she said nothing. The ballet was spectacular. None of the four had ever seen anything like it. Men and women dancers did indeed walk, prance, and twirl around on their tips of their toes. The music was enchanting and all four truly appreciated the performance. Zoran and Zdenka began to realize just how much was truly deficient back on Adapazan. Arts were so lacking!

"We have to bring culture and civilization to Adapazan!" Zdenka exclaimed to Zoran, when they were finally back in their room.

"Absolutely. Music, dance, ballet — I never knew that these existed before! Our planet must be completely backwards, in the sticks!"

"No," Jarka intervened, "Kazimir has been doing nothing but conquering and subjugating our people. Once he is gone, we can then bring Adapazan out of its dark ages."

The rest of the week's meetings were down right boring and mundane. It held little of consequence for Zoran's group. However, Baroness Anita, encouraged by the enthusiasm of Zoran and Zdenka, took them to other cultural events in the evenings. She took them to a play the next night. A return trip to the ballet followed that and then a choral performance. However, the last night of their stay was the formal dance and once again everyone had to be there. Nothing could keep the four from the dance floor now!

After the dance, Barons Milan and Viktor dropped by Zoran's room. "Word with you nephew," he began. Zoran offered them a seat and they all gathered around the two older men.

"Okay, mission accomplished. However, now come Kazimir's countermoves. We've sent out spies to Dorum and to his other allied planets in hopes of getting some advanced knowledge of their next move."

"So it is not done yet?" Zdenka reacted a bit unnerved.

"Not by a long shot. He has two targets now: Zoran and Lida. If he can somehow have Lida killed, he can name a new heir. However, with your recognition, he has much larger worries, which we feel takes the pressure off of Lida. Our money is on their attempting to somehow take you out, Zoran. If you die, then by our own rules, your Circle is up for grabs. That is, it must have a Duska. If you are eliminated, he will try to install someone else, such as Baron Bogdan's son Strom, for example. Only then will he be highly likely to come after Lida with his full might."

"Yes, but surely they won't mount an all-out assault on us? It took him a whole couple of years to build up and make his attack on Sholov Province. Either way he goes, there are three more provinces between his lands and Brn," Zoran pointed out.

Baron Viktor replied, "We've considered this. Yes, overland directly — yes, it may well take him several years and at a terrible cost, considering our promised armies and your use of dragons. It is my best guess that he has weighed that cost and found it prohibitive. He is not a complete fool. The best advice that I can give you is to stay alert for other actions. Perhaps a Shadow Walk of an army directly to the gates of Brn. Perhaps a number of assassins. His objective is not necessarily the capture of your Circle but rather your death, Zoran. Please stay alive. All depends upon your outliving Kazimir. He knows this too."

"Yes, he knows that we know this," Milan picked up the discussion. "Hence, we are going to arrange to make him believe that we are planning an assassination of him. He has spies in our lands as well, as do his allies. We intend to make sure that they learn of some assassination plots against his life. Don't worry; we are not about to really assassinate Kazimir, but he doesn't know that. Our objective is to make him paranoid about attempts on his life, directing much of his energies off of you, Zoran. We're trying our best to indirectly aid you."

"Bottom line," he finished up, "is stay alert to all manner of unusual ways that they could get to you. We don't believe that it will be an overland assault, marching through three other provinces to get to you. That's what we are saying. And for heaven's sake, if anything does come up, let us know immediately. We will help you in any way possible."

"Thanks uncles. We really appreciate all that you are doing for us and for my twin sisters," Zoran admitted freely. "Someday, perhaps I can repay you." Both men smiled, indeed both knew that day would come. They were politicians, after all, powerful ones at that. The men shook hands and left.

No sooner had they gone than another knock on their door startled them. Zoran opened it to find Baron Alvaro standing there. "Baron Archmage Zoran, Baroness Archmage Zdenka. My wife and I would like to give you some parting presents — a small token of our friendship. You see, just because we are Neutral does not mean that we are your enemies. On the contrary, we just do not want to get involved in interplanetary conflicts. If you will come with me and bring along Archmage Karel and Mage Jarka, Baroness Anita is waiting for us. Oh yes, you should also bring along your General of Security as well." He had a twinkle in his eye.

Dutifully, the small group followed the Baron down many corridors and finally out into the large courtyard where Anita was waiting for them. "Ah, so good to see you once more, Baroness Zdenka. Alvaro and I wanted to give you some parting gifts to remember us by, and we do so hope that you will come and visit us as soon as you can, though we know right now you face many problems at home. From me to you and your beautiful companion, I have three of the latest fashion dresses like the one you wore and three matching pairs of the new heels as well." Both women were pleased, though Zdenka still had not gotten used to walking in the heels. They thanked her profusely.

"Archmage Karel, here are six of the finest hawks on Alta. We've heard that you are a master falconer, a small token of our new found friendship." Karel examined the birds in their cages and was very nearly speechless. No one had ever given him such a royal present before. He shook Alvaro's hand vigorously.

"General Lavos, please accept this crate of the finest bastard swords on Alta. We both know that such will be most useful for you as you build up your protective forces for the young baron here." Now it was Janos' turn to be impressed, and he gave him a hearty thank you.

"Finally, baron, Alta is horse country. We produce some of the finest mounts in the Federation, though others may dispute our claim. Please accept my donation of six fine mounts. Two are stallions and the rest are mares so that you may breed them, if desired."

"Thank you, Baron Alvaro, thank you. Indeed, you may not believe this, but until now, I didn't even own a horse! These will be very timely and valuable to us. Thank you for your incredible hospitality. I never expected such kindness. If there is anything I can do for you, let me know." As soon as he said this, he realized that he had been totally setup! This was precisely what the baron had desired.

"Well, there is one small matter. I have asked Brother Jiri to build us a new Circle of Ascension here on Alta. He has agreed to do so. However, he is not sure how soon he can get to us. If it is not too much trouble, why just give him a nudge that we will really appreciate it as soon as he can build it for us. See, a simple matter. I'm sure that most all of the barons had asked him to build another one for them as well. I suspect that he'll want to build those for your allies first, so when that is done, we would love to be next in line. And please, come back for a visit any time that you can. Alta has much to offer you. Friends?" he offered his hand.

"Sure, friends," Zoran shook his hand. "I'll chat with Brother Jiri. I suspect that he has already made some promises to others, but if he hasn't, I will put in a good word for you. Truly, I speak for Zdenka as well; we both have been very impressed with Alta and with you and your wife. We look forward to coming for a visit, once the home front is stable. Thank you again for your gracious gifts."

Back in their room, Jarka commented, "Okay, I now know the precise routes that we traveled here and can duplicate them anytime. Say, that's pretty magnanimous of them to give us all such presents."

"Well, he wanted Zoran to attempt to move his request for a new Circle ahead of whatever he may have worked out with Brother Jiri. Small price to pay if anything comes of it. Pure political move," General Janos replied.

"Well, at least we have made one new baron friend," Zoran commented. "I am beginning to suspect those that are Neutral are merely neutral in interplanetary conflicts, not necessarily neutral in good versus evil tyranny. That is something that I did not know before."

"You will need to study the six Neutrals thoroughly, Zoran," Karel declared, "before you can make an honest overall appraisal."

Chapter 20 Spring's Problems

By the 1st of April, Brn was a hive of activity. Already, Aldrick had brokered the move of about a hundred more gold dragons from Voss. Each of the ten warlord provinces now had around ten dragons to protect them. The smaller provinces had fewer, such as Orlovia, as well as the bitterly cold province of Tratky. Larger ones had a few more. In each, one dragon was appointed the leader and maintained communication with that warlord's Mage. Aldrick secretly maintained contact with all these dragon leaders. Unknown to Zoran, at this time, Aldrick was also acquiring some gold dragons for several other planets, Gladno and Valtr among them.

The physical shipment of the emergency grain shipments for Tratky was handled by Duke Stefan. Neither Baron Viktor nor Milan wanted to risk Zoran handling the shipment because of rising fears that Baron Kazimir would seize this opportunity to kill Zoran. Indeed, their spies had already begun reporting troop buildups on all of the enemy planets.

Brother Jiri and Priestess Anezka had not returned from Alta with Zoran. Instead, he went to Gladno with Baron Milan. His objective: build a new Circle of Ascension for him. He hoped to begin construction of Baron Viktor's new Circle towards the end of the year.

Archmage Zdenka now had her hands full. Saturday was the spring Picking time once again. All week before Saturday, she was a nervous wreck, according to Zoran. "Have I got the check lists ready, Zoran? How many should I pick? Archmage Nadia suggested that I take only four, but what if there are many good candidates? How am I going to choose them, really Zoran? I know the questions that she used, but what if there are a lot that pass the test? Am I really going to be able to train them, do you think? What am I forgetting?"

Poor Zoran, all he could do was to continually support her and help calm her fears. Six advanced students of Archmage Oldrich were still here and Zdenka was now going to be their teacher, though Nadia had promised to help her with anything she might need. Indeed, Archmage Nadia had spent a good deal of time with Zdenka, instructing her on what to do. Marek was still the door warden, though he hoped to work on his topmost spells this year. Perhaps this would be the year that he achieved Archmage status; he certainly hoped for it. He'd also volunteered to help her out with the other students, which she greatly appreciated.

Making matters worse, she could not just go to the Stodgy Inn by herself to conduct her Picking. Since she was now a baroness, she would be a prime target for Zoran's enemies. If they could get to her, they could use her to get to him. Thus, the Archmages and Mages worked out a plan. Jarka would cast Invisible and take up a station behind where Zdenka would be seated, guarding her rear. Karel would be Invisible and perched just above the door to the inn, surveying and studying all who entered the inn on Saturday. Zoran and the twins, also Invisible, would station themselves near her, yet out of the way of those in the inn. Finally, they put all of the protection spells possible on her, before she went into the inn on Saturday. Bernard had already gone into the inn the night before and was pretending to be spending the night there. He would be scouting out all of those staying at the inn and be sitting at the bar during the Picking.

"Well, here I go," Archmage Zdenka said to Mage Marek on Saturday morning as ten o'clock approached.

"You will do fine, Archmage," he said softly and encouragingly. She cast her spell and stepped into the center of the Stodgy Inn. A dozen had come for this year's picking, eight young women and four young men. Most of the men of Brn were now engaged in the fortress construction and its supporting tasks. The pay was so good that few could refuse this golden opportunity to make double their usual income this year.

Zdenka walked to the middle of the room and made her announcement. "Hello everyone. I am Baroness Archmage Zdenka Vladislov. Once again, it is Picking Time, when we accept new students into our magic school. This year because of the extensive construction that is going on, I will be accepting only four students. If the construction has subsided next year, I will accept the usual dozen. If you are not chosen this year, please try again next year. Age is not a factor to gain entry into Brn Tower. Now then, those of you who wish to apply, see me at yonder table, one at a time please." She walked to the very same table at which Nadia had sat and chosen her.

One by one the hopeful young teens came up to her. She noticed that a pair of twin girls was present; both had long brown hair and oval faces. She found it difficult to tell them apart. Their clothes were in a terrible state, a patchwork of patches. That they came from a very poor family was more than obvious. Yet, as the first one sat nervously before her, she could see that they were clean.

"And what is your name?" she asked.

"Markéta Tehov, your Archmage-ship," she replied timidly, totally uncertain just how to address Zdenka.

"I'm glad that you decided to come for the Picking. Now then, I have a little situation to describe to you and then I will ask you some questions about it." Markéta nodded, fingering her long brown hair with long slender fingers. She guessed that Markéta was perhaps fourteen.

"You enter a room only to find a table with a bag containing one thousand gold coins in it. Sitting at the table is a young man who is bleeding badly from a sword wound. You see no sword in the room. Cowering against the back of the room is young mother shielding a small child. What do you do?"

"Oh my, so much gold. I've never seen more than one gold coin that my mother once had. What do I do? He's going to die if we cannot stop the bleeding. I can use part of my dress to make a bandage somehow. I have to get him to the doctors. Is there a doctor anywhere nearby?" she replied, compassion flowing from her eyes.

"Very good, Markéta. You are chosen. Please take a seat over by that man at the bar. His name is Mage Barnard."

"Oh! Really? Me? Accepted? Oh thank you, thank you. Oh, please, you must pick my sister too, please? We are never parted," she begged.

"Well, that depends on her. She will get the same opportunity as everyone else." Markéta seemed satisfied and moved over to Bernard, who began talking with her.

Her sister came next. "Hi, what is your name?"

"Karina Tehov, your Archmage-ship," she replied in an nearly identical tone of voice. Zdenka asked the same questions of her.

Much to Zdenka's surprise, Karina's reply was word for word, emotion for emotion the same as Markéta's! Quite amazed, she said, "Well, your answer is identical to your sister's. You are also chosen, but how is it that your answers are so identical?"

"We always know exactly what the other is thinking, your Archmage-ship," she replied timidly, as if perhaps she had done something wrong.

"Fascinating, Karina. We must talk about this at length. Please go join your sister with Mage Bernard."

A boy answered that he would take the gold and then go in search of a doctor and use the money to pay the doctor. Zdenka cast her Forget spell on him and politely asked him to try again next year when she would be taking more students.

A bit later, she chose a fifteen year old girl with short black hair and an infectious smile. Her name was Jitka Liten and was already a seamstress, but wanted to see if she could learn magic as well. The last person to come up to her was Gustav Tava, a lad who had turned sixteen. His father had trained him as a blacksmith. He was well-muscled, but had found smithing not to his liking. Now he had a chance to learn magic, which he hoped that he would like. He too was chosen.

Just as Zdenka was about to tell the four what to do next, Archmage Karel's Message spell contacted all of the mages. "Help outside. Got me an assassin red-handed. Little help, please, Jarka!" Instantly, the Invisible spells cancelled, surprising the four new students and the bar keeper himself.

"Stay here kids. Bernard, guard them. Karel's captured an assassin outside the inn. Be right back!" Zdenka exclaimed, and joined Jarka, Renata, Emil, and Zoran as they raced to the inn's doors.

Outside, Karel had a man entrapped in a mass of sticky Webs from his spell. Six of his hawks were perched on the horse rail nearby. The man's eye sockets were bloody and empty, hawk claw marks covered his bearded face. "Hawks helped me out. He's now more or less harmless as he can't see. Jarka, what do we do with him? I don't want to get poisoned." Karel was more than angry. He'd spared no punches stopping the assassin from entering the inn — that was abundantly clear!

Jarka cleverly and cautiously removed the assassin's daggers and short sword. She checked his boots and pant legs, disarming him of his two concealed throwing daggers. "Who sent you to kill Baroness Archmage Zdenka?" she spat on the wed-tangled man, thrashing about in terror and pain.

"None'o you damn business," he screamed, wildly trying to free himself.

"Should we torture him to find out?" Karel asked. "I can figure out some painful means!"

Zoran laughed, "I'm sure you can, Karel. No, I have a better way, the Duska way."

"No!" the man screamed, his voice going up an octave in high pitched terror!

Everyone looked at Zoran. He realized that none knew what he was talking about, but that the assassin did. "A Duska can read men's minds, though I have never done it yet. I guess there is always a first time for everything. Here goes." He wanted to put his dear friends and wife at ease about this revelation of a Duska skill. They might suddenly believe that he had been probing their minds all along.

Zoran concentrated. However, something was very different about his mental skills now. Admittedly, he'd not used anything but his Shadow Walking, communication ability, and danger warning skills for a very long time. Still, something was vastly different. At first, everything in his mind turned sky blue, the color of his Circle's thread. Peculiar, he thought. Then, he focused on the man before him and to his surprise he found that he could easily slip into the man's mind and thoughts! He'd learned how to do this from his sisters, but it had always required his utmost concentration. Even then, the images and thoughts were faint and hard to decipher. Now, the images were vividly real; the man's thoughts, quite clear!

"Ah, he was sent on behalf of Kazimir by Bogdan. He was supposed to kill Zdenka," Zoran reported to his friends.

Jarka spat on him once more. "Bastard. Death is too good for you!"

"What do we do with him? We cannot turn him loose," Zdenka asked, torn between the man's injuries and the fact that he had been intent on killing her.

"We need to send Bogdan a clear message!" Karel angrily declared. "I know, let me remove his arms too and bandage them up. Then, we send him back to Bogdan!"

Unable to stomach the retribution being put forth, Zdenka went back inside to her new students. Emil said quietly, "It is too dangerous for you to Shadow Walk to Bogdan's castle. Your Uncle would have a fit. Please allow Renata and me to return him to Bogdan on Rehor."

"Okay, thanks, Karel, Emil, Renata. Well done all of you." He went back inside to check on how Zdenka was handling this attempt on her life. Karel was true to his anger. Two quick whacks and the man's arms were removed below his elbows. A quick pair of tourniquets stopped his bleeding. The twins changed into their normal dragon forms. Emil picked up the man in his claws, and the two dragons swooped gracefully into the sky and then disappeared. Meantime, Karel and Jarka cleaned up the mess.

When they were done, the twins returned. Renata said, "That's done. We took the opportunity to test out our fire breaths once more."

Emil chuckled, "We gave the Baron a wake up call and burned quite a few of his men in the process." Karel laughed loudly, and they all went inside to escort the new students and the others back to the tower.

Meanwhile inside, Zdenka was quite shaken by the assassination attempt. "I am truly sorry, Zdenka, to have brought this down on you," Zoran consoled her.

"I know you are. I knew what I was getting into when I married you. I do so love you, Zoran. It's just the awfulness is only now coming home to me. I will be okay. I am just glad that my new students didn't have to see it. I'm okay."

A bit later, Zdenka began introducing her new students to life in her tower. One of the first actions she did was obtain new dresses for the twins. By late afternoon, all four were beginning their initial studies of the history of magic and of Adapazan. She now spent her time with the older students.

Meantime, Karel and Zoran held a discussion with the engineers on the fortress construction. Karel had come up with a bright idea several days ago. Zoran held a conference with his friends, and all agreed that it was a brilliant one. Now the two set about seeing how it may be accomplished. Essentially, Karel had suggested, "Look. We have dragons protecting us, but let's not put all of our eggs in one hen house. We know that there are other kinds of dragons on Voss. What happens if Kazimir or Bogdan gets their hands on some of them and sends them here to attack our new castle and fortifications? We have seen the damage that the teens can do to stone with just their bodies. Remember how they nearly caved in the exit from Mikolas' castle? Well, suppose our fortifications get attacked by some other dragons. We ought to build in some additional protections."

"My idea is to put an impenetrable Force Wall down the middle of all of the wall sections and then inside the castle-manor house walls and on top of the roofs. Make the spells permanent and you've got a hidden extra measure of protection. What say you all?" Everyone thought Karel's idea was sound, practical, and brilliant. At this point in time, Zoran and Karel had to work out its implementation with the five top engineers.

The high, impassable, rugged mountain valley just behind the Wizard Tower and northern walls of Brn was filled with work crews. Like ants, they cut through the hard granite, leveling off the surface which the outer walls would eventually surround. The stone that they removed was carefully cut and polished and stored for use in the wall construction proper. Another crew had just begun assembling the first section of the mile in circumference walls. Each section was fifteen feet long and would be three feet thick at its top, each rising fifteen feet above the ground. Three hundred fifty-two such sections were required, yielding nearly two hundred fifty thousand cubic feet of stone to be quarried, shaped, polished, and set into position.

The forty work crews that the two barons had sent would require nearly ten years finishing the outer walls, ignoring the inner castle and manor house! However, the barons sent along ten Mages who would use their magical spells to help the workers, cutting the time down to one year for the outer walls to be finished. Zoran began to fully realize just how indebted he was to his uncles Milan and Viktor!

While they were discussing the alteration of Karel's, two workers came running up to their chief engineers. "Come quick! We've struck something important. Gems, we think." Everyone rushed after the two excited workers. At the center of the area being cleared, where the base of the castle was going to be positioned, workers having removed a good deal of stone, discovered two ore bearing veins, running on down into the mountain. The jubilant workers quickly pointed out what appeared to be a large green gemstone affixed to the rocky vein and nearby was a clear, white crystal in a similar vein.

Zoran sent off a Message spell and shortly an enormous gold dragon swooped down, landed, and changed into the familiar form of Aldrick. Naturally, the workers all stopped to stare at this incredible sight. "What have you found?" he asked curiously.

"Well, that's what I need you for — have a look see. Valuable gems perhaps, at least we think so," Zoran replied. He kept his fingers crossed. Could he be this lucky? Obtaining enough money was a major problem he faced. Aldrick squatted down and began examining the green stone. "Yes, it is an emerald! Looks like they've uncovered a vein here. Now this other is a diamond, Zoran. You need to carefully extract these. The emeralds are particularly prone to breakage when you try to break them free from the stones to which they have grown. You need to mine these veins carefully."

"Well, I have not got any miners around. Those who can do this are up at the mountain mines beyond the Dark Forest. Would you be interested in doing the mining here for me?"

"Certainly. I can use this opportunity to train my twins properly. What say you to our keeping a quarter of what we find?" Aldrick struck a hard bargain. Zoran, however, readily agreed. He needed all the help he could muster.

"Deal."

Aldrick was surprised that Zoran had not bargained for a lower price, and he felt a bit guilty having asked such a high price. "We'll throw in the cutting of the gemstones as well. It will give my twins much valuable experience. They must know how to precisely cut a raw stone so as to bring out its true inner beauty. Sofie, the twins, and I will get on it now, if we are not going to be in the way."

The plans for the castle portion now had to be slightly revised to allow for the two working mines in its basement. The excavated rock the dragons generated was used in the construction of the walls, so it did not go to waste. However, easy access had to be provided in the castle plans for the mines once it was built.

While they were reworking the plans, Jarka made a suggestion. "Based on what I have seen with the other Baron's Circle of Ascension protections, I think that we can do it better. Suppose that we cast and make permanent a Mind Maze spell in the corridor just before the Circle's room. As long as one speaks the password, nothing happens. However, if someone should try to sneak in via your Circle, when they reach the Mind Maze, they will become trapped in an endless maze until we let them out. That ought to stop any assassins trying to sneak in that way." Oh, Jarka was brilliant, Zoran thought. He readily adopted her idea and thanked her profusely for coming up with an excellent use of magical spells.

The next day, Mayor Bogdan Oldrich came to visit Zoran. "Baron, about these road improvements. We've drawn up these plans and I would like to make sure that we are going to be meeting the proposed needs. As you know, the mountain peaks here in Brn Province pretty much dictate the path that our roads must take. I know that it is a long, circuitous route to get to Ves, Valy, and Veklov Provinces from here. We are in the very north of our province. The mountains and Dark Forest rather force us to go very nearly to the southern edge before we can go east or west to Valy or Ves." Zoran examined his proposals and decided that they would suffice.

"Have you coordinated with the other three provinces to make sure those will be the routes that they will be improving? We don't want our improved roads to wind up in some isolated valley of Ves Province," Zoran asked.

"Not exactly, but those are the only real road into those provinces from here. Can you contact those warlords and make sure we are going to meet up with their improved road systems?" Zoran agreed to do this.

"Now then, the cost of these improvements. Brn treasury is unable at this time to finance all of these improvements at once. Nor do we have the manpower to do three at the same time. I believe that we can finish one of these road improvements yet this construction season."

"Okay. I suspect the other warlords will be having similar problems. Let's see if we can get the improvements made to Veklov Province. Next year, the two east-west side spurs to the other two provinces can be done. How's that?" Mayor Bogdan was pleased and left to attend to the details. This was going to be a major expense for Brn this year; he'd have little left over for anything else.

That night, Zoran began having nightmares. At least he called them that. In the middle of the night, he awoke in a hot sweat. He'd seen a mermaid swimming around a Circle of Ascension. Somehow the mermaid was drowning and he was trying to help her, but continually failed.

"What's wrong?" asked a very concerned Zdenka, who had been awakened by his thrashing in their bed. She saw that he was dripping wet. "Are you ill?"

"Bad dream. No, I'm fine. Just had a nightmare, that's all. Mermaid was drowning and I couldn't save her."

"Dear, there are no such things as mermaids. It must be your imagination at work. Maybe you are working too hard. Maybe all of the stress you are under — what with all the assassinations and war threats." She tried to invent a plausible explanation. He agreed with her and they went back to sleep.

Since the assassination attempt on Baroness Zdenka, Karel had adopted a new policy. He's been highly successful at thwarting the assassin by virtue of being both Invisible and perched high on the roof of the inn. From that vantage point, he'd seen the assassin coming. Now each morning as the sun rose, Karel moved to the top of the tower, some five stories above the city and the construction site behind the tower. Here was where he kept his dozen falcon cages. Each morning, as well as evening, he would release them and allow them to hunt and get some exercise. While they were doing so, he cast his most powerful spell, changing into a giant falcon himself. While circling high over the town, his falcon vision showed all warm blooded bodies down below. Workers coming to the construction site predominated.

Karel's thought was to continue to hunt for further Invisible assassins who might be making a sneak attack on the tower. Anyone about below who had cast Invisibility on themselves would show up with his falcon sight. He could now see in the infrared band as did his hunters. Once the town became a bustling hive of activity, Karel would transform back and call back his many falcons and join the others for breakfast. Thus far, he's seen nothing out of the ordinary.

Near the end of April, while they were eating breakfast, Baron Milan made mental contact with Zoran. *Zoran, we just got word from our spies that a large force of shock troops is on the move. We don't know where they are headed or how many there are. Reports suggest that a number of Mages are with them. Stay vigilant, nephew.* He thanked his uncle and promised to be so.

"Gang, that was my uncle. He reports that his spies have detected a large force of shock troops and Mages are on the move. Stay alert today. They may be headed here," Zoran relayed the news. All day long, everyone was on high alert, spells at the ready. However, Zdenka continued her lessons with her students. If an attack came, she would join in the defense. Nothing happened all that day.

In the middle of the night, Zoran again had his mermaid nightmare, waking Zdenka once again. "It's always the same. I see this mermaid swimming around a

Circle and she is drowning and I am powerless to prevent it," he explained, wiping the sweat from his face. Zdenka just snuggled with him. She'd run out of things to say. After all, mermaids did not exist. True, the Mages could cast Breath Water spells and stay underwater for hours, but there were no mermaids on any planets.

At dawn, Karel once again let his falcons lose and transformed into his giant falcon form to join them. As he soared high above the nearly deserted streets just beyond the entrance of the Archmage Tower, he suddenly spied invisible forms materializing. At once, he cast his Message spell to the others.

In bed, Zoran suddenly had a vision of a Circle of Ascension activating and men in plate armor with broadswords and shiny helms were being transported. He awoke with a start. Just then, Karel's warning message blasted into his mind as well as all of the other Mages and General Janos. Archmage Karel dove for the safety of the tower's barbican lined top and transformed back into his normal form. Then, he hastily cast numerous protection spells on himself. Invisible, he crept to the edge and peered down into the broad street below.

Hundreds of Kazimir's best shock troops, their plate mail armor glinting in the early morning sunlight, began marching rapidly towards the tower. In the rear, hovering above the mass of men were five Mages, Archmage Milos, and Baron Kazimir himself. The Baron was heavily encased in his best suit of armor and was at the very rear of his small force.

Boom! The Archmage cast a Disintegrate spell on the wooden doors of the tower, splintering them into kindling wood. The Baron's plan was obvious. Rush the tower before anyone was awake and take them all down while they were confined within the constricted space of the tower. Karel took careful aim and determinedly cast his spell. Suddenly, Archmage Milos' head had a three inch hole bored completely through it. He died instantly from Karel's Disintegrate spell, catching the small army and Mages totally unaware. Of course, that revealed Karel and his position to the other Mages, who unleashed a volley of devastating spells his way. Karel was faster and he dodged back out of the way and cast a Fly spell and then Invisibility. Quickly, he flew off to the right of the tower as more spells landed on the top of the tower. Several Web spells covered the area from which he'd launched his attack.

Zoran and Zdenka were sleeping on the fourth floor when the alarm came. While she cast protective spells as rapidly as she could on Zoran, he got dressed and grabbed his swords. He cast a Magical Door spell and stepped into the first floor, just out of sight of the main door. Already he could see the leading wave of shock troops a mere ten feet from the gaping hole where the door had been. He cast his most powerful Ball of Fire spell. He spotted Marek, the door warden, nearby. Marek saw what Zoran cast and duplicated it, adding his exploding ball of flames to Zoran's, doubling its effect. Men dropped like flies before the door.

However, the shock troops behind the incinerated ones continued their forward momentum. They knew that the battle was theirs the very moment that they could set foot inside the building. No more flames could be cast in such a confined space. Meanwhile, Karel hovered and aimed his next spell carefully. Another Disintegrate spell blasted a hole in the center of another Mage, who crumpled to the ground. He'd aimed for the Baron, but his Duska sense warned him of the impending attack, and he dove and rolled out of the way, leaving his Mage to take the spell in his chest.

Suddenly, two windows on the fourth floor splintered, glass shards, reflecting sunlight, tumbled slowly to the ground. Two large golden dragons, the twins, came flying out of the windows. At once, they swooped and let lose two blasts of their fiery breath upon the troops about to enter the tower. Simultaneously, Zdenka appeared on the rooftop amid the remnants of the sticky Webs. She shot a Disintegrate spell at another Mage, downing him, but becoming visible herself. She dove for cover, fearing instant retaliation from the remaining three Mages.

Bernard and Jarka planned their first attack carefully, based upon the action before them. Both teleported to a position behind the three hovering Mages, whose attention was totally toward the tower, frantically lobbing spells at the last known position of Karel and Zdenka. Another pair of Balls of Fire came from Zoran and Marek from just inside the open door.

Just as Jarka and Bernard launched their attack, Aldrick and Sofie came flying in to go to work on their mining operations. Seeing the battle, they swooped in and added their fiery breaths to those of their circling twins, further roasting the shock troops. Jarka's carefully thrown dagger pierced the back of the neck of one hovering Mage; he collapsed onto the ground. Bernard's Disintegrate spell removed the back of the head of another Mage. Jarka's subsequent volley of Acid Missiles struck the remaining Mage in the back of his head. He died instantly.

Baron Kazimir whirled and prepared to duel the two Mages. He saw the look of total confidence in Jarka's eyes and instantly Shadow Walked himself back to his castle. Her throwing dagger missed his forehead by a split second. Once again, his Duska sense had kept him alive.

The dragons circled the mass of burning men, continuing to breath fire down upon them. They were taking no chances. At last Zoran called out to them that the battle was over. Only then did the dragons cease. Emil called out, "We're off to eat. This has made us hungry!" Zoran chuckled. One by one the defenders stepped out of the front door or down to that area, except Bernard and Jarka, who were already examining the fallen bodies of the Mages, making doubly sure that they were dead. As the flames died down, but not the horrid stench, Zoran saw the remains of two hundred fifty of Kazimir's best shock troops. Not one had set foot in the tower. Now all of their students began peering out of the windows as well as hundreds of townsfolk, who began congregating to see what had happened. The stench was awful; many were nauseated. It was that bad.

"Anyone hurt?" Zoran called out loudly. A chorus of no's gave everyone immediate relief.

"Kazimir was the only one to get away," Jarka yelled to him. "I just barely missed him. He's a hard man to kill."

"He's a Duska," Zoran yelled back. She grinned. Well, she knew that. That was the reason she did not go after him first. He would very likely avoid her attack and perhaps fell her in the process. Instead, she took out the next most dangerous ones, his Mages. "Hey, that's Archmage Milos!"

"Yes, I took him out first," Archmage Karel declared. "He was the most dangerous man on the field of battle that I had any chance of getting. He had to go.

Pity I didn't get the chance to get Kazimir, though."

"He would most likely have just dived out of the way in time, and your spell would have been wasted," Zoran explained. Karel began wondering just how one could kill an enemy Duska anyway. He angrily swore to find out.

General Janos, who was out walking among the fallen shock troops, called out, "Interesting, Zoran. Dragon breath is so hot that it has melted their armor and weapons! None of it is worth salvaging. What a mess to clean up before breakfast."

"I know. Have your men stack them up in a pile of four. I will get rid of them myself," Zoran decided. As a pile was made, he cast his Vanish spell on them, dropping them just above the sun, where their remains vaporized instantly. However, it took him an hour to get them all disposed of and only then could the rest of the scene be cleaned up. With all the Mages working together, casting numerous Create Water spells, the whole main street before the tower was finally washed clean. Many of the cobblestones would now need to be replaced, because they had cracked under the intense heat of the dragon's breath. One side note, this outcome convinced everyone in Brn that indeed their new baron and his dragons would protect them from Baron Kazimir. Zoran now had the entire town one hundred percent behind him.

Finally at ten, the group sat down for their very late breakfast. General Janos and his men set about replacing the doors and the two broken windows. After eating, Zoran then made contact with his uncle telling him the outcome.

Zoran, that is the best news I've heard in a long time. With his Archmage and remaining five Mages dead, he is out of magic users! That has to cripple his ability to wage war! Glad none of you were injured. You are an amazing nephew!

Say uncle, I've been meaning to ask you something. Does any planet have any mermaids on them?

He detected his uncle laughing. *No, there is no such thing as a mermaid. Now the water world of Asami does have women who swim underwater going after pearls. That's their biggest money making enterprise, pearls. No mermaids, sorry. Why do you ask?*

Been having strange dreams. Guess that's all it is. Thanks for the timely warning.

The next night, the nightmare returned and this time, Zoran told Zdenka what Baron Milan had told him about Asami and their pearl industry. "See, I told you that there is no such thing as a mermaid," Zdenka pointed out. Nevertheless, as the days passed, the nightmare continued to plague him.

On May Day, Bernard and Jarka were married in a simple ceremony held at the Stodgy Inn, where they had first met many years ago. "Where are we going to go for our honeymoon?" asked Jarka coyly the day before May Day.

"Beats me. Where would you like to go?" Bernard replied.

"Well, when I was in Alta, I heard all of these tales of just how fabulous the water world of Asami is. Delightful sandy beaches, warm sunshine, tropical breezes, perfect weather nearly every day. It is a vacation planet," she replied.

Since Zoran had not yet taken Zdenka on a honeymoon and hearing Jarka's desires, he spoke up. "Then, it's settled. Zdenka, you and I and the Dragans are going to honeymoon together on Asami! Kazimir is not likely to do anything against us here in the near future. I'm not really needed here at the moment, though I have yet to deal with the Yeller problem. That can wait. Let's have our honeymoon on the vacation planet."

"Are you sure, Zoran?" she asked conservatively. It would not do to get her hopes up immediately.

"Absolutely. With Bernard and Jarka with us, we ought to be plenty safe. Besides, no one will know that we are going but us. We've only just now decided to go there. It should be safe for a few days, maybe a week. What say you? Marek, Karel, the twins — anyone can substitute for you with the students for a few days. Please say yes my love," he begged.

Now convinced that he meant it, her enthusiasm sprang out. "Fantastic!" she jumped up and hugged him tightly. Jarka was also very pleased. She was going to a tropical paradise!

"Dear, what do we wear there? What should we pack?" Zdenka, ever practical, asked what now came into her mind.

"Let's take nothing. I'm sure that we can buy whatever is appropriate there," he suggested. Honestly, he had no idea whatsoever what they ought to take. He'd never been there, only hovered above it during Shadow Walks.

Chapter 21 Asami

After the wedding ceremony was finished and the new couple congratulated by everyone in the tower, Zoran sat down and focused his mind on Asami. He soon made contact with Baron Hajime. *Hi, Baron Zoran here. Say, Zdenka and I and another couple would like to take our honeymoon on Asami.*

An excellent choice, I might add. You and lovely Zdenka are most welcome. In fact, please allow us to host your complete honeymoon! Baroness Lami will not hear of it if you insist on paying. Please, allow us to show you our world. When would you like to come?

Wow! Thanks, yes, we would be delighted. Jarka and Bernard just got married a few minutes ago. We'd like to come now, unless you need time to prepare for us. However, I must request that until we leave, you keep our presence a secret, as much as that is possible. Baron Kazimir has attempted to assault our tower a few weeks ago and before that Baron Bogdan attempted to assassinate Zdenka.

Yes, I have heard about both. Terrible treachery and from your own father too. Despicable tyrant. Were you hurt?

Not at all. No wounds on any of us, though the Baron lost two hundred fifty of his best shock troops, his Archmage, and all of his remaining Mages.

Incredible. That must be most devastating to him. Yes, we will keep your visit as secret as possible. After all, I have my reputation at stake. If anything happened to you or your party while on Asami, why, our tourism industry would suffer an immense blow. Politics, eh son?

Politics can be useful. Thanks. Where should we arrive? I've never been to your world. Can we get whatever clothes are needed when we come? We have no idea what to wear or bring.

Leave all that to Lami. When you approach, look for the largest island. It is called Shimamori. You can't miss it. There is no other island anywhere near its size. My fortress and castle is on the northern edge of the island at our largest city of Paru. When you approach, you will see a large yacht and docks. Land on the docks and I'll be waiting for you. Give me a half hour to prepare for your arrival.

Thanks a bunch, Baron Hajime. We four really appreciate your kindness for our very special time.

"All settled gang. All expenses paid vacation on a tropical paradise island! Baron Hajime insists that we pay nothing. Bring nothing, he said. He'll provide what we need. We leave in a half hour. All right!" The others whooped it up. Jarka was extremely excited about this trip.

Zoran decided that the fewer people that knew about this short trip, the better. Hence, he did not even tell his uncles. Only his trusted friends in Brn knew of their trip. Archmage Karel was put in charge and the four joined hands a half hour later. Zoran began his Shadow Walk once again, taking them with him. Into the black void they stepped. Zdenka and Jarka fought valiantly the nausea that swept over their bodies. Bernard just closed his eyes and pretended it was nighttime.

Soon, a blue dot appeared ahead in the total blackness. Slowly it began to grow in size until it became huge. Now those with open eyes could see Asami, the water world. This planet was almost entirely water, one monstrous ocean from pole to pole. As they drew even closer, a myriad of tiny islands began to appear, tiny against the sea of blue. Zoran moved slowly around the world, looking for the large island. At last he saw what had to be his destination, an island perhaps a hundred miles long and fifty miles across. Sure enough at the northern edge, as he moved closer, a large city sprang into view. Paru. He moved down towards it and spied the large yacht and docks. A moment later, he landed the four nicely on the docks.

"You can open your eyes now, dear. We are there," Jarka teased Bernard.

"Oh, wow. It's beautiful," he exclaimed. He felt a bit sheepish, but then he had not gotten ill during the trip.

Baron Hajime walked up to them. He looked so vastly different than he had at the High Council that they hardly recognized him or his wife! Gone were the fancy blue suit coat with twin tails and the billowing blue dress. He wore blue shorts; his chest was bare; flip-flops were on his feet. Baroness Lami wore shorts as well, revealing her nicely tanned and shapely legs. She had on a top that barely covered her breasts, leaving her middle section open to the warm, balmy air. She, too, wore flip-flops. However, what caught their attention was the huge string of creamy pearls about her neck and matching pearl earrings.

The air was moist and balmy, about eighty-five degrees. A gentle sea breeze fluttered strands of the baroness' long black hair. "Welcome to Asami!" Baron Hajime exclaimed, shaking Zoran's hand first, then the others. The baroness gave each a hug and fake kiss on each cheek in turn.

"We are most honored indeed that you have chosen our humble planet for your honeymoons," she said cheerily. "Come on inside, and let's get you changed into something cooler before you melt in your heavy clothes!" She got no argument from the four.

Their castle and fortifications were made of imported gray granite. Here at Paru, the island rose a whopping fifty feet above the sea level. The constructions themselves were built to withstand heavy storms, and its walls were just ten feet tall. Even the castle itself only had two stories, but it was a sprawling complex with many smaller stone buildings. They were given a pair of adjoining bridal suites, and Lami had already set out traditional planet clothing for the four. A half hour later, all four wore the typical blue shorts and flip-flops, with the women also wearing a skimpy blue top identical to Lami's.

Their hosts then led them to a dining room, where Lami had drinks already prepared for their guests. Sipping their delicious drinks, whose taste was enchanting, Baron Hajime chose this opportunity to tell them, Zoran in particular, a bit about his world. Although he was classified as Neutral, he wanted Zoran to be favorably inclined towards him. Hence, this vacation gift was really a political maneuver for him.

"Ah, much better. I see Lami's choice of island clothes suits you four well. Comfort, that's the key here in the islands. By the way, do you realize that your Circle of Ascension is the eighteenth built, not the seventeenth? Ours here in this castle is the seventeenth," Baron Hajime coyly began his history lesson and in politics.

"What? Eighteenth? Wait, are we missing a planet?" Zoran asked, suddenly quite confused. To his knowledge, there were only sixteen planets in the Federation, sixteen Circles — well now seventeen counting his new one.

Hajime grinned, knowing that he had Zoran right where he desired, playing him would be child's play. "Yes, yours is the eighteenth. Mine here is the seventeenth, the last Circle that Bandar Zar ever created. However, there are only sixteen planets in the Federation. You see, Asami had to have its rebuilt. Let me tell you our story." All four listened to his tale, none more so than Zoran.

"Baron Asami, who discovered this planet more than two and a half centuries ago, had Bandar Zar build him a Circle of Ascension. Asami, as you have seen, is an ocean world. Yes, we have many yachts that sail the seas. You are sitting on the largest land mass on the planet." He paused, allowing them to show their surprise, though it only confirmed what they had seen as Zoran had shown them, while he was trying to find this island.

"Yes, Shimamori is the largest island and this city, Paru, is the largest. Our world has two hundred thousand six hundred and five islands scattered around the blue waters. Most lie within a thousand miles of the equator. None are anywhere near the poles. Indeed, you are sitting on the highest point on Asami."

"Wow. Do you have storms here?" asked Zdenka, starting to understand the world a bit better.

"Yes, that is our biggest problem, always has been. We get squalls nearly daily in the equatorial zone, but that's just rain, refreshingly warm usually. Each fall, we have a hurricane season. Sometimes these hurricanes wreak havoc on our low lying islands. We've had islands completely disappear during a hurricane. Back in the days of our founding by Baron Asami, that is indeed what happened. A hurricane completely obliterated his fortress and castle, submerging two thirds of the then largest island. Today, only a long, thin strip of that original island remains. It is called Shima Yubi. Our second largest city, Tesaki, lies on the extreme eastern edge of the island. We call that our get-away island. You can walk or ride an open carriage for a hundred miles along the thin strip of island that yet remains. On either side, but mere feet from the grassy knoll on which the road lies, are some of the best beaches we have to offer. Spectacular. It is remote and isolated, perfect spots for honeymooners. Yet, you can easily return to civilization in Tesaki."

"Along this thin strip, the swimming is superb. The waters are warm and shallow, allowing you breathtaking views of underwater life which thrive here on Asami. I highly recommend that you spend some of your private time riding along that strip."

"I do hope that you like sea food, for that is our main dish here on Asami. All grains, for example, must be imported and are thus highly expensive. In Tesaki inns, you can find some of the very best the sea has to offer. Indeed, Asami exports all manner of produce from the sea, from delicious sea weeds to a tremendous variety of fish to the exotic, such as squid and octopus and oysters. I suspect coming from Brn on Adapazan that you have rarely eaten much ocean fish. Hence, you might try the delicacy called swordfish. Those fillets taste remarkably like your steaks. In fact, I once made a gaffe at the High Council, complimenting the baron on such quality swordfish, when in fact it came from a cow or so I was informed."

"I highly encourage you all to travel that road and go for long swims. Since you are all Mages, you can cast water breathing spells and truly enjoy and admire the teaming underwater life which is so abundant here on Asami."

"Oh you certainly must!" Baroness Lami interrupted her husband. "You've never seen anything like our underwater world. So colorful, so wild, so magnificent. Why there is nothing in the entire Federation of Planets like it. You just *must* spend time underwater!"

Her husband picked up the conversation once more, "Speaking of oysters, I've seen you admiring Lami's magnificent set of matching pearls. Yes, pearls are our number one export, beyond seafood. Pearls fetch an enormous price on other worlds, allowing us to import the many necessities that we cannot produce. In fact, all this stone you see in the fortification and castle came from Adapazan centuries ago. Pearls form our main economic base, along with seafood."

"So I must give you this warning which I give to all our visitors. Searching for pearls is strictly forbidden in all areas but one. We have pearl hunting villages scattered throughout our world. In fact, there is one called Ma-meido which is located at the opposite end of Shima Yubi from Tesaki. These villages are heavily guarded, as you might expect. No visitors are allowed in there. Don't worry; if you drive your carriage to close to Ma-meido, the guards there will let you know."

"However, we know that many tourists would just love to try their hand at pearl hunting. So we have set aside one location for this express purpose. Shimatou is a small island totally setup for pearl diving. There, guides will assist you in finding the best locations to dive and search for the oysters and pearls. You ought to plan to spend one day of your honeymoon on Shimatou diving for pearls. Often visitors find some which make lovely gifts for their wives and girlfriends. Of course, if you wish to purchase a set of pearls, that can be arranged as well. Some barons prefer to just buy a matching set for their wives, rather than dive for the pearls themselves."

Baroness Lima interrupted him, "You must come to our sunahama yakara tonight. Each evening, we have beach parties on our sandy beaches. Food is roasted over a charcoal fire. You just must try our hoshinori kashu, seaweed wine! It is superb. Musicians play and everyone dances barefoot in the warm, soft sands. I guarantee that you will have the time of your life. Everyone does, you know."

"Great! It sounds wonderful. Party time indeed! Bernard, we just must!" Jarka exclaimed. Now they were speaking to her heart's desire! He grinned and squeezed her hand.

"Excellent, we'll come for you at five tonight then. Be prepared to become stuffed and dance until your legs fall off. Oh yes, you can also go for a swim as well. Many do just that as well. Baron Zoran, I think you will rapidly see why Asami is and remains a Neutral planet. We have no mighty armies and no means to equip them if we did. If we, for example, took your side in your battle with Baron Kazimir, there is virtually nothing that we could offer in the way of aid. It is folly for us to take sides, just useless. Yet, we can offer much in the way of friendship and certainly a wonderful respite. Asami has been called the vacation planet of the Federation."

"I understand," Zoran replied, realizing that he'd just been worked over politically. He grinned, "Besides, any army trying to conquer Asami would have an awful time of it. What would they do? Island hop while swimming in their plate armor?" Everyone chuckled at his colorful jest. "No, I can see why you must maintain your Neutrality with all planets. You can count on my support for just that, Baron Hajime." Zoran gave him what he thought the Baron wanted to hear. He hit the mark squarely; the Baron smiled broadly.

"Oh, I almost forgot. Another activity that is quite popular with both tourists and our own people is to go for a lengthy sailboat excursion on the ocean. You noticed my personal yacht when you came, I'm sure. At nearly every town you can rent a yacht and go for a sail. They can be rented with or without a crew to sail them. However, I must insist that unless you are competent sailors, you take one with a crew to sail her for you. There are some very nice yachts in Tesaki. I will send word to the harbor master there so you can take any yacht of your choosing out for a trip. It's on me. I trust that you don't get seasick however." He teased them, for frequently guests did get seasick.

After the meal was done, the four got a tour of the castle and the city of Paru. By the time they had seen the sights, it was time for the sunahama yakara, the sandy beach party. It was everything Lami had said and then more! They dined on an exotic, but delicious meal, heard the most fascinating local music, danced barefoot in the warm sands, and even took a cooling-off swim, before more dancing. It was late before they finally turned in for the night.

In the wee hours of the morning, Zoran had his nightmare once more, only this time the images were even more vivid than before! Somehow his nightmares, he and Zdenka concluded, must have or be tied to Asami! But how and why remained a mystery. He hoped that one night these would end.

The next day, Baron Hajime took them to Shima Yubi and the town of Tesaki, where he had another smaller fortress and castle built for his son, Duke Goro Yoko. "Hi pop! What'sa up?" Goro teased as they walked in on his late breakfast on his patio overlooking the beach and sea. Goro was a young lad, in his early twenties, a splitting image of his father, tall, and thin. He was obviously very laid back in manner, which Baron Hajime disliked.

"You must forgive the insolence of my son," he apologized for Duke Goro. "You embarrass our important guests. Baron Archmage Zoran Vladislov, Baroness Archmage Zdenka, my impertinent son, Duke Goro." He glared at Goro, whose cheery face became instantly serious.

Dressed in very short shorts and flip-flops, he quickly rose and stood at attention, as though he were some soldier being addressed by his general. "Very pleased to meet you, Baron Archmage Zoran! Wow! You are the youngest Baron in the Federation! Way cool!" He shook Zoran's hand vigorously. He then shook Zdenka's hand politely.

His father continued, "These are their friends, Mages Bernard and Jarka Dragan. They are here on Asami for their honeymoon. Whatever they desire, give it to them. Please, show our esteemed guests the very best of times. Where is Kimiko?"

"Sure thing pops," he replied, lapsing back into his cheery manner once more. "She's feeding our baby. Ah, here she comes now." Kimiko had very long black hair and eyes to match. Like Goro, she too wore only very short shorts and flip-flops. She wore no top and her rich full breasts were more than visible.

Hajime grimaced, but explained, "You must forgive them. She is nursing their son. It is our custom to leave a woman's beasts exposed while they are nursing. It is better for the health of their babies and themselves." Kimiko seemed not to notice the stares of the guests and shook everyone's hands as Baron Hajime introduced everyone a second time.

"So glad that you have chosen our island. It is a favorite of honeymooners," Kimiko explained. "Baron, you may rest assured that Goro and I will show these important guests an honorable time." She attempted to counter the annoyance that Goro had already instilled in her father-in-law. She succeeded. Baron Hajime relaxed. He suggested that they try a yacht cruise, sea diving, and a ride along the island. He then excused himself and returned to Paru.

"Kind of stuffy, don't you think? I mean dad," Goro teased, motioning the four to have a seat. "Had breakfast? Probably so, knowing dad. Out here on Shima Yubi, we are totally *not* formal. Fun is the name of the game. Ever been sailing on a yacht?"

"Er no," Zoran replied.

"Okay, that's what we'll do today. That and some sea diving."

Kimiko added, "I'll see that we have a big sunahama yakara ready for you when you get back. Goro, make sure you are not late. Be back by five at the latest. I'll prepare swordfish for you. Most off-worlder's prefer swordfish. I think it tastes more familiar."

"Will you have some of your other delicacies?" Jarka asked curiously. "I'm game to try almost anything. What does octopus and squid taste like?"

Bernard grumbled, muttering, "I'll stay with the swordfish." Everyone chuckled.

By eleven, Zoran's party walked onto the main deck of Goro's yacht. Really, he explained, it was a two masted schooner, though the significance was totally lost on the four. He had a crew of six and before long, the ship tacked out into the open waters. All four stared at the distant horizon and the waters below them, crystal blue.

"Come on; let's lay out in the sun!" Goro declared once they were well underway. "Nothing much to see. Like this." He laid out a towel and then laid down, basking in the warm sunshine. The four followed suit. "Nothing like a lazy cruise in the sun, eh?"

"I admit this is pretty amazing," Jarka volunteered. "I've never seen a sea before, let alone a boat. It is really big, isn't it?"

"Yes, but smaller than dad's yacht. Not much to do around here really, except party on the beach. I mean we do have fishermen and dryers — they fillet and dry the fish and sea weed, pack them, and store them for shipping and such. Rather boring jobs if you ask me. Then of course, there are the pearl divers, but those areas are off limits to all off-worlders. Centuries ago, they caught too many visitors stealing our precious, valuable pearls. However, dad's got one place setup where you can go diving for pearls, but if you find any, they will be small ones."

"Makes sense," Zoran replied.

"Say, do you know that once this island was the largest on Asami? Two and a half centuries ago a hurricane struck with such violence that nearly all the island sunk! Our original Circle of Ascension was here and was lost. No one has ever found it; storm washed it completely away. Had to make us a new one, Bandar Zar did. Zoran, I cannot tell you how excited I am now that you and Brother Jiri Zar have begun to make new Circles! Dad's going to have one built here on Shima Yubi again for me! Not sure just when he's going to build it, though. Brother Jiri wasn't certain on the time. Yep, Zoran, one of these days I will be Baron Goro and come and join you on the High Council! Won't that be something?"

He chatted merrily away for hours. Zoran and friends learned quite a lot from his idle chat. Around two, they dropped sail. "Ah, here we are. I brought you to my favorite reef. You can all cast Breath Water, right?" Zoran nodded and he continued enthusiastically, "Great. We'll go for an underwater swim. You have to see the sights. This spot here is absolutely fantastic. You'll never see anything like it. I promise you. Come on. Cast your spells and dive in. Follow me."

He cast his spell and dove from the main deck making a perfect dive into the clear blue ocean waters. Zoran and friends followed suit, though all four chose to jump into the waters. None had ever dived before and it looked a bit too scary to try. For an hour they swam around underwater. Goro was understating the sights! Multicolored fish, breathtaking coral, undulating seaweeds, the group was mesmerized by the beauty before their eyes. The swim ended all too soon for them. Jarka even got to see a small octopus, something she talked endlessly about for days to whoever would listen to her.

Goro was true to his word and had them all back before the five o'clock sunahama yakara, which Kimiko had prepared for them. This one proved even more entertaining, since only younger folks attended. They dined on ten different dishes, drank more than enough wine, danced, swam, and generally had fun. The party ended at midnight, not ten as with Hajime. Now Zoran appreciated Goro's late morning breakfast. They partied half the night away and slept in to compensate.

Once more, Zoran's nightmare woke him from his deep sleep. This time, the images, the emotions, the feelings were vividly real. Zdenka became even more worried about him, but had no idea what she could do for him. This frustrated her and she resolved to speak to Uncle Milan about it, discretely of course.

Zoran appreciated taking breakfast at ten the next morning. He had a slight hangover from all of the wine he'd consumed at the party. Goro explained, "Well, I suppose that today you newlyweds ought to take a ride down honeymoon road. That's what we call the hundred mile long stretch of island between here and the pearl diving town of Ma-meido. Usually, they drive their own carriage. Honestly, the strip of land is only a couple hundred feet wide the whole way, narrower in places. It is totally isolated so you can stop and do what you like nearly anywhere without being disturbed. All along there, the beaches are perfect on either side of the road, so you can go for a swim anywhere. Now if you want an insider's tip, I'll give it to you." He'd lowered his voice and sounded mysterious.

"Sure thing, please do," Jarka insisted. She had to know what his tip was.

He grinned and whispered, "What most honeymooners do is find an ideal spot and then take their brides in for a swim totally naked. You have to try it; you will love it. The waters are warm, perfect for fun and frolicking. We all do it around here, but don't tell dad. He doesn't like us all doing that." Jarka's face broke out into a big grin. She looked at Bernard, who replied in kind. Zoran knew that this would be the first thing that those two did!

As they were getting ready to go find a carriage, Kimiko joined them, just having fed her son. She said in a matter of fact way, "Ah, going for a carriage ride today. Great. My advice, find a nice spot and go for a naked swim and then have sex. You won't believe how great having sex is while in the warm waters! We do it that way all the time."

"Kimiko, you spoiled it," Goro teased her. "Here I had them all thinking this was a secret mystery and all that." She giggled. So did Zoran and friends. "If you want, you can sleep out on the beaches too. If so, I'll make sure you take along more food and water than you need for just one day."

"How about us taking enough for three days?" Zoran asked.

Kimiko grinned, "Now you are talking! You got it! See, they know what to do, Goro." He chuckled.

An hour later, Bernard sat in the driver's seat of the open carriage. Jarka sat beside him. Two horses seemed eager to get going, while Zoran and Zdenka sat in the double rows of seats behind the two. On the other seat they had numerous water gourds, a sack of charcoal, and enough food for days. Goro saw them off. "If bad weather is coming, I'll let you know. Dad told me to tell you that if he hears of any trouble coming, he'll let you know and you can Shadow Walk home. Just leave the carriage; I'll come get it. Have fun out there. We certainly do."

A half hour later, they left the western edge of the town behind them. Ahead the sandy road ran straight westward. On either side, patches of green grass grew tall and thick for some hundred feet, before giving way to a sandy beach. Indeed, here the island was perhaps ten feet above sea level, if that. The day was sunny and balmy, perhaps eighty degrees.

"Bernard, isn't this just incredible?" Jarka exclaimed.

"Dear, I have long ago lost all words to describe this place! I admit when I first heard about this world, I thought it was going to be dismal, but that shows you how wrong I can be. I'm sure glad that you insisted we come here."

"Well, I can't wait to go skinny dipping! Hurry the horses up some!" Zoran and Zdenka listened to the two chat, but they were already in a passionate embrace.

At lunch time, they stopped and went for a swim, before moving on down the road. They saw no one at all the entire day. When they stopped for the night, Zoran and Bernard estimated that they were about halfway down the island. After they dined, both couples went for a nighttime swim. However, each couple went on a different side of the island. Both couples stripped and headed playfully into the warm waters.

That night, Zoran awoke with his usual nightmare once again, only now it seemed so real that Zdenka had a hard time waking him up. She did her best to not wake Bernard and Jarka. On a hunch, the next day Zoran insisted that they travel on down the road. Bernard had no objection. The two women, Zoran noted, had the most contented, satisfied looks on their faces that morning. He smiled and knew why.

By late afternoon, the island had narrowed considerably, perhaps fifty feet from water's edge to water's edge. From the carriage, they could see everything across the width of the island. Suddenly, Zoran spied a form lying on the beach some distance ahead. "Gang, look there! It looks like a body lying on the beach. Hurry up, Bernard, they might be in trouble," he called out. All eyes stared at the distant form, as Bernard got the horses into a canter, closing the distance rapidly.

"My god, Zoran!" Zdenka exclaimed, "That — that looks like a mermaid!"

Panic seized Zoran. Was he too late to save her? Was she the person in his nightmares? Bernard halted the horses opposite the mermaid, who lay lifelessly on the sandy beach. A bit of her tail remained in the water. She looked like a green fish from the waist down, but was a woman on up. She had no top clothes on and was lying face down in the sand. All four rushed to her side.

"She's alive!" Zoran called out. He rolled her over while Zdenka moved the long strands of her very long black hair off of her face.

"She looks dehydrated," he concluded. Jarka brought a water gourd, and Zoran lifted her into a sitting position, while Jarka attempted to get some water into her mouth. Soon, the woman gained some consciousness and began drinking greedily. At long last, she could speak.

"Help! You must help me! Please, my sister. Help me," she whispered. Her tone was a combination of grief and fear. "I am so weak," she added, now becoming more aware of her body.

"You are in good hands. We will help you and your sister. I promise you. How long have you been lying there on the sand?" Zoran asked.

"Days, I don't know," she replied weakly.

"Okay, food Jarka." The Mage dashed off to the carriage and returned with her arms full of items. Quickly Zdenka and Jarka fixed up some rations, and the two began feeding the mermaid, who greedily ate almost as fast as they could stuff it into her mouth. Zdenka urged her to slow down.

A bit later and with some more water, the woman began to become more coherent. "Now tell us what is the matter and where is your sister," Zoran asked her.

"It's my sister, Chika. She's lost and can't find her way back — I just know it. Please, you've got to help her."

"We will. First, what are you called?" Zoran asked, wondering how he could help a mermaid.

"I am called Akira. Chika's my sister. Our mother, Nao, died a few weeks ago. That's when Chika and I decided to escape. Chika and I found it and she said she could use it to find us a new place to live. She promised she would only be gone a little bit and then come back to get me too, but she's been gone for days now and I can't find her."

All this made little sense to Zoran. He asked, "Just what did you find and how could she use it to find you two a new place to live?"

"It's something magical that belonged to the barons. It's round and got all these different colored bands that glow and move around in it. We thought that it must be what Nao called a Circle. Chika said that we should be able to use it, and she tried and hasn't come back. Please, you must help us," she begged yet again.

Now the pieces began to fall into place. Baron Hajime and Duke Goro had told them that their original Circle of Ascension had been destroyed in a hurricane. Obviously, it hadn't! It was now underwater. Yet, she said that the bands moved. That could only mean that it was still active and operational. However, only a Duska could use it and then only after the person was given the Ceremony of Ascension. It was fatal to attempt it without having the Priestess perform the ceremony! He had no idea what would happen to a non-Duska who attempted to use a Circle. Indeed, he could recall nothing at all about such. Normal people simply could not use it. Yet, apparently, her sister had done so.

"Where is this Circle, Akira?" he asked quietly, though his three companions knew precisely what he was thinking. It was obvious Chika was somehow trapped in the lost Circle of Ascension.

"Down there," she pointed off into the waters. Zoran knew that he could spend days looking for it underwater. He suspected they didn't have days to waste finding it.

Just then, he felt a mental contact being made. Then a second one. *Baron Hajime here.* Momentarily, he received, *Duke Goro here.*

Hi Baron, Duke. Just enjoying your magnificent beaches.

Okay dad. I'll drop the connection.

No, stay with us, Goro. Zoran, I've just sensed that there have been some illegal arrivals on Asami. I have traced their origin point back to Rehor. I am now very concerned for your safety. Shall I send some forces to protect you and your party? These could well be assassins out looking for you.

Thanks for the warning. No, we will Shadow Walk back home shortly. Goro, what about our carriage? I think that we are somewhere near Ma-meido.

When you leave, I'll come and get it later. Not a problem. Did you take our suggestion? He couldn't resist asking.

Sure did. You and Kimiko were quite right! Thanks for the alert. We'll Shadow Walk home in a little while. It has been a wonderful honeymoon. We can't wait to come back for another visit, Baron.

My pleasure, son. Anytime. Both broke their contact.

"Damn, it looks like some assassins from Baron Bogdan are now on Asami. Hajime just sent me an alert. He's detected some illegal Shadow Walking here. I told him that we will Shadow Walk home from here. But first, I have to help these mermaids."

"Okay, gang. Protective spells time," Zdenka ordered and the four cast spells rapidly. Jarka made doubly sure that everyone had the Skin of Stone spell on their bodies. This was one of the best defenses against assassins.

Zoran reached his decision. "Akira, are you strong enough to show me where this Circle is located?"

"Yes, I feel much better now. Please, can you help her?"

"I will do my best. I want you to show me the Circle. As soon as I see it, I want you to come back here. My wife and friends are powerful magic users, and they will protect you until I get back with your sister."

"Thank you. Please, you must take us away with you. We cannot stay here on Asami. Please we will go anywhere. We will do anything that you want of us. Please," Akira was literally begging for her life. That was clear to all.

"We will take you with us off of Asami," Zdenka decided before anyone else could say otherwise. Zoran gave her a smile of appreciation.

"Okay, come on then. I'll cast my water breathing spell, and we can go under."

"Wait until I cast mine," Akira cautioned. All four stared at her in shock as she carefully recited the spell. "Okay, follow me." She crawled into the water and began swimming and then dove under. Zoran followed after her.

"Okay, let's set up a defensive position here. Get all our things ready for an immediate Shadow Walk," Zdenka ordered. The three set to work.

Once the two had dove under the water, Zoran saw how she swam. She did not use her arms, merely her legs and tail in an undulating manner akin to a fish. Yet, she was vastly faster than his kicking and pulling. Zoran just could not remotely keep up with her! She was incredibly fast. He now realized that her tail and big fin made all the difference in speed. Akira glanced back and saw him far behind her and slowed down. Zoran relaxed, thankful that she had.

How far they had gone, he had no way to really judge. As he thought, "I am out of my waters here." He laughed at his own pun. They were at least fifty feet under the surface when she began pointing at something below her. When he arrived, he saw the Circle of Ascension. Zoran signaled for her to return to the surface and waited until she was well on her way, before turning his attention onto the Circle. If he could have spoken, he would have exclaimed, "Incredible! There is my sky blue thread in this one!"

Now what do I do? he wondered as he activated the Circle, stepping into the Shadow world. He needed a Priestess; they were trained in such matters. What do I do? Suddenly, his nightmare kicked in once more, and he now realized that it was not a nightmare at all! It was Chika trying to make a Duska mental contact with another Duska! A totally untrained Duska at best!

I am here. Focus on me and I will focus on you.

Wham! He was totally unprepared for the strength of her connection! She latched on to him for dear life! Slowly he moved toward what he thought was her direction. After what seemed ages of walking in the black void, he finally found her ahead, valiantly attempting to swim, though there was no water here. As he came up to her, she grabbed on to him with her arms and clung to him with all her might! She nearly crushed his ribs!

Quickly, he stepped back out of the Circle. Unfortunately, she did not have her water breathing spell cast and she began to panic. He saw that she was holding her breath but had only seconds left. Zoran then cast his Mystical Door spell and pulled her through it onto the beach, where she collapsed, gasping for air. Zoran canceled his water breathing spell and looked at the four looking at him.

"Any signs of the assassins?" he asked worriedly.

"Goro Messaged me that he saw two assassins arriving at Tesaki. He saw them heading down the island heading our way. They stole two horses and are riding hard. We still have some time before they get here unless they can teleport or fly," Zdenka replied.

"Okay. I've got Chika rescued. Chika, Akira has begged us to take you two with us to another planet. Is this what you two really want?" Zoran asked.

Poor Chika was totally delirious, nauseated, as well as out of breath. She gasped, "Free, we want to be free. Take us anywhere but here. Please. We can pay."

Whether this was a right move or whether this action would ultimately put him on the baron's hit list, Zoran had no idea. However, he acted. "They cannot stand, so Bernard, you carry Akira and I'll carry Chika. Zdenka, you and Jarka hold on to me and hold on to Bernard." Once they were firmly gripping him, he Shadow Walked them off of Asami — their honeymoon abruptly ended.

He felt Chika's terror of the void returning, but focused his attention on Adapazan and then Brn. A moment later, he stepped everyone inside the entrance of the tower. "Let's take them quickly up to our bedroom. The fewer eyes that see them the better," he requested, opening a Mystical Door to his bedroom.

He and Bernard placed both mermaids on Zoran's bed, for want of any place better. "Now what?" asked Bernard.

"They look half starved," Jarka replied. "I'll fetch some food and water. Bernard, you go tell everyone that we are back, but don't say a word about the mermaids." He nodded and the two left.

Akira hugged her older sister, who looked to be perhaps two years older than she, Zdenka thought, if age appeared the same with mermaids. Chika was still pretty much incoherent. "We're safe now, Chika, we're safe," she whispered to her. Chika moaned, but Zoran detected a sigh of relief as well.

Shortly, Jarka returned, her arms full of food and drink. "Okay, men out of here. Let we women tend to their needs a bit." To Zoran, she whispered, "And stop looking at their naked breasts! Men!" He flushed. Was it that obvious? He beat a hasty exit.

Zoran quickly checked with General Janos and Archmage Karel and found that all was well. All had been boringly routine in their absence. He was thankful of that. They chatted a bit and Zoran was brought up to date. He told them about Asami, but didn't mention his two mermaids.

A while later, Zdenka Messaged Zoran, and he headed up to their bedroom. Chika was now conscious and coherent. Perhaps now he could get their story and try to figure out what to do with two mermaids. There weren't any oceans around here or any ponds for that matter. What could he do with them anyway?

When he entered, he found that Zdenka and Jarka had put tops on the two mermaids and that both were sitting on his bed. "Thank you for rescuing us," Chika said. He noted that both women's long black hair had been brushed out, and they looked rather pretty.

He smiled, "Well don't thank me yet. You are on the mountainous planet of Adapazan in the Brn Province, a province of free people. However, there aren't any bodies of water anywhere around here. I'm not sure how long you two can remain out of water or where you can live. The waters around our continent are freezing in the wintertime."

"I'm sorry, we don't know anything about Adapazan. It is enough that you say free people. That's what we want to be, free people," Chika replied quietly.

"But we're not mermaids really," Akira added. "We're people too." Zoran looked totally confused.

Zdenka came to his rescue. "Dear, their bottoms are some kind of man-made skin that covers their legs."

"Can you get us out of it?" Chika asked. "We don't know how. We can pay you. We've both stashed a bunch of big pearls inside our skins."

Zoran blushed. Probably they would be completely naked when the skin was removed. Zdenka again came to his rescue. "We are rather modest people. We only let our husbands see our private areas. That's why he is a bit embarrassed. Dear, you step out a minute, and Jarka and I will see what we can do. If we need help, we'll holler." Zoran quickly stepped out, grateful for her suggestion.

Ten minutes later, Zdenka called out for his help. "Dear, I am afraid that we are going to have to have your help here with this." He was not prepared for what he saw when he entered. The women had managed to peal the skin off of their legs; the fins were now lying in the corner of the room. The women were still lying on the bed. Zoran stared at their legs. Every few inches from the tops of their thighs on down to their toes some kind of metal loops went through their flesh on either leg, binding the legs tightly to one another all the way down to their toes!

After he recovered from his shock, he then examined one ring loop closely. It went through the fleshy part not their bones. Chika had nineteen rings down her legs holding them tightly together. Akira had eighteen. "Well, they look like they only go through the fleshy part, not through their bones."

"Please, can you get them off of us," Chika begged.

"Yes, I have to, but the how must be worked out, Chika. Let's see," he tried bending one open with no luck. "Okay, I have an idea. I'll be back in a minute." He cast a Mystical Door spell and stepped through the door.

"One day I would like to learn how to do that!" Akira exclaimed. Zdenka took this opportunity to chat with them about their spell casting skills. Neither knew what she was talking about, so she prompted them about their Water Breathing spell.

"Oh that was magic?" both girls exclaimed. They had been unaware that it was magic that they were doing. Shortly, Zoran returned with a blacksmith's wire cutter.

"Let's hope that these are soft metal rings," he explained. He set to work on the topmost ring of Chika because it was the easiest to fit into the large cutter's edge. It gave way with a slight popping sound. With a bit of effort, he managed to separate the two halves and then it was a simple matter of slowly easing one side out of her flesh and then the other. "Ta da, one down, eighteen to go."

It took him an hour to free both girls, who could finally move their legs freely for the first time in many years. Zdenka rubbed their legs and holes with a healing salve as a safety precaution, though the piercings were long ago healed. Then, she and Jarka helped them into a dress. Now presentable, Zoran returned to talk at length with them. Suddenly, Asami took on a whole new dark side — one that they had not remotely suspected was there.

Chika began to relate their tale. "Nao was our mother. She and we are called shinjutori, pearl divers. We live at Ma-meido, in the waters there. Just on shore is our communal house. Only women are shinjutori. We slide up onto the beach there and into the protection of the low house. We don't know who our father was. Nao only said he was an important man. Akira and I played there as little girls, running about and having fun. When I was eight, they said it was time that I became a shinjutori. They pierced my legs and put rings in them and then put the fish skin over my legs. Mom taught me to swim. Some man showed me how to breathe underwater. It was awfully scary at first, not having any legs anymore."

"But we could swim much, much faster," Akira broke in. "They did me when I was seven. I didn't want to be left out."

"How many shinjutori are there at your place?" Zoran asked.

"Usually fifty. We are taken out every few days to dive for pearls. Actually they are oysters. That's why we have such long fingernails," Chika explained. Zoran had wondered why their nails were at least three inches long. "We use them to tickle the oysters into opening up so we can get the pearls."

"We are always treated well; we get all the food we want," Chika continued. "Everyone always tells us that we are the most valuable people on Asami and that by our collecting many pearls we are helping to feed lots of people. So we work hard at it."

"But it is dangerous! Tell them about mom," Akira added.

"She's right; it is very dangerous work. No one ever gets old. They die like Nao did. One day a few months ago, a shark surprised Nao while she was collecting pearls. It bit off both of her hands! Oh the blood was awful in the water. Other shinjutori quickly came to her aid and tied ropes to her hands to stop the bleeding. Once we all got her to our home, a man came and gave her something to drink. After that, her arms healed up, but ever since then, we had to be mom's hands. We had to feed her and help her with everything, but she could not do any more pearl diving after that. She tried, but without hands and fingernails, she could only grab an oyster. We had to get the pearl out of it for her. She got awfully depressed and then one morning, she died."

"She told us many tales though. How a long time ago there was this magic circle and that the powerful men and women could use it to go to other places. She told us that our father was one of those who could do this and that maybe we could do it too."

"After Nao died, they brought in another shinjutori to take her place. That's what they do when one of us dies or goes missing for a long time. Then, one day Akira and I went out diving for pearls, and we went a long way from our home, searching for bigger and better pearls. That's when we discovered that Circle thing. We watched its swirling colors and felt its pull on us. We kept coming back when we could and that's when we decided that maybe we could use it to go someplace where we can be free and not have to be a shinjutori anymore. We want to have babies too."

Zoran smiled, "Say, how old are you or do you know?"

"I'm nineteen and Akira is eighteen," she replied.

"Anyway, the other shinjutori told us that the pearls are really valuable and that people in other places must desire them for trade, since you cannot eat them. So we decided to keep some pearls back for us. Zdenka found our pearls when she took our skins off us. We just tucked them inside. When we decided that we must have enough pearls, we went to the magic circle to see if we could leave and go someplace else. I decided that since I am the oldest, I should go first and find us a good place to live. I made Akira stay behind and wait for me to come get her."

"I did, but she didn't come back!" Akira exclaimed. "Not for days and days!"

"I don't know what happened to me. I left Asami but it was all black and I couldn't find anyplace. I couldn't find my way back either! I cried and cried and tried to call out to anyone. Then, I see you coming for me."

"Yes, I heard you calling out, Chika, but I am so sorry that it took me so many days to figure out that you were calling for help," Zoran apologized.

"We are rescued and are now free people, right?" Chika asked.

"You bet you are free people," Zdenka replied before Zoran could.

"You will not be missed? Others won't come looking for you?" Zoran asked the questions uppermost in his mind.

"We have already been missed," Chika answered. "Sometimes shinjutori stay underwater too long and get water in their lungs and die. Sometimes sharks get us, like it almost did mom. Sometimes shinjutori swim too far and get lost and cannot find their way home. A big boat once brought a woman back who went too far and got lost. They bring in new shinjutori all the time. Often the new shinjutori are young girls like we once were. There are no old shinjutori at all."

Zoran's chief worry evaporated. The attrition rate of these mermaids was steep, so that the loss of two more would be hardly noticed. "Okay, you two can stay here with us as long as you desire. We will fix up a room for you at once and get you some clothes to wear. Say, are you able to walk anymore?" He suddenly realized that they might not be able to get around!

"We used to when we were little girls," Chika replied and then tried to stand up, she nearly fell over. Her feet would not go flat on the floor anymore, but her toes did flex well. In time, perhaps her legs would readjust. Zdenka had a flash of insight. She retrieved her tall heels that she had been given by the Baroness and tried them on Chika's feet. Though a little loose, they fit. She had her stand up again. While she needed to hold onto Zdenka for support, she could stand in the high heels. Jarka got her pair and helped Akira to stand.

"Yes, they can stand now with our support. First thing, we need to help them relearn to walk," Jarka announced. Everyone looked quite pleased.

Zdenka then said, "Ladies, suppose that you came home to your protected spot only to find a mother and daughter cowering in a corner. A man was at a table, but was bleeding badly. On the table was a large pouch of pearls. What would you do?" Zoran and Jarka realized at once what she was doing — the picking test!

"Oh, we stop the bleeding," Chika said without hesitation.

Akira added, "Tie something around it like they did for Nao."

"Good. You girls have already been taught one magical spell. How would you like to learn how to cast many, many magical spells?"

"We can? Really? Use much magic?" Akira exclaimed.

That decided that. Zdenka took on two more students. She soon discovered that first she needed to teach them to read and write. It would take them longer than most students, but this gave them new goals and an education, which they totally lacked.

While Bernard cleaned out a storage room for the two and added a bed, Zdenka and Jarka began helping them learn to walk again. With constant assistance, both women regained their mobility in a few days and then were introduced to everyone else.

That evening after dinner, the group discussed their new arrivals. Zoran commented first, "You know, their father must have been a Duska. That is the only way that Chika could have entered the Circle of Ascension. Both were drawn to it initially, so I think that Akira is also going to be able to do it. When Priestess Anezka returns, I am going to have her conduct the Ceremony of Ascension with these two women. We may have just acquired two more unknown Duskas."

"If they take to magic, this will be of great benefit for us all," Zdenka added.

"Yes, but how can we ever go back to that paradise knowing that such wickedness lies under the surface?" asked Jarka. "Imagine doing that to your own daughters!"

"Well, they must have a reason," Bernard replied. "For one thing, they sure can out-swim any of us."

"You can say that again!" Zoran added. "As weakened as Akira was, when she led me to the Circle, she left me in the dust! She had to frequently stop and wait for me to catch up. I suspect that speed has something to do with their reasons. Still, what an awful thing to do to young girls and women."

"Such a short life span!" Zdenka added.

"Well, maybe that's the only way that they can get enough pearls to buy all the things that they need to keep everyone else alive," Bernard theorized.

"Yes, the rest party on the beaches and sleep in until ten, while these poor women risk their lives obtaining the pearls, to say nothing of their legs!" Jarka retorted. She was still angry with those on Asami.

"Besides, dear," Bernard had the last word, "there are no dogs on Asami." Everyone roared.

Zdenka then pointed out, "Do you realize that those girls are likely Baron Hajime's own daughters? Goro is too young to have fathered them. What kind of a man would do that to his own daughters?"

"Dear daughter, he might not be their father," Janos pointed out. "There are many bastard Duskas around on most worlds. Some like Zoran here run off never to be seen again by their barons. Some get disowned, and yes, many barons father children out of wedlock. I even knew of cases where female Duskas had children out of wedlock as well. Women are not immune to lower moral standards either, my dear."

"He's right. Look, a baron might have four children. Only one can inherit his title and position. The others make their own way on their worlds. There must be lots of Duskas running around that we know nothing about," Zoran added.

"Oh, yes, I see your points. Still, what kind of a mother or father would allow this to be done to their children?" Zdenka retorted.

Chapter 22 An Unexpected Visitor

With the young women making good progress, Zoran began to turn his attention to the next major problem to be solved — that of the Yellers. It was mid-May and the construction crews were constantly busy. No one needed his direct assistance so he began to work out how he could uphold his bargain with the warlords.

As he was sketching out options on paper, Lida contacted him mentally from Gladno. *Zoran, Lida here. Assassins came after me and Leo again! Three of Uncle Milan's men were killed this time. They almost got to us!*

Are you safe? Unharmed? Zoran asked, suddenly worried about her safety once more.

Yes, we both are okay. Kazimir sure wants me dead. We've figured out that if he kills me, he is going to name one of his bastard sons his heir. You know that he's had lots of affairs with other women, especially since mom had her accident. What are we going to do?

I have an idea. Hook up Duke Leo with us will you?

Shortly, Leo's mind joined theirs. *She's safe, Zoran. Almost got to us, but we stopped them. Three security men lost their lives though. The assassins are getting bolder with each attempt. Dad's worried, though he isn't saying anything about it.*

Leo, Lida, I have an idea. Why not do what I did? Cleverly disappear and have no one know where you are at, some place that is relatively safe. You can disguise yourselves, use different names or something and secretly come and live here with us. Admittedly, the accommodations are not what you are used to having, but if no one knows where you have gone, you ought to be safe here. We've thrown off one major assault already. Killed all his Mages, so Kazimir is going to be hard pressed to duplicate that action again.

We could come and live with you, little brother?

Sure. If you use a different last name, for example, those of us here can keep your secret, though you will have to be careful that Uncle Milan's engineers and workers don't see you and recognize you.

This isn't good, Zoran. The construction of the new Circle is moving along faster than Brother Jiri expected. I'm going to have to be here in about a month for the formal ceremony that activates it. I'll be a baron then too, Zoran.

So soon? That's great. Once you are a baron and Lida is your baroness, if I understand the rules, then that nullifies Kazimir's heir selection. Lida cannot be a double baroness. It's not allowed. That will nullify her being heir here, then he can select another heir. Lida, you ought to be safe after that.

I'll ask Uncle Milan about that. It sounds right, Zoran. I just have to stay alive until then.

Zoran, I hate to be parted from my Lida, but I am really worried for her safety. This time it was way too close for comfort. Can you take her for a month until the ceremony makes me a baron?

I don't want to leave you, Leo.

I don't want to leave you either, Lida, but I want you to be safe. It's just for a month or so. After the ceremony, we'll be left alone. Please, do this for us, Lida.

Okay. I guess we can chat a whole lot.

Okay sis. Here's what you do. Pack all the things you need and then in secret go down to Uncle Milan's Circle. Go around and around it many times before you head off here. That confuses the trail and no one can track you. Make doubly sure that you have gone around many times, sis. Otherwise, a priestess can see where you have gone. Just tell Uncle Milan that you have gone into hiding until it's safe for you to return as a baroness.

Okay, I'll come tonight after supper. Leo, are you sure about this?

Yes, my love. This way I know that you will be safe. Please Lida.

Okay. After supper Zoran. Thanks little brother. Zoran smiled, he was anxious to see his sister again. He really did miss Rayna and Lida more than he admitted.

Zoran explained what was going to happen to his friends and they set to work clearing out another storage room. "We're rapidly running out of places to put people," Zdenka teased him. "I hope she won't mind our living conditions here. It must be nothing like she is used to having."

"She'll adapt, I'm sure," he replied.

Just after supper, they all gathered around his Circle in the basement. Soon they saw the Circle activating, but Zoran noted that the Circle once again gave him total warning that someone was coming through. Once more he began to ponder the unique bond between himself and his Circle. Many of these effects were not known or perhaps knowledge of same was buried in the old documents of Bandar Zar.

Lida appeared, dressed in a cloak and carrying a pack. He suspected that she had reduced her whole wardrobe into that pack. "Hi little brother!" she rushed to him and gave him a big hug. One by one, she hugged all of the others.

"Well, we have a room fixed up for you. I'm sorry that we can only offer you crude accommodations," Zdenka said apologetically. They led her up to the fourth floor room, next to the two teens from Asami, who came out to see what was happening. Yes, they looked a bit strange wearing light cotton everyday dresses with the very latest in high fashion high heels. The shoes were completely out of place!

Zoran noticed Lida observing this detail, and he introduced the two teens, saying that Lida was a friend who had come for a month's visit. Once inside her room, Lida commented, "Well, Zdenka, this will do fine. Thanks for having me. I'll try to lend you a hand around here. I was still getting my magical training. Ah well, sooner or later I will get that done. Say, what's with those girls and those really high heels? Bit strange."

Zdenka giggled, "Wait until you hear about them! Say, why don't I continue your training while you are here? That way, the time is not wasted?"

"Can you? Oh that would be fabulous! I can help out around here somehow, I'm sure," Lida volunteered.

"Indeed, you can!" Zdenka just had another bright idea. She and Zoran then spent an hour relating the events of their honeymoon, ending up with the rescue of the two mermaids. "They still have the healed holes up and down their legs, but the real problem is that their ankles no longer bend enough for them to have their feet flat on the floor. The only way they can walk is in those really high heels. In time, we are hoping that their ankles and calf muscles will adjust and allow their feet to go flat as they are supposed to. They are now doing pretty well walking. They have to take stairs a bit slowly, but daily I see improvement."

"Can I help them with their reading and writing skills?" Lida volunteered.

"Yes, that's what I had in mind. Glad you thought of that too," Zdenka replied, relieved that Lida had been so observant.

A week later, Lida had already learned three more spells. "Honestly, Zdenka, you are the very best magic teacher I have ever had!" Zdenka, always conservative, didn't truly believe her. After all, she'd only been doing this for a couple of months!

Zdenka kept a close eye on Lida and the two Asami teens. Soon, she was impressed with Lida. Under her care, the two began progressing far more rapidly than before. Lida somehow knew just the right thing to do or say at the right time for Akira and Chika to grasp the material at hand. She began to see that there was more about a Duska than just Shadow Walking and warnings of peril.

Each evening as they dined together, Zdenka saw the strong bond of brother-sister love, similar to that between her father and herself. She resolved to invite his sisters here for visits as often as possible, once they had their castle built. If only this Kazimir threat was over, life could be so wonderful!

Late May, Lida took Zdenka aside. "Do you realize both Akira and Chika are Duska? I mean really Duska! They only lack the Ceremony of Ascension to fully activate all of their potential."

"Zoran said so too. He's planning to ask Priestess Anezka to do it whenever she returns here," she replied.

"Well, if you do it sooner, these two will learn things about twice as fast as they are now. Let me talk to Zoran about it. Honestly, they ought to have had that done for them years ago! Come on, let's go find little brother and get him hopping." Zdenka grinned — how Lida could handle her brother.

They found him studying the maps trying to work out a solution for the Yellers. "Zoran, you positively *must* get the Ceremony of Ascension performed on Akira and Chika this minute!"

"What? Oh, I was, as soon as Priestess Anezka comes back here," he replied, wondering what had set her on the warpath.

"That's not *good* enough. It *is* their birthright, you know. Besides, they will learn everything at least *twice* as fast once that is done. If you don't contact Priestess Anezka this *very* minute, then I will!" Zdenka grinned. She'd never seen his sisters handle him before.

"Well, I figured she might be really busy getting ready to activate Leo's Circle," Zoran replied, wondering if that would mollify her. It didn't.

"I know for a fact that she has almost *nothing* to do at all until Jiri gets it done. She's sitting around being bored. Now you get her here *immediately*, Zoran."

"Okay, okay. If you are sure that she isn't needed there, then okay I will." Zoran replied. He relaxed and made contact with Priestess Anezka.

Hi, Zoran here. Yes, all is well. Say, are you busy right now? Can you take a day off and visit us here in Brn? I have a little ceremony that I'd like you to perform.

Sure. Honestly, it has been rather boring here. I've read all the novels that your Uncle Milan has. About two more weeks, maybe three and we'll have made our second Circle. Incredible, isn't it?

Sure is. Thanks. When can you come?

Give me an hour and I'll drop in on your Circle. Is that okay?

Sure. Thanks a bunch. I'll explain more when you come.

"Okay, sis. She's coming in about an hour. Satisfied?" Zoran teased her.

Lida put her hands on her hips. "Well, it's about time." Then she broke into a laugh, he did too.

They were there to greet Priestess Anezka when she arrived. Again, Zoran had advance knowledge of her coming via his Circle. "Hi everyone. Glad to be back. You know it is awfully stuffy around Baron Milan's place. Much more homey around here. So what's up, Baron Archmage," she used his formal title to tease him a bit.

"I need you to perform two Ceremonies of Ascension." She gave him a totally surprised look. "Come on into the dining room and let me explain." An hour later and three cups of tea later, Zoran had her fully briefed. Lida added her own observations that had convinced her that both girls were Duska.

"Well, the only positive way to know is when I take their hand and walk into the Circle," she pronounced. "Can I meet them now?"

A bit later, the two teens came walking slowly into the room. Although she had been told that they could only walk if they wore the highest of heels, she was still a bit surprised when she saw them. "Come here and chat with me. I am Priestess Anezka Zar." Per her request, everyone left the dining room, leaving her alone with the teens.

A half hour later, the teens, with big smiles on their faces, headed back up to their rooms, very excited. The others entered, Anezka also was grinning broadly. "You are very likely right. Those two ought to have had this ceremony when they were ten or eleven at the very latest! We begin tomorrow at nine sharp. Make sure the Circle is well protected when we do this, Zoran."

"Thanks, Anezka!" Zoran replied. "Say, can I have a private word with you? I've got some unanswered questions that you might be able to answer."

After the others said goodnight, the two were alone. "I've been having some strange connections with my Circle." Suddenly, she gave him her full attention. One by one, Zoran outlined what he considered unusual effects.

"You are right to bring this up with me, Zoran. Forgive me. I ought to have known that something was up the moment that your eyes changed color. These are some effects that must be researched. Allow me to study Bandar Zar's documents more fully. To be honest, neither Jiri nor I have read them in their entirety. As soon as we found the instructions for creating new ones, we went into action and have been doing so ever since. We ought to have read all of his documents first."

"No, you did what was really needed, Anezka. If you had not come along when you did, we would not be in the power position that we are in today. Take your time. None of these effects are causing me any problems — well except for those nightmares, which really was Chika calling out to me. Those are gone now. Let me know what you find out."

"Absolutely, Zoran! I will study them in total detail when I get back. Dumb me, spent all this time reading Milan's novel collection when I ought to have been studying Bandar's documents."

The next morning, everyone gathered beside the Circle of Ascension. Priestess Anezka and Zdenka helped both girls down the many stairs to the basement. Neither wanted any misstep in their heels to delay this vital ceremony. She took Chika first, while Zoran held on to Akira and provided her with some commentary as the ceremony progressed. Specifically, he did not want her becoming alarmed when the two disappeared from view.

Priestess Anezka began her special chant, and at the correct time she took Chika's hand. Together, they slowly began walking around the Circle, stepping on the seventeen colored threads. Suddenly, Zoran was connected to his Circle and was a silent observer of the actual Ceremony of Ascension! Priestess Anezka instantly realized that he was present as well! Another unexpected side effect, she thought. Nevertheless, she continued with Chika. As expected, the teen got dizzy, disoriented, and nauseated. Still, the two continued to walk the Circle. At last, the two entered the Shadows, at which point everyone else saw them disappear.

Anezka led Chika, one by one, to all of the sixteen planets in the Federation of Planets, much as had been done for Zoran during his ceremony. After the trip was done, she repeated it, only this time, Chika began to understand. Her special gland now fully activated. Gone was her dizziness, her nausea. The third trip around, Chika thought, *Well there is one planet that I never want to go back to!* It was Asami, of course.

Anezka then brought them back to the Circle. Chika was all smiles, though quite awestruck. "Wow, sis! Wow!" Next, Priestess Anezka did the same with Akira, but had a much easier time of it, because she had not yet had the misfortune to have gone into the Shadows as had Chika. An hour later, the ceremonies were over.

"Zoran, Lida, I charge both of you to fully train and brief both Duskas about their new powers. I must do some heavy research immediately." She looked at Zoran and he, her. Both knew that his presence with her during the ceremony was an anomaly. It had never happened before. All thanked her and then she departed for Gladno.

Lida took charge of the two teen Duskas, making their training as Duskas her sole objective. Still Zdenka made her take time for her own magic spell training. During the next two weeks, Lida had the teens work on their mental communication skills, to take notice of their special warning of immediate danger, and their ability to Shadow Walk.

In turn, Zdenka noted that the teens literally doubled their rates of learning. Lida had not exaggerated this effect. Now Zdenka began to wonder why this was so, but had no immediate answer, other than it was so. She found herself feeling slightly jealous of Duskas and their skills.

Chapter 23 The Yeller Problem

During late May, Zoran reached a decision. He needed to inspect Dolni Island. Was it inhabitable? Would the Yellers actually be able to survive there? He had many questions and few answers. He announced to all that he needed to go and personally inspect the island.

"Zoran, that's dangerous. Besides, what makes you think the Yellers will move there and how? They are just animals, mean and vicious at that," Karel replied.

"I doubt that Kazimir will be looking for me there. Karel, I think that we humans made the Yellers vicious. At least I got that idea from the history books that we all read when we started. However, I agree, we ought to proceed with caution. There is no telling what we may find there. I was never privy to everything Kazimir was doing. Who knows, he might have some secret fortress there. Ideas on how to proceed?"

"Well, we should go aerial first. Reconnoiter the place before you set foot on the island — that's the safe way. If we go on foot, who knows what we may encounter. Perhaps Bernard has some dogs that can run out ahead and spot dangerous things," Karel suggested.

"Sure, got three good ones," Bernard volunteered two minutes later when Zoran and Karel asked him. "It's a pretty big island from the map, at least the size of Kazimir's entire occupied lands. How are we going to search something that big?"

"Only one real way, we Shadow Walk. If we used our Fly spells we would be at it a year," Zoran replied.

"True, even if I used my falcon form, it would take a very long time to search that large an island. When do we start?" Karel asked.

After informing the others of their plan, Zoran held hands with Karel and Bernard. "Karel, you search to the right of us. Bernard, you search to the left of us, and I'll cover the center. Look for any obvious signs of villages, roads, crop fields — anything that might indicate humans inhabit the island."

"Look for smoke clouds from smithy's or people's chimneys," Bernard added.

"I will take a north-south zig-zag path. Here we go." He concentrated and stepped them into the Shadows. Momentarily, he appeared above the planet and then zoomed down over Dolni Island. He moved in closer until they were several hundred feet above the mountainous island. Below them, dense stands of forests fought the hard granite stone. Here and there they spied streams and an occasional pond. From this height, they could not see if there were animals on the grounds, but they saw no villages or other signs of human inhabitation. However, this was only their first day.

Dutifully, the trio kept at it each day. Zoran was not satisfied until he'd searched the whole island. If the Yellers were going to be relocated here, he had to be confident in his own mind that humans were not here, for both their sakes. On the fourth day of their search, Zoran estimated that their path of zig-zagging had them near the middle of the island, about half way along its east-west length.

"Hey, look over here," Bernard called out. "That looks like a human construction." The three saw what looked like stone blocks, cut with a perfectly straight edge. Zoran moved them in for a closer look. "That's a building!" a shocked Bernard added.

"Can we be seen? Should we cast Invisibility?" growled Karel.

"No, we cannot be seen. We are Shadow Walking. Only an alert Duska could detect our presence. What is this place anyway?" Zoran asked, becoming very curious. Here in the middle of nowhere was some kind of stone construction. He zoomed in even closer. Regular gray granite stone blocks, similar to those used in the construction of Castle Dorumova, lay in a flat square approximately thirty feet across. Trees and brush encroached around the edges and grasses fought for life between the many cracks. None of the three had ever seen anything like this. They could see no signs of inhabitation so Zoran decided to arrive on the stonework.

"What is this place?" asked Karel, after verifying the stone was real and solid.

Bernard, ever cautious, surveyed their perimeter, but could see little into the dense trees that surrounded the square. "Has a fortification wall fallen over somehow?" This seemed the best theory he could muster at the moment.

"I don't sense that anyone is around or that there is any immediate danger," Zoran replied. "I have no idea what this place is, guys. One wall does not a fortress make. Possibly a holy temple of some kind, long unused. Fan out, let's see if there is more to this than what we see here," he suggested.

"If we are going exploring, I ought to fetch my dogs," Bernard volunteered. "They can detect trouble sooner than I can."

"Okay, we'll give you a minute, Bernard. Good idea. We do not know with what we are dealing here on this island. General Janos will have my head if I go around taking chances," Zoran deferred to the stern warnings with which his general had admonished him several days ago.

Five minutes later, three dogs began scampering about, running out ahead of Bernard, as he began exploring what lay around this stonework. Zoran and Karel flanked him, swords drawn ready for trouble. Fifteen minutes later, having dislodged five snakes, they arrived back where they started. "This only gets stranger by the minute," Zoran scratched his head. They had seen absolutely no other signs of anything but the wild landscape around the whole area.

"This is it — the whole construction?" asked a very confused Bernard.

"I hate it when people make these confounded mysteries," growled Karel, his anger rising. "What's the bloody use of having a thirty foot stone wall lying flat on the ground anyway?"

"Well, it's not like this is a stone quarry," Zoran discarded that possibility.

"Hi fellows, we just had to pop around and see what you've discovered," the alto voice of Zdenka came from behind the three. "Wow, what is this place?" She and Jarka had teleported over to see for themselves what Bernard had excitedly described to them when he came to fetch his dogs. One ran up to Jarka and began licking her hand, which she didn't appreciate, wiping it on her dress.

"No other signs of anything around it," Bernard reported. "Told you this was a weird one. We searched about a quarter mile perimeter and found absolutely nothing at all, just pristine forest."

"I've never seen anything like it," Zdenka spoke and then wished that she hadn't. After all, her experience with stonework was extremely limited, so of course her opinion was worthless. Then, she had an idea, conservatively she said, "Perhaps someone was building a temple here and only got the base done before they left. That would explain it."

"Hey, I like that idea," Zoran complimented her. "That's the best idea so far. I wonder who built it and when. The stonework looks amazingly similar to that in Castle Dorumova."

While they were discussing this possibility, Jarka found a stout branch and began tapping on the stone, moving methodically along its surface. Curious, Bernard asked, "What'cha doing, dear?"

"Tapping. Seeing if it is solid all over. Hey, come here everyone!" her tone changed from boredom to enthusiasm. The others gathered round her. "Here, listen to this tap over here and then to the tap at this spot," she asked eagerly.

"Hear the difference?" she asked.

"It sounds different. Maybe it's due to a difference in the stone," Bernard replied.

"No, silly, it's a hollow sound. There is a space beneath this central area. Let's mark out its dimensions. Here, stand here, this seems to be one corner." Bernard moved where she pointed. A few minutes and a lot of tapping later, Karel, Zoran, and Zdenka stood at the three other corners of the hollow area, while Jarka stood by proudly looking at the space they defined. "Ten by ten, big enough for a person to enter. I wonder if there is some secret door that somehow opens. There must be some chamber below ground."

"Could it be a burial ground? Could this be a tomb?" asked Zdenka, wondering aloud what constructions might be hidden in this manner.

"I don't think so," Jarka replied thinking hard. "No head stones, no ornaments, no flowers — no nothing to indicate this was an important person's tomb. I wonder how it opens?"

She began to cast a number of spells. "Well, no magic is radiating, so the opening mechanism must be mechanical. No pull rings, no levers. How does this thing open?" she said getting somewhat hostile about it not revealing its mysteries to her.

"Maybe it doesn't open," Zdenka suggested. "Perhaps, after they put whatever in the chamber, they sealed it up with these stones. Maybe it is a tomb."

"Well, they didn't count on Jarka Mitova Dragan!" she retorted and began casting her Mystical Door spell. After its sixth casting, she added a Light spell. "Ah ha! Now we are getting somewhere. Okay, everyone, there are steps leading down. I've got a door opened inside and a light going. Shall we go exploring?"

"What about the air? Perhaps it is poisonous," Karel volunteered rather worried about charging into some underground chamber with no easy exit at hand.

"I'll bring my dogs along. Keep a close eye on their behavior. If they sense danger, they'll let us know," Bernard suggested. One by one they and the three dogs stepped through her magical door arriving on a long set of descending stairs.

The walls absorbed the sounds of their feet and breathing. A musty smell registered in their noses, but the dogs eagerly trotted on down the steps. "Hey, look at these rotting bags," Jarka commented. One was on either side of the walls. As she touched it, the leather crumbled into dust. A bright light radiated from a stone affixed to the wall. "And there was light!" she humorously declared.

"A Mage has had a hand in here," Zoran declared. "Let's follow the dogs. If you see any more of the lights, open their bags."

"Wait, let me go first! There could well be all manner of traps in here for the unwary!" Jarka exclaimed, pushing Zoran back from the lead.

"Say, are my dogs in danger?" Bernard asked, suddenly worried about their safety.

"They are probably okay, they weigh a lot less than a person. Weight is likely the trigger." She slowly descended the stone stairs. After some fifty feet, she halted. "Ah, just as I thought. A trap!"

"See, Zoran, it's good to have a thief with you," Bernard jested. The others chuckled.

"Only a fool wouldn't," she teased them. "Let's see if I can disarm it. Ah, yes, there. You see, if I had placed my full weight on this step, then the stone would have moved down a bit and something bad would have come flying out from these two holes in the side walls. Spears or arrows would be my guess. It's safe. On down we go."

"Thanks, good work, Jarka," Zoran praised her and followed slowly after her.

One hundred feet below the surface, the stairs opened into a twenty foot square room with ten foot tall ceilings. The dogs were in the middle panting and waiting for Bernard. Jarka found another rotting leather covering and suddenly light began to illuminate the room. "Oh my!" she exclaimed. As the others joined her, they too had similar exclamations.

Stacked against the far wall were five wooden boxes, whose wood had dry rotted. The weight of their contents had then burst the sides. Gold coins, silver coins, gems, and jewelry lay in piles mixed with bits of the remains of the boxes. Against the left wall was a table which held armor and weapons, while against the right wall was another table holding a number of books carefully wrapped in oil coated skins, well preserved. The prints of the dogs were clearly visible in a layer of dust a half inch thick.

"No one has been here for a very, very long time, Zoran," Jarka commented. "How long does it take for a sealed space to accumulate so much dust?" she asked. No one knew, but stared in disbelief at the treasure before their eyes. "Well, don't touch anything. Check for traps. All of you, cast your spells, while I look for signs of mechanical traps," she ordered. They followed her orders, but after ten minutes of searching, no traps had been found. Jarka was finally satisfied and allowed them to begin to examine the room's contents.

Bernard headed for the treasure pile, as did Zdenka. Neither had ever seen so much money and valuable gems and ornate jewelry before. Karel cast a spell and headed over to the armor and weapons pile, while Zoran began examining the oil skin wrapped books. "Zoran! All of these items on the table are radiating magic!" Karel exclaimed, his voice cracking from uncharacteristic excitement!

"All of them?" asked Jarka in total disbelief.

"Yes, all of them!" Karel replied. As he touched the table, the dry rotted wood crumbled, sending the entire table disintegrating to the floor with a resounding crash. Helms, shields, swords, and armor landed noisily on the floor, a cloud of dust rose causing everyone to begin coughing like mad. "Clean! Clean! Clean!" Karel commanded, his spells firing off like a machine gun. The others joined in, rapidly the dust and fragments of wood vanished, particularly from the air.

"That's better," Jarka stated, putting her hands on her hips. "Now, this is the find of a century!" she exclaimed, her enthusiasm returned. "Sacks, we need lots of sacks. Zoran, don't touch your table."

"I'm not. Yes, sacks. Okay, Bernard, why don't you teleport you and your dogs back to the tower and return with a whole lot of sacks," he asked. He didn't need to be asked twice. "I'm going to levitate these books and see if I can keep from wiping out the table. I sure hope these books are not as fragile as the tables are."

Bernard returned ten minutes later to find that Jarka had begun to sort out the coins; Zdenka, the gems and jewelry; Karel, the magical items. Zoran sat in the middle of the room on the floor, a large volume opened in his lap. "Hey, listen to this book's title: _Journal of Baron Valentýn Vladislov, first Baron of Adapazan_. Incredible. This stuff probably belonged to the first baron on Adapazan! It's hard to read, though. The dialect is very different than ours. I have to use a translation spell. This is an incredible find!"

For an hour, the five filled sack after sack, teleporting them back to the tower, only to return with now empty sacks for more. At long last, Jarka made a final thorough search to make sure that nothing had been overlooked, including more secret doors. Alas, she found none.

"Okay, we three will continue our sweep of the island. You two can head back and start counting," he teased, knowing that was precisely what Jarka had in mind.

"I've got to see to my students, but I think I will call a halt and have them all lend Jarka a hand with it," Zdenka added. A bit later, the three continued their Shadow Walk above the island. After three more days of searching, they found nothing else at all. The island was devoid of human occupation, which pleased Zoran, who now knew he had a viable alternative for the yellers.

After diner, the counting finished, Jarka reported that there were five thousand six hundred gold coins, four thousand nine hundred and six silver coins. Aldrick had been called in to appraise the gems and his estimate was four hundred fifty-three thousand gold coins worth. The jewelry he estimated might bring an additional one hundred thousand.

"Okay, first action, divide the gold, silver, gems, and jewelry into eight equal value piles, please," Zoran asked.

"Why?" asked Jarka, confused by this strange request. She was ready to begin her study of the properties of the many magical items.

"Because I want each one of you, including Emil and Renata here to have an equal share of the treasure. I'll give General Janos some of my share. This way, you each have your own money to spend. I know, make sure that the twins only get the large gemstones. They don't want gold or silver," he teased. Both Renata and Emil nodded wildly, about to get what their hearts desired, a pile of gems! Everyone enthusiastically thanked him over and over. Such generosity was nearly overwhelming, to say the very least. Each of his friends just received the equivalent of nearly seventy thousand gold coins.

For the next few days, Zdenka had her advanced students using their Identify spells on the various magical items, attempting to identify just what their magical properties were. It was an extremely good training exercise for them all. While Zoran greatly desired to study the six volumes, he knew that he honestly had to deal with the Yeller problem soon.

"Okay, I've been putting the Yellers off for too long. Tomorrow, I am going over to Zovou Province and see Warlord Petr about the Yellers there," he announced over dinner.

"How are you going to move them? We have no boats?" asked Zdenka, rather worried about his safety.

"They aren't going to go peacefully," Jarka added.

"They are stronger than us," Bernard put in his thought.

"We can always put them to sleep or stun them and then teleport them," Karel stated flatly.

"Dunno yet, gang. I'll have to see."

"Well, we're coming with you," Karel announced in a manner that Zoran could not refuse.

"I'll take all of you, except Zdenka, who has her students to handle. I think General Janos ought to come and maybe a half dozen security men. We ought to be prepared to stay there a few days," he announced.

He sent a Message to the warlord that night. At nine the next morning, the small group teleported over to the most western province of Adapazan, Zovou. There, Warlord Petr welcomed them. He was a burly man, heavily bearded and in dire need of a bath, Zoran thought, as he introduced his party to the rebel leader. Their main fortress was crude by all standards — the smoothly cut and polished stonework of Zoran's slowly forming walls contrasted sharply with the rough and ill-cut stone that formed Petr's outer wall and central manor. Theirs was a life of barest necessities, Zoran realized at once. They eked out an existence, barely.

The furnishings left everything to be desired, he noted, following Petr into his war room, a large, bare-walled room. Blackened oil lanterns long in need of a cleaning valiantly attempted to illuminate the rough map he had laid out on the table. "Yellers occupy all the lands west of here, down to the ocean, we think. We've got daily patrols that go from here to here, keeping them at bay from our meager crop lands. 'Course, that ain't saying much. They barely make enough for half a winter. We are forced to buy more from Ves just to get by. As promised, our new road to Ves ought to be done by first snow. No idea if Warlord Sabina will keep her word and have it connected to yours by then. How much is a wagon of grain going to cost us if'n we get it from you instead?"

"That I don't know off hand. I will check and see. How many wagons could you use this winter?" Warlord Petr took this opportunity to rattle off his long list of supplies that he greatly desired to acquire by any means. He was definitely prepared for this meeting with his new Baron, Karel pointed out, as he copied down the items ranging from grain to cloth to weapons. After lunch and a large round of honey ale, Zoran decided it was time to meet the Yellers.

Warlord Petr loaned him some horses and a guide, but refused to come with him, citing important organizational matters. As they rode along, Karel commented,

"Some organizational matters — I bet he didn't want anything to do with these ferocious animals." Bernard agreed with him. Their guide led them about a half day's ride westward to their perimeter line, which was heavily patrolled. Their well-marked horse trail led northward and southward from this valley. Here, their guide explained that he would await their return. Although the guide didn't say it, Zoran picked up his unspoken words, "that is, if you ever return." Indeed, the warlord and their guide figured this might be the end of their baron. Only fools went after the Yellers directly.

Since darkness would come in about an hour, the Mages cast one of their Safe House spells, which created a large room in which men and horses could safely spend the night free from worry about attacks. The house was extra-dimensional and not visible on Adapazan. Of course, their guide was impressed with their spell and eagerly shared their evening meal with them. From the way he ate, Zoran guessed that the man was having a veritable feast.

The next morning, they cast their Skin of Stone spells on their bodies and prepared to continue westward on foot. "Remember, when we make contact with the Yellers, do not draw your swords. We want to somehow see if we can parley with them," Zoran reminded them of his wishes.

"Let's hope that they understand a few words like my dogs do," Bernard grumbled. He liked this less and less. "They are just animals, after all." Zoran hoped and prayed this was not the case.

"Remember, each security man is to stand next to one of us Mages. If trouble does come, we will teleport ourselves out of here." The six guards appreciated this bit of encouragement, but General Janos had faith that Zoran must know what he was doing. In his mind, a baron always did. Since there were no trails to follow, Zoran headed them up the side of the valley into the next one, hoping that they would not have to travel for days to find them.

After a long struggle to climb up and over the valley walls, they descended into the next western valley. As they reached the bottom and stood admiring the tall, rugged mountains, Zoran's inner senses began alerting him to eminent danger. This he relayed to the others. Suddenly, from behind the pine trees a loud, scary, high pitched yelling accompanied the rush of a dozen seven foot tall Yellers, brandishing large clubs. Zoran saw at once that these creatures, who wore fur loin cloths, had the intelligence to surround them before attacking. That was a good sign, he thought, although General Janos and the others saw this in an entirely different light. Only with extreme effort did the men resist the powerful, self-preservation move of drawing their swords. Zoran raised both of his hands high in the air, hoping that this gesture of submission would somehow be recognized by the Yellers.

The Mages had long since cast their Universal Translator spell. Zoran hoped — no, he had counted upon these creatures having a spoken language. "Peace. We will not fight you. Speak to your leader. Hold. No fight. Speak leader." Zoran called out loudly, as the dozen were now dangerously close to them and within clubbing distance.

Suddenly, one of the tall Yellers stopped and cried out in utter shock and surprise, "Animals speak our language? Hold. Animals can speak?" he addressed Zoran.

"Yes, we can speak your language. I am Zoran. I wish to speak to your leader, chief, boss, the top man. We come in peace. Not harm you. You not harm us. We speak to leader."

Something he said must have sounded funny, because several of the Yellers chuckled. "We never knew wild animals could speak! Leave sharp metals on ground here. Come with us. Glock will be famous now," he said to his men. Zoran asked his party to do as they asked, dropping both of his short swords onto the ground first. One by one, his companions reluctantly followed his lead.

Another Yeller commented, "Glock, they are doing it! You will be famous now. Capture speaking animals!" Glock smiled and gestured for them to follow him. Surrounded by the dozen Yellers who towered over them, to say nothing of their vicious looking clubs, the group followed the one called Glock.

Zoran's group had to almost jog to keep up with the swift footed Yellers, who took long strides. On down this new valley they marched for nearly two hours. Soon, Zoran saw tell-tale smoke clouds drifting upwards towards the billowing white clouds and blue sky. A village of sorts must lie ahead, which he found very encouraging. The others had an entirely different feeling!

Not long after that, they walked into a large village unlike anything they had ever seen before. Hundreds of other Yellers, some old, some young children, came out to taunt them. Uniformly, they all wore fur loin cloths and went barefoot, even their women wore the same thing, their breasts quite visible, startling the men. Their homes were hide domes, round hemispherical affairs. Bent wooden saplings could be seen holding them up. Numerous cooking fires dotted the village.

Glock marched them up to one specific hut, all the while calling out, "Look, the white animals can talk! Come and hear what we found!" As they approached the hut, Glock called out, "Animals, wait here." His eleven men made sure that Zoran and his group did as asked.

Zoran's danger sense was at a continuous low key pitch, which he tended to block out, focusing on just who their leader was and how amenable they would be to constructive talks. Glock opened the hide door and held it open for his leader. Out stepped an elderly woman, taking them all by surprise. Glock said, "Animals, speak to leader. This is leader." He was keeping his speech to short sentences, probably, Zoran thought, because he thought that he was speaking to a dumb animal.

"I am called Zhou. Hunter Glock says that white animals speak. Is this so?" she asked. Her voice betrayed a hint of curiosity.

"Hello, Zhou. Yes, we all speak well. I am called Zoran. I came to talk with your leaders. It is important that we speak." Of course, as soon as he spoke, the whole village erupted into a raucous — wild comments flying in all directions. Evidently, the Yellers thought that the white animals were just efficient dumb animals, as the humans did the Yellers!

She motioned for them to sit by her cooking fire, and she sat down as well. Zoran, smaller in size than she, found it a little embarrassing to find himself staring straight at her breasts. "I am sorry that for years my people have been attacking your people, driving them clear across the land to this location and in the far north. I came to offer your people a new land in which there are none of we white animals, and I will give you my word that we whites will not go there unless you ask for our aid."

"We are called Chou and we once numbered many tribes, before the white animals came with their metal cutters. My grandmother was very angry and ordered many unsuccessful attacks on the white animals. She told me of how the Chou had once been free to roam from coast to coast, but now had retreated to the western half. My mother feared greatly the white animals and sought to gather as many of us as possible together, strength in numbers. Alas, even that has failed. Now I lead my village here to the edge of the world. We have no more room to retreat and must make our last stand here, though we know that we cannot survive." Her apathy touched Zoran. He realized that the centuries of slaughter and constant movement westward had driven them down to anger, then to fear, and now they were in apathy, ready to accept their fate.

"Yes, you and your people can survive and thrive and multiply once more. Across the waters is another land which no whites have touched. It is ten times larger than this area here that your people occupy. To make amends for our butchery of your people for so many, many years, I would like to help all your people move to this new land and get settled there. We have looked the whole land over and have seen no white animals there. I give you my word that in the future, none of us will set one foot into this new land of yours, unless you invite us to come. I know that this is asking a lot of you to trust me that I speak the truth."

"You speak of trust, yet your white animals kill us every chance they get," she replied sadly.

"I know. For that, I am sorry. We thought of your people as also dumb animals too. What I propose is for me to take six of your people to see this new land that I am giving to you. Let them see for themselves if this land is suitable for your people. While I am gone with them, I will leave my friends here with you as hostages to guarantee that I return with your people. Will you agree to let me try to make amends with you and your people?"

"How will you get there? No one can cross the endless waters," she asked somewhat fearfully.

"By magic. How long will your men need to see if this new land is a good one for your people? As far as I can tell, it is very similar to all of the lands here."

"A day perhaps. I will see if you speak truth," she decided. She called out six names, and the men quickly moved to her, standing proudly before her. "You are to go with Zoran here. He says he will show you a new land where we can live in peace. See for yourselves if he speaks truth. I will hold his friends here as hostages until you return. Be back by dark," she ordered.

"But you cannot trust them," one protested. She raised her hand and he was silent. Zoran noted that she held implicit power over the men, concluding this must be a matriarchal society.

"Take these men. Be back by dark. If not, we will kill your men. Go now," she ordered.

"Are you sure?" General Janos asked Zoran.

"Yes, it must be done. I have to show them the land. I will be back by dark," he replied. He had the six men hold hands and then took one's hand and cast his teleport spell, arriving near the northeastern coast, where a mountain stream came down to the sea. He wanted them to see that there was fresh water, which was why he chose this spot.

The men blinked, unable to grasp what had happened to themselves. Suddenly, they were looking at a strange place, a location that they had never seen before. "I will wait here by the stream. You check out the land. Be sure that you return before dark. Yell if you need any help," he explained and then sat down on a boulder to wait.

He watched as the men fanned out and began reconnoitering the area. Now he waited and prayed the land would be to their liking. Hours passed before the men reappeared. Actually, they returned so silently that he was surprised by them. Zoran filed this datum for future reference. These were highly skilled hunters. "We return now," one said to him. After making sure that all six were present, he again teleported them back to their village.

Bernard looked very relieved to see Zoran suddenly appear with the Yellers. "Whew," he muttered under his breath. The six Security Men also visibly relaxed; they had been extremely tense while he was gone. General Janos merely sat back and smoked his pipe.

The six men gathered around Zhou, but Zoran could not overhear their conversation. "Well, how did it go?" asked General Janos. "We've certainly learned more about the Yellers in one afternoon that we have in three centuries."

"Don't know. They scouted around for a couple hours. I hope they liked it. Honestly, if they didn't, I will have to try to find some other solution. I will not be a party to genocide of an intelligent race of people," Zoran stated what his heart told him.

As dusk came, Zhou ended her discussion with her men and came over to Zoran. "You speak truth. Come, dine with us on antelope and berries. Drink honey mead. We talk more." At once, many other women appeared, carrying wooden platters of meat and berries. Others came with wooden mugs and large pottery vessels. Men, women, and children gathered around their cooking fires and sat on the ground, ready to dine. Some brought them over to Zhou and Zoran's group. Zoran carefully watched how the others ate and mimicked them, as did his companions.

When she had eaten her fill and began sipping the strong mead, Zhou began asking questions. "How soon to move? All this?" she indicated with a sweep of her arm.

"Tomorrow, if you like. We can take about three people and one hut at one time. We can make many trips in one day."

"That is good. Better if you take a scouting party first and let them find a suitable place for the village first. Then, take the rest." She took another long drink.

"What about the other tribes?" she then asked. Zoran noticed that her voice had a hint of hope in it, which he took as a very good sign indeed.

"I will need your help with the other tribes. I know that they are scattered all over. Some are grouped as you are here, but in the cold north. Perhaps there are some still in the lands where we whites live. After you see that this new land is good for your people, can you help me to tell others about it so that I can help them move there too?" he asked. He desperately needed her help with this. So far they had been phenomenally lucky in connecting up with someone who would listen to reason. Others might be more warlike.

"You are wise as a mother, Zoran. Move my tribe. If we like it, I will send back others to begin to spread the word. You then help them move. Is this acceptable?" she asked.

"Yes, it is perfect. Thank you for having the wisdom to save your whole people," he complimented her.

"You are more like a mother than man. Tell me, are all white peoples as wise as you? If so, why have they killed us for hundreds of seasons?"

"My own people are as I am. Yet, most whites are not. They believe your people to be wild animals, like bears, and have acted badly. We have bad people too, just as you may have too."

"Ah, we are alike then. We thought that your people were wild animals, stronger than bears. Yet, your people have metal blades. Some of my hunters tell of metal which can cut down trees. Is this so?"

"Yes, they are called axes. Would your people like to have some axes? Would they find them useful in felling trees?" Zoran asked, realizing that perhaps some stronger alliances could be forged through trade.

"Yes, we need many axes to fell trees for huts and fires when white snow descends. You can get these for us? What do you want us to give to you for them?" she asked, eyeing him closely.

"I will give you a hundred axes to show you that we are friends. They will help you get your new village built sooner. Once you have your village built and are ready for the white snows, I can come and visit you. If you need more axes, we can make a trade. Furs would be valuable to us. It will take my people some days to make a hundred axes for you. If you will allow me to send one of my men back home right now, he can return in the morning with as many as he can find. That way, those going to the new land tomorrow can take the axes with them."

She smiled, "That would be very useful. Yes, send your man." Zoran told Bernard to round up all the axes that could be spared and to get the Brn blacksmiths making more to make up the difference. He agreed and cast his teleport spell, causing quite a stir among the Yellers with his magical departure.

Zoran's group was given a hastily vacated hut in which to sleep, though they found it awfully crowded. General Janos insisted that three stand guard over the others during the night, just in case of some trickery. He arranged for a Mage and two men for each shift, but the night passed uneventfully. In the morning, Bernard arrived shortly after sunrise, surprising the villagers once more.

All gathered around him as he opened up a large sack containing twenty metal axes. Even Zhou was quite pleased with the gift. As she organized the moving, Zoran estimated each Mage could take three people plus their hut and meager possessions. By nine, Zoran, Karel, Emil, Renata, Jarka, and Bernard began the first of many teleports. Eighteen men and equipment went with each trip. This first day, they made four trips, depositing seventy-two men on the beach where the fresh water stream entered the ocean.

The next day, one reported that a good site had been found and the major task of moving the whole village began. One hundred eighty were moved each day for the next two days. The remaining fifty followed on the fourth day. As Zoran deposited the last of the villagers, Zhou asked him to return when the moon was full again. Zoran estimated this would occur in two weeks' time. If all went well, she would begin to help him with the other tribes.

At last, Zoran and his friends returned back to their horses, surprising the rebel, who by now thought that he'd just acquired a number of fine horses. "Well, how did it go?" asked Warlord Petr, when they arrived at his fortress.

"I do believe my solution will work. The Yellers are actually an intelligent race of people. They thought that we were nothing but dumb white animals," Zoran explained. "Considering that we have been hunting them down and killing them for centuries, I thought it went extremely well. I will return in two weeks. If all goes as planned, I will have all Yellers moved out of your province as soon as we can. Although it is a tad premature, I do believe that your Yeller problem is a thing of the past. Just don't go attacking any of them for a while, please."

Warlord Petr just didn't believe Zoran at all. Obviously, the Yellers were just a pack of wild animals on two legs. Everyone knew that, except this new baron. However, he would wait. If there was any chance that Zoran would get rid of the vermin from Zovou Province, he had to give him the time. It would save him many men's lives.

When the group returned to the tower, General Janos exclaimed, "Well, daughter of mine, your husband must be God!" As they arrived home, both Zdenka and Lida came running up to them, and he grabbed his daughter, twirling her around. Lida gave her brother a welcoming hug. Janos added excitedly, "He learned more about them in a half day and accomplished more for them and us in a week than the rest of us have in three centuries!"

"Well?" she asked hoping to hear firsthand of their adventures. She was overjoyed that they had all returned safely and didn't say how much she had worried this past week. Even though Zoran Messaged her frequently at night, she was still very concerned for their safety. These were the Yellers, after all.

Janos, Lida, and Archmage Oldrich had Zoran relate all that had happened during their visit. Although Bernard had told them a bit about the encounter, hearing it all from Zoran's mouth cleared up many points. When he finished, Archmage Oldrich insisted that Zoran write a treatise on the Yellers so that future generations might learn the truth. Lida's comment to him spoke mountains, "How could we have been so ignorant, so foolish for so long?"

"Hey how are our two mermaids doing? How are you coming on your spells?" he asked Lida.

"They are doing exceptionally well. I have them both reading and writing at a basic level in just this short time. You have a treasure in Zdenka, little brother. She's the best when it comes to teaching us our spells! I wish Rayna could come here and finish her training too." Lida praised his Archmage wife and he grinned.

After getting a briefing on how the construction was faring that evening, Zoran checked with Duke Leo. There had been a slight setback; his new Circle was scheduled for completion by the 22nd of June. Next, he contacted his other sister, Rayna, who was very glad to hear from him. Zoran briefed her on the Yellers too. Once again, Zoran found himself idle, discovering that he disliked this immensely.

Chapter 24 Enlightenment

The next day, using his Universal Translator spell, he began studying the six ancient volumes from the founding days of the Adapazan Circle of Ascension and his distant relative, Valentýn Vladislov, the first baron of Adapazan. One volume described the construction of Castle Dorumova, and he discovered the location of all its secret chambers of which he knew nothing. Probably Kazimir stored his valuables in some. It was a shame that he or his sisters were not still there; they could go exploring, though they probably would get into trouble with Kazimir.

Another volume was Valentýn Vladislov's diary. This he began reading, skimming over the unimportant details. He learned that his wife was named Karen and that they had two sons. One son had died during an attack by the Yellers. The other son, Rogdan, was named his heir. However, a number of pages later, Valentýn began taking a dislike to his son's slovenly ways. A few pages later, he wrote about no longer trusting his own son! His wife slipped and fell from the rooftop. He attributed the accident to the icy conditions and her infernal study of the stars, which she did nightly. Several pages later, he began to suspect that she might not have slipped. Valentýn wrote that he began a secret investigation. On the next page, he wrote about bringing in mediums to try to contact her spirit and see if she really did just slip on the ice.

Zoran grinned, "Mediums! Bah, probably just told him what he wanted to hear." He read on. He grinned; sure enough, one told him that she had been given a push. The next ten pages were filled with his rambling speculations on who was behind it. Page after page went by, and Zoran began to suspect Valentýn was likely becoming totally obsessed or even slightly psychotic about his wife's death.

Now the pages began describing how he thought his own son was behind it, and he swore that his son would not inherit his ever growing wealth. He wrote, "By the Laws, he inherits the Circle and Castle, but by god he'll not get our wealth!" Now the baron began describing the construction of his secret stash. Just as soon as it was finished, the engineer who designed it and those that worked on it had been killed by the baron. Another page outlined his secret trips to there in the middle of the night, moving all of his valuables out of the reach of his son.

The final pages contained nearly incoherent ramblings about the possibility of his son trying to assassinate him. The last page was almost like reading total insanity. Even the writing became chaotic, bordering on scribbles. Then, blank pages. "Well, either he was assassinated or he died of natural causes or he took a dive off the roof. He really went mad, that's for sure."

Zoran moved on to the next volume and quickly discarded that one. It outlined monthly income and expenses along with numerous trades made with other Federation planets. Two more volumes beckoned to him. One contained a bit of history pre-arrival on Adapazan. While it might be interesting reading one day, it didn't seem material to Zoran. The second one did; it was entitled <u>Notes on My Connection to the Circle</u>.

"Now this is incredible!" Zoran began reading the notes that Valentýn had written. Yes, his eyes had changed to bright red, the color of Adapazan's Circle, just as had his! Eagerly, Zoran continued reading.

> I seem to have total control over my Circle from any distance away, like my Circle is somehow a part of me. I've grown to see it as an extension of me. Bandar suggests that this effect will wear off in future generations. He's apologized for the eye color change. Bandar claims that he was not aware that this would happen.

Further on, he came across the following.

> Yes! I have advance knowledge whenever anyone attempts to use my Circle for Shadow Walking. Coming or going, I know in advance that it is about to occur. Yes! I can prevent such activations, even when I am on Gladno! Incredible.

This is incredibly useful! So I can stop Kazimir if he tries to attack us here via my Circle. Great. Even if I am off-world! Zoran was relieved somewhat.

A bit further, Valentýn noted:

> My connection is even stronger than Bandar predicted! I've just discovered that I have the same advance knowledge when anyone Shadow Walks anywhere within a mile of the Circle! Coming or going, I know about it. Very useful. I have not spoken to Bandar or the other Barons about this fact. It may well prove useful to me.

He read through more mundane notes and several pages later came across another fact that confirmed what Zoran had already experienced.

> I received quite a shock when Rogdan's Ceremony of Ascension was held last night. As Priestess Ari began activating the Circle, I was immediately aware of and a part of and witness to his ascension! It was like part of me went into him or was with him. Conclusion: I will be totally aware of anyone receiving this ceremony at my Circle.

On the next page, fascinated, Zoran read even more.

> My archenemy, Dusan Clav, attempted to sneak into Castle Dorumova last night, via a Shadow Walk. As expected, I had prior knowledge of his attempt. My guess is a few seconds notice. What surprised me was that I somehow knew at that instant what his intentions actually were: to raid my treasury. I reacted by shoving him wildly back into the depths of the Shadows. Today, I received word from his baroness that Dusan is now missing! She had the audacity to ask if I had seen him. Of course, I replied truthfully that I had not seen him.

A bit later, he added a footnote.

> Dusan finally showed up a week later. According to all reports, he looked to be in terrible shape. His clothes were shredded, and he had a number of wounds, none life-threatening, unfortunately. He claims that he somehow got lost in the Shadows. Interesting correlation. I am not going to tell the other barons about this either!

After several more pages, he came across this tidbit.

> Talked to Bandar last night. He is of the opinion that all these effects that the

original owner of a Circle experience will not carry on down to the next owner. He was most concerned about other baron's complaints about having orange and green eyes. He's convinced that our heirs will experience none of this. This is the best news I've heard, since I now suspect my own son, Rogdan, of pushing my wife off of the roof. Treasonous son, poison from the womb! I am very glad that he will not inherit the powers that I have as the original owner. Bandar looked mystified about my cheerfulness over his revelations. I didn't tell him about Rogdan. The fewer that know, the better.

There followed some more rantings about his treacherous son. Then, Zoran came across the most interesting datum yet.

Bandar came to see me. He told me how he sees me morning the loss of my Duska wife and also that I have been seeing a lot of a local barmaid at the Dew Drop Inn, where I get drunk nearly every night. I told him that I cared deeply for this simple woman. He suggested that I marry her. I told him that she was not Duska and that I could therefore not marry her. He kept hounding me and my will failed me. At last, I told him about the treason of my heir, my son, Rogdan. I explained that if I remarried, that unless she was Duska, she could easily be assassinated by Rogdan. I just couldn't face that again, not ever.

Bandar then cast Anti-spying spells and whispered to me. "There is something that you do not know, Valentýn. No one but I know this. Considering your situation, I'll tell you, but you must promise me never to tell another soul." I so swore.

"Anyone, any human that is, can become a Duska merely by having the Priestess perform the Ceremony of Ascension on them. Yes, everyone believes that only we originals, we of Duska inheritance, can have our gland enhanced by the Circles and be able to Shadow Walk and all that. But that is not true. Anyone can. You can secretly have my wife perform the ceremony on your barmaid and make her a Duska. Then, it would be safe for you to marry her. The only limiting factor is age. It is dangerous to perform the ceremony on anyone who is older than twenty-one or younger than ten."

We made preparations to have this done. Unfortunately, Bandar's wife died in what I consider mysterious circumstances. Could Rogdan have found out what we were planning? Worse, Bandar has now gone missing! The entire Federation of Planets is out looking for him everywhere. Apparently, I am under suspicion, since I was the last person to have contact with him here on Adapazan!

This was the last entry in the volume. Zoran stared at the blank page. "So there was treachery even back at the founding of the Circles," he mused. He began to suspect that Bandar had gone to Sholov Province to build a new Circle of Ascension here on Adapazan, one that Valentýn could give to his new wife, his new Duska, one who could fight against his heir and son, Rogdan. Perhaps, Bandar had been killed there by Rogdan as well. Most interesting, he thought. This was a sad commentary on the integrity of the barons and the Duskas.

Now he wondered about giving Zdenka the ceremony. As much as he wanted to, the caution about the age limits held him back. She was approaching twenty-one now. The risk to her life just wasn't worth it. After all, she was now an Archmage in her own right. He also resolved to keep this detail a secret for now. If it became widely known that anyone could become a Duska just by undergoing the Ceremony of Ascension, then the many barons would certainly begin an all-out creation of Duskas, hoping to gain advantage over their neighbors.

That night, Zoran had much to ponder. Zdenka lay next to him, sound asleep, cradled in his left arm. So much he had learned, so much he had done, but mostly it was her. "I love you," he whispered in her ear.

Just then, his inner senses began throbbing! His Circle began sending him data. Two were coming through his Circle right now in the middle of the night! No, they were coming just outside the tower — he'd just sensed their destination point. One was Kazimir and the other — the other's intention was to assassinate him or Zdenka! Zoran didn't hesitate. Using his Duska expanded senses, he imagined swirling them away, off into the Shadows, as Valentýn suggested that he could do. Zoran had the strangest perceptions sweeping over his mind, as though he could somehow "see" the two men in the black void of the Shadows. The others man's grip on Kazimir's hand loosened, and the man, arms and legs spread out, went spinning off — a three dimensional spin, until he totally disappeared. Kazimir, fighting madly, controlled his spin, reoriented himself, and disappeared in the distance. Zoran's senses returned to normal, but he certainly did not!

He wanted to get up and move, but he'd wake Zdenka. He forced his breathing back to normal and then worked to relax his fingers, then toes, then arms, then legs, and at last his whole body. As he finally calmed down, he drifted off into a peaceful sleep, as if this had been but a dream.

The next morning over breakfast, Lida made a strange comment. "Zoran, last night, I had the strangest feeling that the baron was after us here. Weird, I know. Obviously he wasn't."

Zoran decided to say something about it. "Yes, sis, he was trying to get here and do his dirty deeds, but I took care of him and his companion before they actually arrived here. Nothing to worry about." She gave him a strange look and then let it pass, for which he was grateful.

A thousand miles away and at midnight, Baron Kazimir finally appeared in his red Circle of Ascension located in the depths of Castle Dorumova. His clothes were shredded and his body covered in tiny scratches, as if thousands of razor sharp cat claws had attacked him. His long hair was disheveled, and he was frightened, more afraid than he had ever been in his entire life! He teleported directly to his room and grabbed his bottle of whiskey, ignoring his usual glass. He downed half the bottle before pausing, and then collapsed into his overstuffed easy chair.

"God! What happened to me?" he muttered, but no answer came, only the total silence of his room. Slowly, the alcohol kicked in and he relaxed and dozed.

Images of his ill-fated attack on Sholov Province swirled in his mind. There were the fire breathing dragons swooping down. He re-felt his efforts to reach his heir and son, Radek. Now he was holding the burned shell that moments ago had been in the vitality of his life. Now, he saw the shell of a son jumping to his death. A tear formed, but the man detected it not. The funeral of his wife appeared, along with his attempted assassination of Lida. Again, all magic failed and everything went black, as black as the void tonight had been. When the images returned, he saw himself unleashing his most powerful assault group that he had ever fielded, all charging toward the Brn Archmage tower. Dragons again appeared! Screaming, dying bodies flew everywhere before his eyes! Milos died, his Mages dropped like flies. A dagger headed his way as he stepped into the Shadows once more safe. The darkness gave way to this evening's attempt. His top assassin, at least the best one of those still alive, took his hand. Armed with all manner of poisons, he'd swore to secretly kill either Zoran or Zdenka or both. He would not fail. Into the Shadows the baron led him, but then as he zoomed in on the deserted street before the tower, someone else appeared in the Shadows!

Kazimir began sweating profusely. He strained to see who was there, but the figure remained but a shadow among the Shadows. No, it did something! This shadow had wrenched his assassin from him, sending the helpless man sailing off wildly in to the depths of the Shadows, lost forever. He, himself, was sent spinning after him. Only by his powerful will had he been able to regain control of his senses and mind and force them to do his bidding, returning to his Circle at last. He could not see the creatures which had attacked him there in the lost depths of the Shadows.

Baron Kazimir sat bold upright! The alcohol in his system seemed to evaporate in an instant! Someone was out to assassinate him! That had to be it. "Yes, yes, an assassin is lying out there in the Shadows waiting for me! That's what happened. Well, he took me by surprise this time, but I out maneuvered him all right! Damn. Who would want to assassinate me?"

As he sat there, his answer was a very long list. "Think old man! It has to be a Duska! No one else can go into the Shadows. It has to be a master of Shadow Walking. But who? Baron Milan? Baron Viktor?" He named some of his top enemies, but none of them felt right. This shadow person seemed small and relatively youthful; his fellow barons were much older. No, this assassin was dexterous, highly skilled. He ruled them out. "A Duke, perhaps?" He thought of the young sons of his enemies, seeing their youthful faces in his mind's eye. Somehow, he didn't think any one of them was bright enough to have done this incredible thing. At last, he finished off the rest of the bottle and fell into a deep sleep.

The next day, he made mental contact with Baron Bogdan Clav. He told him of his narrow escape. "Honestly, Bogdan, be wary. There really is an assassin hiding in the Shadows ready to assassinate us. No, I am not going mad. I tell you he's real!" He argued with his top ally for several minutes and finally broke off the contact. He contacted his other three allies, but met with similar disbelief. Kazimir gave up. "Sooner or later they will meet this secret assassin themselves. Then, they will come running back to old Kazimir for help!" He headed to his private bathroom. His body was covered in his own dried blood from the night before.

After a hearty breakfast, he sat down at his private desk and began to outline his strategic position. If Jiri was successful in the creation of another Circle, surely Baron Milan would give it to Duke Leo. He'd as said as much at the High Council meeting. Since his announced heir, Lida, had already married Duke Leo, as soon as the Circle was built and activated, Baron Milan would seek recognition of Leo as a new Baron. The High Council would accept it, as it had already done with Zoran. That eliminated all possibility of Lida inheriting his Circle and throne. No one can be a double baron or baroness. The High Council would not stand for that, no way. So in a few weeks, Lida would no longer be of any concern. Well, not unless she divorced Duke Leo. He quickly dismissed that thought. She was in love. She'd never do that, not just for a throne. The fool wasn't politically minded.

For the moment, Baron Zoran was untouchable. "Concentrate, old man. Zoran is not your most pressing issue here. I must be ready to appoint another heir at the fall High Council meeting! The real question is who?" He began thinking of his bastard sons, naturally. He knew that he had fathered two, but there could be more. He'd slept with at least a dozen women over the years. Of course, he would have to choose them carefully, first by age. He knew that they had to be between ten and twenty to undergo the Ceremony of Ascension. Now he had a plan. He called for his advisors and Security General. "I have a top secret, highly critical assignment for you," he began, outlining what he needed done.

At last the moon was full and Zoran saw some action once again. Unfortunately, it was anti-climactic. Zhou met with him; their new land was ideal, according to her. Already, they had begun constructing a permanent village. The remainder of the metal axes she accepted, telling him just how valuable they were proving to her men. Now their talks began on how best to communicate this offer of moving to a new land to all of the other tribes. While she could send out runners to many here in Zovou Province, the other large population of Yellers was totally isolated, way up in the northern Tratky Province. Additionally, there were small pockets of Yellers in many of the other eight provinces.

Zhou explained that, if she could somehow send a runner to the northern lands, those there would not believe the runner. They would insist on speaking directly with his matron, her. In matters of territory and village locations, the Yellers always depended solely on their tribe's matron, who they believed was the mother of their tribe.

Karel actually solved this problem. His idea was for him to teleport some of her runners to the northern province and then himself morph into his giant hawk form, circling above the runners. They would in turn search out and find a prominent village and tell them the news. When they then asked to speak to Zhou personally, the runners could signal Karel, who would then teleport Zhou to their location. Once the talks were done, he could teleport them all back to their new homeland. This she accepted. Zoran realized that she had little choice, since the survival of the tribes depended on their tribal mother. It was her responsibility.

Within a week, the Mages were busy with routine teleportation of the numerous villages of Zovou Province. Karel's plan was set in motion and a week later met with fruition. The first northern tribe accepted the offer. Emil and Renata began to transport them, aided occasionally by their parents. Thus, the Mages were kept busy during the rest of June and the summer as well. General Janos insisted that Zoran stay near the tower, because it was too risky for him to be traveling all over the provinces. Kazimir was certain to have spies among them and send out assassins. Reluctantly, he agreed and allowed his friends to do the teleports.

On the 22nd of June, he sensed another new Circle activating. He added this phenomenon to his list of unique attributes of an original Circle owner. He, Zdenka, and Lida, were the first to arrive at Duke Leo's Circle of Ascension and Castle Damek, named after the city in which it lay. Leo rushed to Lida and she, he. Lovers kissed long and passionately. At last, Milan broke them up and discussed the importance of the day. Zoran watched both Jiri and Anezka accept the praise heaped upon them and was proud of them as well.

Baron Milan stated formally, "At the fall High Council, Leo will become Baron Leo Matous, and Lida will become Baroness. I will have to announce a new heir, that will fall to your younger sister here, Katerina." The fifteen year old teen was very pleased indeed. She had now become a player and not a pawn. Zoran realized that this was precisely what she was thinking!

"A word, Zoran, before you go," Baron Milan requested, taking him aside. "My spies in Dorumova have relayed that Kazimir is now hunting down all of his bastard children. Expect that at the next High Council, Kazimir will announce a new heir, probably one of them. Until then, I suspect you will be safe." While Zoran wondered just how Uncle Milan had gotten spies into the castle, he didn't ask.

"Thanks, I guessed this might be the case."

"Another thing, Zoran. He might be losing his mind over this. We've heard that he has been going around telling his allies that there is now a Shadow Assassin hiding out there in the Shadows. He claims the assassin very nearly got him. We all know that there is no such thing as a Shadow Assassin. Perhaps his mind is indeed going. Please keep sharp; we don't want anything to happen to you."

Zoran smiled; of course he didn't, for that would upset his newfound political gains. "I remain on high alert, Baron." Since other barons began arriving to see the new light brown Circle, Zoran and Zdenka took their leave and returned home.

"Damn! Double damn! I am cursed!" screamed Baron Kazimir. His men had returned from their exhaustive search for his bastard children. They had found three who still lived. One girl was only ten and was of no use. Another was in his thirties and a sergeant in his army, too old. Another was a fifteen year old barmaid, like her mother; she, he dismissed at once. He had had far too much trouble with women to even consider the two girls. "Who is this sergeant?" he bellowed.

"He goes by Damek Kamil, his mother's last name. I've ordered him to report here at noon."

"Very well. Let me know as soon as he arrives. Dismissed." He sighed. "So it comes down to this, putting a bastard older son on the throne and arranging a marriage to a Duska so that he can be baron. Damn, damn, damn."

At noon, Damek was escorted into the Baron's private dining room. He was a veteran fighter, used to giving orders. However, he was now fearful; the Baron wanted to see him personally. Try as he might, he could not envision what he had done so wrong to have called attention to himself! The Baron's soldiers hated to be in the Baron's eye. So many had met ill fates. Hence, fear was his only emotion as he entered the room to face the wrath of his Baron.

He looks a lot like me, thought Kazimir, as he looked at his bastard son for the first time. "Welcome, welcome, Damek. Come and dine with me, your father. I know that I have not been much of a father to you before now."

Damek looked shocked. Indeed, his mind reeled. He called me his son! What is happening? Nervously, he shook the Baron's hand and took a seat. His stomach knotted, how can I possibly eat?

"I owe my career in your army to you, Baron," he finally figured out something to say.

"Yes, and you have certainly distinguished yourself," the Baron replied, although he had no idea if the lad had done anything at all. Until this moment, he'd been a figure on a paper, one of the endless number of soldiers in his army, nothing more. "Now it is time for your just reward, son."

He keeps calling me his son. Why? Reward? Now it comes. I am getting sacked or worse. I knew I should have deserted in Sholov with the other men.

"Son, I have a proposition for you. As you know, my heir and son, Radek, fell victim to the dragons. My daughters have abandoned me and married off-world, long gone from here. My youngest son defies me, having built a new Circle, hoping to take over half of Adapazan. Son, what would you say to becoming my heir? How would you like to become Baron Damek, eh? Like the sound of that?"

Damek's mouth dropped. He stared at the Baron, completely speechless. Kazimir knew well that he had just given the lad the shock of his life and was wise enough to allow him time to absorb the news. At long last, after swallowing three times, Damek squeaked, "Yes, fantastic! Unbelievable, sir! Wait, I am not a Duska, sir."

"Kill the sir. How about just dad? Okay?" While Damek found it nearly impossible to call him dad, he did his best to do so. "Now then, that is our only obstacle. However, it is not insurmountable. You are quite right — a Duska is required on the throne. So we simply marry you to a Duska woman. Then you can be the baron and she the baroness. Perfect, don't you think?"

Still rather stunned, he replied, "Well, yes." He then added, "Ba — dad. But who? How? Will she?"

"Son, you leave that to me. I have connections. I will try to find one that is not a pig," he chuckled. Damek grinned.

"That would be a good idea. I mean I don't want to sound ungrateful, but I doubt that I could bed a homely, ugly woman."

Kazimir roared, "Well said, son, well said. Me either. I will do my best for you. Yes, indeed, son, in a few years, it will be Baron Damek who runs this castle. Yes indeed. Now then, General Damek, I believe that you need to go and see the commissar for a new uniform."

"What?" he was once again shocked.

"Yes, you must be properly clothed. Then, go and see your mother. I wish that both of you will move into our castle here and stay with me."

"What?" Poor Damek was beyond words once more. At last, he nodded and as the baron waved him off, he left the room. As he walked the long halls to the exit, he began to dance a jig. "Me, the baron! Me, live here! Whahoo!"

"Well, that went well," Kazimir muttered to himself, once Damek left. Now came the delicate choice of bride. While Clav had two daughters, both were as ugly as he. No, he had to do better than that. Baron Carwyn Alun of the desert world of Anwyn was a possibility. However, what desert dweller would desire to move to this mountainous, snowy world? Baron Cheng Meerong of the swampy world of Jing might do, but they had yellow skins. No, the best possibility lay with Baron Eckhard Hadwig of the snowy planet Dietmar. Didn't he have three daughters? He couldn't remember well. His late wife, she would know. For an instant, Kazimir missed her presence. Then, he made mental contact with Eckhard.

An hour later, he reached an agreement with Baron Eckhard. His eldest daughter, Brunhilda, now twenty, would marry his son and become the baroness here, allowing Damek to become the baron. At last, Kazimir relaxed. The problem was nearly solved and would be at the next High Council meeting on the 1st of September. Besides, the Castle would no longer be quite so empty.

He resolved to see, no insist, that Damek and Brunhilda marry soon and move into Castle Dorumova. That way, nothing would be left to chance. After all, once their marriage was announced, his enemies may well try to assassinate Brunhilda, leaving him again without a viable heir. Married soon, well, they could still come after her, but here at the Castle under his protections, they would likely be safer from assassins than anywhere else.

That this Shadow Assassin still lurked out there in the Shadows waiting for him also bothered him. The worst case scenario would be for him to be slain without an heir! Then it would be totally up to the High Council to pick his successor. That he could not and would not ever allow! That had happened twice in history, and each time caused a major shift in the power balance among the barons.

Chapter 25 A Long Summer

Zoran missed having his sister around. He missed the excitement of life. Yes, he was bored. Constant vigilance, everyone kept insisting. His Mage friends were daily off teleporting the next group of Yellers to their new island. Zdenka was hard at work with her students. General Janos continued to get new recruits and held daily training exercises. The many work crews with their engineers were constantly working and laying stone. Aldrick was busy mining for gems. Mayor Oldrich was very busy managing Brn's affairs. Not only did the improvement and expansion of their few roads require his time, but the city itself was growing twice as fast as last year. Zoran was reduced to casting a few Force Wall spells, laying them in place and then casting Make Permanent spells on them.

Early July, he received news from Baron Viktor that Baron Kazimir was going to name his thirty year old bastard son his heir and that Baron Hadwig's eldest daughter, Brunhilda was betrothed to him. They were to be married immediately after the High Council fall session recognized Kazimir's new heir. Baron Viktor said that this information was reliable and had come from one of his spies in Hadwig's court. Also, he relayed news that Baron Hadwig now believed that Kazimir had become slightly mad, if delusional. Word was that his allies no longer trusted the Baron. Zoran found this slightly encouraging. No one knew anything about this new heir who went by the name of Damek Kamil. Zoran had never heard of him either.

Finally, the ten warlords began contacting Zoran about trading arrangements. Via a Message spell from their Mage, a warlord sent him word that a trade meeting was desired. Accompanied by General Janos, Emil, Renata, and a few Security men, Zoran began visiting the warlord fortresses, conducting business meetings. Warlord Eduard of Kin Province was the first to request such a meeting. His fortress was bleak and sparsely populated. He explained that most of his men were out manning the huge border with Vraz Province, where Baron Kazimir still fielded a sizeable garrison army on his border with Kin. Not surprisingly, Eduard wanted swords, armor, and then grain, in that order.

"I've put together one thousand drun of gold," he stated. [A drun is roughly 1/16th of a pound.] "We have about five thousand drun-worth of gems. The wagon is loaded and ready for shipment, but the roads to Brn are still not finished nor is it safe to transport such a sum. I do not trust other warlords; besides there are bandits who would stop at nothing to acquire this wagon. What are you going to do about it? When will we get our weapons, armor, and grain?" he asked belligerently.

"I assume that you trust me," Zoran answered a bit testily. He nodded. "I can take your wagon back with me, guaranteeing its safe delivery to Brn. I will then contact the other planets and put together your order."

General Janos broke in, "Baron, you ought to ask what grade of weapons he wishes and the quality of his armor." Zoran grinned and nodded to his General.

"Right, you heard him. I admit that I have much to learn," Zoran replied. Warlord Eduard snickered. He liked this youth, who was not afraid to admit that he didn't know everything.

"Military grade. None of those fancy Duska blades. We have to defend our borders and that means arming everyone I can find. Same with armor. Chain mail tops, forget full body chain mail. That's way too expensive. We'll take ring mail if chain turns out to be too costly or will take too long to make. We need it as soon as possible here. No telling when the Baron will strike. It is summertime and that is when he traditionally attempts to take over another province."

"Okay. Thanks. Eduard, after the devastation my dragon friends cost him last year in Sholov, I don't think that he will be attacking you this summer. I strongly believe that we have yet a little time to prepare," Zoran tried to encourage the warlord. It did appease Eduard, who actually was looking for just such a confirmation of his own take on the situation.

Since the wagon weighed only a few hundred pounds, Zoran was able to Shadow Walk it and his companions back to Brn. He counted out the funds and had Aldrick verify the value of the gems before he began negotiations. As he got ready to actually make the attempt at trade, Zoran suddenly recognized that he had no notion at all of how to proceed! Here was a complete arena in which he knew absolutely nothing! It shocked him.

Uncle Milan, help! Business, this time. Duh, I have just gotten my first request for supplies from Warlord Eduard. Naturally, he wants weapons, armor, and grains. How the heck do I proceed? Who do I contact? Honestly, Uncle, I don't know what I am doing with business affairs!

Baron Milan roared with laughter. With his Duska given telepathy, Zoran could sense his mirth and he flushed. *Relax, Zoran. I've already worked this out. My younger daughter, Dusana, is seventeen now. She has an incredible knack for business dealings. She is betrothed to Baron Tom Witherspoon's son, John, also seventeen and heir to his throne. I've discussed this at length with Tom. We both feel that it is high time that these two get their feet wet with real world dealings. Terra is an agrarian planet, awash in trading throughout the Federation. Hence, it is vital for his son to become an astute businessman. That my Dusana is following in Tom's footsteps has endeared her with Tom. If this is acceptable to you, we will send both of them to stay with you for a year or two to help you get things going there and train someone in how to conduct proper business affairs.*

Uncle, I don't know how to properly thank you. Say, yes I do know. How would you like an ancient magical bastard sword? It belonged to the original founder of Adapazan, Baron Valentýn Vladislov, first Baron of Adapazan. We found a stash of his things.

Incredible, Zoran! Yes, that would be a treasure of treasures! Thank you nephew! Okay, I will tell Dusana and John to make plans to come to Brn. Shall we say in two days' time?

Perfect, just perfect. Oh, please tell them to expect rather crude living arrangements here. We've only got an Archmage tower for accommodations.

I know, nephew, I know. Okay. I'll get on it. Expect their arrival on Wednesday. Thanks again for the incredible gift!

Zoran set to work clearing out another storeroom, next to the room shared by the sisters from Asami. He'd forgotten to ask his Uncle if he should keep the two in separate rooms. He knew how he would have loved to sleep with Zdenka and decided to allow the young couple to make this decision for themselves. If need be, he could put one of them in a smaller room on the fourth floor.

At lunch, he told everyone about their new guests. Zdenka immediately insisted that the two unmarried teens have separate rooms! The sisters volunteered to move to the fifth floor into the room next to Zdenka and Zoran. His crimson face told all that his gaffe was a big one, and he quietly said nothing but thanked the two grinning teens.

With gusto, he prepared the vacant room for the teens and helped them move their few belongings into their new room. A bit later, he'd finished making up the beds, over the protests of Zuzanna, who continually insisted that he was doing her job. "Next, you will be emptying the chamber pots for me," she teased him.

"Oh, do they need emptying?" he teased her back. She threw a pillow at him and laughed.

Five minutes later, it was back to utter boredom for Zoran. However, he then had an idea. Little did he know how pivotal this idea would become to him. He contacted Rayna and Lida. *Say, do you know who Kazimir may have fathered children with, besides mom? I know that he has found one of them and is making this Damek Kamil his heir. We ought to find any other of our half brothers and sisters and get them on our side.*

Super, little brother, Lida replied. The two volunteered to find out. Just how they could escaped him, especially when they reported back with the information in less than two hours! There were two other half-sisters out there. One was called Zuza Vavrin, age ten, who lived with her barmaid mother, Hana, in Chynava, Dorum Province, outside the city of Dorum. The other was fifteen year old girl called Kamila Lota, who lived with her mother, Eva, who was a cook at an inn in Toky, a village not too far from Dorum.

An hour later, highly enthused, Zoran, against all of the protests of General Janos, teleported to the inn in Chynava. Karel, Jarka, Bernard, and Emil came with him, though they had cast Invisibility on themselves and promised to be on the qui vive and remain in the background. The inn was a rundown, seedy one, just right for Kazimir to visit clandestinely of a night. He walked up to the barkeeper. "I'm looking for Hana Vavrin. May I have a word with her?"

"Cost 'u a pint," the burly man replied. Zoran tossed him a coin and he slid a filthy mug of ale over to him. "Hey, Hana, another one to see you." Zoran moved to a back corner table, where he could not easily be overheard.

A thirty year old, pretty blonde haired barmaid, dressed in a provocative but colorful dress, covered with dozens of make-shift patches, walked over to him. She sat down opposite him, sizing him up. Where to begin went through Zoran's mind. "Well stranger, I be Hana."

He noticed that the barkeeper kept a sharp eye on him, as did two other hooded men drinking at another table. "Hana, I want to talk with you about your future. This is extremely important. It's about your daughter and you. Please, is there somewhere that we can go and have a private talk? It is vital that we speak honestly."

"I take men to my room. Give the barkeep a gold and follow me," she replied. Something about this young man pricked her interest. He didn't look like the ordinary kind looking for a quick lay. Zoran tossed a gold coin to the barkeeper, who grinned, bit it, and deposited the coin in his cash box. Quickly, Zoran followed her up the back stairs. He sensed his other Invisible men following him. To hide the noise of their footsteps, Zoran made as much stomping noise as he dared.

She opened a door and beckoned him follow her inside. Such squalid conditions Zoran had never seen before. A young girl wearing mostly rags sat in one corner playing with a filthy doll someone had obviously discarded. He was surprised to see a small boy about her age playing with two broken toy soldiers in another corner beside a dirty bed. The girl, seeing Zoran, immediately got up to leave, tugging on her brother's arm. Evidently, Hana often brought men up here, and the children were trained to quietly leave, Zoran guessed. "Please, allow them to stay. This concerns them as well."

"Well, just who are you and what do you want? Only last week some of the Baron's men came by here. At least they gave me a gold," she stated flatly.

"First, is this Zuza?"

"Yes, she is Zuza and he is Jan. Why?"

"Hi Zuza. Is she the daughter of Baron Kazimir?"

"Why? That's what his men wanted to know. Give me a gold and I'll tell you."

Zoran gave her ten gold coins. That got her undivided attention, as he suspected it would. "I am Baron Archmage Zoran Vladislov, the Kazimir's youngest son. I have a new Circle of Ascension and am representing the Free People of Adapazan. Zuza is my sister, well half-sister. I want to give her the rights to her birthright as the daughter of a baron. I want to help her to become a Duska and to learn as much magic as she can learn. Will you consider moving immediately to my place in Brn Province, where she will be safe and can learn all that she can from my wife, Archmage Zdenka? I will do right by you, Hana. I will see that you are well taken care of. As the mother of a Duska, you should not be living in such a hovel. You should be honored and revered as the mother of a Duska!"

Hana's eyes opened wider and wider. Her face flushed and began fanning her face with her hands. Then, she fainted. "Mommy! Mommy, what's wrong? What did you do to her?" Zuza cried, running over to her mother. Jan did too.

"She's okay; she just fainted. Here, she is coming around, Zuza. The news was a bit of a surprise," Zoran explained. He helped her sit up as her eyes opened.

"Mommy, are you all right?" a worried Zuza exclaimed.

"Yes, yes, dears," she said very softly.

"Mommy, I want to learn magic! Can I? Mommy, please, can I learn magic?" Zuza begged.

"Me too, mommy. I want to learn magic too," Jan added, tugging at her arm.

"Are you playing a nasty game with me?" Hana finally collected her wits. Such an offer just could not be real.

"Allow my companions to enter, and they can vouch for me." She nodded, half expecting to see a bunch of the Baron's soldiers coming to arrest her, though for what, she did not know.

She saw no one entering the room and began to think this was some kind of joke being played on her. One by one, the Invisibility spells were canceled, and she saw Karel, Jarka, Bernard, and Emil standing just inside the door, making the room rather crowded around the door. "Allow me to introduce my dear friends. This is

Archmage Karel, Mage Jarka, Mage Bernard, and Archmage Emil. Now do you believe me?"

Seeing such powerful men and women standing there finally convinced Hana that this was not a joke. "Are you really against Baron Kazimir?" she asked.

"Absolutely," replied Jarka. "I've killed several of his assassins and some of his Mages. You will be safe at our tower in Brn."

"Okay, I will trust you to be who you say, but you must take Jan too."

"Of course, I wouldn't dream of leaving him behind," Zoran replied honestly.

"And train him in magic too," she added.

"Not everyone can learn magic; however, we will do our best with Jan. I cannot guarantee that he will be able to learn magic. With Zuza, once she becomes a Duska, there is no doubt that she can learn magic," Zoran tried to soften what must be a blow to Hana and Jan. After all, only one in ten had any ability to learn magic.

She hesitated a moment, as if resolving something in her mind. "Okay. I can accept that for now. Do you mean for us to leave now? This very minute?"

"Yes, with Kazimir's men around, it really isn't safe for Zuza here. I don't want anything bad to happen to my little sister," Zoran replied.

"What about the barkeeper?"

"Forget him. Pack your things and let's get you safe in Brn," Zoran replied.

It took all of two minutes for them to pack. She had stowed away twenty coppers and had only one other dress. The children had even less. Holding hands, the group teleported to the main street of Brn, just before the Tower. As they arrived, Aldrick and Sofie were flying around the tower, on their way back from feeding.

"Mommy, look! Dragons! Real dragons!" exclaimed Jan and Zuza nearly in unison.

"Then it is true — all the rumors that we've heard about dragons coming to Adapazan and burning up the Baron's army in Sholov are true," Hana said wildly excited with the sight of the two dragons.

"Yes, they are my friends. Emil here is their son."

"You are a *real* dragon?" exclaimed Jan, completely in awe of Emil.

"Yes, want to see?" he said, unable to resist the boy's enthusiasm. He changed into his true form and took flight around the Tower before landing in the street and changing back into his human Emil form once more.

Hana then said what she had been holding back. "Jan is Zuza's twin brother. I never told anyone, not even the Baron's men when they came around last week. I knew that the Baron would take him away from me if he knew about Jan. Please, you must do the same for Jan, please. He is your half-brother."

"Incredible! Put her there, Jan," Zoran offered the lad his hand. The boy took it and they shook. "Absolutely. Both will be allowed to become Duskas and learn all the magic that they can."

"Well, they don't know how to read or write. I don't either," Hana admitted.

"Not a problem. We will have to teach them to read and write first thing," Zoran replied.

"Mommy, when I can read, I will read all the books to you," Zuza promised. Hana smiled.

"Come on; let's go inside and meet my wife, Archmage Zdenka. She's our magic teacher here. This is her tower," Zoran suggested.

Awe. That is the best way to describe the three's tour of the Archmage Tower and the new construction site. Zdenka, of course, tested the two children and found that they were suitable for her training. Out of curiosity, she also tested Hana.

Hana hesitated, and then sighed. "Well, my first impulse is to grab the gold; my children are desperate, but he's bleeding to death. I have to set a good example, so I will see if I can help him and then ask him for some of the gold for my children." Zdenka suspected this might be her answer and smiled.

"Okay, Hana. How about you? Have you ever thought about seeing if you can learn magic?"

Hana was startled. "No. I mean I have always had to work constantly to stay alive. Then, with the twins, it became even more difficult to manage. Do you really think it is possible?"

Zdenka replied. "First things first. We get you three some descent clothes. Then, I am going to twin you three up with two teenagers who are also learning how to read and write. They can help you get started."

"But we have no money for clothes," Hana objected.

"Don't worry. Zoran will be helping to look after his little brother and sister. We could use some additional hands with maid and serving duty around the tower. What say I put you to work part of the time, when you are not studying. That way, you can help out too." Hana agreed eagerly. Hence, Zdenka sent the three off with Jarka to find the seamstress. Her orders: get them each three new outfits and pitch these old ones! She gave Zoran the task of finding lodgings for the new guests.

Since he also planned to see if the other sister and mother would move here, he set to work on the fifth floor. He consolidated the "observation of the sky" room with several others, making two smaller rooms available for the new families. "I am rapidly running out of quarters here," he jested.

After the new arrivals had gone shopping and had a bath, Zoran showed them their new room. Hana had never had such luxury, and Jan and Zuza were very happy with this fine new bedroom. At last, Zdenka took them to the first floor study area and introduce them to Chika and Akira, who took charge of them, eager to help others, who like themselves, did not know how to read and write. Of course they now could do both somewhat.

The next day, Zoran repeated the process, this time heading into Toky to look for the fifteen year old girl called Kamila Lota and her mother, Eva. He found them both working at an inn. Eva, wiped her hands on her apron, and offered him a cup of tea there in the kitchen. She was around thirty-five, but still had an attractive air about her. In her youth, she must have been a rose in this village. Kamila, tall and thin, was working as a waitress, serving tables.

"Well, you are the second person in the last week to come here asking about Kamila. I thought I said everything the last time they were here," Eva began, rather annoyed at having to stop her cooking. Kamila, with her long brown hair, sat beside her mother, curious about this tall man and why he wanted to speak to them.

Zoran introduced himself and gave an almost identical speech as he had to Hana yesterday. "So Kamila is my sister and I want only the very best for her."

"Well, it's about time that someone recognizes her for her worth! Honestly, I was totally aghast at the Baron's conduct. Do you realize that until last week he didn't even acknowledge her existence? Lord knows that I've tried. Sent him letters at least twice a year about her. Nothing until last week. Then, nothing even came of that." She rattled on and asked pertinent questions about how she and her daughter would be accommodated, how well she would be treated, and so on. He did his best to satisfy Eva's curiosity.

At last, Eva agreed, but they would need time to pack their few things and arrange for another cook to come finish up the stew for the evening crowd. Around noon, Zoran was finally able to teleport the two, along with his friends, back to Brn. Zoran found that Eva and Kamila were slightly better off than the Vavrin's, at least their clothes were acceptable. As a cook, she'd earned just enough to keep them alive, not much more, though. However, Eva proved to be an excellent cook; their cook at the Tower greatly appreciated her help in the kitchen. The number of mouths to feed continued to grow.

Both Eva and Kamila joined the others on the first floor, since they needed to learn to read and write as well. That night, Zoran contacted Priestess Anezka once more. Via telepathy, he sent, *Got three more for you to give the Ceremony of Ascension to, my half-brother and two half-sisters!*

On Friday, Priestess Anezka performed all three ceremonies, which activated their special gland. Now they had their birthright, true Duskas. Lengthy education would now commence in earnest. Zoran took a sense of pride in what he had done. True, the two twins were a little young for the Ceremony of Ascension, but times dictated the need.

On Wednesday, Duke John Witherspoon and Dusana Matous arrived. He was a tall, thin lad, but quite handsome. Dusana looked much like her mother, with curly brown hair and charming eyes. While their dress was more suitable for a court than an Archmage tower, they merrily began to make friends and did not seem troubled by their relatively Spartan accommodations. Their first request was to meet and see the dragons. Next, they wanted a complete tour of the new construction site.

After lunch, both began to tackle his trading situation, outlining what planet offered the best deals on what commodity. Zoran took copious notes. All this was totally new to him. By Friday, they had worked out the best trade on such short notice. The following week, they began accompanying Zoran, as one by one, the other warlords began requesting that he come and setup their trading arrangements. Their work occupied them for all of July and into August.

During this time, Dusana and Chika became friends, and Dusana discovered that Chika was a whizz at math and a keen observer of the value of things. Thus one afternoon, Dusana approached Zoran, "You know that you need a shrewd business person here don't you?" He nodded. "Well, unless you have other plans, I have the perfect candidate for you, Chika. She is a natural at it. True, she has tons to learn and all her magic training ahead of her, but seriously, Zoran, you ought to allow her to be your business advisor." He agreed and Chika was very pleased with this. From that day on, Dusana and Duke John took her under their wing, teaching her all that they knew about business dealings and trades. In the middle of August, the two finally departed, having handled all ten warlord trades. They had Shadow Walked the goods and funds between worlds, with Chika accompanying them. No one would allow

Zoran to do it — far too dangerous for him, what with all the assassins gunning for him.

By the time that Chika finished her magic training, reaching Mage level at twenty-two years old, she was the best business trader in the Federation of Planets. No one struck a better bargain than she. Always, she knew just when and how hard to press another. Zoran suspected it came from her Duska senses.

Also, in late July, Lida and Rayna both came for a short visit. They wanted to meet their younger brother and two sisters. After they had returned to their planets, both women sent their siblings an extensive wardrobe of court dresses and suits. Zuza, Jan, and Kamila were incredible pleased with this, naturally.

Additionally, Jan wanted to learn to fight as any young boy his age did. Hence, an hour each day was devoted to learning to handle a sword. General Janos was given the charge of training Jan. Additionally, Zoran insisted that Chika, Akira, Zuza, and Kamila also learn to defend themselves from attackers. Assassinations were common place and he wanted to give them the best chance of survival. He owed it to them, even if Kazimir did not.

Finally, late one night in the middle of July, Zoran was awakened by his inner senses. His Circle notified him that someone was attempting to Shadow Walk, arriving outside the Tower. Again, he found himself automatically in the Shadows observing who was coming. No mistake, Baron Kazimir himself was probing his defenses! However, the Baron was being cautious. The instant that he detected Zoran's presence, he fled, returning to his Circle in Castle Dorumova. Unknown to Zoran, Kazimir was now more than ever convinced that there was some Shadow Assassin lying in wait in the Shadows looking for him!

Chapter 26 Fall High Council

As the 1st of September drew close, Zoran and friends began their preparations to journey to Terra, an agrarian world, home of Baron Tom Witherspoon and Baroness Abigail, close allies of Zoran. This time, the chances of assassination were drastically lessened. Once more, the men would need their finest suits, while the ladies, their finest ball gowns and highest heels. As before, Karel would act as his advisor, with Bernard and Jarka behind him. General Janos decided that he ought to remain and safeguard the construction and Tower. Instead, Emil and Renata went in his place as their security personnel.

Zdenka and Jarka were wiser this time. Knowing that they would need to be wearing the most fashionable very high heels, they began practicing walking in them the week before, taking tips from Chika and Akira, who had to wear them so that they could walk. Their ankles and calves still would not allow their feet to rest flat on the floor, but they could walk effectively now in their heels. By now, the teens were very adept in their heels and gave Zdenka and Jarka some excellent tips. Both women vowed to look as graceful and elegant as the other baronesses and women at the council.

At last, the evening before the meeting and with bags packed and shrunk, Zoran Shadow Walked his group to Terra. Specifically, he zoomed in on their egg shaped continent. Although barely dusk there, as the land grew closer to them, neatly tilled fields dotted the horizon. Soon the capital city of Heddingham dwarfed their view, eight perfectly straight roads ran out of the city — a perfect compass rose. The city was huge by Adapazan standards, at least three times the size of Dorum. Located in the very center where the eight roads met lay Waterton Palace, the home of Baron Tom Witherspoon.

The sprawling castle complex, built from brown stone, occupied several acres, including a grass pasture land for their many horses. Zoran estimated the enclosed space behind the outer walls, complete with parapets, to be ten times the size of his new fortifications. Impressive. The eight roads arrived at eight double barbicans, heavily guarded entrances to the grounds. Instead of one castle inside the walls, Tom had three very large ones, connected with each other by second and third story stone bridges, the lower ones some fifteen feet above the ground below them. An enormous stone platform with miniature parapets lining three outer sides was their landing location. Great entrance gates allowed access into the center of the three castles. Here Zoran finally ended his Shadow Walk, landing the seven gracefully upon the stone.

Baron Tom, aware of Zoran's arrival, was there at the great gates to greet him. Baroness Abigail, Duke John, with Dusana Matous holding his arm, waved as the seven landed. "Welcome to Terra at long last, Baron Archmage Zoran, Baroness Archmage Zdenka, Archmage Karel, Mage Jarka, Mage Bernard, Archmage Emil, and Archmage Renata," Baron Tom called out formally.

As each took turns shaking hands, Zdenka and Jarka couldn't help notice the dresses worn by the Baroness Abigail and Dusana. Abigail's bright yellow dress, with many colored flowers, flared out at least eight feet in front of her body. Giant hoops draped the yards of material into a perfect shape. In stark contrast, their waists seemed impossibly tiny; their bosoms, large. Baroness Abigail had her hair up in what could only be described as a bee hive, complete with many embedded flowers. Dusana wore hers curly and long, though it was fluffed out, making her head seem much larger, proportionally.

In contrast, the dresses of Zdenka and Jarka, wearing the fashions of the spring council meeting, only flared out some five feet. "Oh, dears, you must try the newest fashions! Don't we look fabulous?" the Baroness chatted with Zdenka and Jarka. "These ball gowns are now the latest fashion, though I admit these corsets are terribly tight. Doesn't Dusana here cut a magnificent figure in her pink satin gown?" The young woman broke into a broad smile.

"They are a bit much to handle, but Duke John cannot seem to let go of me," Dusana whispered coyly to Zdenka and Jarka. "Oh you two simply must get one of these new gowns with all of the accessories for the big dance tomorrow night!"

"Oh indeed you must! Dusana and I have picked out dresses for each of you, my small gift to welcome you to Terra, Zdenka and Jarka. You don't mind if we don't address each so formally, do you? Just call me Abigail. Now then, Dusana picked out the colors. She got them to match your sky blue one, Zdenka. Yours is cherry red, Jarka. I do hope that you like them, though it takes two of us to get into them, and it takes ever so long to get dressed. But you will see. After you get settled in, we'll come by. I'm terribly sorry that we did not know that you were coming, Renata. We'll get you a dress tomorrow, if that is acceptable to you." Abigail chatted on and on.

Renata, unused to such formal court dialog, interrupted the Baroness. "Excuse me, Abigail, but I am happy with my dress. Thank you for the kind offer. A dragon is far more interested in that lovely green emerald on your neck. It is absolutely beautiful!"

"Oh, why thank you, Renata. Yes, it is quite large. Tom got it for me on our twentieth wedding anniversary. You know, Tom now has twenty golden dragons flying about Terra, protecting us from attacks. I am so glad that your kind is so willing to help us."

Renata grinned, "Oh we do almost anything for gems such as yours. I'm sure that the dragons will be very happy here if there are more such gems to be found. Say, I wonder, do you have a gem store in this city where I could exchange my smaller gems for treasures such as yours?" she asked, her gem lust exceeding her court knowledge.

"Well, I'm sure that we do, Renata. Say, I will ask Tom about it and let you know tonight when I come by for the ladies. If so, why, I will personally see that you can get to that store. Oh, I see the men are waiting on us. Shall we show you all to your rooms?"

While the ladies were chatting, Tom took Zoran and Karel aside. "Say, Barons Milan, Viktor, Aldo, and Etienne want a word with you two before the morning's meeting. Since my wife wants to abscond with your women after we get you settled in, what say that we all get together? We can relay the news and have a sample of our excellent ales. Here on Terra, we make some of the finest stouts and dark ales in the Federation, though others may dispute it." Zoran agreed and they waited on the ladies.

As the men escorted the women inside, Zdenka noted that both Dusana and Abigail walked even slower than she and Jarka. Why, she didn't know. That thought left her as she began taking in the marvels of this splendid castle. The walls of the halls were covered in elegant, historical tapestries, each one telling a story in the long history of Terra. Magical lighting illuminated these works of art. Zdenka and Jarka had never seen anything like this before.

Bernard and Karel were more fascinated by the standing suits of plate armor, artistically arranged at various nooks along their passage. "This is the housing castle. Next door is the meeting castle, where spacious rooms hold our meetings and where we will be dining. Oh, yes, the giant ballroom is in that one as well, Baron Tom pointed out as they slowly walked down the halls, the clicks of the women's heels on the stone floor providing the only other sounds.

They had a suite of rooms, all quite large. Indeed, everything about Tom's castle was large. He explained that Waterton Castle had been designed around holding High Council meetings. Thus, no expense had been spared in its construction. Their suite consisted of a huge living room, two baths, and five bedrooms, far more than they needed. Zoran noted that it was luxury all the way. Everything about Waterton Castle spoke of extravagance. Evidently, Terra was a wealthy planet indeed. Chika later explained to Zoran that Terra and Cosma, the agrarian planets, provided much of the various grains that the other planets needed for survival. Over the centuries, they had become rather wealthy indeed.

A half hour later, Abigail and Dusana, arm in arm, returned to their suite to pick up Zdenka and Jarka. Abigail whispered to Renata, "It's all arranged. Tomorrow evening, Tom will arrange a special gemstone showing solely for you and Emil at the finest gem stone store in Heddingham!" This greatly pleased Renata, who took Emil aside and told him of her arrangement. He was likewise very eager to go.

"Zoran, Renata and I need to make a quick trip back to the Tower. We'll be back in about a half hour." The glow in their eyes told all. Only the thought of fine gems produced that glow, that and of course powerful magic. Both left the room after the ladies left.

"If you will take my arm, please," Abigail asked Zdenka. "The only problem with these new dresses and heels is that we always needing a balancing arm. Honestly, I have to admit that Dusana and I are having a challenging time with these outfits. Still, the effect upon our men is more than worth it." Jarka took Dusana's arm and the pairs slowly walked down the long hall.

A bit later, Tom came for the men. Zoran, Karel, and Bernard followed him to a side meeting room, where overstuffed chairs, small work tables, and a huge bar occupied the elegant space. Plush rugs covered most of the floor. The other barons were already here, sipping a dark stout, some smoking their pipes.

"Ah, Zoran, well met once again," Baron Viktor said, as they entered. "Come, try this dark ale. Superb. We have much to discuss."

Zoran's comment spoke volumes, after taking a sip of the ale. "Incredible! Best ale that I have ever tasted! I think I need to make a trade with you, Tom!" The men laughed; Bernard was in heaven, trying each of the ten different types of stouts and ales. Karel gave him a glare stare and contented himself to a mug of the ale that

Zoran had. He needed to keep his wits about him.

"Okay, to business," Milan finally said, putting the pleasantries aside. "We've gotten the preliminary schedule for the meeting. It is a bit strange. Baron Kazimir is holding an official wedding just before the opening statement of Tom's. Apparently, he's found a wife for his bastard son, Damek Kamil. Baron's Eckhard's eldest daughter, Brunhilda, will be marrying him. Why? Well, Kazimir is going to nullify his heir, Lida, just after the presentation and acceptance of Duke Leo as the newest baron. We expect that he will announce that Damek will be his heir. Of course, we will launch a formal protest, in that Damek is not Duska, but we all know that is just a formality. As long as Brunhilda is his baroness, she will be in charge of his Circle."

Viktor added, "Zoran, it has happened three times in the past — a baron who is not a Duska, that is. Usually, it is the baroness who is not. Yet, in this case, it is going to be very strange indeed."

"Why so?"

"Well what do you know of this Damek?" Etienne spoke up.

"Not much at all," Zoran replied.

"No one does. That's the point. Our spies tell us that he was a mere sergeant in the Baron's army — just a mere platoon leader, now become a baron," Milan continued. "As far as we know, he knows virtually nothing about being a baron, his duties, his responsibilities, or even magic!"

"The man is way out of his league, way out of the waters!" Etienne broke in.

"About the stupidest idea I've ever heard of," put in Viktor.

"Doomed to fail utterly," Aldo added. "I don't see how he can possibly measure up to the task of being a baron. Lord knows how much you didn't know and you were a Duska and an Archmage when you became a baron. No offense intended son."

Zoran grinned, "None taken, Aldo. "I am the first to admit how little I know about many things. I cannot thank you enough for the use of Duke John and Dusana. They have been utterly invaluable!"

Milan resumed control, "Hence, it is our guess that two things will occur. First, Brunhilda will likely take control of most things. Second, we suspect that Kazimir's allies will be sending a large amount of, shall we say, advisors to Dorum. He will need Mages as well as business and financial advisors."

Baron Viktor concluded, "And this will make Baron Damek a mere puppet of our enemies."

"Which means, Zoran, that it will really be Baron Eckhard who is running Castle Dorumova," Milan finished.

Karel looked at Zoran and then spoke up, "Is that good or bad?" He kept Zoran from having to ask this embarrassing question.

"Depends," Milan answered. "Bogdan is a brute, similar to Kazimir. Eckhard is sly, cunning, devious, and underhanded. He's probably the most powerful of our enemies, save perhaps Cheng. We've feared that Bogdan would simply bring in his army and try to smash his way to Brn by brute force. Eckhard is far more treacherous and devious."

"A snake in the grass," Etienne broke in, cursing the man.

Just then, the door opened and two couples entered, ending their meeting.

"Ah there you are little brother. I see the barons are keeping you hostage," Lida said coyly as she and Leo entered, followed by Rayna and Stefan. Zoran noted that she too wore this latest fashion ball gown that billowed out some eight feet in front of her body. She held tightly onto Leo's arm. Her dress was a gorgeous blue, while Rayna's similar dress was emerald green; both were satin. His sisters looked very elegant indeed. Zoran rushed over and gave them both a long hug.

He then formally shook Leo's hand, "Congratulations, Baron Leo, Baroness Lida!"

Duke Leo was very pleased that Zoran acknowledged his new position, though it would not be formally recognized until the morning's High Council session. "Thanks. I have the prettiest baroness in the Federation," he replied, squeezing Lida's hand.

"Oh just you wait. I'll have the prettiest baroness in just a few more months," Duke Stefan protested. Rayna grinned. Soon the five were chatting, catching up on the news.

When Zoran got the opportunity, he whispered to Leo, "We need to have a very private talk about you and your Circle." They agreed to find a time when they could sneak away from the others.

When the men finally returned to their suite, they found the dragons had returned as well as the ladies. Their bedroom was now filled with their new dresses and undergarments. "You have to wear all of this?" exclaimed Zoran in surprise, as he and Zdenka went into their room for the night.

"Somehow they all go together to make their newest look, but I sure don't know how! Honestly," her mellow alto voice which always enamored him continued, "I am dreading that corset thing and those heels, Zoran! Just look at how tall their heels are. Abigail said that the sides of the boots really, they are hardly shoes, are steel re-enforced so that we cannot twist our ankles. Zoran, I'm going to need your arm constantly, if you want me to wear that outfit."

"You don't have to, love, not if you don't want to," he said, "I love you just like you are."

"Yes, I know, but baronesses must uphold the highest fashions. Everyone else looks up to us. At least that is what the other baronesses are saying. I don't know if that's true, but even Lida and Rayna are wearing these new outfits. I will look out of place if I don't and I don't want to embarrass you."

"Honey, you can't possibly embarrass me. Even when our castle is finished, it is going to be utterly plain compared to those that we have seen."

"True, still, I will give it a try, only promise me that you will always hold on to me."

"Of course, love."

"Say, Abigail has lined up special events just for us and Leo and Lida to attend all week long. Of course, there is the formal opening night ball tomorrow night. Then, we go to a play, then we go to the music concert, then there is a night of ballet, then there is the choral night, and finally the closing ball. She's got all of our evenings all lined up. I'm excited about the balls and the ballet. How about you?"

"Dances, you bet. I love nothing more than to dance the night away with you, my dearest. The ballet we saw last time was intriguing. I wonder how they can walk around on the tips of their toes like that. Pretty amazing, don't you think?"

"I'll show you what is amazing!" She pulled him into their overly large bed.

At seven the next morning, Abigail and Dusana, along with two personal assistants arrived to help get Zdenka and Jarka into their new outfits. Meanwhile, Zoran and the others donned their fancy suits with twin tails. Looking as formal as possible, Zoran liked his image in the mirror. Now they had to wait on the ladies. Breakfast was at nine and the wedding was at nine forty-five, minutes before the opening ceremony hosted by Baron Tom. Zoran wanted to see the wedding; he had a vested interest in observing the new couple.

It was almost nine before the ladies appeared from their room. Zdenka, holding onto Abigail, moved slowly into the room and took Zoran's arm. She looked incredibly gorgeous. The sky blue satin dress, though enormous, was an eye catcher. Her waist looked so tiny, he thought. "I can barely walk! This corset is so tight I can hardly breathe! What these women do for fashion! Don't let go of me, please!" she whispered to him. Jarka, dressed in her cherry red matching satin dress, took hold of Bernard's arm. Bernard gaped at her and whispered something into her ear, which caused her to blush. Indeed, Bernard never took his eyes off of her the rest of the day. Jarka finally teased him calling him her little puppy dog.

As they all headed into the castle next door for the meeting, Zoran commented, "You didn't eat much breakfast. Are you doing okay?"

"Can't. I'll say this, you sure won't get fat wearing this outfit! If I have to walk much further, I swear my knees will give out. Oh, she said tiny steps, maybe that's it." Zdenka was having a hard time adapting, he noted and was glad that he did have to wear her outfit.

Slowly they made their way to their assigned seats. Once seated, Zdenka took stock of the other baronesses and their dresses. Over half wore this new style outfit, she noted, and all of those women were being as cautious and slow as she and Jarka had been. In this, she took comfort. The others wore the style of dress which she had worn when she came here. Those ball gowns only billowed out some five feet in front of their bodies. Even more interesting, she noted that all of the other women were constantly noticing everyone's dresses, particularly those wearing this new fashion. So these women were being observant of the dress code; this she found interesting.

At last, some musicians played the traditional wedding music found nearly uniformly among the planets. Baron Kazimir and a man in his thirties, both wearing the finest blue suits, entered and then Baron Eckhart entered with Brunhilda on his arm. Baroness Gisela followed, holding onto the arm of a youthful teen, presumable her son. Zdenka noted that Brunhilda also wore this latest in fashion type of dress, only hers was pure white, naturally.

While the simple wedding was conducted, both Zoran and his friends studied the new couple intently, as did many others in attendance. His brother, Damek, more closely resembled the late Radek, tall, well-muscled, and sporting a moustache. Zoran noticed a close resemblance to both himself and Radek. No doubt he was their half-brother.

Brunhilda was twenty-one now, equally tall, probably because of her heels, he thought, thin and of average attractiveness. She had curly black hair worn shoulder length. Even from this distance, he could see her overly long fingernails, painted blood red. Her countenance suggested that she was a woman used to having her way. Zoran guessed that she would tend to be the bossy, take charge, type of woman, an asset which Damek would need at his side.

When the ceremony was over, both moved to the Visitor's Area, joining Duke Leo and Lida. At this point, Baron Tom rose and gave his opening welcome speech. Once that was done, he dove into the first item of business. "Brother Jiri Zar and Priestess Anezka have finished construction of another Circle of Ascension. This one is on Gladno. The owner of this newest Circle is Duke Leo." A loud round of applause followed.

"Per our rules, at this time, the High Council is obligated, per our rules, to pronounce Duke Leo as Baron Leo Matous. Hearing no objections, I give you our newest baron. Baron Leo Matous and Baroness Lida Matous, please come and take your rightful place at the High Council." No one objected.

Gracefully, as if born for this moment, the young couple gracefully, albeit slowly because of Lida's outfit, moved over to sit beside Baron Milan's group. Zoran didn't recognize the man who quietly slipped in with them, his advisor.

Baron Tom continued, "Brother Jiri wishes me to announce that the construction is well underway for a Circle of Ascension on Valtr. He expects it to be done before spring. Once finished, he will commence construction of a Circle on Alta. Perhaps by our spring meeting, we may have two more barons at our table." A polite round of applause signaled their acceptance. Zoran noted that Baron Alvaro looked very pleased and gave Zoran a nod of appreciation. Zoran wondered whether or not Jiri had decided to do Alvaro's next because he had put in the good word for Alvaro. He made a mental note to ask Jiri later.

Next, Tom gave Baron Kazimir the floor. Zoran noted that the Baron's eyes were bloodshot. In spite of the fact that the portly man was well dressed, he sensed a great tiredness, a heavy weariness emanating from him. "At this time, since my appointed heir, Lida, has become a Baroness on Gladno, per our rules, she can no longer be my heir, unless she will rise and divorce herself from Baron Leo Matous. Will she do so at this time?" He did not look at his own daughter.

"Don't be ridiculous. I will do no such thing," Baroness Lida retorted.

"Thus, my choice of heir is no longer valid. I take my right to name another heir. I chose my son, Damek Kamil, to be my formal, legal heir to my throne. Yes, as many of you know," he stared at Zoran, "Damek is not a Duska. Yet, I point out that his wife, Brunhilda, is a Duska. Thus, this is a legal heir."

"I protest," Baron Milan rose and objected. He listed his reasons. However, Barons Alvaro and Hajime quickly pointed out that this situation had occurred thrice before in the past. As long as his wife was Duska, the rules allowed Damek to become a baron. As expected, his protest was voided. Primarily, Milan wanted to be on record opposing this heir. It was purely politically motivated. The other barons realized that this heir, should he become baron one day, was totally ill equipped to handle the responsibilities of his post. Many Neutrals expected that Damek would become their very weakest baron and thus their vote was uniformly in favor of Kazimir's request.

That settled, Damek and Brunhilda were allowed to sit with Kazimir acting as his advisors. Now the meeting settled into complete boredom, as far as Zoran was concerned. The rest of the day, the barons took up several petty beefs several had with other barons. None of it concerned Zoran in the slightest.

That evening, the formal opening ball provided both entertainment and a time for quiet political discussions between the barons. Zoran finally realized that most of the real decisions were made at these times, not during the actual meetings! Twenty musicians began playing from a raised gallery at the far end of the elegant ballroom. The highly polished oak planks of the floor reflected the magical lighting coming from incredibly ornate chandeliers. Zoran and Zdenka moved onto the dance floor immediately; Jarka and Bernard were right behind him.

By now, Zdenka's feet were killing her, as was the tight laced corset. Still, she said nothing. She had a passion for dance and would allow nothing to interfere with her evening in the arms of the man she dearly loved. The dancing couples presented a colorful panorama, the huge dresses were definitely a showcase, adding beauty to the large gathering.

Before long, others began cutting in, requesting the next dance with either Zdenka or Zoran. As Baron Alvaro cut in, handing off Baroness Anita to Zoran, he whispered, "Many, many thanks for putting in the good word for me with Brother Jiri. How about that? We are next in line. I owe you, Zoran. Ah, Zdenka, you are the flower of the dance floor."

As he took the arms of Baroness Anita, also wearing the latest in fashion, she said, "Yes, thank you so much. Our son can now have his birthright without waiting for our demise. I am so glad that Zdenka has taken a fancy to our latest fashions. Though I must admit, I find these are a wee bit too much to handle. How's everything in Brn?" she chatted away.

A bit later, Baron Hajime and Baroness Lami broke in on their dance. As they exchanged partners, Baron Hajime whispered, "Please accept my apologies for those assassins ruining your honeymoon. I do hope that you two will come visit us again. To make amends, I will give you another week of all expenses paid on Asami."

While dancing with Hajime, Zdenka, thinking of the mermaids, Chika and Akira, commented, "We know about your shinjutori, your tortured mermaids. How dare you permanently clamp their legs together and force those awful fish tails on them and make them search for your pearls? I think that is just terrible mistreatment of your young women."

Baron Hajime flushed. "How did you . . ." He didn't finish his sentence and Zdenka would not have answered his question anyway, though she knew what he wanted to ask. He quickly regained his composure. "You misunderstand our shinjutori. Please Archmage, allow me to explain."

"I'm listening," she said quietly.

"Our shinjutori, our mermaids, are perhaps the most important women on our planet. As you have seen, we have nothing but a few scattered islands, yet our population number in the millions. How can so many be fed and housed? Only by buying off-world all of the commodities everyone else takes for granted can we possibly survive. We buy grain, tools, clothing, wood, everything but what we can take from the sea. We have no ores, no gems, no mines from which to extract gold and gemstones to trade. We have only the pearls from the oysters. These lie deep under the waters of Asami. Originally, men and women dove for them, but many could not swim either deep enough or hold their breaths long enough and drowned. Oh so many, many have drowned diving for pearls."

"By selecting out the very best of our maidens, we have made them into shinjutori, teaching each one to cast the Water Breathing spell. Their tails are absolutely vital for them to be able to swim farther and faster and deeper than any of us. Honestly, a shinjutori can swim probably more than twice as fast as the most ablest of swimmers. The shinjutori hold a singular position of great honor and pride among our people, because of their ceaseless work and donation and sacrifice, millions of Asami can live and survive. We owe our shinjutori our total survival. Because of the pearls that they find, we can purchase all the off-world things we need to survive."

"Without the shinjutori, Asami would perish within a few years. We treat them with our highest honor. So please do not think ill of us for wanting to survive."

"I see. Well, I admit that I had not seen the bigger picture. Still, I think that you ought to give those women some choice in the matter of whether or not they want to be mermaids. Perhaps you ought to consider allowing them to retire after five or ten years of pearl diving. Allow them to experience life the way the rest of your millions do."

"Ah, Archmage, I will consider your suggestion. Perhaps, when we next meet, I will have such news for you. It has been such a pleasure dancing with you. Your new gown meets with my approval. You look just stunning in it. Zoran must be proud to have such a beautiful wife and companion."

After many more 'Excuse me, can I have this next dance' requests, Zoran suggested that they cut in on his brother and new wife. "You talk to Damek and I'll sound out Brunhilda." She agreed.

Soon, Zoran took the arms of lovely Brunhilda. He noticed that she too now wore this latest of fashions. Her satin dress was emerald. "Congratulations, Brunhilda. Looks like we are now neighbors. I love your new dress."

"Thank you Baron. Neighbors, yes. I am amazed that your wife can keep up with the latest fashions. After all Brn is *so* out of the way! Warlord country is *so* dismal, isn't it? Downright primitive by our standards. *So* uncivilized. We *owe* it to them to bring civilization to them, don't you agree?"

"Most certainly we do. I prefer peaceful means, however." She didn't respond, so he continued. "How do you like my brother, Damek? You will, of course, be the power behind him and support him when he becomes the baron, right."

"Certainly, he is not a Duska, as *we* are. He knows so little about our ways. I *do* hope that you do not send your dragons to murder him like you did your brother Radek."

"My dragon friends are here only to help protect my Circle. For the record, I did not send the dragons to murder Radek. He was with Kazimir as he and his army murdered and slaughtered all of the free people of Sholov Province. Wars are nasty affairs, completely unforgiving. I tried to talk Radek from following in Kazimir's footsteps, but he would not listen."

She chose not to respond, but said, "Well, just so the record is straight between us. If you send your dragons to attack Castle Dorumova, my father will send his entire army from Dietmar to help defend us. Don't get any wild ideas just because

Damek is not a Duska."

"I wish no ill to my brother at this time. Besides, if you haven't heard, I have neither a fortress nor an army."

"No, you have the dragons," she replied, slightly envious, slightly testily.

Meanwhile, Zdenka was dancing with Damek. "You dance well, Damek. You ought to come and visit your brother sometime. I know that he would really like to meet you. Until recently, he didn't even know that he had a brother."

"Would he permit that? I mean, having Brunhilda and me come to Brn to visit? I don't want to be burned to death by your dragons as Radek was."

"Of course you would be safe and welcome to come. Just expect far cruder accommodations than you have at Castle Dorumova. I've only got the Archmage tower at the moment."

"So I have heard. I'm an old soldier, used to field conditions. I'll manage. Say, can I ask you something personal?"

"Sure, but I may not answer it," she replied cautiously.

"You and I are rather in similar circumstances. I mean neither of us are Duska. Have you found it hard to learn what is required of you as a baroness?" he asked what was troubling him the most, Zdenka guessed.

"I knew nothing about Duskas, courts, barons or baronesses. Yes, it is a challenge to learn enough fast enough. I rather imagine your position is far worse than mine. After all, the baronesses here seem to be more worried about the latest fashions than ruling a planet."

He chuckled, "Aye, they certainly seem that way. Even Brunhilda was very worried about wearing just the latest in fashion today. Yet, she knows what she is doing with the Circle and all that. She is good with magic, though she is not an Archmage, like yourself."

"I understand. I am sorry that you were cheated out of your birthright to be both a Duska and a Mage. Kazimir is not much of a father in my opinion," she added.

She touched a sore spot with him. "That is true. He didn't even know I existed until he needed me for his token heir. Mom didn't tell me that he was my father until I was twenty-one. By then, it was too late for everything. Yet, if I do become baron, that is something."

"Yes, I do hope you do not then follow in Kazimir's footsteps and be another tyrant over our people," Zdenka decided to probe into his intentions a bit.

On this, he was cagy. "I hope not to be a tyrant either." Just then, another couple broke in on them, desiring to dance with Damek and Brunhilda. Zoran gladly resumed dancing with his wife once more.

At long last, and not too soon for Zdenka and Jarka, the dance ended. Once in their rooms, Zoran and Bernard were needed to help the two women undress and change into more comfortable attire. Without her asking, Zoran began giving her feet a good massage. Bernard, seeing what Zoran did, followed suit.

A bit later, the twins returned from their shopping trip. Both were extremely happy and had to show everyone their new mammoth sized gems. Zdenka's comment hit home to both. "Those are of such high quality that you could enchant them with all manner of magical properties." This had not occurred to either, and they both set off to work up what spells they could infuse the gems with and how.

"Dragons sure love gems," she said as the two turned in for the night.

Zoran had just gotten to sleep, when his Circle and inner senses forced him wide awake. Someone was attempting once again to Shadow Walk to the area of his Circle. No, it was Kazimir, he detected. As before, he found himself partially in the Shadows observing, picking up on the man's intention: to arrive on the street before his tower. Just as Kazimir was about to arrive, Zoran moved towards him to drive him off. Again, the Duska inner sense warned the Baron, who instantly fled for his life! Zoran's eyes closed and he again fell into a deep sleep.

Zoran noted Kazimir looked incredibly haggard and run down, when he arrived for the morning council session. Try as he might, he could not figure out what the Baron was attempting to do by coming to his tower so late at night. He brought no attacking army or assassins with him. It made no sense to him, as did the day's meeting. The rest of the week was spent on mundane things, hardly worth having them all together, Zoran thought. Like Zdenka, he began to long for the evening's entertainments, carefully arranged by Abigail.

That evening, Zoran escorted Zdenka to the fancy carriage, designed especially for women wearing such wide dresses. Dozens of such carriages were in a line, waiting for the guests. Tom and Abigail took many other couples with them to see the latest stage play in the largest theater in Heddingham.

Zoran simply lifted Zdenka in and out of the carriage, for which she was grateful. The play about farmers and their lives was interesting because both knew next to nothing about the agrarians and their world.

This was repeated the next night, as the carriages took them all to the same theater. This evening a forty member music group performed dozens of pieces for nearly two hours. "Somehow, we just have to get musicians in our castle," Zdenka insisted. Zoran heartily agreed, though he knew not just how this could be done as yet.

Both Zdenka and Zoran looked forward to the next night's affair, the ballet. For ninety minutes, they watched enthralled as the dancers, men and women, walking, prancing, and dancing on their toes told the story of a traveling musician and his trials and tribulations. Knowing just how much these two loved the ballet, Abigail arranged for the two of them to meet the main two dancers back stage after the performance. It is hard to say who was more impressed, the young dancing couple or Zoran and Zdenka. They chatted for nearly an hour, inquiring how they learned to dance on their toes.

Years and years of practice was the routine answer. However, Gail added, "For novices who yet do not have the feet and ankles strengthened and who want to experience ballet dancing, we know of a shoemaker who makes special boots. If you like, I can send him to you." Thus, the two returned home with a pair of these special boots to try out in their bedroom later on.

The next evening, they were treated to a choral concert. The evening was divided into three sections. First, an all-women's choir sung for thirty minutes. Next, an all-boy's choir sang in their unusually high voices — nearly angelic was the common description. Finally, a large mixed choir of some one hundred men and women sang four and eight part songs. Leaving the theater Zdenka commented, "Wow! Wow! Wow!" Abigail was quite pleased.

Back at their room after the concert, Zoran and Baron Leo finally had time for a private conversation. After casting preventative spells, Zoran asked, "Observed any special connections that you have with your Circle, Leo?"

"Other than my eyes changing? Sure glad that you alerted me to that one. Well, it seems like I can sense things with it." Zoran smiled, good lad. He spent an hour outlining all of the "special connections" that he had so far discovered with his own Circle.

For this information, Leo was exceedingly grateful, thanking him profusely. "I owe you a big one, Zoran. Thanks! I'll let you know if I discover anything else going on with me and my new Circle."

Late afternoon of the last day, once the meeting adjourned until the spring session, Milan cautioned Zoran once again. "Look, now that Baron Eckhard has a vested interest in Dorumova, you had best be on a sharp lookout for all manner of plots, especially assassinations. I'm sure that Eckhard will want to somehow shore up his hold over Adapazan. I think he believes that he is about to conquer your planet." This Zoran didn't need to hear.

What he found interesting was discovering that Gladno, Valtr, Cosma, Terra, and Gonda now had between twenty and thirty golden dragons living there. Each Baron had signed a defense pact with them and was paying the dragons in large gemstones for their services.

That night, Zoran related this to Zdenka. "You know, I sometimes wonder if I did the right thing, bringing the dragons to Adapazan. It has hardly been a year and now they are on five other worlds."

"Yes, you had no choice, Zoran. Besides, these five are our allies, but that's not what is troubling you, is it?" she astutely asked.

"No. What if the other worlds somehow get other dragons, different species, such as the red dragons, to come to their worlds? I may have opened the flood gates to the ruin of the whole Federation."

"Oh don't be so hard on yourself. You did what you had to do. Come to bed."

Chapter 27 Winter's Treason

The October's early snow fell on Brn, as it did various places around Adapazan. The warlords had their grain for the winter. The two large pockets of Yellers were now gone, leaving only isolated groups in the other provinces. These he would handle somehow in the spring.

Twice more, Zoran detected Kazimir attempting to Shadow Walk to his Tower. Twice more, as he moved towards him to intercept him, Kazimir fled in a panic. Still Zoran had no clue of the Baron's intentions. Was he somehow testing him and his defenses? He had no answer.

A thousand miles away in the comforts of Castle Dorumova, Damek was finding life a bit annoying. First, his father was growing increasingly strange. His obsession with a hidden Shadow Assassin was discussed nearly every day. Of course, no one had ever heard of such a thing, which greatly annoyed Brunhilda, who reported the Baron's growing madness to her father back on Dietmar. Damek found the best way to deal with Kazimir's outbursts was to offer him a strong drink. It shut him up, anyway.

Beginning in October, Baron Kazimir began to make plans for an all-out assault on Brn. "Son, there is one thing that I must do for you before I die and that is to eliminate Zoran, my ill-gotten excuse for a son! Now, I have a pact with Baron Eckhard. Come spring, he will be sending along a huge army. Together, we will take Brn away from them! We must make our plans, son."

Bit by bit, the Baron created his three dimensional model of Brn Province. Kindly, Eckhard had lent him a Mage, who went Invisible, Teleported to the province, and cast Fly on himself. Slowly, he began to obtain the data needed for the model that the Baron was constructing. "Find their weakest point, son. That's where we shall strike."

During the winter, Kazimir worked his remaining soldiers, getting them as prepared for a great battle as he could. No one dared mention the dragons to the Baron. At the beginning of the training, one soldier did. It was the last thing he ever said; the Baron killed him instantly. "You fill fight and die for me or I will kill you right now!" the Baron swore at his commanders and soldiers. Damek attempted to become as invisible as possible at these times. He had spent nine years as a soldier of the Baron's, working his way up from a buck private to sergeant. He knew well what fear was going through the minds of the soldiers. They had seen thousands slain at Sholov and knew that nearly three hundred of the very best of them perished as they attempted to storm this very same tower last year. None wanted anything to do with the dragons, yet to say anything meant instant death by the Baron.

Hence, unknown to the Baron, many soldiers began slinking off in the middle of the night, heading for the Wild Lands beyond the reach of Kazimir. Of course, his commanders also knew of the desertions, but none dared even mention this to the Baron. He would take his wrath out on them! Worse, they had no Mages anymore. They would be facing numerous Archmages as well as Mages and dragons. The assault was pure folly, but they continued to drill their men in spite of this.

Married life with Brunhilda was not going well for Damek either. She was bossy and condescending to him. Over and over, she barked, "Look, you are not Duska. I am. You do what I say or else!" Now at night, he preferred to stay up and drink far into the night with Kazimir. At least once the old man started drinking, he didn't speak. Damek became more and more unhappy with the turn that his life was taking.

Often during the battle planning sessions, Kazimir and Brunhilda left him totally out of their conversations! Once he attempted to point out a small flaw in their planning. Both told him to mind his own business and go for a walk. Useless, that's how Damek began feeling. He was adrift in a tempest and knew not what to do. Was there anything even that he could do? Daily, he grew more and more convinced that he was nothing but a mere pawn, of little or no value whatsoever. He took to brooding even more.

As Yuletide approached, Damek made a last ditch attempt to melt his relationship with his wife. On his own, he searched the shops of Dorum and bought her what he thought was a very fine diamond necklace. In his own defense, it was the finest diamond that he had ever seen.

At dinner, he decided to give it to her. "My love, I got you a Yuletide present. I hope that you will like it." He handed her the nicely wrapped box, and for an instant he thought that he had done it. She looked like an eager child opening a present.

As she opened the box and saw the diamond, her face fell. He felt crushed even before she spoke. "Ah, tiny diamond. Not worth a whole lot. I have far better ones in my jewelry box. Thanks anyway, Damek. The thought was nice at least." He stared at his plate until the other two left the dining room to return to their three dimensional battlefield of Brn.

Midnight of the first night of Yuletide, Baron Kazimir decided to make one more attempt at Shadow Walking. As he began to arrive at his usual location outside the Archmage Tower in Brn, once more he saw his nemesis, the Shadow Assassin coming towards him! Once more he fled into his own Castle, badly shaken up once again.

When he arrived, both Damek and Brunhilda were waiting for him. "I saw the Shadow Assassin again! Damn him to the Eternal Fires!" He did not notice that Damek had his broadsword out and pointed at the Baron. Behind him Brunhilda kept making faces and motions towards Damek.

Her body language kept saying, "Go on! Do it! Stab him and let's get this over with!" The night before, she had finally taken Damek to bed with her and shown him a wonderful time. Once finished with pleasure, she told him, "The next time that Kazimir attempts to Shadow Walk and play around with this insane madness of his and this non-existent Shadow Assassin, it is time to strike. Have your sword out and when he returns, stab him through his heart. He is a Duska, but now he is an insane, mad Duska. When he comes back, he will be totally confused and quite mad, oblivious of what is going on around him. That is the time for us to strike and get rid of this incompetent, insane, old man. Be ready, Damek. For once in your life, do what is right. We cannot continue with this madman around. Do you understand, my dearest love? With him gone, it will be just you and I. Things will be much better. You enjoyed it tonight, didn't you?"

Oh, she played him well. He did enjoy her pleasure, and he did see the need to get rid of Kazimir. The man was quite mad, quite insane, he had to go. But he was a Duska. He knew well that he stood no chance at all of even scratching the Baron, not with his inner sense of emanate danger. The Baron would know instantly that he was about to stab him and would launch his own brutal counterstrike. Damek would be killed at once, just as he had seen so many soldiers slain in the last couple of months.

Ah, but now, now it would be different. His Duska, his wife, would be there to back him up. Her plan made sense. He'd seen the Baron return from these Shadow Walks, seen the condition the man was in, but normally just gave him a bottle to drink and shut up about it. Now, he could take an action, one that would eliminate this mess, this continual invalidation of him. Thus, he agreed to do it. Brunhilda gave him a warm hug and passionate kiss, further solidifying his resolve.

Now that the time came to actually thrust his sword through this pitiful man's chest, he was frozen to the spot. Not because he was terrified of going into battle. No, he was a trained soldier. Kazimir looked and was pitiful, a madman. Yet, he was his very own father, who had sought him out and gave him the opportunity of a lifetime, a chance to become a baron! He could not thrust his blade, no matter the ever-growing wild gestures of Brunhilda, still standing behind Kazimir. He just could not slay him, not like this, not in this way.

Absolutely furious with Damek, Brunhilda took action of her own accord. All along, she had suspected that her husband would not be able to perform even this simple a task! He was an idiot and a fool, a mere foot soldier promoted to a baron. Already, she had formulated a variation on her original plan to kill Kazimir. Seeing the frozen Damek standing there looking like an idiot, Plan B kicked in. She would deal with Kazimir and then kill Damek. Both would be eliminated. She would then tell her father and everyone else that the two men turned on each other and killed each other. She would then be in total control of Castle Dorumova and its Circle. She could then choose her own man to be the baron and she would choose wisely!

Brunhilda drew her dagger and made a lightning thrust, aiming to place her blade between his shoulder blades, severing his heart. She wanted a quick kill. As her body began its lightning move, Kazimir's inner sense of eminent danger kicked in. However, as distracted as he was, and the fact that his body was now old and out of shape, he was not fast enough. His hand drew his own blade, but he felt her dagger diving deep into his back. Kazimir performed his last lightning fast move. He whirled and brought his broadsword up in one last desperate thrust, slicing open her gut from her navel to her heart.

Brunhilda gasped and her hands frantically attempted to hold her insides in, to keep them from pouring out onto the floor. The Baron's blade dropped, clanking solidly on the stone floor, his eyes closed, and he slumped to the floor. He was dead when his body met the cold, hard stone. Brunhilda screamed and screamed, but her hands were unable to keep her guts inside the huge cut. Now her arms felt cold, oh so cold. They no longer seemed to move properly. Useless, she thought. She looked at last up at Damek with a shocked and terror-filled face. Her eyes saw a man staring back at her, equally shocked. Now her legs felt cold, numb. She felt her body falling to the floor. She tried in vain to resist, but the floor offered her relief. Standing was so difficult. Perhaps if she lay down, she could stop the bleeding. When her body met the unforgiving stone floor, she was dead.

Damek continued to stare in a complete and utter shock. True, he's seen men die, many men. It was not the death of the man and woman that paralyzed him. Rather it was the magnitude of who they were and what unexpected actions had occurred. He continued to stare, unable to move a muscle. Yet, he now sensed that something else had stayed his sword arm. Something warm, friendly. Kindness, but he knew not what this was.

It was ten o'clock when Kazimir attempted his last Shadow Walk to Brn. Zoran lay in bed with Zdenka, not yet asleep. As his Circle warned him of the approach of Kazimir, Zoran found himself once more half in the Shadow World, on an intercept course to prevent the Baron from arriving outside his Tower. He saw the Baron perceiving himself and watched as the madman fled in terror. He was still half in the Shadow World as the Baron arrived, standing before Damek, whose sword was drawn. Zoran, still partially connected with the withdrawing madman saw Damek and Brunhilda. Curiosity got the better of him or perhaps it was yet another instinct or property of his unique connection to his Circle. No matter, he remained partially in the Shadows watching what happened.

He saw her urging Damek to strike, saw him refusing to do so. Damek was his brother. Zoran could not let his own brother slay their father. He entered his brother's mind and re-enforced his brother's resolve to take no action. Then, he saw Brunhilda make her Duska, lightning fast move, saw the Baron react too slowly. Again, he stepped in and as the Baron was about to fail in his last sword move, Zoran gave his father's muscles a little extra push from the Shadow Land. Kazimir's sword struck true. Without Zoran's intervention, it would not have cut Brunhilda.

When both bodies finally collapsed onto the floor mere seconds later, Zoran Messaged his friends. *Teleport to Castle Dorumova immediately! The Baron's been assassinated! Meet me in the main dining room there!* Message sent, he stepped out of the Shadows and into the room. Using his most powerful spell, he lowered the Baron's protections against others directly teleporting here. He took hold of his brother's arm and helped his body sheath the sword. Then, he moved him over to a chair and had him sit down.

At last he spoke, "Well done, brother. You have maintained your own integrity and honesty. I am proud that you did not do what Brunhilda asked."

"Zoran? You? Here? How? She — she killed dad! Dad killed her!" Damek finally found his voice.

"I know. I saw it all from the Shadows. My friends will be here momentarily. We will keep you safe from harm and retribution." Thirty seconds after Zoran appeared in the dining room, Zdenka appeared, still in her nightgown, spells at the ready. Seconds later, Karel, Bernard, Jarka, Emil, and Renata also appeared.

"Oh my!" exclaimed the conservative Zdenka, seriously shocked by what she saw.

"Damn, what happened here?" exclaimed Karel, the moment he apparated in the room.

"I'll be!" Jarka calmly stated as she arrived. "Bit of a mess. Is Damek all right?"

"He's in shock, but is unharmed by their duel" Zoran replied. "We have a real mess here. For once, I don't know what to do."

"Well, silly, get a hold of Milan or Viktor immediately. Karel, Emil watch the hall. Don't let anyone in here," Zdenka ordered, as she saw Zoran concentrating.

Uncle Milan. I need your help instantly. Please come to Castle Dorumova, the Baron's private dining room. Home in on me. Brunhilda's killed Kazimir and he has killed her. I need your help, please sir.

On my way. Don't let anyone else into the room, certainly none who live in the castle. I'll be there as soon as I get my pants on son!

"He's coming soon," Zoran reported. "Don't touch anything until he gets here."

"Backstabbed, just like a woman," Jarka commented.

"Yes, but you are also a woman and a thief and you backstab all the time," Bernard teased her. For once, Jarka didn't retort, but broke out laughing.

"I mean just like a *woman*, not a woman, silly." Both chuckled.

A minute later, Baron Milan and Baron Leo stepped into the room from the Shadows; both had their swords drawn, ready for action. Looking at the mess, both sheathed them. "What happened here?" Baron Milan asked.

"I was in the Shadows, still watching Kazimir. He tried to come to Brn Tower again tonight around ten. I followed him back here and accidentally saw the whole thing. Brunhilda tried to get Damek to stab Kazimir when he had returned from the Shadows, but to Damek's credit, he refused to do it," Zoran explained, omitting the fact that he had lent a hand to his brother's refusal.

"Brunhilda then drew her dagger and did a Duska lightning stab in his back. He whirled around and ripped her open as he died. They killed each other, while Damek stood by helpless to react as fast as a Duska can."

"I see. Well, their wounds and positions and the lack of blood on Damek or his sword backs this up. What a mess! Baron Eckhard will blow a gasket when he finds out! Hell, Kazimir's allies will all rave about this one. We best handle this properly and legally. It is not every day that a baron and Duska are slain. Leave everything to me. You and Leo help the others keep all local personnel out of this room," Baron Milan ordered, taking charge. Leo and Zoran joined the others at the doors. There was no chance of anyone getting past Emil or Renata, but Zoran decided this was best left in the hands of Milan.

Ten minutes later, the other barons began arriving. Purposely, Milan notified Eckhard last of all. Thus, when the father arrived, all of the other barons had already come. "My daughter! What madness is this? Who has slain my precious daughter? I'll kill them with my bare hands!" Eckhard screamed.

"Calm yourself, Brunhilda has already had her revenge. Look for yourselves. She stabbed the old man in his back and his blade unfortunately has ripped her open. Lightning moves for sure. You had trained her well, Eckhard. Look, her dagger pierced his heart, a perfect Duska strike. No shame on her. Damek had his sword out, but could do nothing. They obviously used Duska moves. Damek had no chance of preventing his wife's murder by the Baron," Milan explained, slightly altering the events to ease the grieving father and prevent further questions that might be hard to prove.

One by one, the many barons examined the crime scene and stated their belief that she had indeed stabbed Kazimir in the back, hitting him directly in his heart. The Baron's bloody blade had obviously cut her open. Finally, Baron Alvaro spoke, "Barons, are we all in agreement on what happened here?" A chorus of yes's filled the room. Eckhard was the last to speak. "Yes, it is plain. I taught her well. She struck a true blow. Woe to me the day I agreed to allow her to marry his son! The blame of her death lies on my head. I am so sorry, Brunhilda. So sorry."

Softly, Milan said, "You may take her body back with you now, Baron. Go with our deepest sorrow for your untimely loss."

"Thank you, Milan. I won't forget your kindness." He picked up her remains, cast several spells on her, the last shrinking her very small. Finally, he nodded to the other men and Shadow Walked back to Dietmar.

"Well, we will certainly have some major business at the Spring High Council meeting," Baron Alvaro commented to Milan as he too left. One by one the other barons nodded and left.

When they had all gone, Milan let out a sigh of relief. "Whew, that went well, better than I expected. I was really worried that Eckhard would challenge the scene. Since he did not, I suspect that he may have given her the order to attempt to kill Kazimir. Interesting possibility."

"Thanks for your help, Uncle. What do we do now?" Zoran asked, very much impressed with Milan's handling of the situation and the barons. That he altered what had happened so successfully was not missed by anyone present, except Damek.

"First, Damek must now make the announcement that the Baron and Brunhilda are dead. Normally, Damek would now become the new baron and have full and complete authority over the castle and realm."

"Yes, but he's not a Duska," Zoran protested.

"Quite true, that's what makes all this a mess. He has no choice now but to act as if he is the Baron of Dorumova. He must make the announcement and see to issuing of orders. If the Generals will go along with this, then we are all safe. If they reject his authority, we will have to take immediate action. Eckhard will be watching Dorumova very closely. If the Generals reject Damek, undoubtedly Eckhard will come back here with a sizeable force, claiming the castle and Circle now belong to him, vis a vi his daughter."

At last, Zoran turned his attention onto his brother, who had been sitting quietly in the back corner, totally forgotten all this time. "How are you doing, Damek?" he asked.

"Useless, pretty much useless, brother. Why?"

"Well, now is your real chance to make a difference in our world. Stand up and take charge here. We will all support you. If you don't, Eckhard will likely be returning with an army and try to take over this whole castle and province. You don't really want him running your country, do you?"

"Well, no. Treacherous bunch. Zoran, I am a pawn. I have no idea what to do or say. Can't you step in and do it?"

"No big brother, I cannot. I am considered an outlaw here, their enemy, as far as Kazimir taught them. You are his heir. Since he is dead, at least for now, they will consider you to be their new baron."

"But I don't know a damn thing about the stupid Circle thing or even magic. Nada, nothing."

"The Circle is safe and right now needs nothing. Magic is not needed either. What is needed is that your Generals, your men out there, they need guidance, a leader. You were a sergeant. You know how to give orders to soldiers. Go give them those orders. This I know that you can do. Go do it, big brother." At last, Damek smiled.

"I like the sound of that — big brother. I see your point. I'll do this, because I really don't ever want to see Eckhard again, not ever! Will you come with me?"

"Okay, but I had better be Invisible. The Generals might think that the Castle is under attack if they see me."

Damek chuckled. "Hell, and they've been plotting a huge battle to take your tower come spring."

"Bet the men are scared of the dragons," Zoran teased.

"So much so that there has been rampant desertions among the ranks, though no one dared tell Kazimir about it. You know, she wanted me to kill him, don't you." Zoran nodded. "Well, when it came down to it, I just could not kill him. For once in his pathetic life, he did something good for me. I just could not kill him because of that."

"I know; you were very wise not to have drawn his blood. Come on; we've got Generals to address." Quietly, Zoran's friends cast their Invisibility spells and followed along behind them. Only Jarka and Milan remained, watching over Kazimir's body.

At the end of the long hallway, a guard stood sleepily on guard duty. "Guard! Make haste. Go find the bugler and have him sound General Quarters. I must speak to everyone immediately!" Damek barked his first order with enthusiasm.

A few minutes later, bugles sounded throughout the castle, and Damek stood on the second floor balcony overlooking the large assembly grounds below. Soldiers, officers, and the Generals came rushing out of their barracks, partially clothed, swords drawn ready for action.

Speaking as loudly as he could, Damek said, "I have vital news for everyone. Brunhilda has just slain Baron Kazimir in his dining room. Kazimir in turn has killed Brunhilda. The many barons have already been here and have verified the slaying of both. As you all know, I am my father's heir, so that now makes me Baron of Dorumova. My first orders are as follows. The spring assault on Brn Province is off. There will be no battle. For now, we are at peace with Baron Zoran." In spite of themselves, the relief boiled over! Wild yelling and cheering drowned him out for several minutes.

"Second order, since it is Yuletide, I want all soldiers, except for the castle guards, to take the next month off of active duty. Go home and spend this time with your families and friends. I promise you, no more wars. Not for a long time. I would like my Generals to visit with me at ten tomorrow to discuss security arrangements before they go home as well. Please, go enjoy the holidays!"

The wild yelling, clapping, and cheering made any further orders impossible to deliver. If he had any more, Damek forgot them for now. He stood there tall and proud, waving his hands along with his fellow soldiers. He knew precisely what this news actually meant to them. He had been one of them until just months ago. At last, the men headed back to their barracks. Many packed up and left at once, before their Baron could change his mind.

Damek turned and headed back inside, bumping into the unseen others. "Er, how was that?" he asked, as Zoran and the others became visible once more.

"Perfect, big brother. I do believe that you are in charge. Of course, the meeting tomorrow with your Generals will tell all, but I think that they have already accepted you as their baron."

"But how can I be baron?"

"Let's worry about that later."

"But I don't really want to be baron, Zoran. I haven't a clue about how to do it."

"I know. Please, let's worry about that tomorrow."

Back in the dining room, Milan told Zoran, "Now he ought to be buried as soon as possible. Do you want a state funeral?"

"No, he was a tyrant right up to the end. However, he ought to be buried in the family burial plot."

"I'll see to that in the morning," Damek offered. "But what do I do now?"

"Well, I for one am going to go to bed. It has been a long, eventful night," Baron Milan replied. "Zoran, I'll come by tomorrow afternoon and we can discuss things with Baron Damek then. Okay?"

After he left, seeing Zoran and friends about to leave, Damek suddenly became fearful. "What about me? Will I be safe in here alone? What if Eckhard tries something? I cannot even get a hold of you."

"Emil, will you volunteer to stay here with Damek tonight and protect him if need be?"

"No problem. I will wander the halls and make sure no ill comes to him."

"Thanks, we'll come by tomorrow and talk more Damek. I am proud of the way that you handled things here tonight. Well done, big brother." Zoran's comment had his intended effect; Damek smiled. Then, they vanished from sight.

Back in their tower, everyone was now totally awake, so they raided the kitchen. For a while, everyone discussed this unexpected turn of events. Finally, sleep overcame them all.

Chapter 28 Aftermath

Early the next morning, Zoran took a hasty breakfast, before the onrush of Zdenka's students. When she came down, she found him sipping his tea, deep in thought. As she sat down, he looked up and said, "Damek didn't want to kill Kazimir. He was resisting Brunhilda's orders. I know, I helped him. I was sneaky and just enter his mind and re-enforced his own choice."

"You did what you had to do, Zoran," she replied, sitting down to eat.

"Yes, and now I feel that I am facing the biggest decision of my life."

"How so? Isn't everything over now? I suppose Milan will have someone else become the actual baron," she replied, afraid that she was sounding terribly ignorant of this court situation.

"I hardly know the man, Zdenka, but he is my brother."

"Well, so was Radek. Look how he turned out?"

"That's precisely my point. Would Damek be another Radek, if given half a chance?"

Jarka walked in, her black hair a disheveled mess, sleep still in her eyes. She'd heard the last of their conversation and chose to answer Zoran. "Oh that one is an easy question."

"Oh, morning Jarka. What do you mean easy?" Zoran turned to look at her.

"Yes, easy. Suppose that it was Radek there — you know, standing there with the broadsword and not Damek. Would Radek have done it — stabbed Kazimir?" she asked, taking a long drink of juice, and then wiping her lips.

"Yes, yes he would have. Radek always wanted to be the baron. With Kazimir so — well mad — he would have seized his chance, probably sooner," Zoran replied. He brightened up, "I see what you mean. Damek didn't. Well, I will give Damek a chance. Thanks oh wise Mage," he teased.

"No, it's a thief thing, not a magic thing. Got to understand people's motives, Zoran. Magic can't do that. Um, pancakes!" She helped herself to a pile from the platter that Hana just brought to the table.

Zoran grinned. "Okay, here's the plan. I think it's time that Damek met the rest of his family and they, he. He's already met Lida and Rayna. We'll take Jan, Zuza, and Kamila to meet their older brother. Based on how that goes, I'll work out the rest. Thanks, Jarka."

A half hour later, Zoran gathered the three together. "Gang, we have an older brother to meet. I know, he's our half-brother, but still he's our brother. He's much older than all of us. His name is Damek Kamil, and at the moment he is acting as the Baron at Dorumova. Shall we all go and meet him?" They had no objections and certainly were curious to meet him, especially the young twins.

Zoran Shadow Walked his friends and the kids directly into the main meeting room of Castle Dorumova. None of the three had ever been inside a real castle before and were awestruck with what they saw here. Suits of plate armor, tapestries, fancy tables and chairs, even the plush carpet was noticed. "Ah morning Damek. I've brought along the rest of our family. We've one more brother and two sisters."

"This is Zuza and Jan Vavrin, they are ten years old and are learning to read and write now."

"Very pleased to meet you, Zuza and Jan. I'm your big, older brother, Damek," he shook their small hands. Zoran watched his reactions carefully. He seemed to enjoy meeting them.

"Gee, you really are old, Damek!" Zuza exclaimed wide eyed.

Damek laughed, "Yes, I'm three times older than you, but not so old that I can still tickle you guys." She let out a squeak.

"Can you show us the castle, please? We've never see a real castle before," Jan pleaded.

"You bet."

"And this pretty teenager is Kamila Lota."

"Hi, Damek. I'm learning to read and write too."

"You are going to be a very pretty lass. Yes, I know, our dad never did much for us. I didn't learn to read and write until I was twenty-one and in the army. As a soldier, I had to learn to read the orders. I must admit, Kamila, I don't read very well. I get stumped on the big words. Would you like a tour of the castle too, Kamila?" Damek asked.

"You bet! I've heard adults sometimes talk about this castle. I never dreamed that I would ever be inside it!" Off they went. Jarka decided to tag along, just in case, while Zoran and the others headed for the study. The sounds of three excited children echoed through the halls.

A while later, the jubilant kids returned. Jan said, "Zoran, guess what? Damek says that we can come and visit him anytime we want. I told him that we can all Shadow Walk here. How comes he can't do that? Is he really too old to learn?"

"Yes, Kazimir ought to have given him the proper ceremony, like I did with you kids. He didn't. However, Damek might just possible be able to learn some magic spells. Of course, he'd have to learn to read and write much better."

"Zoran? Are you teasing me? I'm thirty years old," Damek replied.

"You have our father's blood in you. I know it is rather old to get started, but there is always the chance, if you are willing to try."

"Thanks, brother. I owe you. I have to meet with the Generals in a few minutes. It shouldn't take too long. We can talk more then."

"Okay, I need to get the kids back to their lessons. Zdenka here will have my hide for keeping them from their studies. We'll drop by in a couple of hours, round lunch time, okay?"

With that, the group returned to their tower, just in time to meet Baron Milan and Baron Viktor, who had come to meet with Zoran. They took tea and biscuits in the second floor dining room.

"We've been going over the Federation Legal Rules," Milan began, "to try to figure out this mess."

"Yes, it is highly irregular for a baron to die and his appointed heir also to be at that time technically invalid. There is no question that at this point in time, Damek will not be permitted to become Dorumova's baron. He is not a Duska and no longer has a Duska wife," he explained.

"Now if Damek can marry a Duska woman before the Spring High Council meets, he would then become qualified to be the baron," Viktor added. "Is there any real chance of that?"

Zoran shook his head. "Damek does not know any one that meets that criteria. He's already had one arranged marriage which did not work out well. I doubt that he could be convinced to do it again, even if we could somehow find someone in time."

"Yes, that is the conclusion that we both reached. He's thirty. It would be criminal for us to marry a teenager to him," Viktor admitted.

"So what do the rules say happens next? Does the High Council just vote someone to take over Castle Dorumova?" Zoran asked.

"Well, if all else fails, yes. It will take a majority of the High Council to approve such an appointment, once such a person is found," Viktor answered.

"But before it goes that far, the rules clearly state that, in the event the appointed heir is invalid at the time of appointment, then the eldest remaining son, who is valid, may become the heir. Failing any valid remaining sons, then any remaining eldest daughter, who is valid, may become the baroness. If none meet that criteria, then it falls to the High Council to pick someone, as Viktor said," Milan finished up.

"Well, that is interesting. There is one more valid son and two daughters," Zoran explained. "I took your advice and rounded up the other known offspring of Kazimir's. Jan Vavrin is only ten, but he is Duska now. Priestess Anezka performed the Ceremony of Ascension. I had her conduct it for all three. His sister, Zuza, is also ten. Finally, Kamila Lota is fifteen. We've got three valid candidates."

Milan grimaced. "Bastard son and daughters will be the argument our enemies will put forward."

"Can we argue for them?" Zoran asked.

"Certainly," Viktor replied. "Jan would be the likely candidate, though he is too young. Isn't there a regency rule for under-aged heirs?"

"Yes, somewhere, let me see." Milan produced his copy of the rules, a hefty sized manual, which he had shrunk to transport it. Unshrinking it, he began to rifle through the pages. Zoran noted that the pages were well worn from extensive use. He realized that he ought to have a copy of the Federation Rule Book. Viktor promised to send him one soon.

"Ah, yes, here it is under Regents. It says that, if the valid heir is not yet eighteen, then the Circle can be held for him by an appointed Regent," Milan read.

"Yes, that's all well and good, Milan," Viktor complained, "but who can be the appointed Regent? And who appoints him?"

"One moment, I haven't been over these rules in years, Viktor. Let's see here." He rifled the pages back and forth. "Ah, a Regent can be anyone whom the under-aged, valid candidate chooses, subject to the following. A Regent cannot at the same time be another baron. While it is preferable for the Regent to also be a Duska, it is acceptable if he or she is not. If the Regent is not Duska, some provision must be made for the protection of the Circle of Ascension."

"Terrific, all of the bases are covered, Zoran. We present to the High Council that the legal new baron of Dorumova is Jan Vavrin. His Regent can be Damek, with Kamila acting as Duska, when needed," Baron Viktor replied, greatly relieved.

"By golly, this will work! Will Jan accept becoming the baron? Will he allow

Damek to be his Regent? Will Kamila volunteer to act as his Duska when needed?" asked Baron Milan.

"I don't know, but I sure don't see why not. Should we present this to them now?" he asked.

A few minutes later, Zdenka brought all three children into the dining room to meet with the barons. She cleverly stayed, most curious to hear what transpired. Zoran did the talking. "Jan, we've been studying the Federation of Planet's Rule Book to try to find out who the next baron of Castle Dorumova and its Circle of Ascension should legally be. It's you, son. You are the next qualified heir of Baron Kazimir."

"But Damek is so much older. Why isn't it his?" Jan asked, confused.

"Because he is not Duska and you are. The baron must be a Duska or have a Duska wife. Damek's Duska wife died, so he can no longer be its baron. Are you willing to become the next baron of Castle Dorumova?"

"Me a baron? Have my own castle? You bet, wow! Wait until I tell mom! We can live in a castle!" Jan was exuberant. What child of ten would not be?

"Now you won't actually get to be the baron until you have your eighteenth birthday. Meantime, you must learn to read and write and learn your magic spells and how to be a baron," Zoran explained. "In the meantime, you need to have someone who actually does run the Castle for you. That person is called a Regent. I cannot be your Regent because I already am a baron here. However, Damek can be your Regent. He knows how to deal with the army and has lived in the castle and how to run it. Would that be a good choice for your Regent?"

"Sure, he'd be perfect, only I wish you could be it, Zoran."

"I know, but I can't and he can. Now then, there is the Circle of Ascension there that must be considered. You know that it has to be very well protected. It is what gives the barons their powers. For that, you need a Duska to help you. If it is all right with you, how about having Kamila be your Duska helper with the Circle?"

"Sure, she's really nice."

"Kamila, are you willing to take on this extra responsibility, ensuring the safety of his Circle of Ascension?"

"Wow! Super, but I don't know much about it, excepting we had that Ceremony with it."

"Not a problem. I'll get you trained up on it fast. Really, there are only a few things that you must know how to do — protection spells, which any Duska can learn quickly. I'm sure that you can manage it. Thank you, Kamila." She beamed, for she was now going to become an important person at this fabulous castle!

"But I'm left out," complained Zuza.

"I know, sis. How about you get trained to help out Kamila when she needs it? You can be her backup Duska. How about that?" Zoran improvised. This totally appeased Zuza; that she had a part to play was all that she wanted. She sat tall in her chair now.

"Okay, then it is back to studies with you all," Zoran said. Grinning ear to ear, Zdenka lead them back downstairs.

"Okay, let's clear this with Damek next. If he agrees, then we must fill out our formal request and send notices to all of the other barons. It is vital that our request gets to them before Eckhard figures out some way to take control, vis a vi his daughter," Milan explained. Hence, the three Shadow Walked over to Castle Dorumova.

"Hi Zoran. Oh, hello barons. I have a little lunch prepared," Damek greeted them as they materialized in the study.

While they dined, Zoran explained the rules and their solution. "Wow, Jan can legally become the next real baron here? That's great. We get to keep it in our family," Damek seemed greatly relieved that these men were not going to try to convince him to continue as baron.

Zoran then explained the need for a Regent and a Duska to monitor the Circle. When he found out that Jan wanted him to be his Regent and that Kamila would deal with the Circle business, Damek was very pleased. "Now that *is* something that I can do. For once, I am given something I can manage on my own! Thank god for that! Yes, I would love to be his Regent."

"Good, good. The whole thing must be approved by the Spring High Council, but it seems that we are totally legal at every step. It ought to be approved. If you will excuse us, we must get this drawn up properly and submitted before Eckhard comes up with some devilish plan of his own," Milan replied. He and Viktor made a hasty exit.

Alone for the first time, Zoran said, "Well, brother, you inherit our father's mess. You have a golden opportunity to begin to set things right here."

"Yes, there has been far too much bloodshed on Adapazan. Let's not have any more wars, not for a very long time. My Generals are completely behind me. Say, I don't know where any of the baron's secret chambers are located, much less his treasury. I have to pay these people soon. Ideas?"

Zoran spent the next week going over every inch of the Castle. First, he dispelled every spell that Kazimir had cast upon the rooms. Together, they pitched the possessions of Kazimir, such as his clothes — cleaning house, Damek said. All of the secret chambers Zoran managed to locate, though more than once, he had to consult the ancient volumes of the original baron. Once Kazimir's protective spells had been dispelled, he recast new ones, and gave Damek the key word that allowed him access without dispelling said spells.

His week actually turned into several weeks work. He'd forgotten just how large the castle complex actually was! By February, Castle Dorumova was now completely in the hands of Damek. The Archmage tower there was another matter entirely.

In February, the combined Archmages and Mages finally gained entrance, having at last cracked Archmage Milos' protective spells. They spent the whole month carefully identifying and dispelling all of his protections that he'd place on the various rooms and contents. Once it was safe, they then cleaned house here as well.

Zdenka carefully examined all of the books and scrolls to see if any were useful to have at her tower. To everyone's amazement, Archmage Oldrich's collection greatly exceeded what Milos had. Only two volumes did she confiscate for their use. Once they finished at the end of February, Zdenka cast a protection spell on the main entrance. When a new Archmage could be found for Baron Jan, the tower would be given to him or her.

The 15th of March was now only two weeks away. Much hinged upon this High Council. The balance of power shift was nearly complete.

Chapter 29 The Spring High Council Meets

Per Baron Milan's request, Zoran took his party to the High Council around three in the afternoon the day before the meeting. He wanted to hold a private meeting with him. This time, the event was on the desert planet of Anwyn, home of one of Zoran's enemies, Baron Carwyn Alun and Baroness Elain. Besides Zdenka, Zoran took Karel, Bernard, Jarka, and General Janos, who added three Security guards as well. Back home, Emil took charge of their defenses, while Renata continued teaching the students their magic lessons.

Anwyn was an arid planet, that is the largest land mass, several thousand miles long and a thousand wide, was dry. Sandy deserts and scrappy, arid hills predominated. That is not to say the continent was without water. While many oases dotted the desert, two huge rivers, running north to south, roughly divided the continent in thirds. One river was Y-shaped, called Aeronwy or wy-river. In the north at the Y lay the capital city of Aeron, where Baron Carwyn's castle was located. The port city of Rhian lay at the mouth of this great river. The other river was called Ysbail. It was shaped like an enormous Z, hence it was the Z-river. At the two bends lay the other two large cities of Tarren in the north and Seren in the south.

Zoran carefully Shadow Walked his party to the wy-river and then zeroed in on Aeron and the sprawling castle and fortifications there. Because it was early March, the weather was not yet unbearably hot; rather the temperatures were in the low eighties during the nearly always sunny days. As they drew close, date and fig trees could be seen along with a large number of palm trees rising like stark sticks above the bleak, barren, brownish sands. Their landing point was a large brown stone platform, centrally located within the secure walls of the fortification, some distance from the sprawling castle complex. The castle itself was only two stories high, but was quite large. Land they had aplenty here. Besides there was no reason to erect taller buildings for the land here was quite flat.

As they arrived, the dry air was quite noticeable compared to the snow which still covered the high country of Brn. Baron Carwyn and Baroness Elain were there to welcome them, along with their three teenagers. He was tall and thin, perhaps thirty-five, with short brown hair and moustache. Carwyn was handsome. He wore native dress, a white robe and sandals. His wife was perhaps a year younger, with very long, straight brown hair and a pale oval face. Everyone's skin was a light tan from constant exposure to the hot sun.

"Welcome to our home and Anwyn. This is the Castle Aeron. My wife, Baroness Elain, my eldest son and heir, Cadfael." He was fifteen and a splitting image of his father, though smaller. He carried a wicked scimitar at his side. "My charming daughters, Beanwenn and Ceri." Both dressed like their mother and wore their brown hair long as well. All the women wore court ball gowns similar to those that Zdenka and Jarka wore, not the latest in fashion, rather the ones that billowed out only five feet. Zdenka was thankful that she remembered that Elain had not worn the latest fashion dresses on Terra. Hence, she and Jarka, while they brought those confining dresses and heels, chose to wear the more practical gowns.

After exchanging pleasantries, Baron Carwyn said, "Baron Zoran, my condolences on the death of your father. I would very much like to speak privately with you before the High Council opens tomorrow. Baroness Elain wishes you to dine with us and the other early arrivals at five. Perhaps we can get together for a word after dinner?"

"Thanks. Yes, we've never really had an opportunity to chat, one on one. I know that my Uncle wishes to speak to me as well. Shall I contact you when I am free?" he replied politely.

Carwyn agreed. "Come, let us show you to your rooms and then perhaps you would like a tour of our fortress?"

"Thanks. Sure, I'd love to see your place. Already I can see that Anwyn is vastly different than our mountainous Brn," Zoran replied rather formally. The Baron led the way, escorting them into the extremely large castle complex. Their suite of rooms was on the second floor. From the signs on the doors that they passed, all of his enemies and many of those that were Neutrals were given suites on the first floor. Theirs was between the suites occupied by the Matous and by the Pavels. Once settled, they got their tour. Zoran noted that the Archmage tower was the tallest building in the complex and even the city, rising a full five stories, round as expected. He wondered just why wizard towers were cylindrical in shape.

Baron Milan and his party were already present, and he chose to meet with Zoran just as soon as his nephew returned from the tour. "It is as I expected. Baron Eckhard is also submitting a claim for your father's castle and Circle. The High Council will allow him to make his formal presentation first, and then we make ours. His claim can only be his youngest son, Burkhard, who is now eighteen and of age to become a baron. He is betrothed to Baron Bogdan's youngest daughter, Cede. If they marry, it will further unite those planets, the Clav's and Hadwig's. Adolf, Eckhard's heir is already married to Bogdan's daugher, Greta."

"Can his claim override ours?" Zoran asked, becoming worried that their plan would fail.

"Not very likely. However, if we did not have a good basis, then, yes, his may well win the day. I don't think that we have too much to fear from his claim. Now let's get some dinner."

After diner, Zoran and Carwyn held their private meeting. "It's about time that we had a chat, Baron," Carwyn began his carefully planned discussion. "How is the construction of your fortress coming along? It's been nearly a year now, since construction began, right?"

"Yes, the outer walls are up and the castle construction has begun. I'm afraid that ours will be only a dim shadow of everyone else's fortresses and castles. We just don't have the funds or the time to construct as elaborate ones as everyone else has. I'm impressed with yours. It is so expansive."

"Yes, space we have aplenty here on Anwyn. That, and a whole lot of sand. You don't need sand, now do you?" For a moment, Zoran thought he was serious, and then the grin told him it was a tease. Both men chuckled. "Sand makes fine glassware. Anyway, Zoran, you mentioned a key element, lack of funds. You see, you should not consider us here your enemies. I know that Barons Milan and Viktor have convinced you that it is us versus them, with the rest being politically Neutral."

Zoran nodded, he stated the obvious.

"However, that is not the complete picture. Between you and I, Zoran," he leaned forward as if revealing some secret, "it is more like the 'haves' and the 'have-not's.' Really, that is what a lot of these alliances are all about. You see, Adapazan is really with our alliance, the have-not's. Your planet is mountainous; it's difficult to find much land on which to grow crops. Grains, in particular, have to be imported. It is the same with us here in the desert. We have hot sands and not much else. On Dietmar, Baron Eckhard's planet, snow predominates, nearly year round in much of his world. I cannot imagine living in cold temperatures year round. Then on Jing, Baron Cheng's world, swamps prevail. Nearly all of that planet's land mass is swampy and marshy. He does grow a lot of rice, I'll give him that. In many ways, Rehor, Baron Bogdan's planet, is much like your own, mountainous and rugged."

"You see the bigger picture? We are the have-not's. Admittedly, Asami, Baron Hajime's water world, at least has pearls in vast quantities so they can import nearly everything a man must have to live. On Chana, Baron Aryeh's desert planet, they have vast diamond mines and trade such for staples. Gerde, Baron Adolf's mountainous world does have sufficient plains to grow sustainable crops, and he has plenty of gold mines. These three are Neutral. While they are not wealthy planets, they are able to get by."

"Now you take Gladno, Valtr, Cosma, Terra, and Gonda. All of these planets are awash in nearly everything that makes life survivable and pleasurable. All five planets are extremely wealthy. Have you not noticed that Cosma and Terra supply much of the grains that sustain so many other planets? These planets have gotten rich off of the rest of the planets. They are the have's."

"So you see, it is not some grand scheme of Good versus Evil in play here. It is a game of the have's versus the have-not's. Really that is what it is all about. Adapazan is a have-not planet, which is why your late father was aligned with us. Our objectives have always been to get a better compensation from the wealthy planets. Have you not noticed the wealth, the triumph of the arts on Gladno, Terra, and these others? Whereas here, it is mere survival that occupies our daily lives. We have no time for the arts, not on the scale that you saw on Terra, for example."

"I know that Baron Milan is your Uncle and that Kazimir, the old fool, totally treated you badly, forcing you into exile. Perhaps, that was for the best. After all, you were able to rescue Brother Jiri, and he's begun to create new Circles for the first time in over two centuries. Did you know that Milan and Kazimir were half-brothers? They had the same mother. I think that is in part why Milan has been so hard on Kazimir, sibling rivalry."

"Now I know that Baron Eckhard is grief-stricken over the sudden death of his daughter. He is obligated to submit his petition for control over your father's Circle. It was his daughter who was to inherit it, you see. He owes that to her memory. All would think less of him if he did not submit his petition. I know that you are also planning to submit a similar petition, though I am not yet privy to your particulars. We will all find out first thing in the morning."

"I'm sure that the High Council will decide on the one which had the best merits. I'm sure that Milan and Viktor have filled your head with notions that we may be planning an invasion of Adapazan to take the Circles by force of arms. Am I right?"

Zoran didn't think that answering would reveal any secrets. "Well, as a matter of fact, they have. They are pledged to send their armies to help me defend if you launch an attack against Adapazan."

"We are the have-not's. Why would we do such a thing? What is to be gained? Only political votes. Nay, rather we ought to be assaulting Cosma, Gladno, and Terra. They are the have's. Watch your step with those barons, Zoran. In many ways, they are using you for their own ends. They would much rather go to fight a war on Adapazan than on their own planets. We only seek a better equity between the planets of the Federation."

Zoran decided to speak his peace. "Well, there is the slight matter of suppression, slaughtering, slavery, and brutality that Kazimir wreaked on Adapazan. I am totally against that. I stand for the Free People of Adapazan. There is more to all this than mere inequity of riches, baron. Never have I seen worse conduct than that committed by Kazimir. If there ever was an evil man, he was it, though I've heard that Bogdan is a close second. I've not seen this kind of inhumanity to mankind, this kind of suppression of free will on Terra, Gladno, or even Alta." He decided against speaking out against the mermaids of Asami, because such knowledge might not be widely known.

Zoran finished up, "My fight is not about money, riches, or wealth. Mine is about the freedom of our people. I will fight against anyone who tries to crush our freedom and free will."

"You will get no argument from me on that point, Baron. Such a noble attitude is most commendable indeed. However, I should also point out that Adapazan, like Rehor, is rather an inhospitable world, filled with warring primitives, a harsh world that must be tamed if civilization and broad scale survival is to be brought to such wild lands. Into such wildernesses, only the strong survive. Baron Kazimir and Baron Bogdan are hardy pioneers, fighting anyway they know how, with limited men and resources, trying to tame a wild and primitive world. Sometimes, their methods may seem too harsh to our eyes, but the end result should be what they are ultimately judged by. I personally admit that many times, I thought that Kazimir went too far in his treatment of others. And I often told him so, just as I frequently do Bogdan. In the final say, do the ends justify the means? If they can take a primitive, harsh, wild planet and turn it into a civilized, cultured world with a high survival potential, then I tend not to look too harshly on the means."

"You might have a different view if you were the one being suppressed, slaughtered, or turned into a slave," Zoran countered.

"Aye, son, I might at that. I promise you that I will continue to be vigilant with Bogdan and continue to try to moderate his ways. I just wanted you to have another point of view on the alliances of the High Council. In my opinion, it is not Good versus Evil. It is political, the have's versus the have-not's. Just something for you to ponder."

"I know my wife will be doing her best to give everyone a good time each evening. She's spent years working on the entertainment. Just realize that Anwyn is not Terra. We do not have such expansive arts as they do. Our people must work just to survive. We have little free time for the arts. She's worked long and hard to put together three wonderful evenings for everyone."

Zoran was curious, "Say, how often does a planet get to play host to the High Council?"

"Until you came along, and now Baron Leo, with two meetings a year and sixteen planets, each planet plays host every eight years. This matter is on the agenda this time. We must decide what to do now that more and more new barons are joining us," he replied. The two chatted a bit longer, before Baron Carwyn had to leave to welcome more arrivals. Indeed, most were arriving this evening.

In the privacy of their suite, Zoran told his friends what Baron Carwyn had to say. Most found his explanation fascinating. None of them had considered this point of view before. In many ways, it did make sense.

At ten the next morning, Baron Carwyn gave his opening welcome speech. His was short, and he quickly got down to the business at hand. "First, Brother Jiri Zar has completed a new Circle of Ascension on Valtr. I give you Baron Viktor Pavel."

Baron Viktor rose, "It is our great pleasure to announce that the new Circle is fully functional. My son, Duke Stefan and his wife Rayna are there in the Visitor's Area. It is my wish that they become Baron Stefan and Baroness Rayna. Both are fully qualified in all ways."

After a round of perfunctory applause, Baron Carwyn asked if there were any objections or challenges. Hearing none, the High Council voted unanimously in favor. Carwyn then announced, "Be it here known that this Circle of Ascension belongs to Baron Stefan Pavel and Baroness Rayna. You may come and take your place at the council table." While the group again applauded, the two took their seats beside Baron Viktor, who was very pleased indeed.

Carwyn continued, "Brother Jiri has informed me that the Circle on Alta is nearing completion. Further, he expects that by the fall council, he will have the next new Circle on Terra finished. We should expect to introduce two more barons at our fall session. Now then, the next action must be to address the vacancy of the Circle of Ascension at Castle Dorumova due to the untimely death of Baron Kazimir and Brunhilda, the wife of his heir, Damek. In acknowledgment of the fact that at this time Damek has not married a qualified Duska, his claim to the throne is void. Thus, the position must be filled by the High Council. In this matter, Baron Eckhard, father of Brunhilda, wishes to make his petition first. I have granted it, as it was his daughter and Duska that was slain. Baron, you have the floor."

Baron Eckhard rose and spoke solemnly. "Such a sad day we face, when a baron passes away leaving his Circle unmanned. This is why we strive so hard to have guaranteed heirs to the throne. Had he left us just such an heir, we would only have to give our approval and move on to more pressing matters. However, in this case, we must fulfill our sworn duty to man up this Circle of Ascension."

"To that end, I am petitioning on behalf of my late daughter, Brunhilda, who was designated the Duska of Dorumova, in the event of Baron Kazimir's death. As you may know, my eldest son, Adolf, has long been declared my heir and thus cannot be considered for this position. My youngest daughter, Greta, is married to Bran Clav and Bran is the designated heir of Baron Bogdan. Thus, she is also ineligible by our rules. My youngest son, Burkhard, is now eighteen and of age. He is, of course, fully Duska trained. It is my petition that the Circle of Ascension in Castle Dorumova be given to Burkhard, based on Brunhilda's former position as heir-designate. I hope that you will give this your strong consideration in her memory. Thank you." He sat down. Several Barons clapped for him.

Carwyn then rose and announced, "Baron Milan, on behalf of Baron Zoran, will make another formal petition."

Baron Milan rose and began his well-rehearsed presentation. "Federation Rules are quite precise in this particular situation. First, let me point out that Brunhilda was only heir-designate, she was never officially baroness, and thus her claim is secondary, according to our rules. Likewise, per our rules, if Damek Kamil at this time has remarried a valid Duska, it would be our obligation to declare the position his. Damek has chosen not to do so. Thus, his claim to the throne is invalid, just as Baron Eckhard has said. We do not argue that point. However, the rules clearly state that, in the event the appointed heir is invalid at the time of appointment, then the eldest remaining son, who is valid, may become the heir. Now that also fails because Zoran, Lida, and Rayna are all holding similar positions at other Circles. Failing any valid, remaining sons, then any remaining eldest daughter, who is valid, may become the Baroness. If none meet those criteria, then it falls to the High Council to pick someone."

"Yes," called out Baron Eckhard, sensing that Milan was playing into his hand. "We must choose someone."

Milan raised his hand, "Ah, but there *is* one more valid son and two daughters!" All three are valid Duskas, as certified in the documents you have at hand by Priestess Anezka Zar. Thus, per the above mentioned rules, the baron position should go to the son, Jan Vavrin."

Zoran glanced at Eckhard and saw his face grimace. Milan continued. "While Jan is a Duska, he is only ten years old. So now we must review the Regency rules that cover the situation when an heir is too young to assume the throne. Those rules specifically state that, if the valid heir is not yet eighteen, then the Circle can be held for him by an appointed Regent. Thus, we come to the matter of how a Regent can be appointed. The rules again state that a Regent can be anyone whom the under-aged, valid candidate chooses, subject to the following. A Regent cannot at the same time be another baron. While it is preferable for the Regent to also be a Duska, it is acceptable if he or she is not. If the Regent is not Duska, some provision must be made for the protection of the Circle of Ascension."

"Heir designate Jan Vavrin has asked that Damek Kamil be his Regent, running the Castle and its affairs until he is of age. Further, he has asked his sister, Kamila Lota, assume the task of protecting the Circle of Ascension until he is old enough. Kamila is now sixteen and a fully trained Duska, who can perform those duties that a Circle requires. Both Damek and Kamila have agreed to fill these positions."

"In summary then, our petition is that Jan Vavrin be appointed heir to the throne of Castle Dorumova and the Circle of Ascension therein. Further, that Damek Kamil be appointed his Regent and that Kamila Lota be appointed his Circle Protector until such time as Jan reaches the age of eighteen, at which time, both Damek and Kamila will be relieved of their positions and obligations."

Baron Eckhard rose, fire in his eyes. "I must also point out that all three of these are bastard sons and daughter of Baron Kazimir!"

Baron Milan rose, "The rules do not make any exceptions. It clearly states sons and daughters. Marital status is not referenced at all. Your protest is invalid, but duly noted by all of us."

Now the floor was thrown open for discussions. Bogdan, Carwyn, and Cheng all spoke in favor of Eckhard, punching in the bastard son aspect. They argued that the High Council had an obligation to enforce strict moral codes, that this would reflect on the lowering of Federation morals, and similar such arguments. Barons Viktor, Aldo, Tom, and Etienne all spoke in favor of Baron Milan's request. Each argued that in no way at all did it violate any of the Federation rules of succession and that the rules could not and should not be broken at this time.

During all this, Zoran watched the faces of the six Neutral barons, curious of their reactions. On the surface, the argument of morals versus bastard sons and daughters sounded good, but Zoran suspected that many of these men had fathered sons and daughters out of wedlock. Certainly this was highly likely in the case of Asami and Baron Hajime — as witnessed by Chika and Akira, the mermaids. He saw that most of the Neutrals were enjoying immensely watching this power struggle between the two sides!

Finally, as the noon hour approached, a vote was called and Milan's request was approved by a vote of eleven to four. Adapazan was not allowed to vote, and Zoran had to abstain since he had a vested interest and they refused to count half-votes. Baron Carwyn announced the request as passed and said, "Regent Damek, you may take your seat on the High Council. However, as it is close to noon, let us adjourn for lunch."

Barons Milan and Viktor were extremely pleased with the outcome. The political balance of power, which used to be five versus five versus six neutrals, had now completely changed, becoming six versus four versus six neutrals. Over lunch Milan pointed out that such a dramatic shift in the political balance had not occurred for over a century and a half! Hence, this was a very significant shift indeed.

During the afternoon session, they tackled the problem of where to hold the High Council meetings in the future, now that more and more Circles were being built. A number of ideas were put forward, but the unanimous decision of the Council was to continue their eight year cycle, visiting each planet in turn. However, when it was a planet's turn to host, it would be up to the multiple barons there to determine at whose castle it would be held.

That evening at the opening night dance, based on lunch time chats with the other baronesses, Zdenka and Jarka chose to wear their latest fashion billowing gowns with the extremely high heels. Over half of the baronesses wore theirs and both women desired to join them. However, they continue to wear their more comfortable gowns during the daytime, as did the other baronesses. The dance was acceptable, though the musicians were nowhere near as good as those at the other dances they had attended.

Later that night, Barons Milan, Viktor, and Zoran met in private. Milan said, "Well, we've accomplished what can only be called a miracle. Now our task becomes to keep little Jan alive for another eight years! Undoubtedly, our enemies will send out all manner of assassins. If Jan is killed, Eckhard's request may well be adopted, unless you can find some more unknown bastard sons and daughters," he teased Zoran.

"I will keep them at our Tower as much of the time as I can. Besides for many years, Jan, Zuza, and Kamila will need to study and train. All three have many years of magic training ahead of them. I'll keep them safe."

Viktor spoke his mind. "We should keep a vigilant eye on Bogdan and Eckhard. There is still a strong likelihood that they may attempt an invasion of Adapazan. This is especially so, since Damek is now seen as a weak leader, to say nothing of the army casualties suffered in Sholov Provence. You certainly don't have an army yet. Do not rule out an aggressive military action against the whole of Adapazan, Zoran. I certainly would not."

"In that case, I really ought to see if I can have another twenty dragons living around Dorumova. The treasury there can easily support them," Zoran concluded, very worried about just such an attack. Indeed, their position on Adapazan was tenuous at best. Only the dragons stood between their freedom and an invading army. Whether or not his allies could get significant armies to Adapazan to counter an invasion in time, Zoran did not know.

The next evening's entertainment consisted of an hour and a half of Anwyn traditional belly dancing with very exotic costumes that revealed too much, as far as Zdenka was concerned. The men thought otherwise. The next night was a traditional desert fiesta. For this event, all of the women and men were given local costumes and went barefoot in the warm sands. Bonfires provided both illumination and heat for roasting their meal. Local musicians played afterwards, with the attendees given lessons in the local barefoot sand dancing. Zdenka and Jarka were most impressed with their traditions and loved the sand dancing. The third night was a play and this night they again wore their latest fashion dresses. The play was called Haves and Have-Nots and told the story of these two cultures in conflict with a balance achieved at its end. Zoran realized that this was really a political play, with many subtle undertones reflecting the current politics and situations going on within the Federation.

When Zoran left after the next night's closing dance, he realized that he had actually learned a considerable amount from this meeting. Not from what was said during the long, mostly boring meetings, but with his chat with his enemy and seeing first hand their culture and life. He realized that he truly needed far more data about the other planets and their situations. Once more, Zoran realized how much he did not know. What Zoran didn't know was that many others in power did not know that they did not know!

Later that night and home again, he and Zdenka looked out over their construction site. The walls were finished and the sides of their new castle were now five feet tall. They began to see their rooms and halls taking shape. Another year and they may well be able at last to move into their Castle Brn, as Zoran named it. She chose this time carefully and whispered into his ear, "I'm pregnant."

"What? Wow! Fantastic! I'm going to have a baby!" he exclaimed.

"Ah, dear, it is I that will be having it. You are just the dad." He laughed at her tease, picked her up, and twirled her around in circles, before passionately kissing her. Life looked happier than Zoran ever imagined it could be.

The End.

Other Books by Vic Broquard

Without Warning (fantasy)

The Trident Series: (fantasy)
      Volume 1 The Trident and the Book
      Volume 3 The Trident and the Scepter
      Volume3 The Trident and the Resurrection

The Adventures of Elizabeth Stanton Series: (science fiction)
      Volume 1 The Evolution of the Path
      Volume 2 The Great Messiah
      Volume 3 Of Kings and Queens and Troubadours
      Volume 4 Chaos in the Aftermath
      Volume 5 Power Plays
      Volume 6 Age of Exploration
      Volume 7 Abducted
      Volume 8 The Emperor and Empress
      Volume 9 A Job Worth Doing
      Volume 10 Degradation
      Volume 11 The Second Crusade
      Volume 12 When Worlds Collide
      Volume 13 Dark Ages

The Lindsey Barron Series: (fantasy)
      Volume 1 The Rod of the Apocalypse
      Volume 2 The Board of Governors
      Volume 3 The Crown of Moses
      Volume 4 Dominus for President
      Volume 5 The National Health Care Program
      Volume 6 States Justice
      Volume 7 Cross and Double-cross

Zoran Chronicles Series: (fantasy)
      Volume 1 A Dragon in Our Town
      Volume 2 Dragons, Power, Courts, and War

Planet of the Orange-red Sun Series: (science fiction)
      Volume 1 When Kingdoms Fall
      Volume 2 Dark Ages
      Volume 3 Age of the Towers
      Volume 4 Difficillis Exitus
      Volume 5 Age of the Lords
      Volume 6 The Renegade Tower
      Volume 7 Rebellions
      Volume 8 The Aliens Return
      Volume 9 Power Struggles
      Volume 10 Guilds, Genetics, and Gods
      Volume 11 Magi, Witches, Swords, and Superstitions
      Volume 12 The Voyage of the Eagle's Seed
      Volume 13 Justifications
      Volume 14 Responsibilities

The Return of the Wizards: Twelve Companions – The Making of Wizards (fantasy)

www.ingramcontent.com/pod-product-compliance
Lightning Source LLC
Chambersburg PA
CBHW082033170626

46817CB00010B/3142